CLOTH GIRL

CLOTH GIRL

Marilyn Heward Mills

TIME WARNER
BOOKS

First published in Great Britain in 2006 by
Time Warner Books

A CIP catalogue record for this book
is available from the British Library.

Hardback ISBN-13: 978-0-3167-3188-1
Hardback ISBN-10: 0-3167-3188-9

Typeset in Caslon by M Rules
Printed and bound in Great Britain by
Clays Ltd, St Ives plc

Time Warner Books
An imprint of
Little, Brown Book Group
Brettenham House
Lancaster Place
London WC2E 7EN

A member of the Hachette Livre Group of Companies

www.littlebrown.co.uk

For Beatrix, with love

Acknowledgements

I am indebted to my first readers Karen Scott and Jane Stone for much valued early enthusiasm and assistance. Deepest gratitude also to my marvellous agent Christine Green for her unwavering belief and for making things happen at all; to Dietra Cordea, for whose early confidence I am eternally thankful; and to Rosie de Courcy, for her brilliance. I could not have written this book without the faith and support (which too often I take for granted) of my friends and family.

For wisdom is more precious than rubies,
and nothing you desire can compare with her.
Proverbs 8:11

PART I

The Gold Coast, British West Africa

March 1937

Chapter One

Robert Bannerman, still happy to display his body in the privacy of his compound, walked on to the upper veranda of his house with a towel wrapped around his waist. Later on in life, he would put on weight, but for now his body still showed the benefits of having led an active life in England, where he had participated eagerly in most sports, making up for his mediocrity with fervour. In his opinion, his only personal sporting failure was that he had never learned to swim. The truth was that he was afraid of water. When he was a boy, he witnessed a childhood friend drown in the sea, which scarred him with the unwavering respect that comes from recognising one's uselessness in the face of a vast unconquerable. What a peaceful death once the waves had silenced the screams. Anyhow, it would be inappropriate for a man like Robert to be seen swimming in public. There were things that he could not do here that he might have done freely, without a care in the world, back in England, where he had been anonymous and unaccountable; here, he was a pillar of society, respected by many, and the least he could do was try to live accordingly.

He stood gripping a cup of tea in one hand and surveyed his household while his extended family and servants carried out their tasks. He had always wanted his work and play in one place, and as he watched the stable boys and trainer working with the horses and his children playing in the yard, he felt he had achieved that. It had definitely been worth returning home; he belonged here.

He had turned to go back into the house when he noticed a girl whom he did not recognise in the courtyard below. He was transfixed. He did not want to stop looking at her, and for a while took no notice of his wife, Julie, who had appeared beside him and was talking to him. Reluctantly, he turned his head towards Julie, allowing his eyes to linger on the girl as long as he could. He looked at his wife fleetingly, long enough to recognise the contempt in her face, and then turned back to look at the girl again. Julie stood and stared with her husband for a few moments. Then she took the unfinished cup of tea from his hand and stormed into the house.

Matilda stood in Lawyer's compound looking around anxiously for Uncle, clutching the bundle of documents in her hand. Her brow was glistening with sweat, and her palms were damp. She transferred the bundle from one hand to the other so she could wipe her palms on her dress. There was a strong scent of warm horse manure, which mingled with the smell of burning coals and cooking food. The smell of sweet, thick cornmeal made her stomach rumble.

She had never been inside the grand house or its compound before. Built on a corner plot, the house and compound were bigger than they seemed from the street. She squinted to protect her eyes from the glare of the sun, which was rising confidently in the sky, and looked around slowly. The house was a two-storey wooden rectangular building painted the colour of dirty honey. It had a low-pitched roof covered with corrugated-iron sheets, which glittered like a mirage. On both levels, two huge glassless windows, flanked by big blue shutters, opened on either side of a door on to a covered veranda that ran along the width of the building. From where she stood in the light, the rooms upstairs seemed to be in darkness.

Along the far side of the compound, opposite the gate, were stables for Lawyer's cherished racehorses, which Matilda had often seen being ridden to or from the racecourse. One horse had stretched its neck to rest its head on the stable door as though in exhaustion. There were several people in the yard. A thin man with a wizened face sat on a shaky wooden bench in the middle of the courtyard

4

underneath the shade of a gigantic neem tree giving instructions to two boys who were grooming horses. The boys moved slowly in response to the man; the heat from the tropical sun, even though it was still early in the morning, discouraging any hurried activity. Two mongrels with tick-infested, patchy fur, one of them with oozing eyes that were plagued by flies, lay on the ground perilously close to the man's feet. One of the dogs neglectfully allowed a stray paw to touch the man's leg and received a sharp kick from him in return. The dog yelped in disgust and moved away the offending limb but failed to move far enough to ensure that he would not intrude in the same way again. Next to the man, an old woman sat heavily with a fat, happy baby on her lap. Whenever the woman shuffled her feet and readjusted her bottom on the hard seat, the bench wobbled, although neither the man nor the woman seemed to notice.

A woman was washing a little girl underneath a running tap close to the house, paying no attention to the child's screams as she scrubbed her all over with a sponge, covering her entire face and body with foamy soap. Soon, she would have talcum powder doused all over her just like her brothers, who had survived their wash and were now playing on the lower veranda in the shade of the house, their smooth bodies still streaked with white powder, like blackboards smeared with chalk. Several dazed chickens wandered around the yard, pecking at the dry brown earth, hoping to find the kind of juicy worm that did not thrive in Lawyer's compound. They clucked persistently in a self-assured manner that was irritating, unaware that they were only ignored because one day soon they would form a special meal for the household.

Matilda was eager to keep a safe distance between her and the dogs. Breathing in deeply through her mouth, she moved cautiously towards the old woman and stood close enough to her to avoid having to speak loudly and risk being told off for being disrespectful.

'Please, good morning. I am looking for Uncle Saint John. Please, do you know where he is?' she asked in her polite voice.

'Lawyer's clerk?' replied the woman in a hot, bored voice, without really looking up. Before Matilda could reply, she continued, 'In the office,' pointing with her chin in the direction of an alleyway that ran towards the front gate.

'Thank you.' She nodded and walked in the direction the old woman had indicated.

As she approached the office, Matilda could not help wishing that Lawyer would be there. She was curious to see what he was like close up. She had seen him occasionally as he drove past in his car, and she had heard a lot about him, in tones often covetous but always reverential. Outside the office, she paused to look at the sign that stood at the front gate with the inscription in peeling paint: 'Robert Bannerman, BA (HONOURS), Cambridge University, ENGLAND, Barrister-at-law & Commissioner for Oaths.' Matilda knew what the sign said because her uncle had told her many times. He often recited the words, merged together but with the appropriate emphases, in his singsong, heavily accented African-English, not pausing until he had reached the full stop at the end.

She went round the corner and up the steps leading to the office. She saw through the open double doors that Uncle was alone. He was hunched over a desk covered with piles of books and papers, studying a document and looking bewildered. The office was dark and gloomy, a serene haven from the noise and brightness outside. An unlit bulb hung from a lead in the ceiling. The only light in the room came from an old green lamp on the desk. Shelves, heavy with rows and rows of hefty, dusty books, lined the walls. The gold lettering on the book spines was fading, but apart from the big Bible that the minister had on the pulpit at church, these were definitely the most impressive books that Matilda had ever seen. The cement walls of the room were cracked in several places and had probably once been white, but with time, dust from the earth outside had yellowed everything, enhancing the dimness of the room. Piles of paper and folders tied with pink ribbons covered most of the floor and every surface in the room. In the corner was a large dark-brown leather armchair that had seen better days. It looked comfortable. Matilda was amazed; she had never seen such a grand room or so many books in one place.

'Excuse me, Uncle,' she said softly.

Saint John looked up, and when he saw her, he grinned with his whole face and took a deep breath, pushing back his shoulders as if shaking off some imaginary burden. 'Oh. It's you,' he said. 'Come in, come in. Lawyer is not down yet. Come and see my lovely office.' He gestured welcomingly. He was sweating, constantly wiping his brow with a folded handkerchief that had once been white. Saint John was short and eager. If it is ever fair to generalise, then he had a typical fisherman's physique – stocky with well-defined strong arms and oversized calves. His head was shaped like a cocoa pod with a conveniently positioned bald patch, which he did not yet have to confront on a daily basis. He had a moustache to emulate his employer's and wore the same brown-flecked, gabardine wool suit to work each day. It was one of Lawyer's old Oxford baggie suits – oversized pleated trousers with a three-inch waistband and wide lapels on the jacket – which Saint John's wife had altered, taking up the sleeves and trousers a little crookedly and a little enthusiastically, so that too much of his socks now showed above his shoes.

Matilda walked into the room, relieved after all that Lawyer was not there, and turned to look at the wall behind her, which was covered in framed cartoons of men in red gowns and wigs. There were several gilt-framed photographs of Lawyer. Matilda breathed in the cool musty-paper smell, relishing the calm of the room, and peered closely at the grainy black-and-white paper, wondering how much it would cost to have such enormous pictures taken. The album at home had two small pictures in it. On special occasions, Matilda's mother carefully took the album out of its protective box and proudly showed off the small, shadowy photographs, which were now browning with age and desperate to curl in submission to the humidity. In one of them, Matilda's parents, Ama and Owusu, looking uncomfortable and dressed in their best clothes, smiled uncertainly, almost quizzically, into the lens. The second portrayed Uncle Saint John and his wife looking startled. Matilda and her sisters joked secretly about how Aunty Amele was staring slightly agape, with a hint of fear in her face. And at every given opportunity, Matilda's mother reminded Aunty Amele exactly what it had cost the family to capture this unrefined expression, which was, to be frank, quite upsetting, apart from being a waste of good money. But to destroy the photograph would have been even more shameful, so it remained in its rightful place in the family album for all to see.

Matilda wondered when she would be able to have her portrait

taken, and if she would look as nice in print as Lawyer did. She
noticed her reflection in the glass of the picture and focused on it.
She had recently reluctantly become aware of her appearance. She
had been told she was fine-looking and shapely, and everyone commented on her complexion, which was a shade lighter than her
sisters, a colour that her mother, who constantly reminded her to
avoid standing in the sun unnecessarily, had told her was a distinct
advantage for a girl. Her face was round, childish, with dimpled
cheeks, large brown trusting eyes and a full mouth with a lower lip
that curled downwards somewhat, revealing the soft pink of her
mouth. All her friends and female relatives praised her neck; it was
long and had two rolls of flesh, a beautiful neck, they said.
Embarrassed by what she saw, she blinked and concentrated on
Lawyer's image again.

But the man on the wall looked at ease, like someone used to
having his picture taken. In one shot, he was sitting on a chair, probably in a studio, smiling comfortably and holding a roll of paper tied
with a ribbon. His other hand was majestically positioned on his
thigh. Matilda took an imperceptible step closer to the wall and
examined his face. It was not black-black, as very dark children,
likely to be alternately pitied and teased by their friends and families, were described. He was a refined brown-black, the colour of the
bark of a neem tree, a little lighter than Matilda herself. His face was
square, and his head, covered in black hair, had looser curls than
anyone Matilda knew. She envied his sisters if they had hair like his.
Hair like his grew fast and long, lending itself to the more intricate
hairdos that Matilda longed for: long braids that would reach her
shoulders, or, better still, which would venture down her back. But
her hair would never grow that long. Unconsciously, she reached up
and stroked her head just behind her ear with her fingers. As a
schoolgirl, Matilda's hair had to be kept short, just a little longer
than was acceptable for a man. Her tight, springy curls, which when
pulled straight at least trebled in length, was the most inflexible of
African hair and could not be combed into submission without some
pain. She thought her friend Patience would think Lawyer was
handsome, but she thought that he had stern eyes. They were bulbous and sleepy, and his long nose and mouth – accentuated by a

trim moustache, which made him look quite distinguished – were much thinner than Matilda's.

'Please don't touch anything,' warned her uncle.

Matilda walked over and handed him the papers.

'These are the law reports. They contain important cases that Lawyer reads when he is preparing for court,' Saint John explained, waving grandly at the books. 'Lawyer is a very clever man.' He told anyone who would listen to him, and many who would not, about Lawyer's qualifications, emphasising their exceptional brilliance – the sign of a great man, a good man, actually. Saint John Lamptey believed emphatically that the fact he worked for such an out-standing individual was an indication of his own importance. Look how his place in society had been raised to a level which, it had to be said, was far beyond where one would have expected the son of a fisherman to reach! That Saint John should take pride in his employer's achievements was simply not something to be questioned.

Matilda turned back to the wall.

'Uncle? Please, what does that say?' She pointed to the caption at the bottom of the photograph.

'Cambridge University, 1928,' he replied without hesitation. 'The best university in the world.'

She turned to look at another photograph, a group of men all wearing similar gowns to the one Lawyer wore in the individual portrait. Matilda counted four rows of six or seven people. She leaned further forward and saw that one of the people in the front row, who were all seated, looked like a woman. Lawyer was not hard to find. His face, the only black one, was there in the third row, right in the middle of the picture. Everyone in the photograph looked happy, but he looked ecstatic. He seemed to be smiling more energetically than most of the others, who Matilda assumed were his classmates. She wondered whether it took a particular type of courage to be the only one of a kind. But the expression on his face was not that of someone who thought he did not belong.

Matilda had only seen whites from a distance. The colonials did not live near Jamestown, the part of Accra where Matilda lived. Jamestown, named by the English who originally settled there, was

9

a neighbourhood, not a town, on the Atlantic Ocean, just southwest of Accra proper, inhabited almost solely by the Ga tribe. The Ga people were renowned for their fishing skills, and they often lived up to their reputation for being aggressive, but they described themselves as sophisticated, mainly because they had had hundreds of years of exposure to Europeans and also because Accra, the administrative centre of the Gold Coast, which was part of British West Africa, was Ga territory.

The Europeans had since moved on to leafier suburbs nearer to Christiansborg Castle, the Governor's base, and Matilda, who rarely had reason to go anywhere beyond her immediate environs, had never spoken to a white person. Looking at the photographs, she wondered what whites were like, whether their skin felt as it looked, cold, translucent and fragile, and whether, amongst themselves, they too had colour distinctions indiscernible by her, such as white-whites or even yellow-whites, or whether they were all simply white. She also wondered whether there was any truth in the rumour that white women were happy to be thin and that they did not mind being flat.

'Well, now you have seen the office, you'd better get back to help at home and let me get on with my work,' said Uncle, interrupting her thoughts.

Dismissed a little sooner than she would have liked, Matilda set off.

Robert Bannerman belonged to the educated elite of the Gold Coast. Unusually, he came from a family of educated men. His great-grandfather had been sired by a British merchant and a local girl and had been sent to school in England. Through the generations, the Bannermans had continued to educate their males in this way. After primary school in Accra, Robert too had been shipped off to boarding school in England, and then to obtain a law degree at Cambridge. He had been away from his country and family for many years when he returned as a barrister to claim his rightful position of privilege and power.

Robert had loved his time in England unashamedly, and he still esteemed anything English, but he knew that there was really only one place where he would be able to be the man that he was destined to be. Now, only five years after his return, he was one of the most respected lawyers in the colony.

No one, least of all Robert, was sure where the Bannerman family's money came from, or questioned how there was enough to educate its sons in this lavish manner. There were rumours that their progenitors had been involved in the slave trade, but this was not something that Robert gave much thought to.

He turned to go back into his room when he saw the unfamiliar girl walking towards the back gate. He caught only a glimpse of her face as she walked past. He watched, transfixed. She had big hips that swayed from side to side as she glided in a way that belied her generous proportions. She walked lazily, scraping the heels of the unwieldy sandals as she moved, scooping up dust and dirt to sit moistened between her toes. Robert didn't want to stop looking at her. He wanted to know in which direction she would go, hoping for some clue as to who she was, but she disappeared behind the big wall.

He remained distracted all morning, wondering about the girl. He was slightly more irritable than normal with Julie and with the maid who brought him his breakfast. Surely his reaction to the girl was the usual excitement that precipitated the chase he would embark on as soon as he knew who she was.

'Lawyer, it is time to go or we will be late.' Saint John was running up the stairs to the veranda where Robert sat contemplating his breakfast.

Robert noticed that they were already nearly an hour late. 'Morning,' he replied gruffly.

Saint John hovered next to Robert while he drained his cup, then the men made their way down to Robert's car, a dark-blue Austin 16 four-door saloon with maroon leather seats, footrests and picnic tables that folded out from the back of the front seats, which had arrived from Liverpool only a few months ago. On a day like today, typically sunny and hot, the sun visor above the front windscreen was a wonderful accessory. The driver spent a considerable amount of time polishing the car each morning, and today it gleamed in the sunlight as though in gratitude. The driver held the door open while Lawyer climbed in and sat behind Saint John, who was seated in front, tall

11

and puffed with pride. As the car eased slowly out of the compound and on to the unmade road, several small children stopped playing and started waving at it. They saw the car almost every day, but it had lost none of its magic, and some of them ran beside it until it reached the main road, waving all the while and trying to catch a glimpse of their toothy grins reflected in the sleek hulk of the car as it rolled along gracefully.

Robert and Saint John, ignoring the children as usual, were engrossed in a discussion when Robert saw the girl buying something from a street vendor at the edge of the road just ahead of them. His desire was unmistakable and oddly overpowering. He leaned forward and shook Saint John's shoulder vigorously.

'Do you know that girl in the green dress? She was at the house this morning.' The driver had slowed down close to where Matilda was standing and was preparing to turn into the main road. Robert continued to shake his clerk's shoulder as though that would force a reply from him. 'That girl there. Do you see her? Find out who she is.' No one in the car could have misunderstood the excitement in his voice.

Saint John looked out of the window in the direction Lawyer had been gesturing. The frown on his face lifted in recognition. 'Lawyer, that is my niece Matilda. My favourite. A good girl.' He was nodding his head to emphasise his words and grinning with idiotic pride, taking more than his fair share of credit for the girl's allure.

The driver crept on to the main road and increased his speed a little. He drove gingerly, even though there were few motorcars on the streets.

Robert could not stop thinking about the girl, whose name he now knew. His usual style would be inappropriate. To seduce his clerk's niece and then walk away would fall outside the behavioural code by which he strove to live. But he was overwhelmed by how fiercely he wanted her. Certainly, she would not be the first such girl to have this effect on him. Yes, he had married well and had acquired precisely the sort of wife for the kind of man he was; stylish, educated, bright, and with the right background. Julie was very English in her ways, which Robert liked. In some ways, she was even more English than he, which was an advantage for their children. They would attend English-speaking schools from the start, none of this vernacular nonsense to confuse them. He wanted them to be brought up well, to acquire the superior tastes he had, and Julie was the right mother for all that. And she was presentable, which helped a great deal. She knew what to wear, what to say and how to comport herself without his input. Even her name, Juliana, had always impressed him with its ring of imperialism, but he too had succumbed over time, albeit unwillingly, to the abbreviated form that she preferred. So why, as soon as he had returned to the Gold Coast from his studies, and ever since, it had to be said, had he needed to dally with girls so far beneath him? Girls he usually met in secret, girls who satisfied something in him that Julie, with all her finesse, was unable to. He shrugged and stared out of the window, allowing his thoughts to return to Matilda. He began to consider where and how they could meet in a way that would be best for all concerned. There had to be a solution; he just had to think of it. Or, alternatively, he thought, I could simply allow this desire to run its natural course unaided. There was, after all, no likelihood that he would cross paths with the girl again soon.

Two days later, Robert was fed up with being plagued by exciting thoughts of her. While they were preparing for a case, he asked his clerk to send for Matilda.

'Tell her to find the papers for the Acheampong case, which you took home.'

Bewildered, Saint John asserted that he had not taken those papers home. They had to be in the office, although he had to admit that had not seen them in a while. Anyone looking at the piles of papers and files in the office would be suspicious of Saint John's claims that he always knew where any particular piece of paper was. Yet, time and time again, he astounded Robert by the speed with which he found the necessary documents.

The message was dispatched. Robert was edgy with anticipation. He wondered whether the girl would be as he had remembered. Time passed slowly. Robert wondered whether the girl would come. And if she did come, what would he do? He would cross that bridge when he got there, he thought eagerly. For the third time, he called for the boy who had taken the message to Saint John's house and again asked him, 'And when you got to the house, who did you talk to?'

The boy's answer had not changed since he was last asked the question. 'Please, I saw Sister Matilda and asked her to find the papers that Uncle left in his room and to bring them here as soon as possible. I told her that if she cannot find them, she must come and tell Uncle.'

There was nothing to do but wait. The silence was tense. Saint John continued to search the office, visibly concerned that his filing system should let him down so decisively, particularly in circumstances where he could not share the blame with anyone if the documents were indeed missing.

Robert continued to pace up and down the office with a mixture of exhilaration and intense irritation. How preposterous was it that this young girl had rendered him so weak over the past two days? He had intended asking Saint John how old she was, but something had prevented him from wanting to know. He convinced himself that her school uniform wasn't necessarily a true reflection of her age. Girls in this country go to school at all ages, he reflected. There is no legal age limit for schooling, no legal start date. In fact, he would have to stop thinking of her as a girl; she was probably a woman; it was quite possible that she was already eighteen. When the girl's outline appeared in the doorway, he was walking away from the door with his back to her. He reached the wall, turned round and saw her standing there. He smiled. She was lovely. More striking than he had remembered in the image of her that had occupied his thoughts unceasingly since he first saw her.

'Come in.'

Matilda took a hesitant step into the room and stood just inside the doorway, blinking while her eyes adjusted to the darkness of the room.

Robert could see that she was anxious. Naturally, she had not found the papers, and she probably expected to be in trouble now.

'Did you find them?' Saint John asked.

Matilda shook her head and pursed her lips, waiting for the onslaught.

'Don't worry about the papers,' said Robert, not taking his eyes off

14

the girl. He could sense his clerk's perplexed expression. 'I have just remembered that I took them upstairs yesterday. Go and get them.'

Saint John hurried off.

'Sit down.' Robert gestured to the armchair in the corner.

Matilda could hear her heart thumping as she walked towards the chair.

'Don't worry,' Robert continued, 'the papers are upstairs. I just wanted to see you.'

Matilda frowned. She tried to swallow, but her mouth was dry. She wondered whether she should say anything. But what could she possibly say to this man? To Lawyer? She tried to sit on the very edge of the armchair, but she slid down into the wide seat. The chair was not as comfortable as it looked. She knew she was frowning and tried to smile but couldn't. Her palms would not stop sweating, although she kept wiping them on her school uniform. As soon as they were dry, they needed wiping all over again. It seemed the safest thing to keep looking at the floor. If only he would turn away from her, then she might dare to have a good look at him.

Robert stared at her. She was indeed handsome. Untouched, he could tell. Her innocence increased his desire.

'What is your name?' He couldn't think of anything better to say.

'Please, Matilda,' she replied, still avoiding eye contact with him. For what purpose did he need to know her name? she wondered, and why was she here? She also wondered whether he was like the men her mother warned her about. 'The older they are, the more you need to remain on your guard,' Ama had often said.

'Well, Matilda, I am Lawyer Robert Bannerman. Your uncle talks highly of you. How old are you?' Not being able to say what he wanted was alien to him, but he knew he had to exercise restraint for now.

'Please, fourteen,' she said, pinching her fingers.

'So, when will you finish your schooling?' He stared at her more closely now. Fourteen was rather young, even for him. She was a child still.

'Please, I will finish next year.' She looked longingly at the door, wishing her uncle would hurry up and return so that she could leave.

'And when will you be fifteen?'

'Please, on the twenty-first of May is my birthday.'

Robert smiled and considered what she had said. In about two months she would be fifteen. Clearly old enough. He chewed his lip. There was no law prohibiting him from seducing her now, only his blasted inconvenient principles. And his irksome clerk, on whom he had come to depend quite heavily these days.

Saint John rushed into the office clutching the elusive papers. He looked pleased. 'Lawyer, you were right. I have found them. They were in your room.' As soon as he saw Matilda sitting in the armchair, he shouted, 'Get up. How dare you sit in Lawyer's chair? Did I raise you to be disrespectful?'

'Saint John, it is fine,' said Robert. 'I told Matilda to sit down. We were just talking. Your niece is not disrespectful; in fact, I can tell that she is very polite.' He turned to Matilda and smiled. A smile that normally got him what he wanted. 'Thank you so much for coming, Matilda. You can go home now.'

Robert did not take his eyes off her as she hurried out of the room. He had made up his mind. He would have to have her; it was clear that this desire, these thoughts, so overpowering that they made him dizzy, had to be satiated. He was prepared to go as far as, well, as far as marriage even, if that became necessary.

Matilda set off to the local school where one of the teachers was giving English lessons over the holidays. She was relieved that Lawyer had let her go in time for her lesson, but as she walked, she pondered the strangeness of their meeting. She had gone to the office filled with fear after searching in vain through Uncle's things for the documents that the messenger had said were supposed to be there. It was odd, and very unlike her uncle, who never misplaced Lawyer's papers at home, that she could not find them. He normally kept work papers in one place only – on the table in his room – and no one was allowed to touch them. Matilda knew Uncle, and probably Lawyer too, would shout at her if she did not find them, and yet she couldn't; there were no papers anywhere in Uncle's room. And there weren't many places to look in the sparsely furnished room. There was a bed in the corner underneath the window, through which a small amount of light filtered after finding its way between the little houses, which were barely three feet apart on either side of an alleyway. Beside the bed was a table and chair on which Uncle Saint John and Aunty Amele battled for space, she for her cheap ornaments, jewellery, bottles of scent, yellowed with age, and her English Bible, which she could not read, and he for his newspapers and, when necessary, for Lawyer's documents. There were two chests side by side on the floor in which Uncle Saint John and Aunty Amele kept their clothes. The whitewashed concrete walls had been dirtied with smudges of miscellaneous unidentifiable substances over the years, and on the wall between the bed and the table, Uncle Saint John had sometimes scribbled things when he could not find a piece of paper. Other than a crucifix, which hung above the head of the bed, the walls and the undulating cement floor were bare.

Despairing at the thought of having to go to the office empty-handed, she had begun to look in the most unlikely places. She had bent down to look under the bed. It was dark and dusty and filled with clutter: some shoes, a battered brown suitcase, a box of books. Each time she pulled something out from underneath the bed, her nostrils filled up with disturbed dust, which promptly resettled wherever it could. She had even sneaked a look in the chests on the floor. When she opened the chest filled with Aunty Amele's clothes, the scent of camphor escaped first, then the smell of crisp new cotton. There were several bundles of unused printed batiks, possibly left over from Aunty Amele's dowry, neatly piled in one corner of the chest. Matilda could not resist running her hand delicately over the top bundle before she closed the chest.

When she arrived at his office, she had quickly noticed that Lawyer was much taller and imposing than he had seemed in the photographs. Matilda had been taken aback when he asked her to sit down. She had never been offered a seat in the presence of any of the adults she knew. It did not make any sense to her that he should want to see her. She could not imagine why such a prominent lawyer would have time to be interested in a girl like her. She panicked as the thought materialised. Please God, let him not be interested in me, she thought, then smiled at the ridiculousness of her overactive mind. Yet, try as she could to make sense of it, she remained perplexed about their encounter. She would tell Patience about it.

Patience would be impressed and would certainly have some theory or other about the meeting.

Matilda was going to start learning English that morning. It had taken a while to convince Uncle Saint John that she should learn English. He said that the education she received at her school, the local mission school, was sufficient. There, lessons were conducted in the Ga language. The missionaries, originally from Switzerland, were here to spread the Good News and to raise healthy converts; intellectual advancement was not really part of their mandate. So, in addition to religious studies, they concentrated on teaching the girls handicrafts, domestic science and other necessary skills for motherhood.

Uncle Saint John had said he could not see any reason why Matilda would ever need to speak English, but his sister, Matilda's mother, Ama, had a gift for making everyone around her do what she wanted and so Matilda was going to learn English.

Before accepting defeat, Uncle Saint John had cautioned the women in his house one final time. 'Mark my words. You go ahead and over-educate the girl and you will see how you will just complicate everything,' he said. 'It is not as if I am against education; after all, am I not educated too? But the wrong education is dangerous. What is the use of educating Matilda as if she is a British girl? So that she starts to wear British dresses? So that she abandons her culture? Too much education is just a hindrance for a girl who is only going to be a wife and mother.'

'Yes, yes,' Ama had replied. 'But it might improve her marriage prospects. Anything that might improve those prospects must be done.'

Matilda had stood with her hands behind her back in the corner of the compound as Uncle Saint John spoke, rejoicing internally as it became evident to her that her mother was getting her way. But it would be a bad idea to appear too victorious, so she scrunched her lips to repress a smile. She ached to know more than how to cook and sew, and she had a nebulous notion that there was a world of knowledge she could not access because she could not speak English, a world she was determined to enter some day. The first step would be to learn English, and then she could start her journey of discovery, to find what, she did not know. To date, her schooling had been haphazard; whenever she was needed to run some errand or other or help her mother at the market, she had to miss school. It was the same for all the other girls, and the teachers could hardly penalise them for their absences.

Today, as she walked towards the school, she wondered why her mother was in favour of her learning English; they rarely wanted the same thing, making Matilda careful to conceal her real desires at all times.

As Matilda entered the schoolyard, she saw a group of girls all in the same green school uniform she was wearing. They were being entertained by the vivid gestures of one girl who was holding court. She wondered what made-up stories Patience was telling this time.

The schoolyard was an area of red-brown compacted earth surrounded by a low brick wall. The soil, thirsty for the rainy season that was due in a few weeks, defied the elements by sprouting patches of grass that browned as soon as they emerged. The girls were sheltering in the shade of two mature mango trees, which stood proudly, close to the centre of the yard, where they were beginning to sag under the weight of their ripening fruit. Scraggly pink and white frangipani shrubs were dotted around the periphery of the wall, the legacy of a teacher who had been determined to beautify the school and had supervised while pupils planted them some years ago. Not much aftercare was given to the plants, however, and in time, only a few survived.

The classroom block was a long, single-storey concrete building, which was divided into four rooms. The roof sloped away from the covered veranda that ran along the length of the building, so that when it rained, the rainwater was channelled away from the entrance to the classrooms. Each room had three gaps in the walls on either side, which served as windows. On a normal school day, when classes were filled with pupils of mixed ability and age, those sitting closest to the windows had to concentrate to hear the teacher in their room, especially if the teacher in the next classroom was particularly enthusiastic.

'Hey! Matilda,' Patience shouted as she saw her friend, waving frantically at her.

As soon as Matilda was close enough, Patience grabbed hold of her arm. 'Wait till you see the teacher. I tell you he is handsome,' she continued almost breathlessly, with her eyes wide open.

Patience dramatised the most minor events, particularly if they involved men, and Matilda had learned to take little notice of her most of the time.

'You always think about the wrong things,' she said. 'We are here to learn English, not to find husbands. Our elders are doing that job full time for us, and they don't want our help. Hello, everyone.' Matilda recognised most of the girls from school. 'You won't believe where I have just been,' she whispered to Patience.

'Tell me, then.'

'Lawyer Bannerman, you know, the one Uncle—'

'Everyone knows who Lawyer Bannerman is.'

'He sent for me today,' said Matilda, enjoying the amazed look on her friend's face.

'Just like that?'

Matilda told the story, but before she could finish, Patience interrupted. 'He must have seen you somewhere and decided that he likes you. What are you going to do about it?' she asked, grasping Matilda's arm with both of hers.

'Don't be stupid, Patience. I am not looking for a boyfriend. And if I was looking, he would not be so old. And he is married. I don't want to be a second or third wife.'

'Whether or not he is married is irrelevant. If he can support you and your children . . .'

'Anyone would think that your head is filled only with husbands and babies. As for me, there are things I want to do before I settle down. I want to be educated.'

Their conversation was halted by the sound of a bell. Looking in the direction of the noise, Matilda noticed a man standing outside one of the classrooms ringing the school bell vigorously.

'Hurry,' said Patience, pulling her friend's hand as she made her way towards the classroom block. 'I want to sit right at the front.'

Patience was successful, and she and Matilda sat at the desk nearest to the teacher. From this close, Matilda could not help but study the teacher while she waited for the lesson to start. He was rather small and nervous-looking with black horn-rimmed glasses that seemed a little too big for him. He was very dark and had very short hair. Matilda noticed that his white shirt was immaculately pressed. She took this to mean that he was overly preoccupied with his appearance, which seemed to her a little at odds with his otherwise scholarly look. Probably he just had doting women at home who were concerned on his behalf; none of the men in her house ironed their own shirts. They considered the effort of heating the coal iron beyond them, and if Matilda or one of her sisters did not iron her cousin's clothes, he simply went out looking like a crumpled envelope.

Anyway, Matilda was really not interested in men. She was here to learn English. Her dream was about to come true. But she was prepared to admit, if pressed again by Patience, that this teacher seemed nice. At least, he would make a change from the fat, frightening women who taught her at school. Women who seemed to believe that girls were incapable of retaining any knowledge unless they were sufficiently caned. Matilda had always believed that to be a teacher, one had to have a cruel streak. How fortunate that the teacher who had been scheduled to teach this class had become ill after the pupils had already paid for the course. Matilda was certain that her mother would have been less keen for her to attend a course taught by a man.

The man introduced himself as Mr Mensah. It was an Ashanti name, and Matilda wondered whether he spoke Ga, and if not, how he was planning to communicate with his class.

Mr Mensah interrupted Matilda's thoughts. 'Welcome to our English classes. I am glad to see so many of you here today. As you know, Mrs Bonsu has been admitted to hospital and so I am privileged to be your substitute teacher. I hope you will find my tuition beneficial. English is the language of the British Empire, and therefore of our world. It is very important that you, as the future mothers of our country, are able to read and write it. Many illustrious works of culture will be available to you when you master this sumptuous language.'

Mr Mensah must have noticed that there were sixteen girls staring at him blankly, some with their mouths open. He was speaking in

English, and his audience did not understand him. Although most of them knew some basic everyday English, they did not recognise his luxuriant vocabulary. Even if they had, he spoke clearly, intonating the words correctly for the most part, which made the sounds unfamiliar to the girls. He smiled at them, revealing a gap in his upper front teeth, and started speaking very slowly and carefully, nodding in time with the words as he wrote what he said on the blackboard. 'I will not use conventional methods of teaching; I will converse with you as a friend about things that interest me, and you will increase your vocabulary and your general knowledge that way.' He looked approvingly at Matilda, who was fervently but hesitantly copying down everything that he wrote as though she might not have another chance. He pointed at her. 'You. What is your name?'

Matilda was taken aback. She was used to teachers calling on someone who had put up their hand to answer a question. She rose slowly and held on to the desk. Why had she listened to Patience yet again? She cleared her throat. 'Plis, Mateelda Quartey.'

'Good, good, good. You see, you understand more of this language than you may realise.' He was wagging his finger at the class, raising his eyebrows to the ceiling, smiling and nodding his head all at once. 'But remember, when you are conversing with a British man or woman, he or she will not expect you to say "please" all the time. Needless to say, you must be cautious not to abandon your respectful duties to your superiors when you speak to them in English.' He turned back to Matilda, who was waiting keenly to be told she could sit down and stop being the centre of attention. 'So, what is your age now?'

Matilda frowned slightly and bit her lip. What had he said? Was she allowed to tell him in her language that she did not know what he had said? She felt tongue-tied and stupid. 'Plis, erm . . .' Mr Mensah turned round to write the question on the board. Matilda looked at Patience, who looked serene, like a person daydreaming, and gave her a nudge, but her friend just shrugged unhelpfully.

Mr Mensah turned to face his pupils again. He smiled at Matilda and the rest of the girls. 'Aha. Wait. How old are you?'

'Fourteen,' Matilda answered quickly, relieved that she understood this question at least. Please let her sit down.

'Well done. Sit down, Matilda.' He was writing her age on the board for all to see. He wrote it twice. 'Fourteen √. Fourteen X.' 'The correct way to say this word is *four*teen.' He was pointing with a stick to the word on the board with the tick next to it. 'This way is wrong,' he said as he tapped the word with the cross. 'Everybody repeat after me, *four*teen.'

And they did. Repeatedly and in unison, each time stressing the second syllable of the word just as Matilda had done, becoming progressively sure of themselves, saying the word louder each time, all the while smiling back at their teacher because they were pleased with their effort.

Finally, Mr Mensah shook his head and held out his hand to stop them. 'Enough, enough. We will simply have to remain on the alert to this pitfall and, over time, improve your fearful diction.'

When the lesson ended, Mr Mensah asked the girls to practise some of the words they had learned that day and to take every opportunity to speak English at home with each other. 'The BBC Empire Service is an invaluable service that I recommend to you. Borrow your fathers' wireless sets whenever you can and listen to the broadcasts.'

It was home time. Matilda stood up, feeling slightly light-headed as she did, almost like a person who, parched, had drunk too much water far too quickly.

Chapter Two

Audrey Turton awoke to the bright sunshine with a dull head. She rolled her fragile body away from the window, stared briefly at her white bedroom wall through the tiny holes in the mosquito netting that draped the bed and closed her eyes again. She resolved not to drink a drop today. It was no fun waking up in this fogged state, with her senses so painfully heightened. It just didn't seem fair that one could go to bed engulfed in what felt like heady happiness and awaken so desperately low.

Already, she could feel the heat encroaching from outside. A fan whirred ceaselessly above her, but all it managed to do was distribute the warm air efficiently. The brightness increased as the sun rose steadily. How wonderful if it rained today for a change, proper rain that soaked the ground and washed away the dust, if for once it could be dull, not predictably sunny. She moaned. Today, she would love nothing better than to curl up on one of the old chairs in her mother's kitchen with a nice mug of cocoa. She rolled on to her back and listened for something, but in the stillness, all she could hear was her own gentle breathing. Distant cocks had stopped crowing, and Alan's dogs kept birds away from her garden. Heat had absorbed the sounds of life and left the atmosphere densely quiet.

The days passed slowly here; yet somehow, without her noticing, a whole year had slipped away since she arrived in the colony. How many more would slip by her like this? she wondered. And there was no sign that they might be able to leave soon. Alan was happy here and appeared to have no reason to rush off elsewhere. 'Give it time, darling,' he had told her. 'You simply need to acclimatise.' But Audrey knew she had made little progress on the road to acclimatisation.

She climbed out of bed and rang the bell for Awuni, the steward. She had introduced a little bell to the servants shortly after she arrived – her mother, who had known a woman who had spent a stretch of time in India, had suggested it might come in handy – and found it more tolerable than hollering for them whenever they disappeared inconveniently. They were the bane of her life, the useless servants. Having servants was, she imagined, a little like having small children one could not control. She had been trying to train Awuni for long enough now, and he was still far from ideal. His redeeming grace was his seemingly endless energy, and his ability, at least outwardly, to serve her happily. That and the fact that he had been the most suitable following a long line of disastrous hires. She had dismissed Alan's steward, a useless fellow with not a spare brain cell, within weeks of her arrival, which had amused the ladies at the club no end. Not long before, at one of the first tea parties she attended, she had informed the gathering about how she wanted to get to know the natives, and not just as servants. 'I find it a little decadent,' she had said, 'to have people at one's beck and call day and night.'

It was Polly Aldridge who had said haughtily, 'Oh, we have heard it all before, haven't we, girls? Let me give you some advice regarding servants, Audrey: they are not your friends. You'll rue the day if you give them an inch, if they think you are weak. I am sure you'll be bossing them about like the best of us in no time at all.'

Audrey had looked disbelieving, and Alice Jenkins, who had since proved the kindest of the bunch, had said, 'She *is* right. They have to know who is in charge or else they really will make your life miserable. They don't expect anything different from you. And actually, they have a much better life working for us than they would otherwise.'

There had followed a steady supply of boys, each highly recommended by other employees of expatriates. As she found out later, they were relatives hauled in from distant villages in the hope of finding a job for which they would pay the job finder some commission, but none of them had lasted more than a few weeks. Some left in tears saying that they could not bear to be treated as her slave, others she had marched out declaring unfit for sophisticated life, suggesting they return to their village. Indeed, it had not taken long for her to conclude that if Europeans had not stumbled upon Africa, these natives would still be living in a happy undiscovered state, blissfully unaware of the civilised world; such a fatalistic and uninspired lot of people would be hard to envision without first-hand experience.

'Awuni!' she screamed at the top of her voice. She needed coffee. Where was that damned servant? She had ventured out of her bedroom clutching her dressing gown around her thin body when she saw him scurrying towards her.

'Sorry, madam. I went to toilet.' He was breathless and did not seem to notice the revolted expression this information brought to her face.

'I hope you washed your hands with soap,' she said, sickened. She refused to speak pidgin English with her servants. After all, was not one of the Empire's aims to educate the negroes and to advance civilisation? 'Make me some more coffee. This is cold and disgusting,' she said, motioning at the tray of breakfast things that he had set out for her at seven that morning in accordance with her strict instructions, even though she now found it hard to wake before eight, and sometimes even nine.

'Yes, madam. Right away, madam,' said Awuni cheerily. He was a small man with sinewy arms and legs, which bowed through his crisp white uniform. He nodded at her and grinned slightly before picking up the tray and hurrying off into the kitchen with his bare feet slapping on the brown linoleum.

She flopped on to the sofa and stretched out her legs. It was going to be hot today. She looked around the space that had become her home, wishing once more that she could rip off the mosquito netting that covered the large windows at either end of the room, which restricted the breeze as well as light. It was a standard government bungalow on stilts set in an acre of land. There were two bedrooms at the rear of the building, one at each corner, and a simple bathroom. To this day, Alan still emerged from it on occasion full of praise for running water and flushing toilets and regaled her anew with stories of his time in the bush.

The living area was spacious and stretched the width of the house. Over the year, she had tried to lessen the impact of the dark, chunky mahogany furniture Alan had had made when he was stationed in Ashanti before she joined him, but the room was still sparsely decorated. Within weeks of arriving, she had taken up Alice's offer of sewing lessons, and together they had embarked on making some brightly patterned cushion covers. Alice had been incredibly patient, but in the end, much like a mother who thinks her child's help is more of a hindrance, she took over and did the sewing while Audrey watched, often cigarette in one hand, cool drink in the other. Alice had suggested a few times since that they try some curtains, but Audrey hadn't enjoyed sewing and didn't have the energy to try, even though she longed to replace the old lacy things that fluttered ineffectually in the windows.

It was surprisingly quiet this morning. When she had first arrived and met all their servants, she had wondered whether she would ever have any peace in her own home with all these people coming and going. Apart from the steward, there was Cook, whose name was Kwame, a small boy who helped him, a driver and Hassan, the gardener, whose face still terrified her. He was from one of the northern tribes and had long, thin tribal cuts on his face, which Alan had explained were done at birth with knives and were considered beautifying. Fortunately, he never said much to her other than 'madam', by way of greeting, when he revealed his toothless, diseased gums.

Audrey began to hear the distinctive sound of tuneless, lively whistling getting progressively louder. She sat up, startled, just in time to see her husband appear in the doorway.

'Well, good morning, my darling,' said Alan loudly, striding through the open doors. He clasped her shoulders firmly and kissed her cheek. Alan's dogs, a pair of Alsatians, excited to have this extra time around their loving owner, stayed at the door wagging their tails and hoping to be let in. 'How are you today? Sleep well?'

He was an energetic man who never sat still for long; just watching him hurry around in the heat sapped what little energy Audrey thought she had. Whenever he smiled, his green eyes twinkled in his tanned face. He was tall and trim with broad shoulders, and he still exuded vigour and healthiness, rather like an advertisement for tropical living. Even his hair, which at home was a nondescript brown, had been washed by the sun to the colour of bright sea sand and now glinted in the light.

'Yes. Thank you.' Audrey realised what she must look like and wanted to escape to the bathroom.

'Let's have coffee on the veranda. It is such a lovely morning,' he said as he shuffled papers on the table. He looked up and, smiling again like a man assessing his perfect world, said, 'I want to make sure everything is ready for tonight. Don't want any last-minute hitches, do we? Not with the new governor coming. I'd like to make a good impression on His Excellency.'

Audrey felt her stomach drop. How could she have forgotten it was today? It must be her blasted head; the dull ache made thinking straight impossible, blocked her thoughts from flowing freely. Oh, she hated waking up like this!

When Alan first suggested it was time they had some kind of do, she had been enthusiastic. That she might feel the slightest apprehension hadn't occurred to her, even though she had never thrown a party and her parents were not great entertainers. The idea of having guests in her home made her mother almost ill with anxiety, which Audrey had never quite understood. For inspiration, she had thought back to the parties she could remember, imagining what she might do differently so hers was one everyone remembered, even though Alan had suggested they keep to the standard format: drinks and nibbles. In her opinion, none of them had been distinctive. She would like hers to be memorable. It seemed all rather simple: food, booze, good company and a jolly hostess. What more could there possibly be to it?

She had lain awake in bed thinking of ways she could make sure that the party was a huge success. She realised it would have been nice to have a soirée for close friends to start with, to practise on. Yes, one needed to stretch one's imagination when listing 'close friends' in a place one had only lived for a year, but it would have been ideal.

She had put Alan in charge of the guest list, and he seemed to have invited absolutely everyone. 'We can't really leave them out,' he said when she asked why so and so was on the list. 'We are too small a community to be overly selective. And Mother always says you never know where or when you are going to need someone, so it's best to be nice to everyone.' Audrey had smiled, veiling her desire to roll her eyes upward.

Over the last couple of days, she had begun to feel anxious as it dawned on her how much of a trial this was going to be after all. The party had become the main subject of conversation at the club, where the women were open about their keenness to see what she would wear, how her staff performed and whether or not the new governor, who had been in Accra for less than a month, would come. And with all the kindness of a thorn, that awful Polly Aldridge had remarked, 'Finally, we get to see how *you* do things.'

From the outset, she had known it was important to Alan that they make the right impression, but she hadn't imagined *she* would care what they all thought; she didn't ordinarily care what anyone thought of her. She knew that it was this trait that had alienated her from a fair number of the women here. She had refused to blend in, to become another one of them, with their awful hobbies of sewing and knitting – it was so bloody hot, yet many of them knitted away incessantly – and, worst of all, amateur dramatics. She had refused to take part in the pantomime last Christmas or to help with the costumes or the programmes. Polly's right-hand witch, as she referred to Frances Winram, an overly competent woman with pretty features, had persisted in presenting her with various tasks. To each, Audrey simply said, 'No, thanks,' while remaining pleasant. Alice had piped up, 'I think Audrey just wants to settle down properly first. I am sure she'll play her part next year.' Audrey had intended correcting this statement when gentle Alice pressed firmly on her foot to shut her up. She was surprised when Alan mentioned over dinner one evening that she was the only woman in the British community who wasn't taking part. She shrugged and smiled at him. 'Not really good at that sort of thing, darling,' she had said. 'Next year then, maybe,' he'd responded. He continued with his dinner, oblivious to her fury. She wouldn't do it, this follow-the-leader game that the other wives played unquestioningly. She simply couldn't. She had always hated conformity, and she couldn't be submissive when she thought it was what was expected of her. It had made life at school awkward. Her parents had tried to be supportive, to understand her apartness, the individuality that meant so much to her, but her mother knew it would make Audrey's life unnecessarily painful.

Last night, Alan informed her casually that the Governor and his wife were definitely coming, and she had to admit she was a trifle nervous. He smiled and said, 'Don't worry, darling. It will be fabulous, and you'll shine,' which only jolted her nerves further, so she had to pour herself another gin. The Governor hadn't met the wider British community outside of the castle, so his presence would be an honour.

Gathering her dressing gown tightly around her now, she thought: What is the worst thing that can happen tonight? It is only a party, for heaven's sake! Get them all sloshed and they'll only remember the good bits. If there are any bad bits to forget, that is. 'I need some coffee,' she said almost to herself. 'Where on earth is that idiot of a steward?'

'Darling . . .'

'Yes, I know, I shouldn't insult the servants. I'll go and make myself decent,' she said as she escaped out of the living room.

She leaned against the sink in the bathroom and stared at her tired blue eyes. She leaned further into the mirror. More freckles. Once, there had only been a few scattered on her nose; now, they were all over her face. She scrubbed them violently and brushed her hair. She had always thought it was her best feature, sheets of thick, straight brown strands that had paled pleasantly in the sun, but which went lank and wavy in the worst humidity.

She put on a fading sleeveless floral dress and applied copious amounts of her new cologne, breathing in deeply the pleasing citrus scent. This simple routine, which she followed several times each day, never failed to lift her spirits. Now she felt primed to face Alan.

'You look nice,' he said, interrupting his whistling to look up when she walked on to the veranda. He rose to pour coffee. 'I have just been speaking to Awuni; it looks like he has everything ready for this evening.' He handed his wife a steaming cup. He stood for a moment stroking his chin and grinned at her. 'I am rather looking forward to tonight, aren't you?'

Audrey smiled. It was hard not to be affected by his enthusiasm. 'I suppose I am. It *is* my first party here. But what is the Governor like? What's his wife called again?'

'Edith. Lady Smythe to you and me. They're charming. There really is no reason for you to fret.'

This very suggestion, which he kept repeating, was beginning to make her worry.

'Parties are probably more of a chore than anything else for them. They certainly won't be judging your performance. I am the one who is likely to be scrutinised; he's my boss, after all. Anyway, Mother always says parties are a lot easier if you are well prepared. And we are. You'll impress him by just being you, my darling. And with your jelly . . .'

'Oh yes! My *pièce de résistance*. I must make it soon,' she said with a playful shrug of her shoulders. 'Promise you'll be home early tonight.'

'When have I ever let you down, darling? I'll be home with plenty of time to admire your new dress,' he said, smiling.

He was handsome when he smiled, thought Audrey, looking briefly into his shiny eyes. Why couldn't she simply be happy to be here with him? She turned away and tried to control her thoughts from wandering off in the wrong direction. No time for self-pity this morning. There were flowers to cut, servants to supervise and two large jellies to make. For him, she would try to make a good impression on the Governor and his wife, to throw a party that the expats would remember and that would make Alan proud. There must be no snags, not tonight, she pleaded.

Audrey stood on the veranda and waved as the driver manoeuvred the car round the small circular patch of grass at the front of the house and down the gravelled driveway towards the road. When he was out of sight, she slumped back into the wicker chair, allowing her arms to dangle beside her. She shut her eyes and tried to think about all the things she had to do before the guests arrived that evening. How convenient it would be to know how many guests one was expecting, she thought, sighing loudly. She started listing chores in her head; she liked to test herself like this to see if she could improve her memory and concentration: jelly, crockery, Cook . . . Whenever she lost her train of thought, she started all over again: make jelly, check crockery, flowers, send Cook to the market . . . She must have been sitting for half an hour when she felt something soft and wet on one of her hands, which made her jump up and scream. One of the dogs had licked her hand. She stood up, shocked, and tried to steady herself. Funny that the servants did not come running to see if she was being murdered by savages. Admittedly, there were no savages, but that was not really the point. Could she not reasonably expect them to protect their madam? But she knew that they had likely tired of coming to rescue her, because her screaming had never signalled real danger yet. For instance, whenever she came unexpectedly close to one of those horrible but harmless translucent geckoes in a dark corner of the house, she screamed out loud. She also screamed when she saw cockroaches, which were larger than she had imagined possible, and evil-looking, with their shiny brown bodies and long, waving feelers. Once, she had found a small grass snake sunning itself on the veranda and she had screamed for a very long time. She had continued to scream even after the gardener and Awuni chopped it up, laughing all the while. And she had screamed hysterically when they fed the fresh meat to the dogs.

Already exhausted, Audrey went back into the house, warning the dog to stay outside. Jelly. She had to make the jelly first. Or should she first talk to Cook about the food? She was beginning to think that being a hostess was perhaps not as easy as she had believed.

She strolled to the kitchen, which was housed in a separate building in the back yard. Basically equipped, hot and never as clean as she would have liked, Audrey found little reason to spend any time in it of late.

It had been different in the early days, when she'd been eager to explore every inch of her strange new home and make it hers, to own it. These days, she was happy to let the servants reign in the kitchen, which seemed to give them untold pleasure.

She remembered her first morning, when, thirsty, she had wandered there in search of a cold drink. Alan had told her the back of the house was the servants' domain. She had thought it strange that her kitchen should be demarcated in this way. It was fine for him, he never cooked, but she would have to, and she wanted to make sure the servants realised from the outset that she was reclaiming this part of their property.

There was no grass at the back, only hard, bare ground, which she had heard the boy sweeping earlier. At the far end of the property was a small concrete rectangular block, which housed the boys' quarters. Alan had warned her that it was a definite no-go area for them. 'It is rather basically equipped, but they seem happy enough. It's probably better than they have in their own homes.'

The kitchen was halfway between the house and the boys' quarters. As she approached tentatively that first morning, Cook appeared in the doorway.

'Good morning, madam. Are you looking for somethings?'

She smiled warmly. 'I wanted to see the kitchen. And yes, I'm dying for a cold drink.'

'Madam, please don't say you are dying. For what you say with your mouth often enough will for sure come to pass.'

'What?'

'I said, please don't say you are dying . . .'

She laughed. 'Oh, I am not superstitious. Can I get past please? I really am dying for a drink.'

'There is no need for madam to come in here,' he said as he moved aside.

Audrey looked around the small room. It had a cement floor and whitewashed walls. There were two large windows at opposite ends. The equipment was simple: a small cooker and wood-burning oven for baking, a small fridge and a few cupboards. At home, she had only ever assisted her mother in the kitchen, but things would be different here: she would be in charge. She went to the fridge and pulled it open.

'Eh, please be careful, madam!'

She turned. 'What is the matter?'

'We don't open the fridge for just any reason at all.'

'I want something to drink,' she said, peering into the fridge. It was mostly empty. She opened the ice compartment and was pleased to see some ice trays.

'Madam, I beg you please to tell me what is your wish and I will send the boy with it.'

She felt awkward; wasn't she perfectly capable of getting herself a drink?

'Madam, please return to your house,' he said, pointing with his fat fingers outstretched towards the house. 'Please, we will bring you a refreshing drink.'

Audrey had returned to the house feeling like a child told off for trespassing.

How it used to irritate her that she should feel unwelcome in her own kitchen! But it bothered her less now. It was generally too hot to cook, and she had quickly come to realise that she didn't like being in such close proximity to the servants. No matter how often she told Cook to go away when she was in there, he found some reason to remain, to linger and peer into her pots and pans, making her invariably ruin whatever she was cooking with his scrutiny.

As she approached now, she could hear him screeching, his voice interspersed with loud slaps. She hurried her steps and turned the corner to see him hitting the small boy on his head with both hands. She watched, wondering what he had done this time to deserve a beating. She had learned that it was best not to interfere too much in the hierarchy of her servants, as little of it made sense to her. The small boy was a cheeky youth whose name Audrey could not pronounce, and she referred to him as 'you there' or 'boy' on the odd occasion she needed to speak to him.

'Madam, I caught him red-handed. Eating the chicken,' said Cook, hitting the boy one last time. The boy must have thought his ordeal was over now that Madam had arrived, and he had dropped his hands from his head, leaving his face open to receive the full force of Cook's hand. Audrey had oftentimes marvelled at the stoutness of Cook's fingers and hands. They were in keeping with the rest of him. He was a rotund, short fellow who had a large belly that swelled over the white apron that he always wore tightly bound across his hips. He had a pock-marked, very black face, with cheeks that looked as if they had been stuffed with something so they poked above the contours of his face. His lips were full, but each turned outward so that his mouth looked as if it was painted with smudging

34

lipstick. Usually, he grinned incessantly, revealing incredibly pink gums, but today, he looked angrier than she had ever seen him.

'Stop! I beg you stop. It is enough, I beg,' the boy cried.

'Shut up, you disrespectful boy. I will tell you when it is enough. Stealing red-handed, I tell you, madam.'

'I have come to ensure that everything is in order here,' said Audrey.

'Madam, as you know, you do not need to check on me. I have been in this service before now for nearly fifteen years. Before you, I was with—'

'I know your impeccable history, Cook,' said Audrey, 'but it never hurts to check everything is in order. This is my first formal party, and I want to make sure that it goes well. I am sure you understand.'

'As you wish, madam.'

'Have you got all the crockery you need?'

'The small boy from Mr Griffis's house brought a box full just now. We have plenty of everything now.'

'And Mr Griffiths knows about this?'

'Madam, Mr Griffis will know about it when he eats from his own plate tonight.' He laughed. 'Don't worry, madam, this has been our system since many years, and no one complained before now. We will not break anything. In fact, before Mr Griffis wakes up, before dawn even, his plates will be back in his cupboards safely and soundly.'

'As you say,' said Audrey, sighing. Simply talking to him tired her out. 'Do we have enough ice? And the food, how is that coming along? Can we talk about the menu now? You have put me off long enough, and I really need to know what you are planning to serve tonight. The Governor will be here, you know.'

'Madam, I assure you from the pit of my heart that I have cooked for governors present and past on many more occasions than I can recollect . . .'

'Yes, you said. So what *are* you cooking?' It was hot in the kitchen, even though there were two large open windows at either end, and Audrey wanted to go back into the house.

'For the delight of your guests this evening, I will prepare smoked fish pâté on toasted breads, prawns with cucumber relish, chicken and fish pieces.' Kwame stood with his hands clasped before him, his chin raised defiantly. 'Yes, and assorted fried vegetables such as yams and plantains. And special pork surprise.'

'Well?' Audrey said, waiting for him to continue. 'What is the bloody surprise?'

Kwame flinched visibly. 'It is, as I said, a surprise, madam. You will only have to trust me.'

Audrey rolled her eyes. 'Have it your way.' She resented him behaving like this in front of Awuni and the small boy, who were hovering in the background pretending to be busy. If he were not such a good cook, she would have sacked him a long time ago for his audacity.

Cook nodded. 'So, as I said earlier, madam, everything is all under control. The only thing remaining is the jelly. I have told you that I can make jelly; there is no need for you to make it, madam.'

Audrey told him to bring the ingredients for the jelly to the dining room. 'I will make it myself. You go marketing.' She walked off. 'Bloody servants,' she said between clenched teeth. 'Bloody, bloody servants.'

At least she didn't have to go to the market herself. She had vowed never to set foot there again after Alan had taken her to the large daily market the day after she arrived in the colony. He had been determined she should see the place, describing it as the hub of the natives' lives. He thought it was fascinating and was certain she would think so too.

So she was entirely unprepared for the smells and sounds or for what she saw. The uncovered market sprawled haphazardly in every direction. Rows of tables and stalls snaked unsystematically along rough paths, behind which women sat wearing heavy oversized straw hats to protect their heads from the glaring sun. Already, she was beginning to notice that the tropical heat was different to anything she had ever felt before; dreadfully intense and oppressive, it was debilitating, quickly draining her strength. She understood then why it was still an offence for Europeans to be bareheaded between eight in the morning and four in the afternoon, and she was grateful that she had brought a collection of hats. She could see why walking in the sun, unless absolutely necessary, should be avoided. And the heat exacerbated the smells. A sour stench hit the back of her mouth with a jolt as soon as they entered the market, causing her to blink in surprise.

Then it was as if they had walked on to a stage. From all over the market, eyes turned to scrutinise them, mouths greeted, and hands waved. She stared at the fat market women who had babies on their backs, so tightly bound that only their little faces poked out. Although the market women moved slowly, if at all, especially when carefully turning their heads that were shielded by the enormous woven hats, they chatted loudly amongst themselves with vibrant voices and animated expressions, and seemed to be laughing at her and Alan.

She followed half a step behind him along the unpaved, uneven path, stepping gingerly, as if instinctively aware of unseen dangers. She struggled to hold her breath and maintain a pleasing expression at the same time. As they walked through the bustling market, people called out to them, '*Obronie, obronie*,' and Alan smiled and waved in acknowledgement. He explained that it meant 'white man', and it was a fond term. Soon an entourage of children, encouraged by Alan's friendliness, were following in their footsteps, talking at the couple in their indecipherable tongue, punctuating it regularly with calls of 'Hello, *obronie*', in what they must have thought sounded like an English accent.

Wares ranged from mountains of overripe tomatoes, chilli peppers, white garden eggs and onions to other more ominous-looking foodstuffs that were unrecognisably desiccated. There were live animals, wizened chickens trussed up in cages that were far too small, scrawny-looking goats and sheep tethered and waiting for a rich customer. Alan pointed out fish that had been laid out to dry in the sun so that their tails and heads curled in an attempted meeting. The fish were covered with large flies, which no one was bothering to do anything about, and they smelled sour and most definitely inedible. Audrey grimaced and instinctively raised her hand to clamp her nose in disgust, but quickly realised that it might be best simply to continue to hold her breath and look courteous. She began to realise she had been naïve to think she might get to know the natives.

'You can get all sorts of things here – bush meat, which the locals love, and which I must say is not bad at all considering the animal

37

looks a little like an overgrown rat,' he said authoritatively. Audrey felt her stomach turn. Alan reached for her elbow in a reassuring gesture and said, 'I promise on my life that I will never make you eat anything that unfamiliar. Cook only serves us chicken, beef or lamb. And lots of *fresh* fish,' he said, laughing.

She laughed weakly, and her lungs filled with the rancid scent.

They passed some stalls selling what Alan said were traditional medicines. Audrey could not make out what was being sold. Everything looked brown and unfamiliar. She blinked, trying hard not to shut down her beleaguered senses.

'Vital animal parts, lizards, birds, snakes and other amazing things that are used in the traditional religious rites,' Alan explained with the excitement of a ten-year-old boy. 'Come, let's buy something.'

Audrey could not believe her ears, but before she could formulate a protest, Alan was haggling in pidgin English over a pile of tomatoes with a large woman wearing voluminous African clothing. She started waving away flies from her tomatoes, which previously had been left undisturbed, while she argued with Alan over the price. When he paid, the woman reached into her vast bosom and pulled out a rolled-up handkerchief, which she carefully unwound to reveal a neat bundle of money. Audrey's eyes must have been as round as plates because she noticed that the children were pointing and laughing at her.

As they walked off towards yet another part of the market, a scrawny boy with bare feet and a confident, cheeky grin came up and slipped his dirty hand in Alan's. The two of them walked along like this, holding hands as if they were father and son, Alan looking down at the child like a benefactor. When the boy's friend tried to take hold of Audrey's hand, she clutched her handbag firmly and folded her arms in defence, a forced grin on her face.

At the gate to the market, he stood to say goodbye to the children. She was stunned, but he stood there with his hands in his pockets smiling happily as he savoured this glimpse into the lives of the people he was here to govern.

Why was he at ease in this strangeness, this hovel that he had brought her to, where children were urinating into exposed sewers, and women were openly feeding babies from flattened breasts, where armies of flies, attracted by the filth and germs and the stink, hovered first on children's scabs, then their urine, then the piles of food that they would eat? How could he be unperturbed and even enthusiastic about this cesspit that the civilisation of the British Empire had obviously not reached? And how could she learn to feel the same way, with her mouth coated in microscopic particles of stench, despite her efforts to protect herself from it, and with these dirty children bent on touching her white skin? With the utter awfulness of it all?

Later, she trembled as she washed away invisible grime. She vowed never to go to the market again. Not ever. She would never see what it was about the smells and sights that appealed to Alan. She began to worry that she had made a huge mistake. This place was not going to be an adventure, it was life, her life, and her life had always had more than its fair share of tedium.

In those days, she still believed that round the corner was a cleaner, greener side to Africa, a vibrant idyll, quite unlike the reality she had so far encountered. Now, a year on, she still hoped occasionally to find the Africa she had dreamed about, but with disconcerting regularity, she tried again and again to understand how she had ended up here in the first place. How had one fateful visit to Cambridge to see Cousin Freddy led her to this God-forsaken place where she sometimes seemed to be losing grip of her mind?

It was shortly after her twenty-first birthday that she met Alan while on a visit from Stonebridge in Suffolk. Now that she was working as a secretary for an accountant who was an old friend of her father's, she could afford to make more frequent visits to see Freddy. It was nice to leave home even for a few hours; that perfect, wet, green village where everyone smiled and nodded at everyone else stifled her. And her visits gave her an excuse to avoid jam making or fruit preserving with her mother, which she no longer enjoyed.

It was a mild day, perhaps the warmest that year, and Freddy was playing in a cricket match. When the match was over, Freddy introduced her to his friend and team-mate Alan Turton. He was tall and strong with incredibly broad shoulders and shiny green eyes. In his cricket whites, his face looked sunny. He had a lovely thick moustache, which he fiddled with whenever he laughed, which was a great deal, a magnificent barrel of a laugh, Audrey thought. And he spoke with a confident clipped voice, asking her about herself and listening captivated to everything she said.

She began to visit Cambridge regularly, and several weeks later, they were alone one afternoon when Alan told her that the Colonial Office had offered him a position in the Gold Coast. He seemed euphoric. He showed her where the colony in West Africa was in his atlas.

'They want me to go as soon as the colonial service course is over,' he said.

She was looking at the map of the world and thinking how small England looked.

'I'll be leaving in a couple of months, Audrey.' He was biting the inside of his lower lip and trying to get her to look at him.

She said cheerily, 'I'll write to you . . .'

He gripped her wrists suddenly. 'Marry me.'

'What?'

'Marry me, Audrey. Please?' He lowered himself on to the floor clumsily.

She held her breath and looked down into his eyes, which were straining up at her. He plainly wasn't joking. Marry him? She had not seriously considered marriage. West Africa? She *did* like him. A lot. 'Gosh,' she whispered, her cheeks stretching into a wide smile.

'Audrey?'

'All right, then.'

He jumped up and embraced her. 'It will be perfect. All that space. The heat.'

'Me off to Africa! Wait till I tell them,' she said, giggling.

Audrey told her parents about Alan. A short engagement was hardly uncommon, but she told them, quite calmly in fact, so they had no idea that inside her heart was pounding with such vehemence she was sure they could hear it, that in less than two months she would be married to someone they had not yet met. Someone who was about to set sail for deepest, darkest Africa and who clearly thought it a reasonable request that they should send her to join him. Someone they did not even know. And surely she hardly knew him?

Her father spilled hot tea all over his grey flannel trousers and spluttered moistened fruitcake on to his hand. Then he placed his teacup on the table quietly and excused himself, mumbling incoherent words.

Looking pained, and wearing a cherry-stained apron, her mother had a clipped talk with Audrey about the condition, not always easy, that is marriage, which she said would only be compounded by unfamiliar situations and circumstances, such as the heat, the wildlife, the illnesses, the distance from home. She emphasised the words 'distance from home', which as far as Audrey was concerned, she needn't have done. Audrey struggled to hide a smile. The most appealing thing about this situation would be that very distance, as though the further from home she went, the greater her chance of adventure. Her mother cried reluctantly and left the room.

The wedding was planned with no mention of Africa and occurred a week before Alan sailed. The gathering at Stonebridge Town Hall was quiet and small. Audrey had bought a new dress. Made with delicate beige chiffon, it had long sleeves and a lace-trimmed V-neckline. Cool enough for a late September afternoon in Stonebridge, she thought it might also be suitable for long African evenings. She met Alan's family for the first time at her wedding and immediately thought his mother was too bossy. But nothing could trouble her that day; she had Alan beside her, and his exhilaration and self-assurance were contagious, setting at ease everyone who came in contact with him.

The Colonial Office refused to let Audrey travel with her husband. It took months to organise a trip to Africa, they said, and when Mr Turton had been posted, there had been no Mrs Turton. She would simply have to wait a while. She was inconsolable. Worse still, neither of them knew when she would be able to join him, so she had anticipated him leaving with a heaviness that swelled as the day approached.

Standing alongside the boat train that would carry Alan from Paddington to Liverpool, Audrey breathed through her mouth to stifle her tears, and her lungs filled with the thick, cloying smog that clouded the air. A shrill whistle blew, and the platform began to fill with the sounds of chaotic goodbyes – tears, shouts, cries of farewell, a screaming baby. A man in the next carriage leaned out of the window to cling on to his sobbing fiancée. Two guards began to shout and wave at the passengers as they walked along the train slamming doors and blowing their whistles. The train puffed. Audrey clutched Alan. He kissed her then dashed into the train, closed the door and reached to her through the window. The train started to move, and the young fiancée next to Audrey began to wail and wave with a handkerchief, which she pressed to her nose and mouth intermittently. The woman's make-up was streaming down her face, which was contorted in pain. Audrey made an effort to swallow the lump that had thickened in her throat as she watched the gleaming black train inch away from her. The funnel screeched and spat twirling steam; the wheels chugged and chugged faster; Audrey stood and waved gently until she could no longer see her husband. Around her, people shuffled back to their lives. She wiped a tear away and shoved her hands into her coat pockets. Well, I must be *in love* with him, she said to herself and smiled faintly.

From then on, everything around her revealed itself as mundane and uninspiring; her friends appeared tedious and monotonous, home dreary, and her parents increasingly irritating. Now she wanted only to be gone, to be on her way to Africa. She felt like a bird impatiently poised for flight but unable to take off because it was encased in a glass cage that was dangling tantalisingly from the top of a tree.

On her last morning at home, she had looked through the rain at the cluster of trees at the bottom of the garden, the birthplace of her dreams. Africa with Alan. Her mother was mistaken, she would cope marvellously. She said to the empty room, 'I'll show them.'

On board the ship that was bound for Africa, Audrey scrutinised the cabin that was to be her home for the next two weeks. Each bunk had a wall light directly above it, and there was a lamp on the bedside table. There was a desk and a chair, a built-in wardrobe that was large enough to fit all the clothes she might need on the journey and a dressing table with a triptych mirror on the wall. The walls were covered in a dark, glossy wood veneer, and the floor was covered in carpet that had a large green swirling pattern repeated against a brown background. Through a tiny adjoining door, there was a surprisingly spacious bathroom.

Up on the boat deck, she looked out at the peninsular towards the mouth of the river and the open sea beyond, fused seamlessly with the drab, overcast sky. Her hair blew wildly. She took a deep breath and held it. Africa was waiting for her way beyond there somewhere with Alan. Thinking about him made her tingle; her face beamed. She was startled by a persistent loud horn. She stood against the railings, pulling her coat tightly about her, and watched well-wishers descend the gangplank and merge into the crowds on the jetty.

The distance between Audrey and everything she knew began to swell. Her lips began to tremble, and her exhilaration lessened. I am going to see Alan, she told herself. This is the adventure that I wanted. She opened her mouth wide to fill it with tastes of the country she was leaving – the muddy river, black smoke from factories close by burning rubber and coal, the cigarette unsmoked in her hand, fresh fish – and her stomach heaved.

When Liverpool was an indistinguishable lump on the horizon, she went to her berth and sat on her bunk. She picked up the 'Gold Coast Handbook', which the Colonial Office had sent with her ticket. She remembered how her parents had exclaimed when they had seen the price of the ticket and how she had quickly calculated that it amounted to nearly six months' wages. She knew too that, to start with at least, Alan's wages in the colonies would only be slightly more than her secretarial wage, but he had assured her there was little to spend money on out there. She flicked through the slim pamphlet and read, 'You are to cultivate an impassive and philosophic temperament, as irritability, a very frequent product of the climate, makes a man uncomfortable and has, undoubtedly, a bad influence on general health. Moderation in all things should be the rule of the Tropics.' No wonder they picked darling Alan, nothing ever agitates him, she thought. She read on, 'A healthy man should get physically exhausted each day and should experience the sensation of pleasurable fatigue. However, in the Tropics, work is performed in a leisurely manner, and the climatic conditions are not conducive to activity. The tendency to lead a sedentary existence and remain idle is great and if indulged leads to nostalgia, tedium, isolation and over-consumption of alcohol. For all these conditions, the appropriate remedy is vigorous exercise.'

Absentmindedly, she turned to the section entitled 'Tropical Health' and became steadily engrossed in the descriptions of all sorts of medical conditions she had never heard about. The section on the tumbu fly, which, according to the pamphlet, laid hundreds of invisible eggs underneath the skin that later oozed out as maggots, made her heave again. Compared to that, the descriptions of sleeping sickness, bilharzia (on which the advice was unambiguous: never bathe in lakes or slow-running rivers, where the worms that cause this serious and deadly disease are rampant), dysentery, typhus and many others seemed rather mild. Suddenly, she realised it was possible that she would die out there, in the White Man's Grave, as Alan's fellow cadets referred to the Gold Coast. As she read on, she became convinced that it would be a most unpleasant death, and some of her father's facts resounded in her head. When he knew that his daughter was indeed going to Africa, he had begun to devour all the information he could find about the place, and every now and then, he would speak over the stillness of the drawing room or the sleepy calm of the breakfast table a fact intended to prove his point, such as 'Did you know that there is no cure for malaria?' or 'That continent is built for darkies, not for whites. After all, it is called the Dark Continent', followed swiftly by some enquiry into what progress Audrey was making obtaining the items listed by the Colonial Office in 'Essential Items for Life in Tropical Africa'. Once, over dinner, he had startled the peace and said he thought it was a shame that she and Alan should waste their God-given talents and brains out there in the heat; heat that must be indisputably unhealthy! Then he had quickly cleared his plate, declined a portion of homemade apple tart and cream and disappeared into another room in the house.

Slowly, the effort she had made over the past weeks to remain hard-headed and determined about the adventure of going to Africa dissolved. Now, watching the grey sea pass by her porthole, she faltered; perhaps she had said farewell to her parents for the very last time; perhaps she might never step foot on English soil again. And did she even know or love Alan, the man for whom she was uprooting herself so spectacularly? 'Stop it!' her mind screamed again and again as she tried to calm the growing panic. But her stomach heaved again, this time violently, and she covered her mouth with both hands and rushed to the toilet, where she gagged and retched repeatedly until she coughed up sour bile.

After two long weeks on board the *Appapa*, most of which Audrey spent below deck suffering from sea sickness, the ship docked about a mile off the shore of Accra, just beyond the tireless surf. When she went up on deck, the heat and humidity hit her like a wave from a fiery furnace. In the airlessness, breathing became an effort, no longer something to take for granted. The sky was blanketed in thick, high clouds and was a hazy, subdued blue. The sea was a similar colour, only fractionally more intense, and together they looked like a sad, faded watercolour, nothing like the vibrant azure blues on travel posters for the Caribbean.

On the distant seashore stood a small gathering among the gangly coconut trees, which swayed majestically, gripping the dirty sand with their meagre-looking root mounds. The trees appeared defiant in the face of the infringing waves, yet all along the beach, marking the site of their prior glory, lay hollowed relics that had eventually succumbed to the ocean.

When it was time to disembark, she had to be asked several times, eventually quite impolitely by the purser, to climb into a chair-like contraption with three other passengers (a mammy chair, he had called it), a snug fit, if you wanted to be close to these people, and Audrey did not. Then the chair was winched up off the deck of the ship and swung over to a canoe that was bobbing alongside. She was terrified to be dangling precariously like that halfway between the ship and the canoe, with the ferocious sea swelling beneath her to reveal its mass. She closed her eyes and held her breath. There was a lot of shouting in a strange language as the muscular African rowers guided the mammy chair safely into their canoe. As soon as the passengers were in the canoe, the smiling rowers paddled furiously towards the shore. The waves were high and frothy, and Audrey was sprayed liberally with warm seawater that instantly left her skin feeling sticky. When the canoe reached the shore, one of the strong African men, his round face glistening with sweat, picked her up and carried her lightly to dry land, where Alan was waiting to welcome her, grinning with delight. He was dressed in his white jacket, khaki shorts, grey knee-high socks and white pith helmet. It took Audrey a few minutes to recover from the shocking manner of her arrival, and she stood flustered and looking silently at her husband. She stared at him; there was something different about him she could not place her finger on. He scooped her in his arms and smothered her face with kisses. 'Oh, how I have missed you,' he said in her ear. Audrey felt a wave of dizziness sweep over her; it was the lack of sleep, she thought, and this incredible heat. It made it difficult for her to be as excited as she had expected she would be. She slipped her hand into Alan's and held him tight. Damp formed where their skin touched. She jumped when one of the natives brushed past her shouting instructions at another; the men in the mammy chair shouted too, while they threw luggage to other men who stood ankle deep in seawater. Each time a case was hurled over, Audrey flinched, but the men were deft and did not drop anything into the sea. Children watched from further up the beach, dancing, waving and shouting at the new arrivals. She took a deep breath of the hot sea air and looked at her husband. What was different about him? He looked fit and brown. His teeth and eyes shined bright; his hair glinted. 'You look very well indeed.'

'Not bad, considering I had my first brush with malaria last month,' he said.

'Alan! Are you all right?' Her throat tightened. Malaria! She was tugging his hand, looking at him in disbelief. He looked incredibly well, not like a man who had recently been close to death. How could he describe it as a 'brush with malaria'?

'It really is not as bad as they make out, you know. A little more quinine and some rest and it quickly passes. It's only a temperature, really, a bit like influenza, I suppose.'

'But I don't understand. How on earth did you get malaria if you are taking quinine? That simply does not make any sense.'

'Massa, we can load?' asked a native man loudly. He smiled at Audrey, revealing large white teeth. She stared at his glossy, round face and blinked.

Alan directed two men to pile her luggage on to a lorry, which had an open wooden frame above the chassis that looked like a cage.

'That is a mammy lorry,' Alan said as he directed another man towards a car with Audrey's smaller bags. 'They import lorries, take them apart, except for the chassis, and then build a new wooden body just like that one. That's how most of the natives get about, on unsecured benches in one of those lorries. They say they're quite safe.'

Each time a trunk was thrust into the lorry, it wobbled, and Audrey wondered whether her luggage would make it to the house. She began to feel clammy; her cheeks were flushed. Her dress clung to her moistened back; she longed for some shade, but there was none to be had on the beach. When all her luggage was loaded, the driver lifted the back flap of the wooden frame and bolted it on either side. Audrey saw written in elaborate letters 'God Knows Why – Trust In Him Alone'. How delightfully simple, she thought.

They drove along narrow straight roads edged with red soil and thick vegetation. There were very few cars on the roads. Audrey sat quite upright staring at everything around her. She felt less dizzy now that there was a constant breeze through the windows. From time to time, they passed groups of women and men snaking along the sides of road carrying heavy bundles on their heads or babies on their backs. When children noticed them, they shouted out and waved and waved. She looked at her husband. Something was different about him. He sounded the same, more enthusiastic, if anything, and he looked the same, if not healthier, most definitely handsome with his tan. 'You've shaved your moustache,' she said suddenly.

'I wondered how long before you'd notice. It was too hot for a moustache.'

'I liked it.'

'Ah, here we are. Home sweet home. What do you think?'

For the last few moments, the car had been travelling along quiet tree-lined streets with houses tucked away behind hedges and shrubs. When the driver turned into a gravelled driveway, Audrey peered between the front headrests to see the house in the distance, her new home. It looked marvellous. She realised that she had not known what to expect. Alan had said the house was nice, but then he was easily pleased. She got out of the car and pulled her damp dress away from the backs of her legs. It was dusk; the intense heat of earlier was falling with the sun. She smiled at him and took a deep breath. The air was dense with the smells of unfamiliar foliage, cooking and smoke from the servants' coal pot, freshly cut grass and dry, brown, baked African earth.

'It looks nice, Alan.' She longed to look around the garden, but Alan pulled her towards the house.

Later, when they were lying underneath their mosquito net, Alan's arms round her and his contented body peaceful next to hers, she sighed deeply. It *was* strange here. 'New' strange, rather than 'bad' strange. It would probably take her a while to get used to it all; after all, this was her first home away from home. She looked out beyond the fluttering curtains at the black sky and listened to the unfamiliar night sounds and her husband's snoring. She looked at him, content even in his sleep; it felt right to be in his arms again. And she could see that he did love her. She pressed her nose against his chin to smell him, pleased that the African air had not corrupted his smell in any way.

Audrey looked at the time and counted just over eight hours till her party. She set to work on the jelly with edgy excitement. Cook sulked through the entire process. In the early days, it had surprised Audrey that he was happy to show his anger when he did not agree with his masters. She always ignored him, which Alice had recommended was the best thing with servants, saying, 'Don't allow them to bully you with their emotions.' Today, he huffed and puffed while he directed the small boy to carry freshly boiled water, bowls, and all the ingredients up the steps from the kitchen into the house and put them on to the dining table. Audrey added lots of gin, gelatine and sugar to the large pot of pulped, deseeded watermelons. It was a recipe her mother had told her about. Apparently, her friend made a reputation for herself in India with her jelly. Pink-gin jelly sounded fabulous, and she had quite fancied the idea of becoming known here for it. With that in mind, she had brought several sachets of gelatine with her from London, which had turned out to be most fortuitous. The Kingsway stores did not stock gelatine, and the Syrian traders had only looked at her perplexed when she asked for it. She hoped she had remembered the recipe right. The jellies tasted more of sweetened gin than anything else, but they looked divine in their moulds – a brilliant fluorescent pink. When they were safely in the fridge, which she instructed the servants on pain of death to open only if utterly necessary, and for as short periods as possible, she sat on the veranda to rest and enjoy a cigarette. She was looking forward to turning them out, showing off her imagination, her culinary ability. She couldn't wait to see their amazement. Just because she didn't bake for the cake sales or make mango chutney, pineapple crumble and papaya jam, didn't mean she wasn't able, that she couldn't do it just as well as the rest of them if she put her mind to it.

Chapter Three

Later that evening, Audrey put on a new dress and stood before the mirror that hung in her bedroom. She raised her arms to shoulder height and turned sideways, running her hands over her hipbones, which pushed out against the fabric a little too much. The blue crêpe material was fan-shaped over her chest so that from a distance it looked as if her shoulders were bare, but the top of the dress was made from skin-coloured net fabric, which her mother had thought would be perfect in the Tropics. She had assured Audrey, as they stood in the fitting room of the women's clothing store in Stonebridge, that it was most stylish indeed and that it suited her. Standing here in the harsh glow of the lone electric bulb, Audrey was not so sure. She cocked her head from side to side in front of the mirror and breathed out deeply. She looked at the clock on the bed-side table and wondered what was keeping Alan. She brushed her hair and twisted it into a loose bun on top of her head, allowing a few strands to fall down her neck. She thought briefly of checking how the preparations were going and how her jellies looked, but she couldn't be bothered traipsing down into the hot kitchen. Anyway, the servants had already proved themselves amply efficient. She had to admit begrudgingly that Cook did have everything under control.

She sighed and said to the empty room, 'I need a drink.' She marched through the living room ringing her bell. 'Awuni!' She looked around the house while she waited for her servant to appear. It looked fine. She had arranged flowers in a dozen vases all around the room. Now the room was overflowing with her favourites from the garden. Large waxy leaves, long furry flowers, pink hibiscus, yellow frangipani, orange birds of paradise on tall stalks, which looked as if they were poised to take off, and many others she still couldn't name.

Awuni came running in, and she looked down at his feet bemused at the unfamiliar sound that came from his for-once heeled soles. He stopped at a polite distance in his freshly starched uniform and crimson cummerbund and grinned at her, with his head bobbing up and down slightly.

'Gin and tonic, please,' she said. 'A large one.' She needed something fortifying.

'Right now, madam,' he said, rushing off.

Wandering on to the veranda with her drink, she stared out into the still, black night. A few electric lights glimmered in the distance, not sufficiently brightly to impede the glow from the stars and the full moon. It was only six-thirty; she could enjoy a quiet drink before they arrived. She took a deep breath. She could smell food. Cook liked the strong aromas of garlic and bay leaf, which he used often, transforming simple foods with these exotic flavours. At least she could be confident that he would not disappoint. She could also smell her jasmine, which poured out its scent at night. It had grown furiously since she had transplanted it closer to the house that first week, and now crept up the wall and trailed along the veranda.

She had spent her first few mornings in the colony exploring her garden. She decided early on that since she could not be in it after dark for fear of being bitten by mosquitoes or snakes, she wanted to be able to smell it when its scents were most profuse. As soon as she could, she set to work one morning digging up a young jasmine plant that was growing near the far hedge, which she wanted to move closer to the veranda. But the earth was unyielding. She went to the kitchen to ask for a saucepan and carried water to and from the tap outside the kitchen to moisten the soil. She realised she was being watched at one point and resisted as long as she could, but eventually turned to see the servants staring bemused. When the plant was well watered in its new home, she began to pull out weeds that were growing around the hibiscus shrubs that grew along the front of the house. In no time, sweat had formed on her brow, and her blouse stuck to her back. Sunspots darted over her eyes when she blinked to wipe her face with her sleeve. Sweat began to pour down her face into her eyes and down her chin. She looked at what she had achieved: a small area about a foot square was now bare of weeds. She puffed and looked at the large expanse of garden. Best have a drink, she thought. She stood up and for a moment everything spun. She steadied herself with a muddy hand. She looked and saw the sun almost directly overhead. Had she really been out this long? She walked to the kitchen as fast as she could. The door was shut. She shoved it, pleased that there was no one to see her in this state, and it opened easily. She took some ice from the freezer compartment and filled a glass with water from the tap. As she drank a second glassful, she read the label on the large stone water filter issued by the Colonial Office that stood on a table next to the fridge, 'J. Wilkinson & Sons Co., Leicestershire, England'. She thought about those factory workers in Leicestershire working away in their stockings and laced shoes, their cardies and scarves. Could they conceive of a place like this? The water had not helped. She still felt dizzy and made her way back to the house slowly. I must tell Alan to put a lock on the bedroom door, she thought, as she stripped off her clothes and lay on the bed.

She had to spend the next seven days in bed. That is to say, she got out of bed regularly but only in order to be violently sick or to use the toilet. At first, she and Alan were convinced it was heatstroke, and she tried to suffer the dizziness and nausea in silence. He was baffled that she had not taken in the advice about the sun, and he was flabbergasted that she had wanted to garden in the midday tropical sun without a hat.

The next morning, she woke up with crippling stomach cramps, and by evening, Alan had to call for the doctor. 'Amoebic dysentery,' Dr Stewart said unsympathetically as he wrote up his notes. 'The reason the CO issues water filters. I am sure in future you will remember that, young woman . . .'

And now where was Alan? She sat in the creaky wicker chair and stared at her gold, high-heeled sandals. Outside, the insects had begun their night-long concert and frogs croaked. She was wearing beige stockings to hide the infected bites on her legs, and already she could feel how hot she was going to be tonight. She sipped her gin, taking pleasure from the cool bitter taste and smiled to herself. Someone had told her once, maybe her mother, that the simple action of smiling could make you feel happy, could cheer you up. It seemed unlikely that a smile would get rid of the vague but ominous ambience that seemed to float about her a lot of the time these days. And why was she always in such a bad mood in the mornings, even on those days when she did not have a hangover? She heard wheels crunching up the driveway. Beyond the glaring headlights that pierced the darkness, she saw Alan's car. She sighed in relief and smiled. She put down her glass and stood to welcome him home.

He bounded up the stairs two at a time. 'So sorry, darling. A late telegram from London. I must have a quick wash,' he said, giving her a kiss on the cheek before rushing towards the bedroom shouting for Awuni to bring him some hot water.

'All ready, sah,' said the smiling servant.

'Wonderful. I promise I won't be a moment, darling.'

She followed him and sat on the bath while he washed his hair and mopped his face and neck. 'I was getting worried,' she said, watching him. He started telling her about his day. As usual, she only half-listened but with a smile should he look up suddenly for some response. 'I'll get you a drink,' she said when he was brushing his teeth, and returned to the living room, where Awuni was hovering.

'Could you get Alan a drink?'

'Right now, madam.'

Audrey looked about her once more, trying to see whether there was anything that she had forgotten to do. Was anything out of place? The house looked immaculate; Awuni and the small boy had cleaned it all afternoon. She admired her cut flowers again. She had decided to swathe the room with hundreds of blooms in a variety of containers and vases borrowed from Alice and the club. But she had to admit that tropical flowers never looked as beautiful outside their natural wild backdrop. Was it because the colours were so dazzling? The garish hues did look best on the vigorous trees and shrubs that grew happily out of the red earth. It was a pity her guests could not simply mingle in the garden amongst the plants, but standing about outside after dark would be unwise. Their visitors would remain safely indoors behind mosquito screens, where coils could burn discreetly to deter those determined insects that had made it past the netted fortifications.

'We're all set, then?' said Alan, walking on to the veranda with his wet hair combed back on his head.

'Oh,' she gasped, 'I forgot to spray the garden. Oh, Alan, I knew I'd forget something.'

'Ah. Well, it's too late now. I'll tell Awuni to make sure coils burn all night.' He dabbed at a cut on his chin.

'You look nice.' She had always liked him in his dinner jacket. It was worth having a party just to see him dressed up like this. 'But aren't you going to swelter in that?'

'It's not too bad, this lightweight jacket, and anyway, as soon as H.E. is here and settled, I can take it off. Just what I need,' he said, reaching for the glass she proffered. He took a long sip and looked at his wife over the rim of his glass. She looked beautiful in that dress, which showed off her figure. Since they had been out here, she had lost some of the curves he had liked, but she still set his pulse dashing, especially looking like this. She didn't often make this much effort. He could see that she had make-up on, and her face glowed. Her sparkling eyes were large, displaying tonight the vulnerability he rarely saw in her, and which made him want to stay close to her. She was easily mistaken as entirely self-sufficient, and it was at times like this that he was reminded that deep inside she was as soft as anything, and that she did need him.

'You look lovely,' he said, touching her dress just above her waist. He rubbed the fabric gently between his thumb and fingers. 'Very nice. If we weren't expecting guests, I'd . . .'

'Alan!' She giggled and stroked his arm.

He kissed her cheek. 'Here's to a successful evening,' he said. 'I didn't tell you, but actually, I've heard there might be an opening at Government House. H.E's aide-de-camp is going on leave soon and . . . Well, I'd love to get out of Education and into the castle, where the real decisions are made.'

'Oh? But how would that help with your next post?'

'I can't think about leaving the colony just yet, but it's unlikely to hinder things.'

'Does the Governor make the choice himself?'

'Almost entirely, yes. It's a rather personal post, after all. He might take advice here and there, you know, from people who've been around longer, but it's his decision. No doubt his wife has a say too, like all good wives,' said Alan, laughing. 'I suspect she'll be inspecting you tonight, to make sure you're not the type to let the side down and all that.'

'Yes . . .' She sighed. 'All the more reason to be on my best behaviour.'

'Oh, you won't be the only one on show tonight. And anyway, look at you! You'll pass outstandingly.'

'Well, they had better be satisfied with my efforts. I *have* tried,' she wailed. It wasn't simply his career that was at stake in this ridiculously closed society, which was worse to some extent than Stonebridge had been, it was her life, her happiness, the prospect of going off to some nicer part of the Empire. Everything was so dreadfully intertwined over here. She gritted her teeth fretfully. But Alan looked calm, eager for the show to start. She breathed in the intense scents of the flowers, the wonderful aromas from the kitchen, she thought of her jelly and the records selected to ensure dancing later. Well, if they didn't like it, they could simply go and get stuffed, she thought, bristling defensively. This was as good as it got from her. And if they found anything to criticise, well then, she couldn't help them.

Alan went to crouch down by the gramophone. He placed the needle on to a record and the house was filled with the sound of jazz. Audrey looked at her wristwatch. Half past seven. Any moment now the guests would start arriving. She took a steadying breath. 'Awuni!'

'Madam,' he answered, rising from behind the dining table where he was still fiddling with glasses.

'Oh, there you are. All set, then?'

He had lined several bottles of cooled Club beer, bottles of gin and whisky, mixers and glasses on the dining-room table from where he could serve guests. Audrey was impressed that he seemed unfazed that no one had told him exactly how many people were expected. 'Another gin and tonic for me. Less gin this time.' The earlier drink had helped, but her tummy had begun to rumble. She had not eaten anything apart from two small cucumber sandwiches at lunchtime. 'Have you got any cigarettes, Alan?'

As he handed her one, they heard a car coming up the driveway.

'Here we go,' he said, putting his arm round her. 'Let's have a marvellous time.'

Audrey thought it sounded a little like a prayer. She called to Awuni and told him to forget about her gin. She took a long drag from the cigarette then stubbed it out as their first guests started walking up the stairs.

They greeted people side by side. Audrey felt secure beside Alan, understatedly suave and unruffled Alan. What on earth had she worried about? Weren't these the same people her social life had centred around over the past year? Well, apart from H.E. and his wife, whom most of the guests hadn't yet met. There were mainly British members of the Colonial Administration Service, employees of His Majesty's Government. Young, eager and ambitious, to most of them the Gold Coast was a stepping stone on the way up, very often the first rung on the ladder. There were of course many other Europeans in the colony – miners, engineers, optimistic farmers even – whom one encountered at the club, but the non-British contingent formed a small minority of the whites here. There were Germans, French and Swiss, Dutch, Italians and Belgians, men here because they loved Africa, not Africans, adventurous, brusque men less attached to etiquette, who played by rules different to those Alan was familiar with. Inevitably, he didn't socialise easily with them, preferring to stick with what he knew and understood best. But he would defy anyone to call him prejudiced. It was nothing to do with outward appearance, and everything to do with culture and shared understanding. He would rather spend time with his friend Robert Bannerman for instance, a native, but a lawyer, a man who appreciated the same things as he did, than with one of his fellow countrymen with whom he had nothing in common. He was pleased that Robert was coming tonight; he wanted Audrey to meet his old friend.

A healthy number of people had arrived, and Audrey thought the gathering appeared quite content. People clutched drinks and chatted as if they had not seen each other in a while, as if they were not gossiping about the same old news. Sir Colin and Lady Smythe had not arrived; perhaps they were not coming after all. She realised she had been hoping they wouldn't. Yet, she thought, as she looked around the room, things were going very well, and if this was all she had to do to get out of here, then she could do it. She had decided to take it slowly with the alcohol tonight, remain in control and all that, but she deserved another drink now, she thought.

She couldn't see Awuni or the boy anywhere. Instead, she saw her friends Alice and Malcolm Jenkins and walked up to them. Alice was thirty-three and had been on the Coast for five years already. They lived in the next house along from Audrey and Alan. What surprised Audrey most was that she was still enthusiastic about life here – not because she liked the country or the people, it had nothing to do with that. She had arrived in the colony, had three small children (a fact that, in Audrey's opinion, deserved a small sainthood) and raved about how wonderful life was here. The daughter of a baker, she had escaped what she described as a deplorable suburban life of chores. 'The heat is a small price to pay for a life of self-indulgent pleasure. Here, I can knit or bake all day if I want to,' she said. 'Or sleep. I don't have to cook, clean, wash or change nappies unless I want to. That, for now at least, is my definition of heaven.' And she had told Audrey that when she had children of her own, she would appreciate what it meant to have servants and nannies galore. Alice was quite happy to stay here, thank you very much, and would only go back to life in cold, rainy England under duress, and she had told her husband as much.

As she approached, Audrey could not help wincing. Alice was wearing a floral backless arrangement that pinched her folds of pink flesh so it looked like squished marshmallow. In Stonebridge, she and this plump, matronly woman would never have become friendly. For starters, there was the age gap. Alice was ten years older, and they certainly would not have met back home. Then there was the apparent lack of communal interests. Audrey still cringed when she remembered their first conversation, at a 'welcome to Africa' coffee morning. She had asked Alice what she did all day long, and Alice had replied, 'I sew, I knit, I crochet. Anything that requires needles, I do!'

Audrey had grimaced. 'And in the evenings?'

'Well, there's the club of course. Monday is bridge, on Friday we have film night, bingo on Sunday, and Wednesday is quiz night. Occasionally, there are dances and parties and dinner parties to host or attend. In the rainy season, the men play cricket, and they are always looking for someone to keep score. And there is the tennis league, swimming galas and the pantomime. Oh, there is absolutely loads to do.'

Audrey had resisted the urge to roll her eyes. She had turned to talk to Polly Aldridge, who didn't look like a knitter with a lit cigarette permanently between her fingers. She had sleek, jet-black hair, dark glasses and was wearing a red halter-neck dress, which matched her glossy nails. But it was clear from that very first meeting that Polly didn't like her. Audrey had been taken aback by her overt hostility at the time. She had always had few friends at school but had basked in the knowledge that most of the girls deemed it an honour if she spoke to them or even smiled at them. She found this antagonism intriguing. Later, when she could confide in Alice, Audrey had asked if she knew why Polly disliked her. 'She thinks you're too pretty for this place,' was Alice's reply, 'or for your own good, in fact,' which had made Audrey roar with laughter and secretly bask anew.

Alice had persisted in spending time with her. In those early days, she had taken Audrey under her wing, shown her where to buy various things, how to treat her servants, made her dresses that were more suitable for the weather than anything that she and her mother had packed and generally proved a rock of support while those first long days of her new life drifted by. Audrey had thought their friendship would fizzle out once she had found her feet, but the truth was, friendship wasn't easy to find around here.

She greeted her friends. 'Promise me you'll dance with me later?' Audrey asked Malcolm.

'Good luck,' said Alice. 'He hasn't danced with me in years.'

'Well, maybe I will tonight,' said Malcolm.

'You certainly are making an impression, Audrey,' smiled Alice.

'Oh yes, my big night,' said Audrey. 'What a load of tosh! It's not as if it is *my* career that is at stake. *I* am not one of their employees they can boss about. As long as Alan is happy, I have done my duty.'

'But you *are*, Audrey.'

'I am what?'

'Well, you and Alan, you know, you are seen as a team. What you do matters, so in a way you *are* answerable to them. I suppose the way I see it, they employ all of us.'

'Well, that may be fine with you, but I refuse to kowtow to them. They don't employ *me*, and if they don't like it, they can stuff it!'

Alice smiled uncomfortably. Audrey's recklessness frightened her. Before Audrey arrived, she and Malcolm had helped their new neighbour Alan settle in. He had been keen to be guided by Malcolm's vast experience, and they had taken to him immediately. He had talked often about his adorable, brilliant wife. When Audrey arrived, well, Alice had been quite frankly a little taken aback. Not with her appearance, no, she was as delightful as Alan had suggested. It was her immaturity, her carelessness regarding grave matters of protocol that betrayed her, and which she feared would betray dearest Alan. Alice decided that Audrey needed mothering. She was convinced that with sufficient understanding, and masses of patience, Audrey would flower. Nevertheless, Alice couldn't help admiring Audrey's gutsiness, which was the only earthly way to explain her friend's steadfast refusal to join in where expected.

'I need that drink now,' said Audrey, interrupting Alice's thoughts. 'I think I've survived the worst.'

'Is H.E. not coming, then?' asked Alice.

'Well, I don't care if they arrive now. Everything is going swimmingly.'

'Malcolm says Lady Smythe is rather formidable. I think we need to be on our best behaviour.'

'That's why I need another drink.' She signalled to Awuni and asked him to bring them two gin and tonics. 'Better make them strong,' she said.

'I shan't, and you should be careful, Audrey, everyone is watching you tonight,' Alice said.

'I don't see anyone looking. Oh, apart from the coven over there. Alice, you should know by now that I don't really care what they think of me. I'll invite the Governor to dance and see if I can give anyone an apoplexy.'

As far as Polly Aldridge was concerned, Audrey wasn't making the necessary effort to fit in, and never had. In fact, the minute she clapped eyes on Audrey she could see she would be awkward and that she wouldn't like her. At that first coffee morning, Audrey had whined on and on and on about everything, it seemed, looking down her nose at what life here offered. She didn't want children, she didn't want servants, she didn't play tennis, she didn't sew, she didn't knit, she didn't play bridge, or do anything useful for that matter, it seemed. And everyone knew Alan wanted children, so how come she didn't? What was it she had kept asking in that insipid little voice of hers? 'What *exactly* does one do here all day long?' Frances regularly mimicked her, which made Polly shriek with laughter.

As she walked up to Alice and Audrey now, she wondered how on earth Alice put up with her as much as she did. 'Hello, girls,' she said, releasing a plume of smoke through red lips. She draped one arm across the top of her midriff and supported the elbow of her other arm on it and dragged some more on her cigarette. After smiling at them for a moment, her heavily shadowed eyes flickered across the room, failing to mask boredom.

'Hello again,' said Audrey, staring at Polly's just-bleached hair, studying her perfectly applied make-up and wondering what kind of underwear hoisted her up so beguilingly. Which husband was she after? Audrey wondered. And how was she so comfortable one minute with black hair and the next showing up looking like Marlene Dietrich? Timo had always struck Audrey as an ineffectual spouse for Polly, which she thought was heightened by Polly's need to tower over him in her ridiculous heels. She had noticed the glances Polly and Alan sometimes exchanged and wondered whether she would be able to tell if *they* were having an affair. Would anyone tell her if her husband was being unfaithful? Alice would, if she knew, but would she know?

'So, congratulations. Good party so far.'

Audrey thought she had what her cousin, Freddy, would call a bedroom voice, curling her words slowly over some large imaginary obstruction in her mouth. 'And everyone's here,' Polly continued, waving a cigarette around as she spoke.

'Why do you sound so surprised?' asked Audrey.

'Oh, I'm not surprised. There is nothing else happening tonight.' She blew smoke towards the tops of their heads.

It was after watching a woman smoking just like this on the Cambridge train one evening that Audrey had her first cigarette. The woman had made it appear so alluring, whetting her curiosity to try it for herself. To this day, she found herself looking to see what brand other women were smoking, because she had never yet found a cigarette that tasted quite as heavenly as they made it look.

'I really need a drink,' said Audrey.

'You haven't got many servants running around with drinks, have you?' asked Polly, looking around for somewhere to put out her cigarette. She stubbed it in a potted plant nearby.

'Please don't do that,' said Audrey. 'That's revolting!'

'Well, there don't seem to be many ashtrays around.'

'I'll go and find one,' Audrey said and walked off. The mere idea of the lipstick-rimmed cigarette lying there on the soil made her itch. How dare she do that? She stumbled through her guests until she found Awuni and told him to abandon his tray and go forthwith to remove the offending item from her plant. He stared quizzically at her so she leaned towards his face and spat out the words, 'Cigarette, you know, puff, puff,' she said, mimicking a smoker. 'Plant, you know, like a tree, flower, the one you water every bloody day, for goodness' sakes. Over there,' she said, pointing in the direction of the offending item. She felt an overpowering urge to shove him towards the pot, but just in time, he nodded and went off vaguely in the right direction.

She helped herself to a gin and tonic from Awuni's tray and added an extra measure of gin because no one was looking. It's only my second. Or is it the third? she wondered. She took a long, cooling sip and went to find Cook, muttering under her breath. It was time for some food. Damn H.E. and his timetable. Wasn't she the mistress of this house? If she thought it was time to eat, then they would bloody well eat.

In the kitchen, Cook was arranging food on trays. He and the small boy were dressed up in their best uniforms and had their little hats on. The small boy was digging in the cool box for more ice. He had large sweat patches on the back of his uniform and under his arms.

'Cook, it is time to serve some food. The guests are hungry.' It was hot in the kitchen and Audrey started to perspire straightaway. She gulped at her gin in a bid to keep cool.

'Yes, madam. We will serve soon.'

'Now! You will serve the food now!'

Cook stopped what he was doing and stood with his hands behind his back in what Audrey understood to be a polite stance. Finally, she was getting through to the man, she thought.

'Yes, madam. We will serve now,' he said.

'Good,' said Audrey. She drained her glass, plonked it on the table and turned to walk back to the house. She turned the corner towards the main building and had to steady herself against the banister while a wave of dizziness swept over her. She felt a sudden chill and wiped her forehead, horrified to see her fingers come away damp. It was the stockings, she thought. My body is overheating. She bent down and undid a stocking. She wobbled a little while she slipped out of her shoe and yanked the stocking off her leg. As she tried to pull off the second stocking, she lost her balance and fell into the shrubbery next to the stairs. She tried to scramble to her feet, but her head was spinning.

'Madam! Eh, madam! Please, are you hurt?'

Audrey looked up and saw Awuni running down the stairs towards her looking startled. 'Stupid question,' she muttered under her breath, as she grabbed the concrete banister and pulled herself up.

Awuni bent down to help her.

'Don't touch me!'

He took a step back. 'I will call Massah one time,' he said, turning to go back up the stairs.

'Don't. I am fine. I tripped on a wretched stone.' Audrey sat on the stair and took off the stocking. When she stood up, she dusted down her dress and brushed her face with both hands, then she walked up the stairs clutching her stockings in one hand and holding on to the banister with her other, aware that Awuni was staring after her.

Back in the house, more guests had arrived, and astonishingly, Awuni and the boy were managing to keep glasses filled. She tried to sneak into the bedroom unnoticed, but Alan rushed up to her and grabbed her hand. 'Where have you been, darling? H.E. and his wife just arrived, they want to meet you.'

'Oh blast! I need the loo first,' said Audrey, frantically brushing imaginary dirt and gravel off her dress.

In the bathroom, she was relieved to see that she looked acceptable. Fortunately, her dress was undamaged. Her face looked pink and glossy. Drops of perspiration were dotted in her hairline. She washed her face with water, wishing that for a change cold water would flow out of the taps. Taking a deep breath, she untied her hair and shook it out, trying to cool her scalp. She brushed it and decided to leave it loose, then she patted powder on her face to soak any further perspiration.

'Are you all right?' It was Alan. He stood next to her, looking at their reflections. 'Come on, they're really nice.' He took her hand and led her back into the gathering, squeezing her hand slightly before letting go.

She followed him up to the Governor, who was a tall man with thinning dark hair and angular features. Audrey scanned Sir Colin Smythe's face. He had quite large sticking-out ears and a trim moustache, and all in all, he was rather nice-looking. She had thought he might be stuffy and unapproachable, but he had a youthful, friendly face. His wife stood primly next to him. She was bird-like, with tiny limbs, thin all over. She wore horn-rimmed glasses, which with her greying hair made her look older than her husband. Despite the heat, she was wearing evening gloves.

'Your Excellency, Lady Smythe, may I introduce my wife, Audrey.'

They chatted politely about the climate for a while. Lady Smythe asked whether the rains were unusually late this year and listened intently while Alan explained that the weather was about to get very much hotter before the rains started, and in fact they were not late, simply completely unpredictable. Edith Smythe thought he was instantly likeable; their briefing had been accurate in that regard. But she watched the way his wife was flirting with Colin. That would amuse him no end. And she's intemperate in many respects, thought Edith, as she watched Audrey help herself to another drink.

'Ah, finally,' said Audrey, as Cook thrust a platter of immaculately ordered food towards them. She glared at him to let him know she was aware he had again failed to follow her instructions, but he smiled back proudly, moving the platter from person to person. She stuffed a piece of breaded fish into her mouth and pricked the roof of it on a bone that Cook had failed to remove. Damn him, she thought.

Alan was glad for the chance to pull Robert into their circle. 'I'd like to introduce Robert Bannerman to you. Robert and I met in Cambridge. Robert happens to be one of the leading lawyers in the colony and also an eminent racehorse owner,' said Alan.

'Welcome to our country, Lady Smythe. I am sure you will come to love it as much as your predecessor did,' said Robert, kissing her gloved hand.

'How do you do?' said Sir Colin. 'I've heard about you, of course.'

'I am honoured to meet you, sir,' said Robert, stooping a little. He turned to Audrey and said, 'Lovely to make your acquaintance at last, Audrey.'

Alan guided the Governor and his wife towards other guests, who were hovering in an attempt to meet the important arrivals, leaving Audrey alone with Robert.

She was intrigued by his sophisticated accent. Not quite British, but then not like the natives usually spoke, with the intonation in all the wrong places. He was tall and distinguished-looking for a native too. But why had Alan invited him? Although he seemed comfortable, much more comfortable than she would be if she was in a room full of blacks.

'You must tell Alan to bring you with him to the racecourse some time, I think you'd like it,' said Robert. 'Our English tea is famous. I of course go every Saturday without fail. Have you met my wife? Ah, here she is.'

He introduced Julie. Audrey was fascinated by the woman's deportment, how she moved her arms elegantly as she spoke. She wore a lavish dress that fitted well her athletic curves. Don't stare, she told herself.

'This is a great pleasure,' said Julie. Then she laughed. 'You're baffled by my accent, aren't you? I can see from your expression, but don't be embarrassed, your reaction is rather usual. I was educated in England, you see, and my parents sent me to finishing school. Actually, my ancestors were English.'

Audrey stared at the woman's face, which was blacker than any she had seen recently, it had a smooth sheen all over it as if it had been lacquered. She wondered just how long ago the woman's English ancestors had existed. She stopped listening to Julie, who was revealing that her father had been one of the first lawyers in the Gold Coast, and surveyed her party happily instead. All around, her guests were having a good time, and the party had visibly loosened up now that H.E and his wife were here. Awuni and the small boy were continually darting about, ducking slightly as they ran-walked, as though that made them less visible. She caught sight of Cook sauntering past her smiling at the food he was handing out. With any luck, no one will choke on a fishbone, she thought, reminding herself to yell at him later. She was feeling quite light-headed and decided she'd had enough to drink. But she had done it, she had survived. Actually, she had done very well, she thought, allowing herself to bask in the success of the night. Just then, she heard a commotion at the door and turned to see Awuni arguing with two men she didn't recognise. They were dressed in almost identical rugged clothing, with big, clumpy boots. Even from here they looked unshaven, generally dishevelled. A few of the guests had begun to turn and stare. Robert asked if she thought she might need his help in any way, and Audrey said no. She looked around for Alan but couldn't see him anywhere. She excused herself from Robert and Julie and walked up to the door, where Awuni stood looking fraught and helpless next to the burly men.

'Can I help?' she asked, smiling to hide her irritation. For all she knew, Alan had met these thugs in the bush and given them an open invitation to their house. Just super, she thought, that they decided to come tonight of all nights.

65

'This men are not invite, madam,' Awuni said.

How do you know? she wanted to ask Awuni. One of the men eyed her up and down quite brazenly. He was wearing an un-ironed stone-coloured suit, which was open to reveal thick chest hair. 'I'm Derek Waller. You must be Alan's wife. You are as stunning as they say,' he said. He had penetrating blue eyes that were set in brown crumpled skin, and Audrey could smell whisky on his breath.

She chuckled and said, 'I am sure you understand, my steward is only doing his job. Did my husband . . .' She faltered. He *must* have asked them, his guest list had seemed to grow daily. 'I don't know where Alan has disappeared to, but he . . . Oh well, I'm Audrey Turton, come in.'

Derek reached for her hand and lifted it to his coarse lips. Audrey staggered backwards surprised, and he tightened his hold on her. She giggled and said, 'Gosh, I must be rather tipsy.' She retrieved her hand and looked around surreptitiously, pleased that the party had resumed around her. Only Alice was staring, making desperate faces at her. Audrey shrugged her shoulders in response. Well, what else *could* she have done?

The other man introduced himself as Douggie and then marched off into the room. Moments later, he had ratcheted up the volume of the music considerably and was calling for everyone to dance, shooing people from the centre of the room to create a dance area. Audrey gasped as Derek pulled her into the middle saying loudly, 'I'll show you what this party needs.' All eyes were on her so she smiled awkwardly. Derek placed his hand low down her back and held her firmly, moving her around with confidence. Where the hell is Alan? she wondered. Derek started to twirl her quite vigorously this way and that, urging her as he did to have some fun. They bumped into someone, whose drink splashed everywhere. Derek shouted an apology to the man over his shoulder but didn't stop dancing. Audrey laughed because she didn't quite know what else to do. Her head was spinning out of time with the rest of her body, unable to keep up with Derek's increasingly fast movements. Eventually, it seemed that her feet had become detached from the rest of her, and she stumbled, lurching heavily against Derek. Suddenly, they had both fallen, Derek on to a sofa, Audrey on top of him. Her head continued to spin, making it impossible for her to tell which way was up. She opened her eyes and saw that her face was in his chest. She raised her head and looked into his laughing eyes, and they both started to giggle uncontrollably. Around them, there was a worried hush. Then she felt hands beneath her armpits, lifting her. The room continued to move around Audrey, and her guests swayed comically before her. Someone was holding her arm and asking if she was all right. She heard Robert Bannerman say in an authoritative voice, 'I think perhaps you gentlemen should leave.'

'Go to hell, you! I don't take instructions from darkies,' shouted Douggie.

A stunned silence filled the room, and Audrey felt herself sober up.

Suddenly, Alan was there too, looking distraught. 'Please leave,' he said, ushering the men towards the door.

'Bloody wogs,' said Derek. 'Our women aren't safe around them.' He was staring at Robert, who watched him calmly, apparently unperturbed.

Julie asked if Audrey was all right. Alice helped to straighten her dress. Audrey thought anyone would think she had been dancing about naked from the glare Alice was giving her. 'I tripped, that's all,' she muttered. 'No crime in dancing with one's guests now, is there?' Alice remained tight-lipped and looked uncomfortable, and Audrey decided to ignore her. Fortunately, within minutes, Alan managed to persuade people to dance, and the moment appeared forgotten.

Audrey had just managed to catch her breath when Awuni materialised beside her and whispered urgently, 'Madam, now we have a problem in the kitchen against which we need your urgent attention.' He looked distressed.

'I thought Cook had everything under control.'

'Madam, it is the thing you made, the gel. It—'

'Oh, my jelly,' she said, glad for the excuse to leave the room. As she walked past guests on her way to the kitchen, she noticed their bemused expressions, how they glanced at her surreptitiously, and could imagine exactly what they were thinking.

'Madam, I tell you that it is not my fault. I am not lying. It is not my fault,' said Awuni, trailing behind her.

67

'What on earth are you drivelling on about? Do something useful and get me a drink.'

'Yes, madam,' said Awuni, who seemed pleased to have an excuse not to accompany her to the kitchen.

Audrey stopped at the door of the kitchen and gasped. Kwame had turned out one of the jellies on to a plate, where it had spread out into a shapeless lump and spilled over the sides. There was pink jelly everywhere. Globules on the table, the floor, smeared all over Kwame's uniform and his hands. He looked as if he had been trying to scoop the jelly back up into a mound, like a child trying to restore a crumbling sandcastle. He had evidently given up and was now filling rows of white china bowls.

'My jelly! What are you doing to my jelly? What have you done?' Audrey put her hands to her face to shield her eyes, which she felt fill with tears. They trickled down her face and splashed on to the jelly-covered table. She covered her mouth so as not to let out the scream that she could feel growing in her stomach, instead allowing a whimper to escape.

'Madam, I am sorry. I could not make it stand up again. It is Kwadzo's fault. He took the jelly out of the icebox to get some ice and forgot to put it back. I have already beaten him, and I will beat him again if you wish.'

'You bloody idiot. You bloody, bloody idiot. I told you to make sure that it stayed in the fridge. What am I going to do now?' Audrey clenched her fists trying to control the desire rising in her to strike the man. 'You did this on purpose. I know you did. You hate me because I tell you what to do. Oh, you imbecile.'

'Madam, please do not insult me. Where I come from, we do not insult people like that.'

'I don't care what they do where you come from! This is my house, and I will speak to you how I wish. If I think you are an imbecile, I will tell you so. Do you understand me?' Audrey tightened her fists further and felt her arms quiver from the strain.

'Yes, madam.'

'What on earth is going on here?' said Alan, walking into the kitchen. Behind him, Awuni stood with a drink in his hands staring at the floor. 'Awuni thought that you might need my help?'

'Pesky interfering whatnot,' said Audrey, wiping her eyes. 'They have purposely ruined my jelly. It's wrecked. What am I going to do?' she said between sobs.

'Come now, Audrey, let's not make a fuss over this. I doubt Cook deliberately ruined your jelly. What a shame, though, they did look superb. But it looks fine in the bowls; perfectly edible to me. And no one will know any different. Do let's leave Cook to it, darling, we have guests.' He started to walk out of the cramped kitchen.

'It is just not fair. I so wanted to surprise everyone.' Audrey took the glass her servant was holding and took a long swig, then she poured some of the drink into one of the bowls. 'There, that looks better,' she said, cocking her head to one side. She scooped the ice out of her glass with her hands and poured the rest of the gin into the bowls. 'They look like floating islands. Get me a bottle of gin, Awuni. What are you waiting for? Quick. Quick. Cook, I want you to pour some gin into each bowl.'

'Yes, madam.'

'And for once, just *do* what I ask,' said Audrey, glaring at him.

'Yes, madam.'

Polly was telling Lady Smythe how she had organised the Christmas pantomime when she helped herself to a bowl of the dessert Audrey's boy was handing round. Lady Smythe declined, explaining to the boy that sweet things did not agree with her. Polly finished her sentence and then looked at the contents of the bowl in her hand. She fixed a smile on her face and stirred silently. She felt obliged to scoop a tiny bit into her mouth. It was like eating congealed gin. She tried not to grimace. What had possessed the woman to serve this?

Audrey saw Polly smiling at her. Well, at least one person is pleased, she thought. And I have another thing to add to the list of things I thought I would be good at but which I seem to be abjectly useless at. And what a long list! It included being a spouse and, in particular, being the wife of a colonial administration officer, living in Africa, managing servants. Now she could add *being a hostess*. She felt wretched, especially for Alan. He seemed untroubled by the gin-jelly fiasco and hadn't seen the dancing, but everyone else had, and she could feel their disapproval even if he couldn't. Oh damn, she thought, sipping her drink.

Alan was turning off the gramophone and was trying to get the attention of the party. 'Thank you all for coming this evening. It is a privilege to have you all here tonight, in particular our guests of honour.' He paused while Sir Colin acknowledged him. 'My wife wanted to keep the real reason for this party a secret, but I think that it would be a shame to deny you all the chance to sing "Happy Birthday".' Alan put his arm round her and started singing, 'Happy birthday to you, happy birthday to you,' and in no time the room resonated with the voices of the guests.

Desperate to cry, Audrey smiled and tried to keep her eyes at a certain level so she could no longer see, dotted on every surface in the room, discarded bowls of pink jelly.

Suddenly, the room was plunged into darkness, and Audrey saw Cook approaching her with a massive cake with several lit candles. She shook her head in disbelief. Her servant was singing 'Happy Birthday' to her, his beaming face glinting in the light of the candles. With all eyes on her, she felt edgy yet elated. How much she would have enjoyed this moment if the jelly hadn't collapsed.

'Happy birthday, madam,' he said. 'I told you never mind about the jelly. We have a big cake. I will serve to your guests right away unless you disapprove.'

Audrey stared with her mouth wide open.

'That would be super, Cook,' said Alan.

'No. Clear away the bloody jelly first,' she hissed.

'Yes, madam. But happy birthday, madam.'

Chapter Four

Saint John made his way to the big house with anxiety pounding in his heart. It was out of the ordinary for Lawyer to summon his clerk on a Saturday, particularly when he had horses racing. As he walked, he revisited the week's errands for any inaccuracies or miscalculations on his part that might have occasioned this summons. He often told his friends how working with Lawyer had improved his own intelligence and sophistication immensely, even though it had only been two years so far. The way he was treated when people realised that he was Lawyer's clerk reinforced his conviction that working for an important person made him equally so. What he did not tell was how he had initially struggled with a job that required him to run errands to the courts and anywhere else Lawyer wanted a message delivered, arrange meetings and help out with paperwork in the office. Lawyer also used him as a sounding board in many private matters. 'I am his right-hand man,' he told his friends. 'It is doubtful that Lawyer can manage without me now, which is why I am doubly watchful of what I say to him. It pays to agree with a wise man.'

Lawyer was waiting at his desk impatiently.

'Good morning, Lawyer. You sent for me.' Saint John took short, deep breaths between his words.

'Sit down. I want to ask you something.' Before Saint John

was comfortable in the armchair, he continued, 'I want to marry your niece. Ask her father whether I can come and knock at their door.'

Lawyer was referring to the traditional engagement ceremony when the hopeful man, together with as big an entourage as he could gather up, descended on the home of the woman he wanted to marry, knocked on the door and begged permission to court her. Over time, this tradition had become more elaborate, and it was now quite usual for the couple to become formally engaged when the 'knocking' took place.

Even as he spoke the words and watched the transformation on Saint John's face, Robert wondered once again whether this was a ridiculous impulse that he was allowing to get the better of him. But he had mulled it over for days now, and there seemed to be no way that he could have this girl without formally taking her as his wife – in the traditional sense, anyway. And he had been unable to stop thinking about her. Even now, he found himself distracted as he thought of how her body moved beneath her clothes when she walked, how her lips curved when she spoke. He shifted in his seat. It was perhaps weakness on his part, he conceded, but he had been unable to come up with any valid reason why this little failing was one he must overcome. He had calmed all thoughts of how his decision might affect his wife, his family or the girl by telling himself that he was only acting in the same manner that his forefathers had. It was actually a form of social service, another practice that propped up society. Taking her as his wife would allow him to distribute his resources more widely; what prospects could a girl like her possibly have otherwise? So here he was, offering to bestow untold opportunity on her entire family, including evidently, the man who was sitting in front of him in deep shock.

Saint John was unprepared for this news, and he was definitely shocked. He wondered for a moment whether he should feel a little appalled; after all, the girl was still only fourteen. But hadn't one of his sisters been married at a similar age? And there was a small matter that he couldn't overlook: such a marriage would link him to one of the most influential families in the Gold Coast. Thoughts flew threw his mind at top speed, and his face remained composed with the polite half-smile that he always wore for Lawyer.

'Wonderful!' He spoke like someone who has forgotten that he is not alone and seemed startled when he heard his voice. A few moments passed and he continued calmly, 'Please, have you informed your wife?'

'Not yet,' replied Robert. 'It is not really any concern of hers.' That matter had yet to be resolved, but then, wasn't he the head of this house? Wasn't his wife experienced in accepting his decisions?

'Lawyer, I am sure that my brother-in-law and my sister will gladly welcome you with open arms. Without a doubt, they would be privileged to agree to such a union.'

'I would have spoken to her father, but I thought you were perhaps better placed as the head of the family?' Robert had not formed a good impression of Matilda's father from Saint John. To be fair, Saint John rarely talked about his private life; in fact, he usually did not talk about anything that Robert had not raised first, and then only to agree with him. But on occasion, probably when he was feeling particularly bitter about having to support his brother-in-law in addition to the man's wife and children, Saint John made an exception.

'A good-for-nothing wastrel' was how he had described him to Lawyer once, 'a good-for-nothing wastrel who is not even embarrassed to live in my house with his wife, who is unembarrassed that he does not have his own house. Lawyer, don't misunderstand me. I know that my sister is entitled to live with me, more so even than my own wife. Is that not what our tradition says, that blood is thicker than water? After all, I am her brother; I can't ask my sister to go and be homeless somewhere else. He should go, but the man has no pride. None. None whatsoever. And what is a man with no pride but a permanent blemish on his family's name? What use is a man who is not ashamed of being a failure for all to see?' He had stopped speaking suddenly when he remembered he was talking to Lawyer and apologised profusely for wasting his precious time.

'When can I tell them to expect you to come and knock? Although I must add that naturally they will not expect you to come in person. Perhaps you could send one of your sisters or aunts? My sister knows how busy you are.' Saint John's eagerness for the match to be sealed was obvious. The sooner the traditional ceremonies were completed, the better for all concerned and the less likelihood of any complications. After all, this was not the kind of offer that one could expect to receive on a daily basis.

Robert was spurred on by Saint John's enthusiastic response to the proposal, not that he had expected anything else. 'My sister Baby is returning from London on the boat next month. I will ask her. Can you tell them to expect a visit and arrange a time?'

He stood up to signal the end of the meeting and walked towards the door of his office with his hands in his trouser pockets. Saint John followed him. For a second, the two men stood in the doorway like equals.

'Right, then.' Robert patted Saint John's back lightly. 'Ask Tetteh to come and see me.'

'Yes, Lawyer,' he said, smiling, as he left the office with his normally heavy shoulders slightly straighter.

It was early in the evening. The breeze had dropped, and heat radiated from the ground, which had been seared by the relentless sun.

Matilda and her younger sisters, Celestina and Eunice, had been given money to buy their dinner and were strolling along the roadside trying to decide what to eat. Many of the residents of Jamestown also bought some of their meals in this way; home-prepared food without the effort of shopping, cooking and cleaning was an appealing alternative to the many women who had numerous mouths to feed. The vendors illuminated their wares with lanterns made from small old tins filled with kerosene from which thick cotton wicks protruded, producing great flickering flames and pungent black smoke. The smell from the lanterns blended with the smell of the freshly cooked food made Matilda anticipate her dinner keenly.

They passed a woman selling *kenkey* – balls of pounded, fermented maize steamed in corn leaves, which were packed tightly in a gigantic aluminium container covered with banana leaves to keep out the flies. On the table next to the *kenkey* was a bowl of small fried fish and another of pepper stew that had been fried until the pepper and shrimps it contained were black and crunchy and swimming in oil.

There was a woman selling freshly baked bread buns, which, apart

from two display loaves that lay unprotected from insects and prob-
ing hands, were stacked high and covered with a piece of old white
lace. Matilda salivated at the thought of sinking her teeth into the
bread, past the glossy crust and then into the sweet, heavy white softness. She tried to remember the last time she had tasted bread,
watching enviously as the woman wrapped up four buns in old newspaper for a little girl who held up her eager hands impatiently.

As they walked towards the next seller, the smell of her food,
pieces of fried overripe plantains, red and oozing fat, filled the air.
Matilda was tempted but knew that their money would not buy
enough of this delicacy for them to have a filling dinner.

They came to the woman selling *wachey* – rice and beans that had
been cooked together slowly until the small red beans had burst
their skins to reveal mushy light-pink interiors and the rice had taken
on a reddish-brown tint. The *wachey*, still steaming, was piled high in
a vast aluminium washbasin, which the woman, just as all the other
vendors, had carried on her head all the way from her home earlier in
the evening. It was packed down with banana leaves, but the woman
had made a little opening in the front through which she could scoop
portions for her customers.

'Let's have *wachey*,' Matilda said, stopping behind the small queue
in front of the food.

'Oh, I don't want *wachey*. Please let's have something else,'
Celestina wailed. She was the youngest sister.

'Shut up,' said Eunice, who was two years younger than Matilda.
'Nobody asked you what you want. Wait until you are asked for your
opinion.' Eunice was peering round the arm of the man in front of
her, trying to see what he was buying to go with his *wachey*. 'Look.'
She nudged Celestina. 'He is buying three eggs!'

Then it was their turn. The woman asked brusquely what they
wanted. *Wachey* too was served with fried pepper stew and, depending on the wealth of the diner, boiled eggs and cubes of stewed goat.
Matilda gazed at the pot of meat. They had enough money for one
piece of meat or one egg; she wished that for a change she did not
have to choose.

'Please, and one egg,' she said.

The woman piled the rice in the centre of a heart-shaped leaf,

75

poured a spoonful of pepper stew on top of it and half-buried the egg in the centre of the rice. Then she folded the leaf lengthways and tucked the ends underneath, making a three-dimensional triangle. Matilda took the soft, warm parcel from the woman, and the three girls started walking in the direction of Uncle Saint John's house, because she did not want to eat on the seats that the vendors provided, where they could wash their hands afterwards in the communal bowl of brown soapy water.

They sat on a low wall, and Matilda opened the leaf cautiously, releasing the sweet aroma of the warmed leaf that had mingled with the smell of the rice, and placed it on the wall between her and Eunice. Celestina crouched down in front of them and watched Matilda carefully divide the egg into three pieces as best she could.

'Oh, I did not get plenty of the yellow bit,' said Celestina.

'Do you only complain?' shouted Eunice.

Matilda swapped her piece of egg with Celestina, whose eyes opened wide with delight.

'You are too soft,' said Eunice, guarding her piece of egg with her fingers.

Then Matilda mixed the pepper stew into the rice. When she was satisfied that it was well mixed, she placed her first finger full of rice on her tongue, signalling the start of their meal. The girls ate hungrily and quickly, alternately shooing away persistent flies from their food and brushing their legs to dissuade thirsty mosquitoes, while trying to keep up with each other until there was not a grain of rice left on the leaf. Then they licked their fingers noisily and rubbed their hands together.

'I am still hungry,' said Celestina.

'Well, you need to eat a bit faster to keep up with us,' retorted Eunice. 'Don't worry, you will learn as you grow up.'

'Here is the rest of our money,' said Matilda. 'Go and buy some *kelewele*.'

Eunice grabbed the money and strode off towards the sweet smell that emanated from the vat of hot oil, with Celestina struggling to keep up with her.

Matilda watched them. In the corner of her eye, she could see Lawyer's house. She could see the yellow electric lights shining, making the building look boastfully bright amongst the small dwellings where meagre kerosene lanterns flickered uncertainly. She remembered the photographs she had seen in his office and all the books – so much knowledge in one place. She wondered what life was like for his wife, for his children. They would not be out here having to choose between an egg and a piece of meat. They would send the maid to buy them piles of *kelewele* whenever they wanted, probably in quantities they could not even eat. If *she* were their maid, she would make sure she bought too much *kelewele* so that there was always some left over for her to eat in the kitchen later. But, she thought, it must be sad not to be able to come out here yourself and choose what you want, at least some of the time. But then again, perhaps their life was so pleasant that they didn't miss outings to buy food.

She remembered her English lessons and the new words she had learned so far; she smiled to herself. Her life was changing, she was growing up, she could feel it, and she welcomed the adjustments.

Saint John was sitting on a stool in the open yard of his house with his wife, Amele, and his sister, Ama. It was even warmer in the compound than on the streets, where there was still a breeze from the ocean. Outside, the darkness was filled with the sounds of life.

The house was below the level of the street, accessed by steep steps that led directly from the street into a narrow alleyway along which several houses, including Saint John's, stood cramped together, ensuring that it was never very quiet. A filthy gutter ran through the middle of the alleyway into which wastewater from the surrounding houses was channelled, and into which children and men urinated regularly. On a very hot day, most days in fact, the gutter, which attracted hordes of flies, emanated a stench that was hard even for those who lived with it to ignore. When it rained – which was not often on the coast – the gutter seemed less offensive, but the earthen path was turned into a hazardous, slimy walkway.

An old wooden door stood at the entrance to the compound behind a step up from the alleyway. Over time, the door had sagged on its hinges, dropping down to meet the uneven ground of the courtyard and required a sharp shove to dislodge it.

The yard was not big, a rectangle of about thirty feet long and twenty feet wide of compacted red-brown earth, surrounded by a wall that was as high as the building itself. In the centre of the yard stood two spindly pawpaw trees, which provided some shade with their fan-shaped leaves.

The house was an L-shaped building containing a few gloomy rooms, which opened on to the yard. The walls of the building formed the boundary of the plot, and all the windows of the house that did not open into the yard opened directly on to the alleyways that ran alongside.

Matilda, her parents, her sisters and assorted cousins and relatives lived here, all provided for mainly by Uncle Saint John, although Matilda's mother did have a market stall selling vegetables. Looking at the house, one might wonder, was there enough room for so many people? But they had as much space as most of the other families in the area. The girls – Matilda and her two sisters, Saint John's daughters, Gifty and Pearl, and two nieces, daughters of a dead sister – slept in one bedroom. When there were visiting female relatives, who often came to stay for undefined periods, they too slept in this room. The girls had rattan mats, which they rolled away in the morning, leaving the room looking spartan. Apart from a couple of wooden boxes, in which the girls kept their clothes, there was one rickety table on which they all kept various belongings.

The boys had a similar room. Saint John had one son, Bright, who was already twenty and had recently moved north to work at one of the gold mines, and two nephews, children of the same dead sister, who shared this room.

Ama and Owusu's room was slightly smaller than Saint John's but otherwise very similarly decorated. Next to their room was a fifth room, used as a storeroom, filled with things that no one could remember or possibly need, but Saint John told them that it was essential to have this additional space. Somehow, having a spare room with undefined or, as Saint John saw it, 'flexible' purpose made him feel wealthier than he was. There was also a latrine and bathroom housed in a concrete block at the furthest corner of the plot from the open covered structure that was used as a food store and kitchen.

While they sat, a mosquito coil burned underneath Saint John's stool, the persistent dark-orange light chasing away the deadly insects. He was wearing a string vest and a pair of slack calico shorts and was trying to read the day's newspaper with the light of a kerosene lantern, but he was unable to concentrate on any collection of words long enough to arrive at a meaningful sentence and seemed to read the same passage over and over again. The truth was, he was as excited as a bride because he was about to share the great news with Matilda's parents and his own wife. They were waiting for Owusu, who had been in the latrine for over half an hour, but Saint John knew better than to rush the man.

Saint John's wife, Amele, wiped sweat from her brow regularly and sighed deeply as though she was being kept from some more interesting diversion. She was short and round with an enormous chest and an even more enormous behind, which from the side made her look like a reversed squat 's'.

Ama had her head in her hands and looked bored; she fidgeted on her stool, unable to find a comfortable position for her thin bottom on the unyielding seat. She looked like her brother, with wiry limbs and a hard face. Her hair was braided underneath her headscarf, and every now and then, she scratched her scalp violently through the scarf.

The women feared bad news; there was no other reason for Saint John to insist that they all gather together like this, and their faces registered resignation.

Finally, Owusu emerged from the latrine with a beaming smile on his face, revealing a gap where one of his lower front teeth had once been. He was a thin man, of average height, with hunched shoulders and a hollow stomach. He had a full, short beard and a full head of black hair, both flecked with grey, wiry strands. He was most probably the oldest person in the house, but because he did not know his date of birth – although given some of the historic events he seemed to remember first-hand, he might have been in his fifties – and because of the general lack of respect that flowed in his direction, this seniority granted him no privileges whatsoever.

Ama tutted and turned her disgusted face away from her husband.

'Well, I shall not waste any more time,' said Saint John as Owusu made himself comfortable on a stool. 'Today, I am proud to be the bearer of the best news that this family has ever received.' His audience looked surprised. Ama raised her head and her eyebrows in hope. 'Our daughter Matilda has had the most fortunate offer of marriage,' he continued, then paused and looked around at his stunned family.

'Go on then, spit it out,' said Ama, sticking her neck out as far as it could go in the direction of her brother.

'You will never imagine. Nor will you believe it possible, even if you imagine it. I am still amazed myself. In fact, the only reason that I have already agreed is that—'

'You have what?' shouted Ama. 'Are you not supposed to ask her parents first? It is not as though you can be trusted in the choice of marital partners,' she said, shooting a glance at Amele.

'Am I not her uncle? As such, I was thinking only of Matilda's future. And anyway, Lawyer will take care of her; she will want for nothing as his wife.' He looked around at their stilled mouths. The news sank slowly, like porous coral in a pond, which eventually reaches the bottom amid a flurry of sand and silt.

Then Ama jumped up from her stool, hugged herself and started dancing around the compound singing, 'Thank you, thank you, thank you,' over and over again, all the while looking at heaven through the star-filled sky. Saint John was beaming with joy and nodding at his brother-in-law. Amele sat wide-eyed and silent, her lips apart.

'Well, I have to say that I think I deserve to take some of the praise for this situation,' Saint John said, talking to no one in particular. 'I don't think she could have attracted such a stupendous offer of marriage without my input. In fact, on my way home, I could not help but think of all the correct decisions I have made regarding my niece. Who would have thought that Matilda learning English would after all be so important? When she has Mrs Bannerman as a rival, believe me, she will need to speak English; I have never come across a more English African in my entire life. How fortunate we are that my father had the foresight to educate me rather than teach me to be a fisherman. You know, I am the first man in my family to be educated, and—'

'Yes, yes, they know. You have told them countless times,' said Ama as she sat back down on her stool and began jigging her hips from side to side in time to a rhythm that only she could hear. 'The dowry. What are we going to ask for?'

'Are you saying that Lawyer Bannerman wants to marry my daughter?' Owusu hardly ever spoke, and they all looked at him in astonishment. 'Matilda is still a child; can't we ask Lawyer to wait a while?' He sounded unsure, not like a man in authority.

They looked at him, mystified.

Saint John shook his head and said, 'At times, I think that accident took not only your tooth and the use of your arm but your senses too.'

Ama stopped her seated dance and looked at her husband. 'We will say yes,' she told him firmly with her eyes squinted. 'And we must send for Aunty Dede at once. This calls for her presence.'

Owusu looked at Saint John, shrugged and said, 'I suppose you can tell Lawyer that he can send them to come and knock.'

'Good, you have got some sense left. I will get a piece of paper to write our demands down. We better strike while the iron is hot.'

Ama had begun describing the sorts of things she wanted in exchange for her daughter and had to exercise a great deal of patience while her brother listed them slowly in his elaborate script.

'Have you written cloth? And jewels? What about scent?' she asked.

'Yes, yes, take your time, I am writing it all down.'

'What else can we ask for?'

'Some food?' said Amele.

'Yes,' said Ama. 'And we should ask for one of the horses too.'

'For goodness' sake, Ama, there is no need to ask for one of his horses as part of the dowry. That is ridiculous. What will we do with it? Where would we keep it? Some gold and beads, some cloth, some spirits, what more do we need?' said Saint John. 'I know that you want something big in exchange from Lawyer, but we cannot lower ourselves and ask for too much. Once they are married, we will all continue to benefit from our relationship with such an important family.'

'Money. Don't forget the money,' Ama said, gesturing assertively at the piece of paper.

So far he had written:

1. 12 pieces of grade-A-quality cloth.
2. 3 sets of jewellery made with pure gold (matching earrings, bangles and necklace).
3. Drink (6 bottles of schnapps, 6 bottles of gin, 6 bottles of whisky).
4. 6 bottles of scent.
5. 12 live fowls.

'Sister Ama, you are lucky to have your daughter marry so well.' Amele sounded a little envious.

'Luck does not come into it,' retorted Ama. 'She is a beautiful girl, and we have brought her up well. Didn't I tell you that educating her would be to her advantage? At least Matilda will be able to hold her own with the first wife.' She was looking at Owusu disdainfully.

'And she has fairness on her side,' whispered Amele.

'Well, I think that is it,' said Saint John, adding a sixth item to the list – a generous sum of money. 'The list is now complete. I will give it to Lawyer in the morning. We should call her and tell her the good news.' He walked to the door of the compound and shouted in the direction of the street to no one in particular, 'Call Matilda for me.'

When she walked into the yard, she was out of breath and had beads of sweat on her forehead from the game she had been playing with her sisters and friends when the summons interrupted them. Similar to hopscotch, it required lots of jumping and hopping, something that Matilda found increasingly difficult now that her breasts had become so massive, apparently almost overnight. The fact was, she had been steadily putting on weight over the past two years, and she often forgot that she was no longer the beanpole she had once been. She had developed curves and dips all over her body that she had not yet become comfortable with. But today, she was winning for a change, and it would be irritating if one of the adults sent her on an errand now. Or could it be that she was about to be told off? That is what usually happened when she was summoned in front of all the adults like this. She could not think what she had done wrong recently, but then, there was often no correlation between her behaviour and a telling-off from her mother. But her mother was smiling and looking pleased with herself. Her father was looking at his shoes intently, as though he had suddenly realised that they were on his feet.

'Sit down, Matilda.' Saint John spoke softly.

She was confused. She was never invited to join them.

'Your mother has some good news for you,' Saint John continued.

She looked at her mother and again at her father. He was still examining his shoes.

'We have some *very* good news for you. Lawyer wants to marry you,' Ama said joyfully. 'Congratulations, my daughter. We are proud of you.'

She was stunned. She tried to swallow, but her mouth was too dry. She looked quizzically at her mother and then her father. He was looking at her now. His eyes were sad, but he did not speak.

'We feel so honoured that he wants to marry you, and needless to say, we have agreed that his family can come and knock.' Saint John was speaking, but the words were a blur to Matilda.

'No need to delay matters, I think,' said her mother. She might have been rubbing her hands with satisfaction.

'You will have everything that you need,' said Amele. 'You are such a fortunate girl.'

'You'd better make sure that you have lots of children for him,' said her mother. 'The first wife has had four children, including twins. Twins, do you hear? We all know how our culture reveres a woman who brings multiple babies into the world at the same time.'

Matilda could not follow the conversation. The yard and everyone in it seemed to be swaying from side to side as though they were in a boat at sea. She suddenly noticed how hot and humid it was, almost as though the air were running out. The noise of the crickets chirping in the dark seemed to drown out the various voices, and a lone frog croaked in a manner that seemed out of place. Several thoughts flowed through her mind in slow motion. She had just been informed that she would become the wife of Lawyer. In a matter of weeks at that. She was aghast. She was not ready to marry or to have children. She did not know him. Naturally, she was afraid of him, who wouldn't be? Yet somehow, she knew that her fate had been settled. Without her. She had to accept it. Or run away. To where? She could not expect to be asked for her opinion, but she had never imagined it would happen like this, or so soon. Her life as she knew it was about to be over. And without warning.

'Matilda Bannerman, wife of Lawyer Bannerman,' Saint John said, interrupting Matilda's thoughts. He had come to stand next to her and put his arm round her shoulders. 'You have done well. You can be proud.'

She wanted to push him away. The feel of his skin on hers repulsed her. She was surprised at the strength of her reaction, but she already realised that each of the adults in this room had betrayed her. No wonder her father wouldn't look at her.

'I will have to be careful or you will be ordering me around just like Madam Bannerman the First,' Saint John continued, chuckling.

'Well, Matilda, what do you say to this news?' Ama asked. 'You should be grateful to Uncle for his help. Without him, you would not have such a fortunate marriage. Left to some others I shall not name,' she said, darting her eyes in Owusu's direction briefly, 'who knows where your fortunes would lie. And we have demanded a nice dowry for you, only the best quality . . .'

'But I am only fourteen.' Matilda had summoned up all her courage to voice these words of rebellion. 'I want to continue with my school, I—'

'Listen here, you ungrateful girl, you will be fifteen soon,' interrupted her mother in a hostile voice. 'I was not much older when I married your father. You are old enough to have children. You are a woman now. And you have had enough education. You can write your name; what more do you want? This is a good offer and we will accept it. We cannot ask Lawyer to wait. Don't you think that there are several others he could marry?'

Matilda looked at her father. Why was he not saying anything at all? She pleaded with him silently, but his eyes had a glazed look, and he seemed to be somewhere far away, somewhere peaceful. Why did he never get involved in the contentious discussions of the household, of which there were many? Why did he remain silent when she needed his opinion? But as the murmur of voices continued reinforcing this abrupt end to her life, and her mind slowly numbed in defence, the scales of childhood fell from her eyes, and she could see why her father had given up trying a long time ago. The one thing he had loved, and in fact been very good at, was fishing. The adventure – tinged with danger, for none of the fishermen could swim – of being on the raging sea in a canoe with other men, the satisfaction of the physical exercise of rowing over the large breakers on to the open ocean, where from the shore, the canoe would be but a dot on the horizon, the feel of the strong sea breeze, watching the sun rise out at sea, and finally, the straining but rapturous teamwork of standing on shore with the other men, often twenty or more, pulling in the day's catch, singing and heaving in unison; that had been his life. But after the accident, when he had injured his arm, he had had to retire. Matilda knew that there were no savings, no security of any kind to fall back on, and she saw that most certainly the reality of having to face the rest of his life as a kept man without escape to the sea had made him ill. Regularly after his accident, and occasionally still, he would wander down to the beach early in the morning when the boats were returning and watch from a distance, breathing in the salty air. Sometimes, he felt able to sing along with the men under his breath, other times, he stood silently, hidden from sight.

His condition, if indeed there was one, might possibly have been diagnosed. But Owusu would never have considered going to see a doctor, probably because he believed that a doctor would just remind him, as did his wife and brother-in-law continuously, that there were several other occupations for a man with only one good arm. So, he had given up on life, before life gave up on him, and had spent his years living as a passive spectator, watching with a mixture of bemusement and confusion as everyone else's life was played out before him. Matilda knew that peaceful look was not there because he was pleased for her. He looks that way because he has taken his mind away from here, she thought. For all I know, he is out there on the sea once more, or asleep in his bed.

'But I am afraid of him,' she said out loud.

'It is not a bad thing for a wife to be afraid of her husband,' said Saint John. Neither Amele nor Ama contradicted him. 'Now tell me, when Lawyer marries you, he is expecting a virgin. Will he be disappointed? Is he going to have to send you back to us in shame? Heh?' Saint John asked.

Matilda was mortified at this implication; she started to cry again and could not speak.

'Eh! Answer Uncle,' her mother shouted.

'Yes, Uncle, I am a virgin.'

'Well, nothing can be taken for granted these days. And there will be no more talk of lessons. From today, consider yourself engaged. You belong to another man who will not appreciate being disgraced. I cannot take any risks,' said Ama.

Matilda's sobs went unheeded while the adults continued to discuss arrangements.

Owusu spoke, startling them all. 'Matilda, go and dry your tears now. It is all right. You will see that everything will be fine.' He was looking at her with impotent kindness.

She started to sob uncontrollably now. She knew he knew it was not going to be fine, but she realised that this battle was over; she had lost with barely a fight, and her pleas had gone unheeded.

That night, before Robert had received formal acceptance of his engagement proposal, he decided to tell Julie about his plans to marry Matilda.

He knocked lightly on her bedroom door and walked in. Julie was sitting on her bed in her peach-coloured frilly nylon nightdress and matching dressing gown, which was demurely fastened with a bow under her neck. It was a hot night, and her nose shimmered with dampness. Julie was very dark, but although she had not benefited from her European ancestors' colouring – when she was growing up, her mother and aunts had often commiserated with her that she had not inherited the lighter skin of her sisters – her features indicated the well-diluted European blood that lurked in her distant past. Her hair was like a well-stuffed pincushion, longer than it looked but patted down neatly around the shape of her head. She had a long face and a high brow. Her cheekbones were pronounced, and her nose and mouth quite delicate. She was slim, altogether statuesque, and she walked majestically, like a woman who has never doubted her worth.

Julie's family were cultivated in all matters English. She had attended the government girls' school in Accra before being shipped off to a cold English boarding school when she was thirteen and then on to finishing school. But when her father, one of the Gold Coast's first lawyers, died, leaving his widow to fend for five young children, her mother, an accomplished pianist, had decided that it would be better for Julie to give up her plans for teacher-training college and marry well. Robert Bannerman had seemed the ideal choice, a young, ambitious lawyer with a similarly glittering background.

Julie was reading a letter, but she looked up and smiled at her husband and started to fold it away. 'Hello. I was just rereading my sister's letter. She has settled down well in London, and she is enjoying her course. I knew that it was the right thing for you to send her there.' Julie insisted that she and Robert speak English together so that their children would learn to speak it. For some reason, unknown even to her, however, she seemed to lapse into the Ga vernacular when she was very angry.

The room was spacious, dominated in one half by a heavy four-poster bed with a bedside table on either side of it. On the far wall near the bed were a dressing table and a chair with a cushioned seat. Several dusty pots and bottles were carefully arranged in descending order of height, with the tallest at the back – eau de cologne and Yardley lavender water, Julie's favourite scents, which she kept in their boxes. There was a small sofa with a low table on which there was a neat pile of magazines – fading copies of *Woman and Home*, *Good Housekeeping* and *Ideal Home*, which Julie had brought back from England with her, and which no one was allowed to touch. A small chandelier with one bulb emitted a warm, golden glow that caused shadows to bounce off the walls.

'My dear,' said Robert, walking up to his wife. He was more nervous than he thought he would be. She looked nice tonight; she was smiling at him, unfastening the bow of her dressing gown slowly.

'No. That's not why I have come,' he said, touching her on the shoulder as he sat down beside her. 'I need to tell you something important.'

'I have something important to tell you too. I—'

'Julie, what I need to tell you can't wait.' She probably wanted to talk about some domestic problem with the maids or the children, but Robert thought chitchat would be out of place tonight. They did not generally talk much, not as much as Julie wanted, or so she told him regularly. They coexisted in some unspoken order of the 'way things should be', each sticking to a carefully predetermined role and taking care never to cross unseen boundaries. Robert thought their marriage was in many ways a success; he knew Julie was aware of his affairs with women who did not care that he was married, only that he would be able to support any children they might have, and who therefore would not give up trying to snare him. She was looking expectantly at him when he said, 'I have decided to take a second wife, and I—'

'I beg your pardon?' she asked quietly. She had tilted her head ever so slightly towards Robert and raised her eyebrows as far as they would go.

He was sure she had heard him, but she cocked her head further, frowning like an old woman whose hearing has deteriorated unexpectedly, and for whom the whole process of listening has suddenly become painful. 'Sorry? What was that you said?'

'I am going to take a second wife.'

Then, as if she had simply needed a little time to react, Julie was on her feet with her hands on her hips and was staring in disbelief. 'What?' Her voice was high-pitched and bordering on hysterical. 'A second wife? Why?' Then, as if the energy that had pushed her up on to her feet was quickly drained, she slumped back down on the bed. 'What am I not providing you that you need a second wife? Do you not like my cooking? Have I not given you four children? Am I not a good wife? Am I no longer beautiful?' Julie was screeching at Robert, waving her hands in the air aggressively, as if she was trying to conjure up answers to her questions.

Although it was late, Robert hoped there was enough activity in the household to drown out Julie's voice. He had not expected her to be this angry. He knew she could be inflexible, but he was surprised at how badly she was responding. He didn't want to lose his patience or his temper, but she was testing him.

Before he could answer any of her questions, she continued, 'This is precisely what I hoped to avoid by marrying an educated man like you. Now you too want to behave like every other uncivilised man in this city.' Her voice was trembling and she had tears streaming down her face. 'What will my friends say? Do you think that I don't know about the child that you fathered last year? At least you had the decency not to acknowledge it publicly. You are less intelligent than I gave you credit for if you think that I can share this house with your conniving sisters while they help you support the child's mother and not find out about it.'

Robert should not have been surprised that Julie knew about his bastard child. His two unmarried sisters lived in an apartment downstairs with its own entrance at the back of the house. It was the right thing that he should provide for them and they might be involved in his family. They had their own kitchen and living space and their own maids. And even he knew how much maids gossip. There were undoubtedly few of his sisters' conversations that didn't eventually get repeated in some guise or other to Julie. For a moment, he looked away from her. 'Well, so you know. There is nothing more to discuss, then. Or do you want me to apologise for something?' He shrugged his shoulders and raised his hands fleetingly. 'I can afford to pay for the child, which is all that its mother wishes. If it makes you feel better to know the details of my private life, I am not seeing her any more.'

Julie shook her head and prepared to say something, but he continued, 'You are acting as if it is unusual for a man like me to want to marry again. As long as I can support another wife and her children, I don't see that there is anything to discuss.'

'More children . . .' Julie shook her head in disbelief. She had stopped crying. 'But we are not like that; we know better. Polygamy is despicable. It is uncivilised. My father, who, let me remind you, was one of the first Africans to practise law in this country, will be turning in his grave. This is not why he sent me to finishing school. Why did you marry me if this was your intention? You knew what I expected from a marriage, a home. My father—'

'Listen! I am not your father. How he lived is not relevant to me. You should know better than to make such senseless comparisons.'

'Robert,' she pleaded. 'I know you have girlfriends, I see you gawping at every woman you see. You think no one sees you, but you're wrong. Have the women, look all you like, do whatever you have to, but I beg you, please don't disgrace me by marrying one of them.' She was looking at him with woeful eyes.

Robert stood up. There was nothing he could say. At times like this, he found it easier not to talk at all.

'Please tell me the real reason. Tell me. Tell me what I have done. Am I a bad wife? Do you no longer want me? Answer me. Please answer me.' She was shaking her head, causing large tears that had welled up in her eyes again to start falling down her cheeks. She tried to brush them away with the back of her hand, but they came too fast.

He answered the one question he felt he could: 'You are a good wife.' He glanced at her. She was watching him expectantly. 'My decision to marry Matilda—'

'Matilda? Who is she? How do you know her? And why are you bothering to tell me when you have obviously made up your mind already?' She put her head in her hands and started wailing like a mourner at a funeral.

Robert remained quiet. This was more uncomfortable than he had imagined. He hadn't anticipated that she would overreact like this.

'Look, it's not as though I am leaving you for her or changing your status in any way.' He considered adding, 'And I never promised that I wouldn't marry again,' but thought better of it. Well, he was simply not prepared to consider the one thing that might reassure his wife. 'Look, you will get used to the idea. I am not the only man in Accra to take a second wife.'

As suddenly as she had started, Julie stopped wailing. She pushed her shoulders back and raised her chin, blinking fast to stop further tears that were tempted to gather in her eyes. 'Well, I suppose since you are going to marry her no matter what I say, I will not stand in your way. But she will not live under the same roof as my children and me. I suppose you have already approached her family?'

'She is Saint John's niece and—'

'Saint John's *niece*,' she whispered. '*Saint John's* niece,' this time more loudly. Then she heaved a sigh. 'That man has never liked me.

I know he thinks that I am haughty because I can't be bothered to speak to him when I see him. I am sorry, but I can't help it if I was raised to know my place and to keep a healthy distance from the servants.' She sighed again and stood up. 'I suppose now he is going to expect me to treat him like a long-lost relative, well, I won't. It is probably best if tomorrow I go and stay with my mother for a few days. You should know that she will now probably never visit our home again.'

Julie had gone to sit at her dressing table and was busy rearranging the bottles and jars, pushing them around, occasionally picking one up and looking at the label as if she had no idea what it contained. Eventually, she picked up a jar of Pond's face cream and struggled to open it. 'Have you eaten yet? I cooked your favourite today – roast pork and rice.'

He was thankful that the worst was over. Clearly, she had remembered her duties as a good wife; she knew better than to make a fuss. He looked up into his wife's face in the mirror. She had been watching him, but she lowered her eyes and started applying the glutinous white cream to her face without looking into the mirror.

'Well, I am exhausted. You see the thing that I wanted to tell you is that I am expecting again. I need my sleep.'

'Oh . . .'

'I am sure you won't mind if I don't get up to see you out.'

Robert stared at her reflection, but still his wife would not raise her head. 'That is good news. Are you pleased?'

'I don't think that is a relevant question, do you?' she said with forced laughter.

Robert longed to go. The room suddenly felt overcrowded and hot. 'I am pleased for you,' he said, walking towards the door.

'What about you? I suppose after five children the excitement wanes a little. Ah, well,' she exhaled dramatically. 'Good night. Sweet dreams.'

Robert paused with his hand on the doorknob. He thought momentarily about going back to her but then realised there was nothing he could say, so he opened the door quietly and walked out. Another child, he thought, allowing himself a smile. At least that would keep her busy.

Julie stared in the mirror and wiped her eyes. She carefully tucked her hair under a net and then continued her nightly ritual of applying creams to her eyes, her face and her hands. She looked in the mirror one last time before she stood up and removed her dressing gown, placing it gently over the back of the armchair. Then she switched off the light and lay on her bed. This was the one thing she had feared might happen to her. She felt an unhealthy loathing rise up in her. She cursed the base side of his personality that allowed him to think she was not enough for him. It was clear that his sophistication was but a thin veneer covering centuries of backwardness that had come before. Now she let the tears flow freely. It was because of her condition, because of all those beastly hormones that had usurped her body that she had cried in front of her husband tonight. She had never before let him see her cry; surely it was not advisable to demonstrate such feebleness in front of a man? But her defences were weakened, and her tear ducts over productive, it seemed.

Matilda looked forward to the arrival of her Aunty Dede. A portly, jolly woman whose fleshy body and fat, smiling face seemed to bring instant cheer to everyone who met her, she had only good memories of Aunty Dede. Memories of laughter and joy. How she loved her visits. When she arrived, she would help Matilda to make sense of what was happening to her life.

And indeed, when she arrived, laden as usual with bags of cakes, *achomo* – the little pieces of deep-fried sweet dough eaten on special occasions – and other food that she must have spent several days preparing, she cheered up the Lamptey household, although it had to be said that Ama and Uncle Saint John appeared happiest of all, and for reasons unrelated to the visit of their big sister. Ama boasted to anyone who would listen about the great fortune that had been bestowed on her family. She could often be seen dancing and singing to herself. And transgressions from the children that would normally have earned them a slap or a beating seemed to go unnoticed.

'So, where is my lucky niece?' Aunty Dede bellowed, waddling into the courtyard. Trailing behind her were two small girls straining under the weight of her bags. She was smiling with joy, her small twinkling eyes tucked neatly into the folds on her round face. Her hair was short and dyed charcoal black so that it looked like a cheap wig and made her skin look reddish. She laughed loudly and stretched her heavy arms to embrace Matilda when the girl went to greet her aunt.

Matilda closed her eyes and enjoyed the sensation of being harnessed in those abundant arms, from which excess flesh dangled like washing on a line.

Aunty Dede pushed her away to take a good look at her niece. She saw that the girl's eyes were packed with tears. She quickly hugged her again and whispered conspiratorially, 'I am here now, don't worry.' She hugged Matilda tighter. 'Don't let them see you cry,' this time more urgently. Then, releasing Matilda, Dede turned to her brother, who was standing by with a look of pride and accomplishment on his face. 'You have done well, then, John,' she said. She refused to use his prefix: 'There are no saints in this family, and as far as I can remember, that is not the name our father gave you,' she would say.

During the usual talk about what had happened in each other's lives since they last met – apart from the big news, which would be discussed in detail later – Aunty Dede asked Matilda to help her unpack bag after bag of goodies, much to the delight of the younger children, who stood observing at a safe distance from the seated women.

Aunty Dede was much older than Ama, who was the daughter of their father's third wife; Saint John and Aunty Dede had been born to his first wife. She lived in a town a few miles from Accra, but her visits always involved her staying several nights. Aunty Dede's children, three sons, were all grown now and had moved to Accra to find work. She had done her duty and raised her children; now she wanted to help raise her nieces and nephews.

When all the food had been carefully stowed away in the kitchen, Matilda noticed that there were still two bulky suitcases that had not been touched. Aunty Dede did not usually travel with so many clothes; she wondered how long she had come to stay.

That evening, as the younger members of the household were turning in for the night, calm and satiated from a day of laughter, Aunty Dede summoned Matilda for a chat.

'Come here,' she said, and again she held her. She had always had a soft spot for the girl, who was tender, not overly strong like her fierce mother. 'I am here now. I will guide you through the map of marriage and motherhood that has been unfolded before you so suddenly.'

Matilda started to cry. Aunty Dede simply held her tighter, as though she could feel the girl's pain and wished to take some of it away.

'All right, all right,' she said gently. 'Enough now. Sit down. I know it's difficult. I was sad when I heard the news. Had your mother told me before they agreed to the marriage, I would have advised her to ask him to wait until you are a little older, but they have already agreed and there is no going back now. We must simply do the best we can; there is too much at stake.'

Matilda began to sob uncontrollably. She had hoped that her aunt would be able to work a miracle and change the course of her destiny; after all, she had always seemed to make everything fine when she was younger. As she cried harder, she began to lose sensation deep in her arms and legs, as if her tears were draining her life away.

'I know that money is not everything, but in our world, it is nearly everything. You must pay attention to the good facts – he is rich, educated and powerful. And I have heard that he is handsome too, which is a bonus.' She winked. 'Do not underestimate what it will mean that you don't have to work or that your children too may be lawyers and doctors. If you are obedient, at least to his face, you will see that everyone will leave you alone. You will experience greater freedom in this marriage than in any other position in our society. Trust me.'

Matilda had stopped crying, but she was sniffing and wiping her wet eyes with the back of her hand.

Aunty Dede handed her a pristine white handkerchief. 'Here, take this. And keep it as a present from me.' It had been carefully ironed. Matilda opened it and a pleasing aroma of perfume escaped.

The women sat silently for a while, listening to the chirping crickets and the partial conversation of two men chatting as they walked along the alleyway outside the house.

'We still depend on men for everything we have. I had to realise very young that in order to have a good life, a painless life, I had to

94

accept my place. I learned to humour my husband very early, to make him think that he was always right. Then he left me in peace. You too have to learn these things. You have to accept that, as unfair as it seems to you, you have no choice in this matter.'

Matilda was listening to her aunt with watery, wide eyes. 'But I don't want to be married yet. I don't want to have children yet.'

'Well, there is no happiness for a childless woman in our world; it is your duty to have children. You might as well get that over and done with. Anyway, you are not too young to have children, even if you think you are. Plus, if their father is Lawyer, you are not doing badly at all.'

Matilda was crying silently.

'Being a second wife can have benefits and pitfalls. I should know,' Aunty Dede said. 'You must always remember that the first wife is not your friend. But try not to make her your enemy either. If you are able to do this, you will succeed in the marriage.'

Matilda nodded obediently.

'And I promise that I will stay here to make sure that at least we can laugh a little while we cry,' she said, her eyes gleaming in the lamplight. She was quiet for a while before she spoke again. 'And I will do all that I can to ensure that you don't have to go to his room until after the engagement.'

Chapter Five

Audrey placed the pink flat of her palm on her forehead as if trying to confirm the source of the pulsating pain, as she made her way carefully to the bathroom. Each step reverberated in her head as blood pounded through her brain. She leaned on the sink and stared long and hard at the ageing face before her. Her skin looked as if it had shrunk overnight, and make-up filled the creases on her face. She pushed her hair, which had long outgrown its last cut, from her face and briefly considered chopping it all off into one of those short styles that emancipated women wore. At the back of the untidy cabinet in the bathroom, she found some headache tablets. She walked to the veranda looking for coffee. She would have it black today, and in peace and quiet. Thank heavens Alan had already gone off to work. In the month since their first party, he seemed to have become less indirect with his recriminations. He would tell her off if she had misbehaved last night. Had she? She probed her memory, attempting to recall a vague chronology of the Governor's cocktail party. What had she done wrong this time? She could remember Alan being frosty in the car on the way home, but not why. She tried to recollect the atmosphere. It hurt to think. She shook her head gently as though to dispel the memory. Tonight. His lecture could wait until tonight.

She gazed at her breakfast. Cook had found fresh eggs at the market, and before her sat a perfectly boiled soft egg and some toast. She stirred the bright-orange yolk and scooped a bit on to her tea-spoon. She enjoyed the warm, creamy taste. She allowed herself another spoonful and then pushed it away. Enough, she thought, and refilled her cup instead. She looked around the house. Was there anything useful she could do today? The servants must have been cleaning for hours. The small boy was putting glasses and bottles away in the cupboard in the living room, trying to be as quiet as possible. Somewhere in the distance, Awuni was singing while he worked. For now at least, the veranda was probably the most peaceful place to be. She looked at the egg wistfully and drank some more coffee. Her head was beginning to feel heavy again. She closed her eyes, and they swam behind their lids. She focused on her breathing while her head steadied.

On days like today, she longed for home, for her garden, to sleep in her old bed. She bit her lip. For a while, she tried to keep the clatter of thoughts at bay. She hated to think what her parents would make of her life here. For the umpteenth time, she contemplated whether this morning might herald the beginning of better days. More positive ones they might even approve of. She forced herself up and went to fetch a sheet of paper on which to write a list. Suggestions to inspire her and focus her mind, maybe to encourage good personal development like her father admired.

1. Dinner party?
2. Help with summer dance.
3. Play?
4. Volunteer for something? (ask Alan)
5. Write more letters.
6. Read more.

She read the list and thrust it aside in disgust. It looked as pathetic written down as it did in her head. She thought of adding one last item – 'write' – but didn't; it was pointless. What would she write anyway? It has been another hot day? I am bored? I am furious with Alan, and even more so with myself? I need something exciting, something adventurous to happen. Exactly; it was inane. The heat and boredom had sapped her imagination, leaving no novel thoughts that begged to be expressed.

She sat in the silence and listened. Awuni had stopped singing and the other servants were too far away for her to hear. The dogs were quiet in their cage at the back of the house, where she preferred them, and there was no wind to rustle the trees. Should she read? Write a letter? Go to the club? Have a nap? The thought of what to do with the day that stretched before her enervated her. And her head still ached in spite of the tablets.

'Good morning, madam,' said Awuni. 'I don't want disturb, but I want clean the floor.'

Audrey opened her eyes and glared at him. He always appeared at the wrong moment. She ignored him, hoping he would go away.

'Madam, you didn't eat the brake fast. Shall I tell Cook to make some food? Maybe some sandwich?'

'No. I am not hungry.'

'But, madam, will you not eat? It is—'

'I said, I am not hungry.'

'Oh, madam—'

'Can't I enjoy a moment's peace in my own house?' asked Audrey, gathering her things. She went into her bedroom and shut the door. Couldn't today be different? Shouldn't today be the beginning of a better stretch?

She had tried so hard at first to be a good wife to Alan and simply join in with his routine, to follow submissively. She was pleased when she saw how grateful he was that she allowed him to be in control. Her mother's advice – 'allow him to be the man of his house' – proved right, and harmony prevailed. But after a few months, Audrey began to find the routine of whiling the day away while she waited for him tedious. And their conversation lacked the fizz that it once had. In the beginning, these thoughts had terrified her. She had refused to believe that a life in this cesspit was the reward for what she now sometimes boldly termed her 'momentary lapse of sense'. But although it amazed her that she and her husband could feel so differently about something so fundamental, she had had to accept that was the way it was. It was hopeless in fact, as well as somewhat ironic, but Alan had fallen in love with the place. And the people. He refused to talk about a transfer and said he would happily remain here indefinitely if this was where he was wanted. Fear caught in her throat when she thought they might stay here for his entire career. At the outset, she had tried to get used to the heat, the dirt, the flies, the boredom, to make some sort of life for herself, but there was something exhaustingly unconquerable about it all that wore her down and made her attempts seem pointless.

She looked at the clock on Alan's bedside table. It was only ten o'clock. A long way from dinner and drinks at the club. A long way from decent conversation. How she yearned to talk to someone interesting. She tried to recollect her conversation with Sir Colin last night. It would probably have been intended to irritate Lady Smythe, who brought out the rebellious side to her nature. Somehow, the way she barely masked her disapproval while pretending that she hadn't noticed anything remiss made Audrey want to annoy her. She groaned, lit a cigarette, got out her letter paper and started to write. '*Dearest Mother* . . .' She sucked on her cigarette, struggling with her earlier resolutions. She took a sip of her coffee but spat it back into the cup because it was cold.

A knock on the door interrupted her daydreaming. 'What is it now, for heaven's sake?' she shouted.

'Madam, I don't want disturb you, but I want clean bedroom,' said Awuni, pushing the door ajar.

'Is there no peace to be had in this house?'

'Yes, madam,' he said, waiting patiently at the door with a smiling face.

'Make me some fresh coffee first. I'll have it on the veranda.'

'Yes, madam,' he said, scuttling off.

She sat on her bed trying to ignore the tears that were clouding her eyes and beginning to stream down her face. That was another thing she had hardly ever done growing up. Crying for no apparent reason. Now she seemed to do an awful lot of it. Damn Alan. Why was he determined to subject her to a life here? She gathered her writing things and went to the veranda, where she sat with her back to the glare of the sun; anything to shield her eyes today. She rubbed her temples with both hands and tried to soothe her nerves. She breathed deeply, slowly. It was best to be calm when writing home. She started on another clean sheet of letter paper.

Dear Mother,

I was pleased to receive your letter and hear that you are all well. And the book! Oh, Mother, it was most delightful to receive a package and then to open it and find something to read. So thoughtful of you. I have already devoured what there is to read here. Fancy me not realising there would be no library. Thank you ever so much for the money. I have put most of it in a safe place.

We were invited to a party at the Governor's rather grand home last night. Very sophisticated! It seems Alan has struck up a good rapport with him, which cannot be a bad thing for his career.

The weather is unchangingly hot, which can be a little tiring at times, but I am getting used to it. Alan thinks I have acclimatised rather quickly, actually. I'll sign off now with fondest wishes and promise to write a longer letter next time.

Yours, Audrey.

PS Send me books whenever you can!

'Madam, here is more coffee. Fresh one,' said Awuni, walking on to the veranda with a tray balanced carefully on one hand.

Oh look, he has learned a new trick, Audrey thought. Hooray, hooray! 'Actually, I've changed my mind,' she said, walking off to her room. She threw her things on to her bed and had a bath. She had just laid her damp body on the bed to dry beneath the fan and closed her eyes when there was a knock on the door and Awuni announced that she had a visitor. Only Alice ever came unannounced. She tied her hair up into a bun and pulled on her dressing gown. When she walked into the living room, there was Lady Smythe sitting on the sofa.

'My dear,' she began, before Audrey had a chance to say anything. 'We need to have a talk.'

Audrey yelled for Awuni the moment Lady Smythe's car had disappeared from view. 'Tell Samson to bring the car round,' she yelled at him. She threw her things into a basket, cursing after each item; her bathing suit and some magazines, and her book too, which she knew was a waste of time, especially in her current state. She never read much these days, not even in her bed, which had once been her favourite place to devour book after book. Flicking mindlessly through magazines seemed about all she could manage. How much harder it would be today with that woman's words ringing in her ears: 'This isn't some eternal holiday, Audrey.' Oh, she could scream! And what exactly did she mean by 'For some reason, I have confidence in you'? Why did they all have this need to interfere in her life? Hadn't she just this morning resolved to try harder? But now she wouldn't. How could she when Lady Smythe had told her to? Please let Alice be at the club, she thought. Seated behind Samson, she closed her eyes and tried to enjoy the breeze that the car's movement brought to her face.

The club was by the sea on a tree-lined avenue, conveniently close to the leafy district where the colonial administrators lived. As the car made its way up the gravelled drive bordered with gigantic palms of varying heights, Audrey smiled. The large compound boasted a lawn of carpet grass, drought-resistant turf with large, tough blades that grew horizontally, creeping along. Even so, in the heavy shade of the many large trees – neems, flamboyants, mangoes and various palms – there were sizeable bare patches of red soil, aerated by armies of large ants. The effect of the shade from all of these mature trees was instantly noticeable; it felt cooler, smelled fresh, clean and altogether more agreeable.

The clubhouse was a brick double-storey building with a sheltered veranda running along its lower perimeters. There were several large rooms including a bar, a lounge and a hall that was used for dances, bingo and film nights, and a warren of miscellaneous other rooms.

Africans weren't welcome, even as guests, which Alan thought was a shame. Audrey, however, couldn't think of anything worse than having natives ogling at her while she sunbathed. This was precisely the type of insensitivity that she was beginning to find irritating. She had once believed that he would always side with her, especially on matters concerning her safety. And how mistaken she had been.

A doorman in fancy uniform and a crimson fez with tassels dangling down his neck opened the door and bowed. She walked past him into the shadowy lobby of the club, where dark floorboards shone and more well-trained staff greeted her with a comforting familiarity. She felt her face and neck muscles slacken further. She always seemed to breathe more easily here for some reason. If there was anywhere she might forget her woes, or shelter from her servants, it was here, in this luscious sanctuary. Lady Smythe didn't hang about at the club, preferring, it seemed, to keep to herself. Audrey walked through the lounge past the notice boards with various announcements, lists for tennis and billiards tournaments, information about cricket games and the upcoming dance. The Colonial Service encouraged daily physical exercise as the best way to stay well in the Tropics, which several of the men were happy to adhere to. It irritated Audrey that *they* seemed to get away with ignoring the related guidance on avoiding excessive alcohol.

She strolled through the enormous covered terrace crammed with potted shrubs, where a few people sat in shabby wicker armchairs drinking. On the large expanse of lawn in front of the terrace, a couple of gardeners in khaki uniforms were tending the gardens, their wet shirts clinging to their skin.

The swimming pool was near the tennis courts and a bowls pitch to the side of the main building. Just beyond, the ocean pounded the rocky coastline, making bathing impossible while refreshing the air. It was approaching midday, and the poolside was deserted. Audrey chose a recliner in the shade of some palm trees and set about making herself comfortable. After a few minutes, she threw her magazine aside and decided to go for a swim. The pool was filled with seawater pumped from the ocean, which had been filtered to remove seaweed and other muck. She lowered herself gently into the dense, warm water. She thrashed up and down in the water until her arms and neck ached, then she lay in the sun with her hat on her face until her body started to burn.

She had just managed to forget about the telling off she had received that morning for long enough to doze off when she heard a voice calling out to her. She shaded her eyes from the dazzle of the sun and looked up at Alice.

Seated in the shade with glasses of cold tonic water, Alice asked how Audrey was feeling.

'Awful. And isn't it hot?' she said, stretching her arms and legs. 'I wonder what I shall do today.' Her days seemed to loom emptier than ever. She sighed deeply.

'You really must get out of the habit of sighing so much. If there is an assured way of depressing your spirit, it is to keep deflating it like that,' said Alice.

They laughed lazily.

'It's just that I am so bored all the time,' said Audrey. 'Each day stretches ahead like a vast hot journey without any interesting scenery or company. This is nice, chatting with you like this, but I can't spend every waking hour here, can I?'

'I could name a few people who manage to do just that,' said Alice. 'I'm sure it gets lonely for you. You know you can come by whenever you want; I am always delighted to see you.'

'You are kind, Alice. Really you are.'

Her friend glowed, always grateful to be acknowledged. 'The entertainment committee needs someone to replace Janet—'

'Never! No committee work for me. Not until I am at least thirty-five.'

'It's the trick to staying sane here. You must occupy yourself with something, even if at first it appears a mindless task. Or we could start up our sewing again, try some embroidery? It's ever so rewarding to finish something.'

Audrey filled her cheeks and puffed.

'And there will be a part in the play you could have. I'm sure you'd have a giggle.'

'Oh, I don't think so.'

Audrey gestured to the steward. 'Let's have some lunch, I'm starving.' The man hovered at a polite distance while the women decided what to eat. 'I need a gin and tonic, and some cucumber sandwiches and fresh fruit,' Audrey said without looking up at him. While he scribbled down their order, Audrey said, 'Why have I ended up here in possibly one of the most mind-numbing places of all? I really don't know how I'll be able to face coming back when we go on leave.'

'Oh, you will!'

'I'm serious, Alice.'

'Are you really?' said Alice, genuinely surprised. 'Have you told Alan?'

'No. But I have started to think it through, you know, what I would do if I stayed there and all that.'

'I am sure you'll be fine when the time comes. Alan loves it here; it would be such a shame if he has to give it all up.'

'Indeed,' said Audrey, sighing. 'Pity he married me. He deserves an altogether more loving, understanding wife.'

'Darling Audrey, don't say that. He adores you.' She hesitated a moment and then asked, 'Are things not well between you two?'

Audrey twirled her glass and took a sip. Should she say something? Speaking words, like writing them down, crystallises them, breathes life into them. She studied the mirage on the lawn ahead instead.

'Auds?'

She forced a chuckle. 'I suppose things have not turned out quite as I expected.'

'But nothing too serious?'

She hesitated and chewed her lip. 'It's just me being silly. Alan is a darling, you know that.' She shrugged. 'There really is nothing the matter, other than that I always feel so drained, and dreadfully low at times.'

'Do you think you might be pregnant?'

'Heaven forbid.'

'It might be just the thing. I think you should have a baby. And do it before you're too old. You might only regret it otherwise.'

'Alice, honestly, I could not think of anything worse than having a screaming brat with a snotty nose running around me and creating more havoc than I already have in my life . . . Obviously, I think yours are quite nice, but children simply don't interest me.'

'As long as you know what you're missing,' said Alice, sounding jaded. 'In any case, I'm glad it's nothing alarming. All marriages go through ups and downs; it's quite normal. Even we have had our wobbles. It can take a long while to adapt to marriage. But you two were made for each other. You'll be just fine, you wait and see.'

Audrey looked at her beaming friend and smiled, wishing she could be as assertive about the state of her marriage.

Meanwhile, Alice was itching to say something about the way

Audrey had behaved at the Governor's party last night. She had promised herself that today she would speak her mind. Carefully and gently, she would be as frank as possible. Audrey needed to hear from someone who cared that she was the joke of Accra. Instead, she ordered a gin and tonic and drank it steadily for courage.

'Has Alan said anything about last night?' she asked without looking at Audrey.

'No. He was gone when I woke up. Why?'

'Oh, nothing,' said Alice, bottling at the last minute.

'I suppose if I could remember what happened last night, I might feel ashamed,' said Audrey, sighing. 'Evil Smythe certainly seems to think I should.'

'She doesn't, does she?'

'Don't sound so surprised, you probably think the same.'

'Don't be silly, Audrey. And how do you know she does?'

'She came over this morning and—'

Alice gasped. 'To your house? My word, what did she say?'

Audrey grimaced. 'That I need to buck up and be more of a wife to Alan.'

'Gosh! Were you terrified?'

'Oh, Alice, she is only human like you and me. Of course I wasn't terrified. What *did* I do, anyway?'

'Well, you did try to command H.E.'s attention for most of the evening. Whenever he tried to talk to someone else, you butted in and joined the conversation,' said Alice. 'And . . .'

'And I had a few dances with him, I suppose . . .' Audrey took a long sip of lemony gin. 'I suppose I'll be the talk of the town again, then,' she said, grinning.

'Audrey, you aren't taking this seriously.'

'Well, I am, actually. I take it extremely seriously that she thinks she can march into my house and tell me how to behave.'

'You fell over. Do you remember falling over?'

'So I fell over, what's the harm in that? I fall over from time to time—'

'You fell over three times, Audrey! For goodness' sakes, you might have Alan sent back home.'

'Well, that won't be a terrible outcome, as unlikely as it is. I am not the only woman to have too much to drink on occasion around here.'

'That's true, but it's your behaviour when you are drunk, Audrey; you make a spectacle of yourself, and . . . you embarrass Alan.'

Audrey looked away and kept silent.

'I am only saying this because I care about you two. It's no good for him or you that you don't give a damn. And you come across as rather disdainful of . . . of us all, actually.'

'Rubbish, I just don't agree with you all.'

'Well, I think you ought to take heed of Lady Smythe. I don't imagine that the Governor regularly sends his wife on that kind of mission. The good thing is they must think rather a lot of Alan, which is marvellous,' said Alice, trying to sound jolly. 'Just think, he might become a governor somewhere one day if things work out.'

'You mean if I don't ruin things for him.'

'I didn't say that . . .'

Audrey stood up and stormed off to use the ladies' room. She couldn't bear the fact that her behaviour was constantly being scrutinised, and that they all thought she wasn't quite making the mark. Sod them all, she thought, as she washed her face with cold water. When she returned outside, there were a few more women by the pool. Alice was talking furtively with Frances and another of the wives, but as Audrey approached, Frances walked off.

It was usual for the wives of the colonial administrators to gather around the pool close to whoever got there first, but today, Frances had set up a separate camp at the other side of the pool as far away from Audrey as possible. 'So, I am being shunned now,' said Audrey sarcastically. 'Really, they are a small-minded bunch.'

'Audrey, you must understand that you are making things awkward for them. They can't be seen to—'

'Associate with an unruly woman who refuses to tow the company line?'

'Well, some of us have children to think about. I mean, I can't afford to have Malcolm demoted or sacked . . .'

'Do you want to go and sit with them?' asked Audrey in an angry voice. She stood up. 'I'll tell you what, I'll go. *I'll* leave so you don't have to choose between your *friend* and those two-sided bitches over there.'

'That isn't what I want. I want you to take Lady Smythe's warning seriously for what it is. I want you to try a little harder.'

'Damn you, Alice. You are not my mother. How dare you tell me what *you* want me to do?' said Audrey, gathering her things once more.

Alice bit her lip and watched her friend go. Couldn't she see the women watching? Why did she not care about creating yet another display? Really, she was exasperating.

Audrey cried all the way home. She was still furious with the Governor's wife for demeaning her in her own home. She relived the visit, now able to retaliate, rather than sit wordlessly and absorb the insulting speech. And she was disappointed with Alice for letting her down, frustrated that she misunderstood her. The reason she had gone to the club in the first place was to have Alice sympathise with her like she usually did. Instead, she had sided with those awful women who were now probably revelling in her expulsion. For that was how it felt, as if she had been driven out of her haven.

When her tears were spent, she got out one of her old notebooks. She had not written anything for a long time. As a child, she had loved to sit undisturbed and scribble, to write randomly whatever occurred to her: lists of things to do, thoughts and desires, letters, descriptions of people, places. Her notebooks had been a place to reveal feelings and thoughts that were easier left unspoken. Once she had outgrown sitting on the damp floor of the small shed at the bottom of the garden, she would sit on the moss-covered bench in front of it in the dank shade of the apple trees and fill her lungs with the smell of musty bark. She wrote whatever the light. This was a skill she was particularly proud of, that she could write, not beautifully mind, but legibly, in any lightless space. She wrote happy thoughts, which she recited to herself, and excerpts from the adventures she fabricated. By the time Audrey reached her teenage years, the loudest place in the rambling old rectory where she had lived since early childhood was her mind. There, she exercised various tones that had no place in conversations with her parents; she could be irritated, impertinent, whining, frustrated or plain rude. And often, in search of respite from the soundless rooms, she would venture to the bottom of the garden in rain or shine to hear birds chirping, squirrels burying nuts, leaves bristling in the wind or under her feet, her unrestricted breaths and her voice.

She had tried to break the habit of spilling her thoughts on to paper, thinking of it as a self-indulgent hobby of her childhood. But this afternoon, there was no one to talk to. She needed to write down her thoughts, how wretched they had made her feel. And as she wrote, she felt the tension dissipate enough to sketch resolutions on how to make her life better. Mostly they revolved round Alan and her, the two of them against the world. She had Alan by her side, one of the handsomest men here, and he adored her. She would adore him back. She wouldn't need anyone else if they had each other. She would show them she could manage without the lot of them.

'Madam, please, you like some tea?' asked Awuni.

Audrey jumped in her seat. 'Awuni, I did not hear you coming. Yes. And some biscuits if we have any.'

He reappeared soon with a tray of tea and a plate with two digestive biscuits. She ate one hungrily. 'Tell Cook he does not have to make supper. I'll cook tonight. Tell him to make sure that he has some fresh chicken if possible,' she said. Cooking might make her feel a little better, she thought, pleased. She took the second biscuit.

She sat on the veranda until it began to get dark. She watched the flame-red sun sink into the horizon. In a few minutes, the sky was plunged into darkness, and the sweet scent of night flowers filled the air. Soon, crickets would begin their all-night concert, and fireflies would be seen darting around restlessly. In the distance, a dog barked, and Alan's dogs barked back.

The next morning, she woke early, still feeling rather light-hearted. She was surprised to see Alan still in bed and not out with the dogs. He played in the garden with them each morning before it became too hot. 'Sets me up perfectly for the day,' he said.

He opened his eyes when she stirred. 'Hello, darling.' He framed her face with his hands. 'Thanks for last night.'

She had made him chicken in a creamy sauce with mushrooms and rice, and to break up the whiteness of the food, steamed carrots.

The sauce had been lumpy, she blamed the tinned evaporated milk she had had to use, but even she had to admit that it had been rather delicious.

'Aren't you going to be late?'

'I am not in a rush this morning. Besides, there is something that I need to talk to you about.'

'Tell me,' she said, turning to face him. He looked handsome first thing in the morning. His hair was all floppy and lovely, his eyes only half open and gentle.

'Well, it's good and bad news, I'm afraid.'

'I am sure whatever it is we can face it together. Tell me.'

'Well, Sir Colin has asked Henry whether I can be released from Education to serve as his ADC.'

'His aide-de-camp? Darling, that's marvellous!'

'Well, it's only temporary, a trial of sorts, I suppose. There's been much insinuation that the current ADC will not return, so I thought I might be offered the post on a permanent basis, with enhanced terms, but I haven't.' He shrugged. 'It's only for eight months.'

Audrey felt her face fall. 'Eight months? So we can't . . .'

'Not until the end of my stretch with him. No.'

'And you can't decline?'

'I can't possibly say no to the Governor.'

Audrey felt her lip quivering and she bit it hard. She sniffed and swallowed. She felt tears tingle and slid out of the bed.

'Darling . . .'

'Oh, I understand, Alan. His bloody Excellency does not ask, he requests!' She went into the bathroom and pushed the door closed. She wanted to kick something hard. As the anger waned, she sank on to her bottom and hugged her knees, crying silently. The walls of the bathroom seemed to be caving in on her. She closed her eyes, but still she felt as if she could not breathe. She stood up to lean over the sink, heaving breaths in and out of her chest.

Minutes later, Alan knocked softly on the door. 'I know you want to go home,' he said through the keyhole. 'And we will, just as soon this stint is over.'

'When will that be?'

'Soon, darling. Please let me in.'

She opened the door. 'When exactly?'

He looked her straight in the eye. 'Well, the current ADC goes off in a couple of months. It *is* a great opportunity. Do try and be happy for me, dearest.'

Her shoulders drooped heavily as she calculated the dates. 'We won't be able to go home until next summer!' she wailed. 'Oh, blast Sir Colin and this bloody country and your stupid, stupid job.' She was pounding his chest with her fists and screaming.

Alan stepped back and tried to grab her hands. He looked disappointed.

'Oh, darling, I'm sorry. I'm so sorry,' she sobbed. 'It's just that I am upset and disappointed. I know you can't possibly turn down the post. It's just . . .'

'I know. Shall we have breakfast?'

They sat in silence. Audrey spread marmalade on her toast and played with it. Several times she lifted it to her face and smelled the tangy orange then put it back on her plate without taking a bite.

'Please eat something.'

'I am not hungry. I shall later.'

'Promise me you will. You're getting rather thin.' He looked at his watch and drained his cup. 'I'd better go now. Will you be all right?'

'Yes, I will.'

As soon as he left, she started to cry again. Large salty tears slipped down her face into the coffee cup that she held by her mouth.

'Madam,' said Cook, clambering up the steps. 'I am going marketing now. What shall I prepare today?'

Audrey stood up and pushed her chair violently so that it fell over. 'I don't give a damn what you cook today or ever again, do you understand?' she screamed. 'Just leave me alone.'

'Is Madam sick?'

'Yes, I am sick. Sick . . .' she couldn't form the words and stumbled off to her bedroom. She had not dared to ask whether they would be able to go on leave directly after his stint as ADC. Why did he not have the guts to stand up to the Governor? Couldn't he see that she was wilting here like a parched flower? That she was slowly going mad? 'Why?' she shouted out loud and punched the pillows repeatedly until her arms ached and her eyes stung from all the crying.

She remained in her bed underneath the fan with the curtains closed for the rest of the morning. She sent Awuni away when he knocked and told him to take the rest of the day off, to go out, 'Away!' She screamed at him so loudly that her throat hurt and the poor man, for once without a smiley face, staggered away. Just the once, she would like her house to herself. She bolted both doors so the servants could not get in. Soon, she felt hungry and thirsty; all the crying seemed to have dehydrated her. In the dining room, the new drinks fridge that she had bought with some money her mother had sent was humming. It was not yet noon, a little early to drink on her own, she knew, but she needed something. She filled a glass with ice and a splash of tonic water and carried it with a bottle of gin to her bedroom. She sat on the bed and poured a large measure of alcohol, which she drained fast. She sniffed and poured some more on the ice that was melting quickly. 'What does it matter if I have the odd gin at lunch?' she asked the room and drained her glass again. 'Remember to drink lots and lots of fluids,' she said in a mocking voice and poured a third drink. A little spilled on her dressing table. 'Oops,' she said and wiped the drops with the bottom of her dress. 'Some music, I think.' She put on a gramophone record and turned the volume up high. She lay on her bed with her feet touching the floor, the cold glass resting on her stomach, and stared at the revolving blades dangling from the ceiling. She must have dozed off because when she opened her eyes she was lying on a wet bedspread with the empty glass next to her, and murky shadows danced on the walls.

Chapter Six

The days after her betrothal passed by Matilda in a haze. She lived in permanent fear of a summons to see Lawyer. For some reason, her mother refused to allow her to continue her English lessons and instead created endless tasks to keep her in the house and busy. After years, it suddenly became imperative that someone should scrub the blackened cooking pots until all evidence of their use was removed, a monumental task that took Matilda more than a week. Then she decided her bedroom had to be scoured as it had never been before. Matilda was the appointed cleaner. She tidied up, making sure she did not misplace any of her mother's personal items, and swept away fluffy mounds of dust. She washed the white lace curtains several times until they resembled their original colour before she hung them up where the sun could finish whitening them.

Aunty Amele sauntered into Ama's room one morning when there was no one around. She stood with her hands folded across her chest and watched for a while as Matilda mopped the floor on her knees. Then she made a loud chewing noise with her mouth and said, 'Anyone would think you were in mourning, the way you go around these days with a face as long as a lizard's tail!'

Matilda looked up from her work. 'Why am I the only one who can see that I am unlucky? That my life is over?'

'You are so ungrateful,' said Amele, shaking her head. 'As they say, those who have too many fortunate things heaped upon them can no longer see their good fortune because they have been blinded by good things. The way you are behaving shows that you don't deserve to have such a nice husband.'

'How do you know he is nice?'

'Everyone can see that he is nice. He is a lawyer, he is handsome, he is rich, and he has many, many children. In fact, why he picked you is a mystery to me.'

'Me too,' said Matilda softly.

'Let me give you one piece of advice. Buck up and don't lose your opportunities; such a windfall will not happen again in your lifetime.'

Matilda wanted to ask what opportunity it was that she now had. What advantage was there in being married to a man she was afraid of, and who already had a wife? But she shrugged in silence and continued with her work. What would be the point? These matters seemed of no consequence to anyone else.

'Anyway, I can see that you have a talent for cleaning,' continued Aunty Amele. 'I think when you have finished this room, you can come and clean mine too.' She walked out.

Matilda sat on her feet. The manual work was draining her. At night, she collapsed into bed, and despite the disturbing thoughts that initially hovered as she pulled her comfortable old sleeping cloth over her weary body, she slept well. She had to be prodded awake by her mother or one of her sisters in the morning, and often she turned away from the light of day and tried to re-enter that haven of sleep. But her mother would not allow her to. 'Now is not the time to become a lazy person,' she said one morning. 'You will have to prove yourself as a worthwhile wife before you can slow down.'

The engagement was still some weeks away. Matilda wondered whether this treatment would stop when she was engaged, which she knew, as they all knew, was really no different to being married. What exactly was the aim of keeping her in the house like this? To ensure Lawyer could not seduce her before he had paid the price? Or so that she would be ready day or night should he decide to send for her? In any event, oh, may God please delay that happening as long

113

as heavenly possible. Or were they afraid of her suddenly falling in love with another man, like in the open-air films that her cousin sometimes went to? Wasn't it just their personal futures that concerned them? She looked around at the room. It looked cleaner, that was certain, but her mother was untidy, dirty in fact, and in a matter of weeks, it would look as if it had never been cleaned. She stared at the brown water in her bucket and the torn rag in her hand. She dipped it once more in the water, laid it flat on the floor and stood on it. Then she shuffled around the remainder of the floor, wetting it, aware that she was only smearing the dirt. No one will know any better, she thought, satisfied, as she picked up the cloth and went outside to throw the water into the drain. Perhaps if her cleaning skills reduced markedly, and for no obvious reason whatsoever, they would stop asking her to clean.

She would go out, she thought, and hurriedly changed out of her house dress. She would say she had to go to the market to buy some food, that she had noticed there were no tomatoes, which was true, and after all, what decent meal can be cooked without tomatoes? She could not hear or see Aunty Amele, so she crept out of the compound and walked straight to Patience's house, where she was relieved to see that for once her friend had come home straight after school.

Patience was pleased to see her. 'Why have you not been attending class these past days? I thought you were the one who wanted to learn English? And when I came to your house the other day, your aunty told me you were out.'

'I have not been anywhere. They do not want me to go out. Everything has changed. My life is over. I have been caught in the middle of a disaster . . .'

'What are you talking about? Come, let us go to the beach and you can tell me.'

Together the girls walked towards the sea, away from their homes, the market, school, and Lawyer's house. Soon their ears were filled with the wondrous sound of the waves. They strolled along the beach, keeping in the shade of bent coconut trees, past several fishing boats that lay upturned on the sand fastened to trees with thick ropes. They were dug-outs, eighteen or twenty feet long, each made from a single tree trunk. They were painted black on the outside and decorated with symbols of abundant life, prosperity and God in bright-red, yellow and blue paint, and with a name or prayer in white. The girls walked until they came to a boat that lay forsaken, right way up and now partly buried in the sand, with the words 'God helps those who help themselves' still decipherable in flaking white paint. Matilda and Patience clambered into it and sat opposite each other on benches that were still intact. Here, they could talk in peace. Here, there would be no adults listening, no errands suddenly remembered, no sisters and brothers, cousins and aunts eager to disrupt their quiet just for the sake of it.

'I can only imagine what goes on here at night,' said Patience. 'Such a quiet spot. It is only a shame that it is not more secret.'

Matilda shook her finger playfully at her friend. 'There is no hope for you,' she said, laughing. 'And there is no hope for me . . .'

'Start at the beginning. What has happened?'

'Lawyer wants to marry me.'

'Oh, merciful Jehovah! What did I tell you?'

Matilda lifted her hands up in frustration. 'Another bystander who can see something that I cannot.'

'When did this happen?'

'Last month.'

'This is good news, as a matter of fact.'

Matilda started to cry.

'Why are you feeling so sorry for yourself?'

'The course of my life has been wrenched from me. I have had no involvement in all these monumental decisions that are being taken around me, so please allow me to be a little sad.'

'Yes, this is new territory for us. You are to be a wife, right? Nothing we do can change that fact; it is as hard as this,' she said, knocking the side of the boat. 'In fact, probably harder.' She looked around. 'There must be a big hole somewhere to make the fishermen abandon it like this. Anyway, what we need is a plan of action.'

'What do you mean, action? What action can I take exactly?'

'You can take certain matters into your own hands. You don't have to sit and wait for everything to happen to you. I know you have no say in the general direction that your life is flowing, but you can decide some of the paths you will take along this mystifying journey.'

'Why are you talking in riddles?'

'My best friend is going to be the wife of a powerful man, why should I not adopt airs and graces to match her new status? So,' said Patience, rubbing her palms together, 'firstly, you have to prepare yourself to meet the Number One Wife. As I see it, that is the first obstacle you have to overcome. Your success in that matter will determine the remainder of your course . . .'

'I am not looking forward to that. I fear—'

'You must not fear! If she sees that you are afraid, she will have the upper hand. She will taunt you like a dog. You know how dogs worry only those people who are afraid of them? You must be fearless in her face, even if she is the face of fear. And if all fails, you must simply do things afraid. After all, you will not die just because you are afraid.'

'I think you are the one who should be marrying Lawyer.'

'I wish. I wouldn't mind marrying him. But to have my friend marry him is the next best thing. And what is it that you fear about her? She is no better than you. She too is only a human being.'

Matilda looked out at the sea and watched the waves in their tireless cycle. The water gathering and rising then lurching on to the sand, foaming and frothing as if it was filled with washing soap and then almost soundlessly disappearing to make way for the next body of water. Day and night, this ceaseless rhythm, this crystal clear evidence of God's handiwork continued, whether anyone was there to see it or not. Matilda admired that in God. He did not seem to care whether or not anyone was there to see how marvellous He was. It seemed that He did not do things just to amaze. He did things because He wanted to, and that impressed her.

'You have your sad face on again, and I don't understand why. To marry and bring forth is what is expected of us. You are being offered both on a golden platter. What exactly is it that you want from life that you think Lawyer Bannerman will not be able to give you?'

Matilda was taken aback by the irritation in Patience's voice. 'I don't know. Love? Friendship?' She smiled, fully aware of how ridiculous she sounded.

'You don't need a husband to give you those things. I am your friend, and as for love, that will come. No wonder your mother is worried about you and keeping you at home. You need a husband for money and children. Anything else is extra.'

'I wish I could see it like you. I just have to try and see it favourably. It is just that I feel too young. You are the one who should be getting married; you have always been more grown up than me. You have been ready to marry for a long time now. Why you have not attracted any offers I don't understand.'

'I also don't understand. But don't worry, I am working on it,' said Patience, winking.

'I don't worry for you,' said Matilda, patting her friend's arm. 'We need to go, it is getting late. I will be in trouble if I arrive home late.'

They walked slowly back towards their lives. A few streets away from her house, Matilda stopped to buy some tomatoes from a young girl by the roadside. The girl could not have been more than eight, but she deftly wrapped the tomatoes in newspaper and counted out Matilda's change, which she handed to her without looking up.

'Tell your mother you should go to school,' she blurted out to the girl.

The girl looked up at them with a bemused expression and said, 'School?' as if she had never heard the word before.

'It is not fair that she has to sit in the hot sun and sell a few tomatoes when she could be learning to read and write,' said Matilda, as they walked away.

'Does she look unhappy to you? Does she look like someone suffering or in pain? School is not the only place to learn the essentials for life, you know. And you seem to forget that not everyone has the fortune we have, the foresighted parents we have.'

'Foresighted my foot,' said Matilda in a huff.

'That is the attitude you have to adopt more often,' said Patience, laughing.

A few paces later, they parted, and Matilda returned home, her spirits lowering again as she neared the door to Saint John's house.

Matilda would always thank God and all her departed ancestors that when she received a message to go urgently to Lawyer's house, she was with her friend Patience.

117

It was late in the afternoon, still bright but past the hottest time of the day. She was braiding her mother's hair. She divided Ama's scalp into tiny, tidy squares, then weaved the strands into tight plaits. It was unusually quiet in the house; Aunty Dede and Aunty Amele had gone out shopping for the forthcoming engagement party, taking Matilda's sisters and cousins with them. Everyone agreed it would take time to prepare for such an important event, and everyone agreed furthermore that it was wise not to leave everything until the last minute. Therefore the adults were seizing every opportunity to gather the things they would need steadily, so the big day would not take them by surprise.

Patience knocked once on the door to Saint John's yard, then pushed it further ajar. 'Please, good afternoon, Aunty,' she said, nodding at Ama in the polite fashion.

'Oh, it's Patience. How are you? How is your ma? I have not seen her for a long time. Come and sit with us.'

'Please, thank you, Aunty,' she said, smiling slightly.

Matilda and Patience's eyes locked briefly over Ama's head, which was enough communication for now. Patience sat and watched while Matilda used the fine comb to make straight squares of hair and watched her hands twist and turn the hair swiftly, as if the hair braiding was the most interesting thing she had seen for a while.

'Aunty, this style really suits you. If I did not know, I would say that you and Matilda are sisters.'

'Oh, Patience,' said Ama, clapping her hands together and beaming. Then she reached up and touched the braids at the front of her head, feeling for confirmation. She lifted the mirror in her left hand and inspected her face and her hairdo more closely. 'Yes, it's not too bad.'

Several minutes passed in total silence. Ama started to hum one of her favourite Methodist hymns and looked pleased with herself. When she got to the chorus, Patience started singing the words:

Aah, maazen larve! Haah ken nit be
Tha thou, ma God, shoo die for me?

Matilda struggled to keep her body from shuddering in delight. Patience's face was a sight to behold; never had she seen her friend look more pious. Patience sang right through the next verse without a break, and when she reached the end, took a deep breath and repeated the refrain. Ama, who was clearly impressed, joined in.

When they had sung it twice, Ama said, 'Your mother has raised you well. I am not sure that any of my children can sing an entire Methodist hymn by heart in English.'

'Please, Aunty, thank you. I like to attend church, and I like to sing praises to God.'

'Matilda, you should be like your friend.'

'Yes, Ma,' said Matilda, sniffing as a tear of joy ran down her face. It was then that they were interrupted by a knock on the door and voice calling out '*Kaw kaw kaw*', which was quite unnecessary, since there was a door to knock. They turned their heads to see a girl they did not recognise standing on the threshold.

'Please, excuse me,' she said. 'I am looking for Mr Saint John Lamptey's house.'

'This is it,' said Ama.

'Please, good afternoon, Aunty,' she said, nodding with respect. 'I have been sent by Lawyer Bannerman to come and call Matilda.'

Matilda gasped and pulled too tightly the hair she had in her hand.

'Eeeh!' screamed Ama. 'You are hurting me.'

'Are you Matilda?' asked the girl, looking at Patience.

'She is not,' said Ama, rising to her feet. 'This is her, my dear daughter.' She was holding on to Matilda's forearm. 'Tell Lawyer that she will be there in a few minutes. By the way, who are you?'

'I am only Esi, the maid,' she said and left.

'I don't think it is right that he should send the maid to call you,' muttered Ama. 'Ah, well,' she said. 'What are you waiting for, Matilda? Did you not hear her? Go and change your dress. Quickly, go!'

'Aunty Dede promised me that I would not have to go before the engagement.'

'Aunty Dede is not here, and furthermore, she is not your mother. Go now!'

In the bedroom, Matilda's hands shook as she took off her house dress. Her stomach fluttered wildly, and she could not think straight.

119

Patience had followed her into the room and stood there looking excited. 'You must wear something very nice. Who knows what he wants.'

'You do, I am sure,' said Matilda. 'What can I wear?'

Patience looked at the box of Matilda's clothes. 'There is not much to choose from.'

'I only have house dresses and a few market dresses. And one church dress.'

'Don't wear your church dress. Maybe your best market dress?'

Matilda pulled out a dress made of green-and-yellow printed batik.

'I am heating the iron for you,' shouted Ama from the yard. 'Come and press your dress. Yes, that is a good choice,' she continued when she saw the garment.

While Matilda ironed the dress carefully, Ama fussed over her hair, patting and prodding it into shape. 'Good,' she mumbled. 'Very good. Yes, good.' She helped Matilda pull the dress on so she would not mess up her hair and then walked around her inspecting every angle. 'Yes. You are ready.'

'Aunty, please, what about some scent?' asked Patience in a meek voice.

'A very good idea. We want Matilda to smell as sweet as she looks.'

When Ama had gone into her room to get some perfume, Patience looked at her friend and wrinkled her nose. 'Well, at least you can start to make some new clothes soon.'

Matilda looked down at the dress, which was too loose and reached her shins. Patience was right; it looked awful, childish even, with a too high neckline and sleeves that were too long.

'You go with her,' said Ama. 'But leave her at the gate. Don't go inside and disturb Lawyer.'

'Yes, Aunty. Matilda, come, let's go.'

When they were out of earshot, Patience grabbed Matilda's arm. 'The time has come.'

'Much sooner than I expected.' Matilda had an overwhelming urge to sit down on the road beside the smelly gutter and cry, but she bit her lip and walked on, trying to listen to Patience's excited chatter. How she wished Aunty Dede had been there to intervene.

When they reached the big house, Patience gripped her hand and said, 'You are about to become a woman, go and be proud. Hold your head up high. Go!' She shoved her friend through the back gate to Lawyer's house. 'I'll wait here,' she mouthed when Matilda turned round longingly.

'Sister Matilda,' a voice called out.

Matilda looked up at the house and saw the maid standing on the lower veranda.

'This way, please.'

Matilda walked towards the maid, who disappeared into the house. As she climbed up four steps on to the veranda, a woman she did not recognise came outside and stood in front of her with arms folded tightly. Matilda took a sharp breath and felt her heartbeat quicken.

'So, you are the one,' said the woman.

Matilda stared in silence. So this was the first wife. She gulped, lowered her eyes in respect and said, 'Please, I am Matilda,' because how else could she answer the question? The one? What one?

'Sit down.'

Surely she had misheard? This was not what she expected at all. But the woman was gesturing towards two seats on the veranda that sat side by side facing the yard. She was immaculately dressed in a pretty European frock with fat pink and red roses printed all over it. The dress had short sleeves and was fitted at the waist, accentuated by a wide belt in matching fabric. She must be on her way out, or maybe she had just returned home. It was not possible that anyone could wear such a beautiful dress at home.

Julie sat and stared straight ahead at the neem tree. Matilda turned slightly to scrutinise Lawyer's wife. Her face was chiselled like an expensive dark sculpture from which her perfectly shaped mouth protruded in a sulk. Matilda wondered why a man with such a wife would want to marry her. They sat in silence for several moments. Without saying a word, muttering a sound, without the slightest movement, Julie radiated a most intimidating mood, and Matilda felt her initial relief at being asked to sit evaporate as fast as water droplets on a hot stone. By the time Julie started to speak, her clasped hands were moist, and her stomach hurt from being pulled into a tense ball.

'I will be frank with you,' Julie began after a dramatic sigh. She spoke softly, even-toned, and anyone observing them would have thought they were friends discussing a trivial matter. 'Why my husband has decided that he must marry again is quite beyond me. And with time, I have no doubt whatsoever that his folly will be clear to him too. I am sure that it has something to do with that disgusting animal lust that resides deep in every male. Unfortunately, all his breeding did not manage to eradicate that baseness from him. Like every man whom I know, telling him not to do something makes him want to do it more, so I certainly will not stand in his way. He will no doubt marry you, believing that he is master of his life and able to have his every wish fulfilled. But I will not allow his desires,' she cleared her throat and continued to stare straight in front of her, 'to interfere with the plans that I have for myself, my children *or* my husband. And I will not allow some ignorant bush child to do so either. As long as you know your place, as long as you remember where you come from . . .' She left her words to hang unfinished while she squinted as if trying to see something on an imaginary distant horizon. 'Am I clear? Well, off you go, then.'

Matilda sat immobilised. She had never been so insulted in her entire life, and by someone who was not entitled to insult her, someone who wasn't a relative, an uncle or an aunt or her mother. Had she met this woman on the street and been spoken to like this, she would have made some attempt to retaliate, to speak her mind, but this was the first wife, a woman she was duty-bound to respect. That the first wife did not like her was unsurprising, although she knew multiple wives could live in harmony and develop sisterly relationships. There was something frightening about this woman, an incredible coldness from within that convinced Matilda she would be dangerous to her happiness.

'Well, what exactly are you waiting for? I asked you to leave.'

Matilda stood on to shaky legs, straightened her dress, which looked even shabbier next to this glamorous woman, and stumbled down the steps towards the gate. Her eyes glistened with tears, and her ears were ringing with the harsh words she had heard.

Patience was waiting on a broken wall outside the house. She stood up as soon as she saw Matilda, grabbed her and said, 'It was very quick. Did he hurt you?'

'Oh no, Lawyer was not even there. It was that woman, the wife. She sent for me so that she could insult me.'

'There are too many ears and eyes here, let's walk a little before you tell me what happened.'

When they were far enough from the big house, Matilda told Patience about her meeting with Julie.

'What a spineless woman she is to send for you like that! She is lucky that I am not the one she has to contend with. And let me get this straight, you said nothing, nothing at all, is that right?'

'Not a word.'

'Why exactly?'

'What do you mean "why?" What could I say? First of all, I was not expecting to meet her today, and when she invited me to sit down there in front of whoever might be coming and going and then proceeded to insult me quietly, I was too shocked to say anything. How exactly was I supposed to respond? "Excuse me, but I am about to become your equal by marrying your husband"?'

'Well, why not? She is no better than you . . .'

'But she is. You should have seen the beautiful dress she was wearing. It looked expensive. And brand new.'

'She is not better than you, after all, the same man, the *very* same man who chose her to be his wife has chosen you also to be his wife. Her behaviour shows that she is in fact very jealous of you. I am sure she is not as beautiful as you. And don't forget that you have youth on your side.'

'She is very sophisticated. I tell you, I felt like a maid sitting in the wrong chair.'

'That is what she wanted you to feel. Oh, how I wish I had followed you. I would have given her a piece of my own mind! Stupid woman!'

'This is going to be as hard as I feared.'

'Who does she think she is?'

'Lawyer's wife.'

'And you will be too. And soon.'

'And she will become my tormentor.'

'Don't take that attitude. You have to fight her back, give her also something to fear. She is no better than you just because she wears fancy dresses and lives in a big house. And all that will be yours too in a matter of days.'

Matilda was struggling to keep up with Patience, who was pounding the earth with angry feet, her fists clenched by her sides. Matilda wished she could have some of the confidence that fuelled Patience in this way. She could see that she was going to need it.

'I will try to avoid her; keep out of her way.'

'Don't be silly. That is completely impossible. How are two wives sharing one husband supposed to avoid each other? And when you have children, will they not play with their other sisters and brothers? I tell you that you must nip this problem in the bud. She might think she has the upper hand, but you must prove her wrong. When you meet her next, you must tell her what you think of her.'

'That she is beautiful? That she is sophisticated? That I am not worthy of sharing her husband with her?'

'You are beginning to annoy me, Matilda! All right, tell her what *I* think of her. Maybe if you say it enough, you too will come to believe it. Tell her that we are all human beings created equally before God Almighty. Amen. That you did not ask Lawyer to marry you, but he chose you, so if she has a problem with the arrangement, then she must take it up with your mutual husband, and finally, and of utmost importance, you are not afraid of her. After all, what can she do? Nothing. Take it from me, the woman is a coward. I am sure she is too proud to have a fight with you like some bush people would do . . .'

'She called me a bush girl.'

'*Aiee!* If I were you, I would go straight to Lawyer and report her. How dare she? You must tell your uncle. If you want, I can tell him for you.'

'No, Patience, I will do something.' Matilda could see that Patience was indeed ready to take the matter to the next level; it was imperative to divert her now. All this would cause was further animosity and plant the seeds for greater turmoil in the already tumultuous relationship between Lawyer's wife and his wife-to-be. 'I will think of something. Leave it to me.' She looked at her friend and smiled.

'Good,' said Patience, nodding with pride.

They walked on, Matilda relieved that she had successfully hidden the concern still heavy in her heart.

Robert sat behind his desk with his palms in supplication, his fore-fingers pressed against his mouth. He only prayed in times of dire need, and he wasn't praying now. In fact, the last time he had prayed had been just before the results of his BA were posted. As far as he could make out, God operated in a timeless vacuum, so he believed he could request things in retrospect. Then, walking along the long, echoing corridors towards the notice board, he had begged for generous examiners and a first-class degree.

He thought the pose grand and intelligent and had used it on many occasions since he had first seen a judge at the Old Bailey sit in this manner while the counsel for the prosecution delivered his summing up. Today, it served to hide his intense frustration.

Until a few moments ago, he had been happily pounding the floor of his office rehearsing the closing arguments of a case. In the background, Bach's Violin Concerto in A minor, one of his favourites, provided the necessary backdrop and blocked out the domestic sounds that he otherwise found irritating when he was trying to concentrate. He kept the volume quite low so he could hear himself clearly, but every now and then, infused by delight, he would turn up the sound, close his eyes and conduct with ardour, stretching out his long fingers and swaying his body as though in a trance. He could work well to Brahms, Liszt, Tchaikovsky or Bach but never to Beethoven, whose music, although some of his favourite, sounded too much like the product of a mad person, passionate and over-wrought. Beethoven's piano concertos were useful when one was in the mood, after a few whiskies maybe.

He walked up and down, inflecting his voice and pitch, using flamboyant gestures, arching eyebrows at imaginary people, leaning in towards them and maintaining the dignified, educated expression that he had practised as a student in front of a mirror and refined in the debating society at Cambridge.

He was representing the defendant in a contractual dispute, and he would have to do everything he could to distract from the fact that they had a thin case. This was one that called for a substantial number of Latin phrases and case names to impress.

His client, Faysal Muhammad, the owner of a Syrian construction company, had agreed to build a shop for the claimant in Adabraka, a busy part of Accra that was becoming busier each year, it seemed. But building work had been delayed and then further delayed. In fact, it had never begun, and three years had now passed since the contract was signed. The building should have been completed two years ago, and understandably, the claimant was at his wits' end and wanted rather considerable damages for his losses, which included the profits and goodwill he would have accumulated by now if his store, The Lord Is My Shepherd Convenient Stores – Your Needs We Meet, had been able to operate. Unfortunately, in the interim, another store had opened across the street, and the claimant knew that his would be an entirely uphill struggle to cultivate sufficient goodwill now that his competitor had such an advantageous head start.

The problem facing the Syrian was simple. The land was the site of a public latrine, and the inhabitants were rather attached to it. The Syrian had tried and then given up trying to negotiate with the people who lived there. He had explained to them the benefit of having The Lord Is My Shepherd Convenient Stores on their doorstep, the benefit of moving the lavatory to a different site, the advantages of living slightly further away from unpleasant scents and disease-ridden flies, but his attempts at negotiation were wasted on them; the inhabitants around the desired spot believed that the spirits who resided on the land did not want the toilets moved. They complained that since the idea had been introduced, and discussions had begun, mysterious illnesses had accosted them, babies had died in higher numbers than usual, and as final confirmation of the spirits' fury, one of the oldest inhabitants was run over by a mammy lorry. The man, so the story went, had been crossing the street to buy some *kenkey* and fish when he had heard the horn of the mammy lorry. He had looked up from the middle of the road and seen, hurtling towards him, the lorry with the inscription 'God Is Coming'. According to eyewitnesses of this tragic accident, the old man had raised his right hand and adopted an amazed expression, as if he were beholding a wondrous sight. He had remained rooted to the spot, deafened to the horrified cries and shouts of the bystanders. The mammy lorry's driver was later cleared of any wrongdoing because he had not been speeding overly, and there is quite simply nothing even the most skilled driver can do when a pedestrian just stands there in the middle of the road and waits to be killed. Evidently, the driver knew that if the lorry had not been quite so overloaded and if the road had not had such a dramatic incline, the truck might have responded to his ferocious pumping of the brakes.

For the inhabitants, enough was enough. The spirits were angry and bloodthirsty. They had to be appeased. There would be no shop, no building of any kind. There would remain in that spot the latrine that for decades had served them and their dearly departed ancestors too.

Robert's client had wanted to argue that the land was to be acquired by the shop owner and not him, that there had been an amendment to the original agreement that the Syrian would buy the land and construct the building. But that term, which all parties understood to be crucial to the performance of the contract, no one had thought to record in writing. Robert had seen straightaway that there would be little point arguing about clauses that no one had documented. Instead, he would argue frustration, one of his favourite legal concepts. The contract simply could not be performed, because there was no land. By implication, there would be no land on which to build the store. No land, no building. He knew convincing the judge would not be easy, but it was precisely this kind of challenge that he thrived on. There was much more pleasure in winning one difficult case than in winning a handful of easy ones.

So, there he was in full flow with the music once again lowered so that he could enjoy his voice and the grand words that slipped effortlessly off his tongue, when his sisters knocked on his door and walked in.

'I am very busy at the moment,' he said, startled.

'This won't take a long time,' said Baby, who had trained as a nurse in London.

'Only a few moments of your precious time,' said Gladys, who unfortunately, was still a spinster at the age of thirty-five.

They sat down in the chairs reserved for clients and waited while he turned off the music. Then he sat behind his desk and stared at them.

'We have heard that you want us to go and engage a girl for you,' said Baby.

'Ah. You have seen Saint John, then.'

'But he did not tell us much.'

Behind him, Robert heard the interconnecting door that led from his office into the house open. Julie walked into the room, smiled sweetly at him and sat down in the leather chair in the corner just in time to hear Gladys ask, 'So, this girl Matilda is how old?'

It was then he adopted his prayerful stance and furrowed his brow. Julie's arrival had flustered him. More so because, after exchanging the briefest of greetings with her sisters-in-law, she sat there with her legs folded over, her hands on her knees, and was staring at him.

'I don't know,' said Robert. 'Of what relevance is that anyhow? They have agreed to the marriage, and you need to make appropriate plans for the knocking ceremony. How complicated can this be?'

'She must be old enough if they have agreed,' said Baby. 'Let's move on to the more important issues, such as timing.'

Robert smiled, relieved.

'Just a minute,' said Gladys. 'I have something to say. My brother, it is not my place to say this to you, but in the absence of our late mother, God rest her soul, I will. To adopt a second wife, in actual fact to adopt any wife at all, should not be done lightly. You have already got a wife; you have already got children, many children. And more coming.' She sounded sad, as though her brother's children existed only to remind her of her childlessness. 'I don't understand why you need to marry again and in so doing have chosen someone who is beneath you.'

From the corner of his vision, Robert could see Julie's shoulders rise with self-satisfaction. 'With all the respect due to you as my elder sister, my private affairs are none of your business. What I choose to do, how many women I marry is my own concern,' he said.

'Eh! You mean you might marry more?' said Baby in surprise.

'How do I know? One can't legislate for these things.'

'Listen, we are not lawyers,' said Gladys. 'And there is no need to waste your big words on those of us who did not go to school in England. Anyway, can't you at least pick a girl who is your equal, such as Julie?'

Julie coughed and stood up abruptly. 'I have to go and see what the maid is doing in the kitchen,' she said as she walked out. This was why she disliked her sisters-in-law. They were even less refined than Robert. How dare they condone the awful concept of a second wife? And in her presence! It was too much for her to bear. She went to the kitchen, where the smells of cooking quickly made her want to retch. She retired to her bedroom feeling even more alone than ever, without an ally. Get this baby out healthily, recover your energy, then they will see who is who, she thought angrily, as she lay on her bed. If this pregnancy was anything like the others, it would soon become quite difficult for her to carry on as normal. And this additional irritation that her husband had obliviously heaped upon her didn't help.

Robert was relieved that Julie had left. He took his cue from her. 'Look, I have a case to prepare for. Speak to Saint John and plan the engagement as soon as possible. I waited until your return, Baby; I am sure that you won't make me regret my decision.' He smiled at her. He could see that his flattery had worked.

'Naturally, we will do what you ask. We only wanted to make sure that this is not an impulsive decision. You know that once we have performed the ceremonies, it will not be easy to extricate yourself from her family or your duties to them.'

'I know. And there is no need for you to point your finger at me. I am not a child any longer. You might be as wise and as beautiful as she was, but you are not my mother. You are my dear baby sister. I am glad that you are back.'

Baby laughed, and Robert relaxed.

'I still have my reservations,' said Gladys. 'But you are the clever ones. You are the ones who were educated abroad. Who am I, a child-less spinster with little education, to stand in your way? If Pa had chosen me to go and study like the two of you, I would certainly not have disappointed him. But there we have it; there is no point crying over the things we cannot change, eh?' She shrugged and smiled forlornly at her siblings and slowly rose to her feet.

When they left, Robert pondered what Gladys had said. His father had decided for whatever reason that it was not worth sending her abroad to school. She had had a good basic education here, but naturally, she harboured some resentment. He walked over to the gramophone and put his record on once more. He felt no sympathy for her bitterness. After all, he wasn't answerable for his father's decision. His sister simply had to realise that life is not always fair.

Chapter Seven

It was a sunny Saturday afternoon, and at Saint John's house, the hot air was thick with anticipation. Uncle Saint John and Matilda's parents, aunts, sisters and female cousins were all scrubbed and starched ready to welcome Lawyer's family to their home for the traditional engagement ceremony. Outside, the gutter bubbled in the heat, releasing a nauseating smell, which wafted into the courtyard with varying intensity.

Ama had spent the previous days directing, instructing, correcting and improving, while her various relations prepared the house for this important visit. Now they could hear the commotion outside caused by the visitors making their way down the alleyway. The family sat on stools and chairs that had been placed in rows on one side of the courtyard opposite seats neatly arranged so the visitors would face the hosts.

The yard had been swept twice that day in an attempt to rid it of some of the dust, and Saint John had painted the bottom of the trunks of the pawpaw trees white to make them look clean. Now the courtyard was awash with the colour of the women's garments, which came out only on Sundays and special occasions. Ornate multi-coloured cloths had been used to make the traditional two-piece outfits the women wore – short-sleeved tops, which sat over straight, long, fitted skirts that made walking difficult. Ama's dress was made with an elaborately patterned purple-and-green cotton fabric with gold beading. The top had very puffed sleeves and a V-shaped neckline, which revealed a sizeable amount of cleavage into which a fake gold pendant disappeared. She had covered her head with a scarf of matching fabric tied in a complicated knot at the front. To complete her outfit, she wore a long piece of the same material neatly folded widthways over her left shoulder. Her new fake gold earrings matched her pendant. They dangled nearly to her shoulders, swinging enormously every time she moved her head, which she did often, enjoying the admiring glances they were attracting. They were made of bright gold-coloured laced metal with a twinkling fringe and were shaped like flat diamonds. And every time she moved her arms, there was a shimmer from the shiny bangles on her wrists. Her face shone, with happiness and with the brown face powder that she had applied liberally that morning, which made her look as if she had smeared herself with cocoa powder.

Amele's dress was made with material that had large orange-coloured diamond shapes and small intense-pink circles thickly embroidered on to soft deep-red cotton. Her top was more modestly cut, with green piping on the sleeves, the neckline and down the front. She too was wearing her best jewellery and a headscarf and looked slightly less pained than usual.

Saint John was the only man in the compound apart from Matilda's father, Owusu. He admired the women and said, 'I am glad I agreed to pay for your new clothes. I think everyone here looks good enough to meet Lawyer's family. Even you, Dede,' he said, laughing at his big sister.

Aunty Dede's cloth was the least sensational of the three, and one she had worn many times before; a simple batik print on white cotton – dark-blue leaves marbled with red veins and stalks, which interlinked the leaves. The bodice and sleeves of her top fitted tightly – slicing her upper arms in two and clearly defining the rolls of her stomach – then frilled out easily over her generous hips.

Saint John and Owusu each wore a huge piece of cloth wrapped under their arms then draped over one shoulder. Saint John had initially wanted to wear his work suit; however, his sisters had convinced him that would not be appropriate. His cloth, which had never been washed so as to preserve the fabric, was intricately textured with symmetrical patterns woven from strands of golden yellow, black and green silky cotton. Owusu's was more sober; a white cloth with raised, woven bars of brown and black thread. Concealed underneath, each man was wearing a pair of oversized calico drawstring shorts.

Outside, neighbours from the surrounding houses stood in doorways or on corners in the alleyway gawping in awe at the arrival of Lawyer's entourage. Everyone had heard the good news and knew the reason these people were making their way gingerly down the narrow passageway, their skirts and trousers lifted high as they stepped from one side to another of the meandering gutter, depending on which side of the path seemed furthest from the stinking drain. A quiet woman's voice said, 'Eh! Matilda has done well, oh!' Children, less inhibited, pointed and commented loudly. The names 'Lawyer' and 'Matilda' were heard repeatedly in deferential tones once the entourage had passed the bystanders who were straining to catch a glimpse of the things some of the visitors were carrying on their heads.

Inside the compound, Matilda's family hushed in anticipation as it became clear that the visitors were gathered outside the door, which today was firmly shut.

'Knock, knock!' shouted someone in time with loud knocking.

'We are knocking! *Kaw, kaw, kaw*,' this time more insistently, so that the door wobbled in its frame.

Saint John, beaming and excited, prepared to stand up.

'Sit down. What's wrong with you?' asked Aunty Dede. 'Ignore them,' she said, flicking her hand in the direction of the gate, as though she was shooing a fly away. 'Why do you want to appear so eager? Have you forgotten that they are the ones who have come to beg for our precious child? Let them knock some more first.'

'Knocking, knocking,' the voice outside persisted, while the Lampteys chatted like a gathering who have been told to chat, so that suddenly they had nothing useful to say to each other.

After several minutes and much more knocking, and when it looked as if the door had been loosened further from its hinges, Aunty Dede called out, 'Who are you? What do you want?'

A relieved high-pitched voice responded: 'We have come to see Matilda's family. We have been sent by our esteemed brother, Lawyer Bannerman, to come and pay our respects to her family and to discuss important matters.'

Suddenly animated, the Lamptey family started talking more purposefully amongst themselves about whether or not to let the callers in. Whether or not Lawyer Bannerman was from a good enough family. Whether or not it would be wise to even enter into discussions with these callers. Through all this, several 'oohs' and 'aaahs' were heard.

'Please, let us in, we beg of you,' cried the caller in an attempt to be heard.

The debate continued inside the compound. After a while, when Aunty Dede thought that there had been enough pondering, she said, 'Come in, then. You are welcome.' She did not sound welcoming.

About twenty members of Lawyer's family trouped into the small compound, many carrying heavy parcels. No one stood up to welcome the visitors, instead, they sat chatting amongst themselves, some even refusing to look up and greet the visitors properly.

Saint John was unable to contain his excitement any further. He stood up and said, 'Welcome, welcome.' He went over to shake hands with Baby, Lawyer's youngest sister, who was heading the group, gripping one of her soft, fat hands in both of his. They had never spoken before Lawyer made his proposal, although Saint John had seen her several times at Lawyer's house. In fact, just that morning, Saint John had remarked to his wife, 'After ignoring me all these years, now she has to come and plead with me to let her brother marry my niece. After all, as they say, the world is indeed round,' and he had laughed to himself.

Eventually, all the visitors were seated with the more important guests closest to the insignificant shade the pawpaw trees could offer.

Saint John tried to introduce his sister to the visitors, but she quickly interrupted him.

'I am Dede, Matilda's aunt. What brings you here?' she asked with an innocent expression and a stern voice.

Baby stood up and wiped her brow with a folded handkerchief. She clasped her hands together and began: 'Thank you for welcoming us into your home, Aunty Dede. We have come on a very humble mission. Our brother, Robert Bannerman, barrister-at-law, Cambridge University, England, saw a very good-looking girl who caught his eye and he cannot stop thinking about her—' Her speech was interrupted by laughter and whistling, and she took the opportunity to wipe her nose and the top of her mouth, where moisture was glistening in the sun.

'It happens to the best of them,' someone shouted from the back of the Lamptey gathering. Everyone laughed. Baby stood, smiling patiently.

'But some fall harder than others,' said another voice from the Lamptey side.

'Well, we understand that she is quite spectacular, this girl,' said Baby, nodding benevolently.

'Indeed she is,' Aunty Dede said without taking her eyes off Baby.

'Yes, yes,' murmured several of the hosts in harmony.

'A fair gem,' shouted one.

'A precious stone,' yet another.

'Good enough for the best,' said someone quite close to the front of the crowd.

'Yes. So we have come here today to ask for your daughter's hand in marriage to our brother, Robert Bannerman, barrister-at-law.'

'I see,' said Aunty Dede, holding her chin between her thumb and forefinger as though she had something to contemplate. 'We will have to ask our daughter whether she agrees to this proposal. Have you brought anything to help her make her decision?' She sounded more like a teacher telling off a pupil.

Baby waved at the parcels that had been stacked in front of her and her hosts. 'We have a few things here that we hope Matilda will find herself able to accept. For instance, we thought she might like this jewellery.' On cue, one of Lawyer's relatives stood up and walked over with a parcel, which she handed to Aunty Dede.

Aunty Dede unwrapped it, and disguising any amazement she felt when she saw the array of jewellery made with what looked like very good-quality gold and beads, she nodded approvingly and handed the parcel to her sister, who was sitting next to her, so that she and other senior family members could also inspect the wares.

Ama took the parcel greedily and held it in her palm, which she pulsed up and down, as though to gauge the weight of the gold. She pursed her lips and raised her eyebrows in admiration. The onlookers started clapping.

'We have also brought some cloth for Matilda,' said Baby, pausing while two more of Lawyer's entourage came forward, each carrying a massive bale of cloth. The crowd clapped in time as the gifts were presented.

Each bale was made up of six pieces of cloth, each measuring twelve yards. There were expensive batiks, richly designed, swirling with happy colours: vibrant greens, dark reds and yellows, oranges like the colour of the fruit, luminous indigos and azure blues. There were hand-woven cloths, part silk, part cotton, textured with brilliant golden yellows and blacks teemed with purples and greens on white or cream backgrounds. There were plain bright cottons with complicated hand-embroidered patterns. And there was lace, white, delicate and involved.

As the gifts were placed in front of the Lampteys, Saint John, who had not stopped grinning from the moment the guests entered the courtyard, nodded in appreciation. There was no mistaking the reaction of the onlookers; many peered over shoulders for a better view, many had mouths open with tongues hanging loose, many gasped – this was indeed the best quality available, and rarely seen in a house like this.

Baby continued with the presentations. The crowd continued cheering as parcels were carried and placed in front of Matilda's family.

When one man placed a cage on the ground in front of Saint John and then carefully removed the cloth that had been draped over it to reveal several plump, lively white chickens staring at the gathering with beady eyes, the applause reached a crescendo.

'But that is not all,' Baby attempted to speak above the noise of the crowd. 'We also have something that we brought especially for the men of the house,' she said, as two men brought forward boxes filled with spirits. 'Something to comfort you when your daughter leaves,' she said, smiling.

Aunty Dede, looking unimpressed, said, 'Very thoughtful of you, but we have not decided whether or not we will agree to the marriage.'

'That's right,' shouted someone.

'Who knows what she will say,' said another.

'We are yet to be convinced,' said yet another.

Soon, there was a chorus of disapproving noises and comments from Matilda's relatives.

'We need to ask the girl herself if she is prepared to accept this proposal,' said Dede.

'Sister Dede, Brother Saint John, we hope our final gift will remove any remaining doubts from your minds.' Baby herself came over and handed them a fat envelope.

Dede opened it and peered in, widening her eyes momentarily in amazement when she saw the number of notes in the envelope. 'Well, well, well. I can tell that Lawyer realises the value of our daughter,' she said, placing the envelope in Saint John's waiting hands.

'We all do,' replied Baby. 'We will be honoured to have Matilda in our family. But before you make up your minds, please let me do my brother the honour of expounding his virtues.' She clasped her hands in front of her like a praying Madonna and continued, pausing at appropriate intervals as though to give additional significance to her words, 'Robert Bannerman, barrister-at-law, graduated with honours from Cambridge University, England, and was called to the Middle Temple bar of London, England, and is now the sole proprietor of Bannerman Chambers of Jamestown, Accra, a highly successful and vibrant operation.' Everyone was looking at Baby intently, as if they were waiting for her to tell them something they did not know. She patted her brow and wiped her neck, where beads of sweat had gathered in the rings of flesh and were periodically rolling down into her cleavage. 'A man whose word is his bond and who is respected by those who know him and those who don't.' A few of the guests murmured in agreement. 'Even though he was in England all these years obtaining a first-class education, he did not forget his roots or his traditions. He insisted that we pay the utmost care today to ensure that nothing is overlooked. Lawyer is indeed a man of great destiny, and we are privileged to call him our brother. We can assure you that you too will be honoured to have him as your brother . . . your son, I should say.'

There was much chuckling at this deference; everyone relaxed visibly.

'We hear you,' said Aunty Dede.

Saint John nodded at Baby in acknowledgement of her speech, and then he turned to his sister and said, 'Ama, I think that you should take these gifts to Matilda and see what she says.'

Ama got up, and Matilda's cousins and sisters, eager to handle the expensive items, came forward to help carry them into the house.

Matilda was hidden in her bedroom with Patience, from where they followed the ceremony without being seen. Initially, she had paced the room anxiously; now she sat quietly and pondered her destiny.

After the initial shock of her parents' announcement, she had secretly been a little impressed that Lawyer wanted to marry her, but she could not articulate the other feelings; the tight knot that had lived in her stomach since the night she heard about the proposal worsened by her meeting with Julie.

She had looked forward to today with mixed emotions. She wondered if it might signify the end of her virtual imprisonment, that she might be free to come and go again as she once had, although being hidden in her uncle's house had meant that any further meetings with the inhabitants of the big house had been avoided. This engagement, a supposedly joyous occasion, would have the two consequences she feared the most: a fresh encounter with Julie Bannerman, and another with Lawyer Bannerman.

She had not been able to eat or sleep much over the past days, and today, she felt rather light-headed. She was nervous about being the centre of attention and performing her role faultlessly. She hoped she would not trip when the time came for her to make her entrance and that Lawyer's sisters would not be displeased with her appearance. She had been up and ready for hours and was uncomfortable in the skirt of her new outfit, which was a little tight around the hips. It was a traditional full-length skirt, which had a drawstring waist that her mother had pulled and knotted tightly that morning. There was a modest slit at the back of the skirt to make walking easy. The top, which was slightly A-line, stopped just below her bottom and had a wide scooped neck and bell-shaped sleeves that came halfway down between her wrists and her elbow. It was made with the most beautiful material that Matilda had ever seen, a gift from Aunty Dede, who had sewed the outfit over the past few days using Aunty Amele's old Singer machine while an audience of little children sat on the ground, watching mesmerised as the fine-looking material become Sister Matilda's engagement dress. The fabric was made up of alternating strips of material – fat bands of emerald-green, shiny, soft cotton, which was embossed with petite symmetrical patterns, and smaller bands of stiff gold that looked and felt like reflective paper, which also had imposing designs in the same shade of emerald green. Her head was wrapped tight in an intricate turban of the same material, and on her feet, she wore her mother's white leather buckled shoes, which pinched her toes but made a pleasing clicking sound on the cement as she walked. Ama had put a considerable amount of brown face powder on Matilda, which she wiped off when her mother was not looking, but which had left a lustrous sheen to her face. Her eyes were lined with kohl, her lips polished with Vaseline.

Patience had not seen the outfit before, and she had spent several minutes touching it when she first arrived, voicing her admiration at the fabric's softness and the smoothness of the shiny gold, which she kept stroking with her fingertips. 'I have never seen such a beautiful cloth,' she said. 'The green really suits you.' She was in her best dress too, made with simple brown-and-yellow printed batik, but she did not wear a headscarf, and her short black hair was patted neatly into shape.

'Look at this,' Matilda had said, demonstrating her clicking heels to her friend as she walked to the wall, swivelled round on the smooth soles and walked back with her mother's borrowed earrings swinging vigorously from her ears.

'So you are going to be Miss Madam now, are you? Always dressed in your best, while I am here in my one pair of brown sandals, which I have to wear, rain or shine.'

'Don't be silly, you know that these are not mine. Nor are these,' Matilda had said, touching the earrings that pulled at her lobes.

'We are still the same; I have simply substituted my usual things today.'

'But I am sure that Lawyer will give you lots of jewellery and clothes. You'd better not forget who your best friend is.' The girls laughed. 'Oh, they are here,' Patience said, walking over to peer through the almost-closed shutters when they heard the knocking. She became engrossed as the spectacle unfolded outside, while Matilda sat on a stool and retreated into her own thoughts.

'You are going to be so wealthy,' she had said, while the gifts were being presented, turning to look at her friend, who was sitting with her head in her hands. 'Oh, cheer up,' she said when Matilda lifted her head to reveal her eyes filled with yet-to-fall tears. 'It won't be that bad.'

'Everybody keeps telling me that it won't be that bad, but it's my life whose path has been changed without any warning.' Matilda was sulking. She was confused by her emotions. She made resolutions almost daily to buck up, as everyone told her she must. She tried to see the benefits that would be hers as the wife of a rich man. She imagined a life with money and power. But then, in sharp focus, she saw, as no one else did, it seemed, that the first wife and the husband were insurmountable hurdles to her enjoyment of any such life. She wondered whether if Patience were in her shoes, she would envy her and think her lucky, rather than commiserate with her. 'I know that I should be grateful, because he is a lawyer and he is rich, but . . . I don't even want children yet.'

'Don't say that! You must have children. You must be proud of this day. All those people have come here because of you.' She chewed her mouth and added, 'They are all going to be so jealous of you, you know? Otherwise, nothing else will change.'

'You are wrong. Nothing will be the same again. My current life is over, before it has even had a chance to start; it is ruined . . .' Sobs swallowed her words. She thought of her childhood, gone without warning, and she felt even sadder. Just yesterday, she had been playing with one of her little cousins, showing her how to make patterns with a piece of string wrapped through her fingers. Matilda had made innocuous movements to reveal a pretty design, and her little cousin, impressed, had clapped for joy. But a sour-faced Aunty Amele put a hasty end to the game. 'You are to be a wife; you need to stop all these childish activities now and remember your place. Do you see your mother or me behaving in that way?'

'They are bringing the presents,' said Patience. 'Don't let them see you have been crying. Come on, quick.' She wiped Matilda's face.

Ama walked into the room and ordered the gift-bearers to put the parcels on the floor.

'Matilda, my dear girl, look at these splendid gifts that you have received. What do you think?' Ama was rummaging through the items with more vigour than she had outside. She was particularly interested in the jewellery. 'I don't think that you will need all this. After all, you can get him to buy you whatever you want when you are his wife.'

Patience was looking at the gifts open-mouthed and wide-eyed. She was about to crouch down to have a closer look at some of the fabric, but Ama gave her a stern look and she took a step back instead.

Matilda tried to seem interested.

'Well, come on, then,' said her mother. 'We need to go and tell them your answer; they have waited long enough now.' She pulled Matilda in front of her. 'Let me look at you. Yes, you're fine,' she said, pulling down the top of Matilda's outfit sharply from behind. 'Your headdress is fine,' she said, patting it firmly. 'Come on, come on.'

Matilda followed her mother out of the room into the yard in a daze. When she stepped into the bright afternoon, she had to blink a few times while her eyes, still stinging, adjusted to the light. The crowd cheered and clapped as soon as she appeared, and as she walked towards the centre of the yard, she smiled bashfully and lowered her eyes to the ground.

Saint John came to meet Matilda, took her by the elbow and led her over to where he had been sitting between Aunty Dede and Ama. 'Sit down, Matilda,' he said, pointing to his seat. 'We need to know if you have a response for Lawyer's family. You have seen the magnificent gifts they brought? So, what do you say?' He was still grinning.

The crowd waited in anticipation as Matilda turned to her mother, who had sat back down, and nodded slightly without looking up. Ama's face broke into a wide smile, and she in turn nodded to Saint John.

'She has agreed to marry your brother,' he said to Baby. Saint John's grin turned into a laugh. A low contended chuckle through which he spoke to himself: 'Marvellous, heh, heh, heh. Splendid!'

'You have done well, my child,' said Aunty Dede softly, so that only Matilda could hear her. She looked sideways at her aunt, but the older woman was staring straight ahead at Lawyer's family with her hands still folded on her lap and her chin up in the air.

'Wonderful,' said Saint John more loudly. 'Please, let us have a drink now. Please, and something to eat too.' He directed the gaze of the guests towards Amele, who had gone to the kitchen, where she was in charge of the food and drink. She was ladling drinks into small calabashes and tin cups, which she then put on trays for the children to hand out. There was water, which the children had collected that morning from the communal tap down the road, carrying it home in metal buckets balanced perfectly on their heads, palm wine, a sweet, milky drink extracted from the tops of palm trees that had a gently intoxicating effect, and corn wine, an alcoholic drink made from fermented corn, which looked like black tea and tasted of burned sugar. The guests helped themselves, draining the vessels swiftly, greedily reaching for more.

Amele uncovered an enormous aluminium cooking pot, releasing the delightful aroma of jollof rice. Cooked in a spicy tomato sauce, the rice was red and moist but not sticky and was a firm favourite, eagerly awaited, judging by the happy eyes and salivating mouths that greeted it when it appeared heaped in bowls along with trays piled high with food that had been prepared over the past few days and nights: chicken fried until the peppery skin was crunchy and the flesh fell willingly off the bones; spiced goat, blackened and desiccated, tasting of garlic and ginger; fried pieces of fat, soft plantain; chunks of crispy, golden-fried yam served with a fresh, lumpy onion and tomato gravy, which was heavily spiced with bay leaves and red and yellow chilli peppers, and finally, sweet and savoury *achomo* and generous squares of plain brown cake, heavy with eggs.

142

The girls served the food, marching to and from the kitchen like soldier ants, until eventually everyone had satisfied their hunger and their thirst.

While everyone else was eating, Matilda sat looking happy, accepting sporadic congratulations on her astonishing match and nodding in response. Her father, who had sat quietly throughout the ceremony, looked at her and smiled slightly. His eyes looked sad, and she smiled back at him, trying to make her eyes happy enough for both of them.

Eventually, the proceedings came to an end, and the guests, fortified with drink and food, left in twos and threes until the Lamptey household was left in peace to ruminate on the success of the engagement.

As soon as she was able, Matilda retreated to her room, where Patience helped her take off Ama's jewellery carefully and then helped her out of her new outfit. She put on her comfortable house dress – a simple sleeveless A-line cotton dress, which had thinned from years of wear. Even though she had not eaten all day, she had been too shy to eat in front of the guests, and now she was ravenous. While her younger sisters and cousins cleared up the remnants of the party, she and Patience went into the kitchen, served themselves a large plate of food each and sat down to eat. At first, the girls concentrated on their food, neither of them saying anything. But Patience was too elated to eat.

'When is the wedding going to be, then?' she asked.

'Soon, I think.' Matilda was shovelling food into her mouth hungrily, pausing periodically to lick her greasy fingers before continuing.

'My goodness me! How can you be so hungry at a time like this?'

Matilda looked up at her friend, licked her fingers again and exhaled noisily. 'You know, I am not even hungry. I am just eating because I don't know what else to do.' She looked at the half-empty plate of food, feeling downhearted.

'Well, I hope you cheer up soon. You don't want to become too fat before you have to do it,' Patience said. Smiling, she continued, 'You are as good as married now so you realise that he can demand his husbandly rights from you, don't you?'

'Thank you for reminding me. I had managed to stop thinking

about that for the first time in days.' And with that, she resumed eating, labouring over each mouthful and sighing regularly.

Patience was right. Lawyer did not wait long to send for her. It was the morning after the engagement and Matilda was washing her clothes next to the bathroom with water that she had fetched at dawn. The pile of dirty clothes on the ground, initially just her own clothes and some of Celestina's, had grown as the adults saw her and remembered items that they too wanted washed – Saint John's shirts, Aunty Amele's house dresses, Ama's blouse and underwear. She picked one item at a time, lathered it using a bar of laundry soap in a bucket with a small amount of water, then rubbed, dipped, rubbed, until she was sure the item was clean. Then she placed it in another bucket filled with clean water. She rinsed each garment twice, wrung it powerfully, flapped it hard, then hung it up to dry on the wire line that was erected between the bathroom block and one of the pawpaw trees. The first set of clothes was nearly dry when she started hanging up the second lot, pausing to stretch her back to ease the pain and lifting her arms regularly to wipe the sweat that was pouring down the side of her face with the top of her dress. She was beginning to wash the last few clothes when the same boy Lawyer had sent to find her weeks ago appeared at the door.

'Sister Matilda, please, Lawyer sent me to call you to come.'

She stared at him for a moment, blinking to protect her eyes from the gaze of the sun and bent down again to continue her washing. Instantly, her mind cleared of all cluttering thoughts, she felt her breath shorten and her stomach clench. She tried to concentrate on the shirt she was washing, but her brief glance at the sun had caused sunspots to gather in her eyes, making orange marks dart elusively around the garment.

'I think you should hurry up; he sounded anxious to see you, if you know what I mean.'

She looked up at him and saw the smirk on his face; he was looking at her, rapidly lifting and lowering his eyebrows.

'Tell him that I am busy; I will be there when I finish washing my clothes,' she said, continuing with her job. She was surprised at how calm her voice sounded even to her own ears. Her hands were shaking, and she felt unsteady. Her heart was palpitating noisily, and she could feel blood thundering through her ears. She wondered would she faint like her sister Celestina had from time to time when she was younger, reflecting how her life might be simplified today if she could suddenly develop anaemia.

'What is wrong with you?' screeched Ama.

Matilda was startled. She hadn't noticed her mother come into the yard.

Ama was shouting and waving her hands violently. 'You cannot keep him waiting for you. You are engaged to him, and if he calls for you, you will go. Now stop what you are doing and go and get ready. Look at how you are sweating,' she tutted. 'Put on some talcum powder and some perfume. And wear a nice dress; you are his wife in the eyes of everyone, and you had better start acting like it.'

Matilda abandoned her washing and walked sullenly towards the house. Her eyes filled with tears. She knew she would have to stop crying like a baby all the time. As she walked past her mother, a tear fell on to her cheek. Her mother slapped her face hard. Stunned, she ran into the house, wondering whether the messenger was still standing at the gate.

'Pull yourself together. I don't want to see any more of this childish behaviour around here.' Her mother was following her. 'Do you think that I like everything that has happened to me in life? For one thing, I have married a good-for-nothing man who cannot even provide for me and I must depend on the infinite generosity of my brother. You'd better wake up and realise your good fortunes. You are no longer a child; you are now a wife. Act like it!'

Matilda was now in the girls' bedroom. Her tears were falling fast.

Her mother stood beside her, arms folded. 'Listen to me. Your life as Lawyer's wife will not be easy if you don't start to act like one. Do you think that the first wife will welcome you with open arms? You will have to fight for your place and respect from his family. Don't be deceived by the sweet talk they spouted here. That was just the engagement. Come on. Chin up. Here, let me help you tidy your hair.' It had been agreed that she could grow her hair now that she was no longer a schoolgirl, and to encourage it to grow, she wore it braided all the time; she had several tiny braids, each about an inch and a half long in its own neat square of hair, which looked like curled prawns fastened to her head.

She walked slowly. Her feet were heavy and unwilling. What would she call him? What would they talk about? Would they talk? What about the other thing? Would she know what to do? Would it be painful? Would he be pleased with her? Her heart was racing, and her palms were sweating. Her stomach hurt. Please that she would not need to use the latrine. She slowed her small footsteps even further.

When she walked through the gate, she thought everyone in the compound stopped what they were doing to stare at her. This was not true, and in any event, it was nearly noon and the midday sun had chased most indoors in search of shade. She made her way to the office, not knowing where else to go in this vast house. And there, waiting for her at his desk, was Lawyer. Matilda was relieved to see a girl standing next to him holding a tray with a plate of toast and jam on it.

'Matilda, come in. Sit down. Would you like some tea?'

No one had ever offered her tea.

'Good morning, Lawyer. Please, thank you.'

She sat rigidly in the leather armchair with her palms flat on her lap, hoping that they would dry. She stared at the floor. Lawyer asked the maid to bring some more tea. She left them alone. Matilda continued to look at the floor, but she was aware that he was on his feet and walking towards her. She felt sick.

'So, I hear the engagement went well. We are more or less married now. What do you say?' He was towering over her.

'Please, I do what I am told.' She hoped he did not think her rude; she simply wondered whether his sojourn in England meant he was out of touch with tradition and he didn't realise she had no choice in the matter.

'Matilda, you are to be my wife. In fact, in the eyes of society, you already are. You can call me by my name, and you don't have to say "please" when you talk to me all the time.' He took her hand. 'Look at me,' he continued. 'You don't need to be afraid of me. I will not hurt you. Would you like some toast?'

Just then, the maid came in with the tea. Lawyer dropped her

146

hand and turned away abruptly. Matilda was hungry and relieved. She could breathe more easily. She had not yet eaten and had only ever had jam once. She was surprised to see how thickly it had been spread on the bread. In spite of her discomfort, her eyes lit up.

He dismissed the maid, who gave Matilda an impudent glance before she left, as if she knew what was about to happen. 'Come here,' he said, pulling her out of the chair. 'The tea and toast can wait.' He led her through the door at the back of the office into a long, dark corridor towards some stairs. They went up the stairs in silence, Matilda too frightened to think, and into one of the rooms, which was his bedroom.

'I have wanted you from the first time I saw you. I have waited until you are mine, and I cannot wait any longer,' he said with a hoarse voice. He put his arms around her and started caressing her with his face in her neck.

His body felt solid against her. She breathed in the fragrance of his cologne, surprised at the softness of his well-shaved skin. Her hands hung beside her, limp and useless. Her heart pounded; she was short of breath. She couldn't see past his body, and he started to undress her hastily. Just don't think, she told herself. Over and over again she thought, Don't think. He stroked her shoulders and her arms, and then put his hands in the dip of her waist. She closed her eyes, not wanting to see any part of her nakedness, and afraid to confront his, but he did not undress himself. His body grew warm and insistent against her, and he cupped her breasts in his hands. When he pulled away, frowning at her, Matilda wondered what she had done wrong. His forehead glistened, and his shirt was clinging to his stomach where he had pressed her against him, and she could see through the wet fabric that he had hair on his chest. 'Come here,' he said, taking her hand and leading her towards his bed and gently pushing her down on it.

She lay rigidly with her eyes squeezed shut, determined not to let them open, ashamed that anyone should see her this bare. She tried to think of things outside this room, the food she would have to cook tonight, the laundry she had to finish, her friend Patience. She heard him undo the buckle of his trousers and let them fall to the floor. She felt the bed sag as he climbed on top of her, and she gasped in surprise. Her body was unwelcoming, but that did not deter him. She grimaced and bit her lip. Then she opened her eyes to look at him and saw that he had his eyes shut. She looked at his face thinking he looked almost as if he was in pain while he moved against her panting and groaning. He smelled now of fresh, clean sweat, and his shirt stuck to her stomach. She was surprised when he held her tightly and released a loud groan, shuddering wildly. Then he was still for a while. Eventually, he rolled off her, unpeeling his damp clothes from her wet body, leaving one heavy leg on top of her thigh, where their sweat could continue to mingle. He did not say anything, and soon she could hear him breathing heavily and dared to open her eyes. He seemed asleep. She stared at him, thinking that he looked harmless with his eyes closed. She took a deep mouthful of air and puffed, like a person finally able to breathe because some respiratory constriction has been removed. She was not sure what she felt; indubitably relief that it was over. She could tell Patience that it was not as painful as they had feared. It was nothing to dread, in fact. She had been embarrassed and terrified, but she had survived. She felt a little proud of her achievement, if that is what one could call it.

She was beginning to feel cooler now that their skins were drying in the warm breeze that came, along with spears of sunlight, through the closed shutters past the fluttering net curtains. She dared to look around her. The bed was colossal, with a soft mattress and an elaborately carved headboard of dark, shiny wood. An electric fan dangled lifelessly from the ceiling above the bed. A bedside table, which was on her side of the bed, had a Bible and two other books on it. She looked at the unfamiliar letters on their spines, wondering what sort of thing Lawyer read in his free time. The cement walls had been whitewashed some time ago, and there were several framed paintings of horses in green undulating landscapes. Most of the floor was covered by a gigantic threadbare red rug with gold-and-green swirling patterns. At the far side of the room, there was a huge wardrobe and a heavy chest of drawers made with the same dark wood, also intricately carved. A pinstripe suit on a hanger was hooked over the wardrobe door so that it could not shut. On the chest of drawers, there were piles of books and papers, bottles of cologne and a wireless set. Two old armchairs just like the one in the office were at the opposite end of the room from the bed, with clothes flung all over them. In between, there was a small table with a gramophone and innumerable gramophone records on the floor.

She remembered the chores waiting for her and wondered whether she could leave.

When she tried to move her leg, still moist and slippery, Lawyer stirred and reached over to restrain her. 'Don't go yet,' he said sleepily. 'I have to get up soon.'

She lay still, thinking what her life had come to. A few weeks ago, she was a carefree schoolgirl. A virgin. Now she was a wife. The word sounded strange in her head. A second wife. And she had done it. She wondered if there had been any blood, but she could not see without waking Lawyer.

He stirred again and, opening his eyes, said, 'I have to go to court now. Go home and I will send for you again very soon.'

Matilda rolled to sit on the edge of the bed. She did not want to stand up and show her nakedness to him again, but her clothes were in the middle of the floor. She walked to them quickly and crouched down to dress; she knew that he was watching her. When she was covered, she headed straight out of the door without looking back. She closed it quietly behind her.

She walked home in a daze, retracing her steps automatically. She felt her reluctant journey to womanhood was now nearly complete. And if the vague family planning lessons she had had at school were correct, she might even already be on the last leg of that journey. Could she be pregnant? She did not know whether it happened straightaway or whether it took a while. An hour? A day? Could it happen the first time? She would have to ask Patience. The idea of becoming a mother was dreadful. Patience might know what to do to avoid it. At least for a while. At least until she had had time to get used to the idea of being a wife.

Matilda was in her bedroom getting undressed when Ama walked in.

'So what happened? How was it, then?'

Matilda felt her skin stiffen and her stomach heave. Then, it was as if the strain of obedience, her sense of betrayal and the fearful and emotional tension of the last few hours caused her usual graciousness to disintegrate. 'I am a wife now,' she said in a tremulous voice. 'What my husband and I do behind closed doors is no business of yours.'

Ama looked taken-aback. But Matilda was even more so. She was surprised that she had dared to speak to her mother in this way and that her mother did not slap her immediately for doing so or call for her uncle to beat her.

Ama did not appear angry. 'Well, well. I hope that you are not going to rise above your station and forget yourself. As long as you live in this house, you are my daughter and you will do what you are told,' she said, her voice becoming louder and louder with each word. 'Do you hear? Do you understand me?' she shouted.

Still Matilda did not flinch. She was not sure where her audacity came from that afternoon. But how could she tell her mother about what had just happened, or that walking home, she was sure everyone knew what she had been doing, that Lawyer had dismissed her without saying much, that she had hated every minute of it, that she was disheartened that this event would occur many, many more times, and she was not sure she could get used to it, and that she was praying she would not get pregnant? Each of these sentiments was certain to start a series of arguments, and possibly result in a beating. The women stood looking at each other for several moments before Matilda eventually lowered her eyes. Her mother chewed on her empty mouth loudly to make a disapproving sound and walked out.

She continued undressing slowly and wrapped a towel around herself. She gathered the pail in which she kept her bar of soap and sponge and carried a bucket of water, fetched that morning, to the bathroom, where she knew she would not be disturbed at this time of day.

The bathroom was a concrete, windowless room, lit only by the daylight that filtered underneath the wooden half-door. Matilda kept her rubber slippers on because the concrete floors were slimy with years of residue. After soaping her sponge, she frantically scrubbed her entire body gingerly, trying desperately to make herself feel clean, taking great care not to drop her soap on to the floor, where it would undoubtedly skid into the gutter clogged with hair and cold, foamy scum. Then she crouched down and kept her eyes tightly shut as she scrubbed away the salty tears that were trying to run down her face. But she only began to weep more, and soon her whole body was shaking uncontrollably. She dropped her sponge and soap, wrapped her arms around herself and wept silently. Eventually, she lifted a pail full of water from the bucket and poured it on to her face. She stood up and continued to shower in this way until the bucket was empty and her body was cool and clean.

Chapter Eight

Polly was on her way home from the weekly rendezvous that left her flushed and glowing like an adolescent. She loved this phase of a relationship, when things were novel and unfolding slowly, when boredom and irritation had not yet surfaced to signal the end.

It was approaching twilight, that precariously brief period before total darkness, and as ever, she was in a leisurely race with the sun, keen to arrive home, or close to the European residential district, before nightfall. The coast road was deserted. Children who had played along here earlier in the day were being bathed and fed; adults who had sat in the shade of the trees watching boats at sea, selling tomatoes and fresh fish had retreated to their compounds. Her friends were safe in their orderly homes having a drink, preparing for husbands and an evening at the club. She basked in the rare aloneness, salty wind blasting out the day's scents.

It was unusual for women to drive themselves around, but Polly needed to escape from time to time in secured privacy. She had learned during her early years in Africa that no matter how discreet you urged a driver to be, he inevitably found willing ears for his stories. And generally, it was the drivers of her friends who listened. What, after all, did the other women think these men talked about for the long hours they sat waiting in car parks? And this was a small society, and priggish too, different to British East Africa, which had been infiltrated by rugged empire-builders who went there to explore and settle. There was a much less significant population of colonials here, serious civil servants in the main with only a smattering of commercial types. She realised as soon she and Timo arrived that it wasn't the kind of place one would easily survive scandal and was careful to keep this part of her life secret. In any event, these rendezvous, and particularly the journey home, provided her with much-needed respite from the exhausting constant mingling. She cared a great deal what people thought of her, which she didn't think was something to be ashamed of, but it could be draining.

As she drove, she pondered plans for a tea party to which she had invited Lady Smythe. So far, her attempts at close friendship with the Governor's wife had been unrequited. Polly was begrudgingly impressed with this apartness, yet had decided she would simply persevere.

As she approached a sharp bend in the road, she slowed down to light a cigarette. The sea was now almost directly in front of her. A red ball of sun swathed in mist dangled above the ocean. For a few hundred yards, she would head into the greying horizon. She slowed further to savour her surroundings when a figure clambering up the steep sandy bank from the beach interrupted her serenity. She peered over her sunglasses and saw it was a white woman. But there was no car parked on either side of the road ahead. She was bemused and wondered who would climb up after her and where they had hidden their car. She considered turning round to avoid an embarrassing confrontation, but it was too late. They were bound to see her, which would arouse unnecessary suspicion. She crawled along, waiting to see what would unfold before her. The woman reached the road and stood up, sending long, brown hair tumbling down her back. Polly squinted hard, more in shock than to strengthen her view. She would recognise that hair anywhere. 'What now?' she asked aloud, remembering that Audrey had been drinking steadily at the club earlier that afternoon, and in a particularly buoyant mood.

Audrey had started to hobble along the road. Polly looked around for signs of someone else, for some explanation of how she had come to be here at this time of near night. She began to feel less jovial. What was Audrey doing here, and why was she alone? Close to her,

153

Polly pulled over on to the dusty kerb and got out of the car. Audrey continued to shuffle along. She was barefoot. Her hair was dishevelled and sandy. What the devil had she been up to? Even by her standards, this was a little bizarre. Polly called out, and Audrey turned slowly, like a sleepwalker, clutching her blouse to keep it on.

'Audrey?' Polly whispered, aghast. Her lip was cut and swollen, the side of her face covered in sand, her glassy eyes staring. 'What the hell happened to you?'

'I can't find my shoes, and there are bloody stones everywhere,' said Audrey, looking at her feet. She raised an arm to push hair off her face, revealing a bruise on the softness of her underarm.

'Oh my God! Who did this?' Polly asked, grabbing on to her to stop her from walking further. She reeked of stale alcohol and seaweed.

'My blouse,' Audrey said in a hoarse voice. 'I don't think I can mend it.'

'Get in the car,' said Polly, suddenly very afraid. 'Quickly!' She bundled Audrey in and started the engine, locked the doors and sped off. 'Native?'

Audrey shook her head.

'White?' gasped Polly.

Audrey nodded.

'Who?' Her heart was sinking.

'They . . .'

'They? How many?' asked Polly, horrified.

'Two.' Audrey's voice had faded to a thin whisper. Polly glanced at her and saw tears roll from behind shut eyes. She gripped the wheel and kept her eyes on the road, determined to get Audrey home as quickly as possible. Thank heavens Alan was away.

Polly was pleased to see Audrey's happy steward appear before she had even turned off the engine. He peered into the dark car, shading his eyes, and Polly opened the car door, shoving him aside as she did so.

'Madam is ill. Go and get some hot water. And a small brandy.'

Awuni nodded, speechless, and disappeared into the house.

Polly helped Audrey out of the car and up the stairs. 'You'll be fine. A warm bath is what you need,' she murmured softly. Audrey sat on her bed looking dazed, while Polly put the bath on. 'Do you need help undressing?'

Audrey stood and walked past her into the bathroom without responding.

'I'll be on the veranda,' said Polly, wondering what exactly had happened.

After a while, she knocked on the bedroom door and pushed it open slowly. Audrey was sitting on the bed wrapped in her dressing gown. Wet, sandy clumps clung to her head. Polly placed a large brandy in her hand. 'I think I should stay with you. I've sent a message to Timo.' Audrey flinched. 'Don't worry,' said Polly, noticing her concern. 'I said you had terrible stomach pain, nothing to worry about, not that Timo would worry.'

'I feel better now.'

'Good. This will ensure you sleep,' she said, handing Audrey a pill.

Audrey swallowed the tablet with a few sips of brandy. 'Thank you,' she said, lowering herself on to her pillow.

'We can talk in the morning,' said Polly. 'I'll be in your spare room if you need me.' She switched off the light and turned to leave.

Emboldened by the dark, Audrey spoke: 'It was that man Derek.'

'Waller?' said Polly, incredulous. She put the light back on.

'And his friend,' said Audrey falteringly. 'They were taking me for a drive. They stopped by the beach and suggested we go swimming. They just laughed when I said I wanted to go home.' She started sobbing. 'Wanted to teach me a lesson, they said.'

Polly was silent, her questions consumed by dread and loathing. Pity overwhelmed her curiosity. Unwilling to come or go, she hovered uncomfortably for several moments between the rooms. Eventually, she heard Audrey's breathing lengthen, and she left her with the door ajar.

Polly slept fitfully in the Turtons' spare bed, and in the morning, she was free for a moment of the sickening knowledge of last night's events. She pulled on her clothes and went in search of the servants, taking care not to waken Audrey. Sitting with a cup of coffee on the quiet veranda, watching the smoke from her cigarette, she reflected on what had to be done.

She turned when she heard a noise behind her. Was it possible Audrey looked worse? Her lip hadn't receded. Her hair was matted and unruly from the night. Her face, drawn and colourless.

'I have a terrible headache; must have been the brandy,' said Audrey, smiling wanly.

Polly summoned Awuni and told him to cook breakfast, motioning silence when Audrey protested. 'You need to eat.' She poured Audrey a milky coffee with lots of sugar and handed it to her with a kind smile.

Audrey sighed and drooped her shoulders. She stared out at her garden. 'I wish Alan was here.'

'It's a good thing he isn't. He can't see you like this.'

Audrey shut her eyes. She wanted Polly to go now, even though she was grateful for the company.

'You're safe, Audrey. They must know better than to show their faces around here again soon.' She couldn't say what she thought, that no sensible woman would clamber drunkenly into a car with two thugs and head to a deserted beach, that Audrey should have realised her temerarious behaviour was bound to have dire consequences. 'You have to put this behind you. You mustn't think about it or talk about it, least of all with Alan. Or your friend Alice,' she said, raising her eyebrows slightly. 'She isn't very discreet, as I am sure you know.'

Audrey looked at her quizzically.

'Well, she isn't,' said Polly with a shrug of her shoulders. 'Tell her and you might as well put a notice up at the club. And trust me, you don't want that. You don't want the police involved, which is what will happen if Alan finds out about this. It would be different if it had been natives, but unfortunately, as it is, it will be your word against theirs. There will be many who attest to the fact that you were horribly drunk and flirting with them, that you accompanied them out from the club quite happily. Unfortunately, you haven't gone out of your way to gain friends, people who might be willing to stand by you now. This could be the thing that destroys you, and Alan, your marriage as well as everything else.' She drank some coffee. 'You've got to concentrate on forgetting,' she said quite vehemently.

'Yes,' said Audrey. How ironic that she should be made to feel indebted to Polly of all people. But she appreciated the small blessing. Alice was kind, but she would probe if she were here, and whitter non-stop about what to do. Polly seemed to realise she didn't want to talk about it, to relive the fear and humiliation, and appeared satisfied with the scant information she had provided. 'Yes, you're right,' she said.

She heard the dogs barking forlornly in their cages at the back of the house and started to cry. She needed Alan. Polly was wrong there, she did need him now. Her crying intensified as she realised how stupid she had been. How much she had let him down. It would break his golden heart to realise that she had put herself in such a dangerous position.

'Here comes breakfast,' said Polly. 'I don't think the boy should see you in this state.'

Audrey went into the bathroom to wash her face, taking great care not to look into the mirror. She needed to get rid of Polly somehow so she could be alone. She splashed some cologne behind her ears and fixed a smile on her face. If she seemed fine, strong enough to cope, surely Polly would go. 'Thank you,' she said as she sat at the table, looking with dismay at the greasy bacon and eggs. 'You've been kind. And you're right. I'll put this behind me. A stupid adventure that went wrong, that could have been much, much worse.' She smiled and, paying no attention to Polly's questioning look, started to cut a rasher of bacon. 'But I feel better now. Much better.' She ate fast, with the help of large gulps of coffee, and chatted happily in between mouthfuls. Her ploy worked, and Polly left soon after breakfast.

Audrey stayed in her bedroom for most of the next few days. Polly visited daily in the early evening, leaving her car out of sight around the back of the house. The first evening, she told Audrey she had informed the girls that Audrey had another bout of dysentery. 'That'll put them off,' she said. 'And give you a reason to see a doctor. Have you thought about seeing a doctor?'

'I will,' said Audrey.

'Good. Don't leave it too long.' Polly took out her book and sat with a cigarette and a glass of beer.

They never spoke much, but it was enough for Audrey. Polly remained soothingly unquestioning, quietly uncritical, while Audrey sat with her legs curled up beneath her, her fourth or fifth gin of the day beside her. By the time Polly rose to leave, Audrey was always calm, quite sedated and certain that sleep would come easily.

Audrey couldn't know that Polly was nursing her own fear. She couldn't tell Audrey that the day after the attack she had seen Derek Waller and his group sitting proudly in the bar at the club laughing about something, or someone, and how her skin had crawled with revulsion on seeing them. She realised how she had been insensitive to Audrey's plight, a little harsh after all. Now she was able to appreciate what ruthless beasts they were when she saw them brazenly enjoying the club. Inside, Polly raged, and wished she had the courage to go and strike Derek on the chin, to shout out about their misdemeanour, but what would be the point of that, other than to bring scandal upon Alan and Audrey, the very thing she was determined to avoid? As she swam up and down the length of the pool, she knew she had to confide in someone, these men were, after all, a threat to all the women. She took a detour on her way home to see the man she knew she could trust most and recounted the story. Later, he told her that the men had been quietly ousted from the club and told never to return unless they wanted to face police charges. They were unlikely to flout this advice, he said, assuring Polly that her friend was now safe, that she was safe.

As the week passed, the reality of what had happened bored beneath Audrey's skin and clawed like a painful irritation. She struggled to cope with an overwhelming tide of despair and hopelessness. She longed for Alan, believing he could restore the life that was before, confident he would ease her out of the turmoil in which fear and loss paralysed her. Then periodically, raging thoughts depleted her: anger that she was here to suffer this awful plight in the first place, fury at Alan for his portion of the blame and exasperation at her inability to alleviate the sense of suffocation caused by an even stronger, still impotent, desire to escape.

At night, once the alcohol had worn off, she was roused from sleep by harsh dreams that left her drenched in sweat. Too afraid to leave her room, she sat in her bed listening to the ticking clock until the sun began its upward rise, casting out shadows once more. Exhausted, it didn't make sense to eat, but she drank and dozed until it was time again for Polly's visit.

The morning after Polly brought a telegram informing her that Alan was on his way home, Audrey began her first ever spring clean. She turned out each drawer and cupboard and polished each and every ornament, including the ivory tusk that she hated. Together with Awuni and the small boy, she washed the windows and the floors, one tile at a time, with Jeyes disinfectant. She boil-washed their bed linen, the curtains and cushion covers and hung them out in the sun, aired their mattress and the entire house. She had Awuni build a bonfire next to the boys' quarters on which she burned piles of magazines and newspapers that she had accumulated. It was well after midnight before she went to bed a little amused at her sobriety. She slept and at dawn rose to continue. She polished the floors with mansion polish, waxed the furniture, plumped up the cushions in their clean covers, returned books to shelves, filled every vase with fresh flowers and poured more disinfectant into the toilets. Her home had never gleamed this much, never smelled so clean; she had never felt as exhausted. Late in the afternoon, she lay on the sofa aching in places she had never acknowledged and slept for several hours.

When Alan arrived in the evening, she stood on the veranda picking her fingernails and tried to look delighted.

He ran up the stairs and scooped her up into his arms. 'Oh, Audrey, you have no idea how pleased I am to see you.'

She held her breath and waited for the feeling of suffocation to pass, but it didn't. She pushed him away and swallowed. She panted gently to dispel the nausea that was building, brought on by the memory of smells: trodden-on, musty leaves and sweaty, leering men. She took a step back. 'I thought you'd need a bath. We ran you one. I think you need some clean clothes too.'

'Good idea,' said Alan.

She watched him walk off. She was sure his shoulders had stooped a little.

159

Over supper, she strained to keep smiling. He had grown a beard, but she could see he was gaunt. 'What have they done to you?'

'Had a touch of tummy trouble out in the bush, lost a bit of weight, I suppose. Gosh, I missed you,' he said, gazing at her. 'It is great to be back,' he said, reaching to hold her hand.

'I missed you too,' she said, while she gently removed her hand from under his.

Apprehensive, he studied her eyes for clues, but she looked away.

She hadn't anticipated guilt or anxiety in his presence. She hoped this awkward unfamiliarity would soon pass. He had brushed his wet hair back from his face and now he looked older, more tired than when he had left. Suddenly, there was a crushing desire to speak. She drew breath, put down her knife and fork. 'There's something I need to tell you, Alan.' She couldn't endure this on her own. He needed to know, to care.

Alan yawned. 'Now? If it is bad news, can it wait? It's just that it's been a bugger of a journey; my old bones ache.'

Her eyes brimmed with tears, and he smiled at her somewhat mournfully. 'It's good to have you home,' she whispered. He looked resigned, or was he simply exhausted? She seemed to have developed an inability to read him. I must be imagining things, she thought. He couldn't possibly know what happened. 'We'll be all right, won't we?' she said as convincingly as she could. I must keep reassuring him, me, us. I must say it every day, several times a day until it becomes the truth.

He nodded as though her question made all the sense in the world. 'It's good to be home after so long.'

That night, she deflected his attempts at intimacy, in the process pushing him further away than she wanted to. Yet how she longed for him to hold her and tease out the fear, to banish the memory, to erase the shame. He turned away, and she laid her hand on his back to prove to herself that he was there, as though she was afraid he would be gone in the morning.

In the days that followed, Alan was startled by Audrey's fluctuating moods. Often, she was in bed when he returned from work, the tell-tale glass beside her warning that sleep wouldn't last the night. At times, she would start crying for no earthly reason in the middle of supper and then disappear off to bed. He found the incoherence hard, when she appeared completely unconnected to her surroundings. She seemed unable to conduct a conversation, and he often found her concentrating blankly on his moving mouth, like a person listening to unfamiliar sounds. Confused by her, and exasperated by the constant rejection, he threw himself into his life to avoid seeing her. He played golf, polo, swam, played tennis and poker. He stayed out late during the week and slept in at the weekends. He tried to ignore her sighs and her wistfulness and talked enthusiastically about his day whenever she appeared amenable. Then, at Polly's suggestion, he insisted they host a dinner party, then another, and lunches catered for by Cook at which they played the perfect hosts. Soon Audrey felt as though she was on stage reciting lines she had learned by heart, acting out emotions elicited by a master director.

Chapter Nine

There was no question of a religious marriage for Matilda, even though she and her family were devoted members of the Accra Methodist Church; they attended faithfully every Sunday and again on Tuesday evening. Polygamy was not something that the minister of that church could openly bless simply because it was widely practised and accepted in society, even by many of its officials. Dutifully, from time to time, the Reverend Minister preached against the tradition of men marrying as many women as they could afford to maintain and tried to encourage his flock to live with one wife only in holy matrimony. But since the very men the sermons were aimed at, men like Lawyer Bannerman, were the most generous supporters of the church, his reprimands were not very wholehearted. And in return, the congregation continued to ignore the Reverend's advice on how to conduct their private lives.

There would be a traditional wedding ceremony three weeks after the engagement. Everyone felt that the speedier the formalities were completed, the better for all. No one seemed to remember that it would be Matilda's fifteenth birthday, a coincidence in any event, since her age appeared irrelevant to everyone concerned.

This time, Robert and Matilda would play key roles in the ceremony. Neither of them was looking forward to it. Robert because it would coincide with race day – the families were insisting that the wedding take place on a Saturday – and Matilda, well, because it would finalise her status as his wife, and in front of a crowd larger and more diverse than the gathering that had attended the engagement.

On the morning of the wedding, Matilda was agitated. She sat quietly while all around her activity bustled. Her mother and Aunty Dede were the chief dressers today. They pulled and stretched her hair into submission, and when it was done, Aunty Dede surreptitiously supplied her with a big cup of corn wine. Matilda had never had more than a sip of alcohol, but she emptied the sweet drink niftily and hid the cup from her mother. Soon, her chest was warm and she giggled a lot, infused by the joyous atmosphere in the house. There were jokes and anecdotes shared freely, and much irrepressible laughter.

'Thanks be to God the first wife will not be here to darken our day,' said Ama. 'I hear that she has gone to her mother's house.' She powdered her daughter's face and outlined her eyebrows and eyelids with kohl.

'Yes, apparently she does not cope well with pregnancy,' said Aunty Dede.

'Well, what does she expect? She is so tall and thin I don't know how her blood can even reach her head, let alone the baby,' said Ama.

'I hear that she faints a lot,' said Aunty Amele.

'I would not like to be so thin. There is nothing for a man to hold on to,' said Aunty Dede, jiggling her flabby tummy. 'Men like women to be sturdy, like our beautiful Matilda.'

'And fair,' said her mother.

'She is right to fear the beautiful competition she now faces,' said Aunty Dede.

Matilda laughed. Heartened by this news, she picked up the small hand-held mirror that lay on her lap and inspected her face. The women had applied deep-purple lipstick to her mouth, which made her look several years older.

So far, her birthday had gone unremembered because of all the preparations for the wedding. No one mentioned it. But she knew her father would not have forgotten it. Although he was almost completely illiterate, at the beginning of each year, he painstakingly copied his children's birthdays from his old diary into his new one. Matilda had seen him do this many times, and when she had asked him once why he did that, he had replied, 'So I can remember what special thanks I need to give to God each day.' Had he given thanks to God for her today? she wondered.

The groom and his entourage arrived in the early afternoon, with a great deal of fanfare. Matilda's family welcomed them like long-lost relatives. Even more members of the Bannerman family showed up this time since the menfolk were welcome on this occasion. There were not enough stools and chairs set out for all the visitors, and those that could quickly grabbed a seat, deferring to the older members of the family and to Lawyer's sisters, who were allowed to have the best seats. Others stood at the back of the compound, while yet others milled out in the alleyway from where they would follow the proceedings.

Robert smiled self-consciously as he followed Saint John to the bridal seats that had been placed at the front of the gathering. He was welcomed with plenty of clapping and cheering by the festive crowd, and several loud comments were made about his appearance. He wore an outfit made from the same fabric that had been used to make Matilda's wedding dress. Chosen by the bride's family, the material was white with chunky, swirling gold-and-silver embroidered patterns. He had winced visibly when Ama and Saint John brought it to his house, although they did not seem to notice. He had hoped he would be able to wear a suit, but they were insistent, and he did not want to establish this relationship on a disagreement that was not really worth a fight. He had paid a small fortune for the material, but he was sure that Matilda's family had bought at least twice as much as they needed for the wedding outfits and that somewhere in this house, awaiting a suitable occasion to have some fancy clothes made at his expense, was the excess.

He smiled to himself as he thought what his chums at the Middle Temple bridge club would say if they could see him now. Thankfully, he had not invited any of his friends to the wedding. Yes, Tetteh, the trainer, was here, and the stable lads and jockeys, they would all be around somewhere in the background. They would attend without a formal invitation. It was a perk of working for Lawyer that his staff could attend his functions, discreetly, and be fed and watered along with the other guests. But his real friends, his equals, the lawyers, the doctors, Alan. Well, this wasn't the kind of do that he wanted them to attend. Quite simply, this wasn't the kind of event that *he* would wish to attend, so why burden them with the obligation? He was only here because the girl's family expected it of him; it was a brief, if hot and slightly irritating, sojourn from his real life.

It was blistering and humid under the canopies that had been erected especially for the day, and Robert, desperate for a drink, was sweating profusely. He wiped his face regularly with a damp hand-kerchief, but the heat was relentless, and he had barely mopped up the moisture when he started to feel more gathering on his nose, above his mouth and his forehead. No breeze whatsoever, he thought, as he watched the still leaves of the tall pawpaw tree.

He turned round when he heard one of his children call him. His sons, four-year-old Edward and three-year-old Albert, were seated in the second row with Aunty Baby and Aunty Gladys, where they would have a good view of their father's second marriage. Edward waved at his father. The baby twins, Sylvia and Bernadette, had stayed at home.

He began to lose his temper, although not visibly, when he had been sitting for nearly an hour and there was still no sign of the bride. As it was, he had arrived nearly an hour later than he had been instructed to. He shifted restlessly in his seat and wondered when the proceedings would commence. The sooner it began, the sooner he could leave; he really did not enjoy these traditional ceremonies any more. He remembered his first marriage, which had been rather different. The traditional engagement at Julie's mother's house, which he had not attended, and which had cost his family a great deal more than the entire proceedings here. He had enjoyed his wed-ding day, the Anglican service and the lavish party afterwards, at which his friends had toasted him and Julie and made lengthy speeches. It was altogether a rather different affair. He smiled. At the time, he had not intended to marry again. Juliana epitomised all he wanted in a woman, and he had actually felt rather proud of their match. He contemplated his current situation. Briefly, he wondered,

Is this a mistake? But he knew it could not possibly be. He had the right, the power, the ability to make this girl his and had chosen to do so. He smiled again. Perhaps Julie was right; it was a reversion to his true ethnicity, which obviously lay deep within him, overlooked but not extinct. But how awful was that? He looked around at all the ecstatic faces. He felt their joy and warmth. He could see the happiness in their eyes, the anticipation in their chests, how they welcomed his presence. How would they feel if he suddenly stood up and announced that he could not marry their precious daughter because he was educated in England? They would laugh at him for his absurd logic. Then maybe they would cry before pleading with him not to let them down.

He looked up when he heard the singing that accompanied the bridal train. Matilda's father and mother with several of their relatives were escorting her towards him. She was wearing a traditional dress with the most intricate headdress. Robert looked at her and thought her beauty was marred by the excessive make-up, which emphasised her age and made her look like a child dressed in her mother's clothes. Again, he marvelled at how this powerful desire he had for her had intensified over the past weeks. He promised himself that he would try to treat her well. He could tell that she did not know what to expect from life, or from this marriage. He did not even know whether or not she enjoyed their time together; she was always quiet, but surely she must enjoy it, and surely she was proud that he had picked her? Now she was next to him, looking down at the ground respectfully, rather than directly at him. Then she was sitting on the stool next to him, still looking at the ground. Suddenly, Robert's senses were assaulted by an overpowering scent; it was the stale, sweet scent of concentrated perfume aged by time and heat. In the airless warmth, the smell was cloying. He realised that he had wrinkled his face in disgust and quickly replaced his thin smile, but he decided he would have to tell her not to use this perfume when she came to see him.

The wedding could begin.

Saint John stood up. 'Welcome, welcome, welcome. Please accept our most heartfelt welcome to you today. We are overjoyed to have you here for the ceremony to marry our daughter to your son. Since it is now nearly four o'clock and the proceedings were supposed to start at one o'clock, maybe we better progress without further ado. We give thanks to God that our venerable family head is here to lead the proceedings today. So, over to you, Uncle Nii Odartey.'

Uncle Nii Odartey was a striking man. His wrinkled skin was very black, almost blue, and it contrasted with his plentiful shocking-white hair. Not only did he have lots on his head but also growing out of his ears and his nose, and on his chest too, sprouting from underneath his cloth. If asked, Saint John would not be able to explain his relationship to Uncle Nii Odartey beyond 'He is my father's cousin', but as the eldest living Lamptey, Uncle Nii Odartey held the position of head of the family, a role he seemed to relish on days like today. No one, including Uncle Nii Odartey, knew exactly how old he was. He must have been in his eighties, but he still had some of his own teeth and could walk unaided.

Saint John helped Uncle Nii Odartey to his feet, and the old man steadied himself and cleared his throat a few times. 'Anyway, there is no time like African time,' Uncle Nii Odartey said to cheers of support from the crowd. His voice was high-pitched and loud. 'Bring the schnapps,' he said, raising a sinewy hand towards Saint John. Although he was very short-sighted, Uncle Nii Odartey refused to wear glasses because he said they would get in his way. Saint John placed a calabash of the clear liquid in Uncle Nii Odartey's outstretched hand, who began in a voice that vibrated, pausing frequently so that his speech was imbued with the significance of the occasion: 'We give thanks . . . to God . . . that we are here . . . today . . . to celebrate . . . the union . . . of your son Robert . . . and . . . our daughter Matilda. As tradition requires . . . so . . . we shall call on our ancestors . . . to bless this union . . . and . . . to bless our children . . . with many . . . off . . . spring.'

The gathering hushed as he started the traditional libation prayer, pausing frequently to pour a few drops of schnapps on the ground.

Drink . . . thousand gods . . . drink, thousand ancestors.
We are here . . . today . . . to bring our children . . . together in
  marriage.
Bless them . . . with many offspring . . . so that they can spill

blood . . . for you . . . in thanksgiving . . . and allow the spirits . . .
   of our ancestors . . . to return.
Curse . . . any evil-minded person . . . who curses them . . . and
   heap . . . misfortune on them. Amen!

'Amen!' declared everyone.

Uncle Nii Odartey emptied the remaining contents of the calabash on the ground and sat down triumphantly.

'Thank you, Uncle Nii Odartey. May our prayers be heard by the
gods and the spirits of our ancestors today,' said Saint John. Then,
turning to the Bannerman family, he said, 'Over to you, Uncle
Theophilus.'

Uncle Theophilus, head of the Bannerman family, and Robert's
late father's oldest cousin, was a lay preacher in the Anglican Church
and an avid traditionalist. He took the calabash that Saint John
offered him and began his prayers, stopping to pour schnapps on the
ground after each incantation.

Numerous spirits and gods, come and drink.
Spirits of our departed ancestors, come and drink.
We are here today for this marriage and to ask for health, peace and
   harmony.
Not for money and riches, just common sense in administering our
   affairs,
So that we will have long life and prosperity. Amen!

'Amen!' responded the gathering.

Uncle Theophilus did not sit down, he continued, 'The fool says
in his heart, *there is no God . . .*'

Several voices chorused, 'Fools indeed,' 'Tell them,' 'Yes, yes.'

Uncle Theophilus acknowledged their support and went on, 'But
I tell you that among us Ga people there are few fools, and certainly
none here today!'

The crowd applauded.

'And I say to you, today show me a man who says to be a good
Christian I must abandon our traditions, and today I will show you a
fool.'

The crowd cheered.

'Obi, bring the goat now,' Uncle Nii Odartey directed one of his cousins.

Robert flinched. This was the part of the ceremony that he had been dreading. Just last night, he had had a row with his uncle over the need to slaughter a goat here today. Robert had voiced, in his most polite voice, his disdain at the habit of sacrificing animals at every given opportunity, and, it seemed to him, totally unnecessarily. 'Don't you think that it is about time we moved away from animal sacrifices and these other abominable practices?'

Uncle Theophilus had gasped. 'With all due respect, Robert, that is a stupid question! Did your years in England erase all our customs from your head? Just because you don't want to see the sight of blood, even though you are happy to enjoy the benefits of sacrifices that were carried out in your name,' he had said, sweeping his arm widely around him, indicating the trappings of Robert's success, 'is not a good enough reason to ask me to abandon my duties, to abandon our ancestors and incur their wrath. This is not a matter that concerns only you, you know. My responsibility is to preserve the lineage of our family; if I fail in my obligations and neglect our tradition, we will be haunted by doom. Do you think that I am fool enough to do that?'

'I am not disputing the need to observe traditions. I believe in tradition so far as it is harmless, but . . . but continuing to sacrifice animals in this manner . . .'

'Nobody is asking you to cut the goat's throat. And you should realise that no road of faith can be well travelled without appropriate sacrifices. I should know what I am talking about. After all, am I not a preacher in the Church? I encourage all my family to be upstanding Christians, to be active members of the Church, even participating fully in the service of the Almighty, but being a good Christian does not mean one has to give up on centuries of tradition. As the Bible says, "thou shalt have no other God but me." Amen! But this is tradition.' He had wagged his finger at Robert vigorously, looking over the rim of his spectacles as he spoke. 'Not for anyone, British or not, educated or not, must we abandon our traditions. The sooner you understand that, the better for you.' Uncle

Theophilus had spoken through clamped jaws and with narrowed eyes.

'I am not sure why you are bringing the British into this,' Robert had replied vehemently. 'I am my own man, educated enough, and a Christian moreover. I know better than . . . than this senseless need to inflict cruelty on animals . . . this waste . . .'

'So you want me to incur the wrath of our ancestors on *all* . . .', he dragged the word out to ensure that it emphasised the vastness of the Bannerman family, '. . . our family just because you are afraid to hurt the feelings of a goat?' Uncle Theophilus looked incredulous. 'Listen. You have voiced your concern. I have heard you. You have your beliefs; I have mine. But more importantly, I have my duties, duties that extend beyond you to your children and all the members of our illustrious family. This marks the end of the conversation.' Uncle Theophilus had shouted this last sentence to make his point.

And that had been the end of the conversation. Uncle Theophilus had stormed out of Robert's office in disgust, leaving him to sit and fume, angry at his powerlessness in the face of this amorphous family that was steering a course that he had no desire to travel. He could attempt to stand by his beliefs and antagonise the lot of them, including Matilda's family – although he was frankly much less bothered about them; they were obviously only too pleased to be assimilated into the Bannerman family, or at least associated with them by virtue of a marriage – or he could go along with his family's expectations and smile and pretend to be happy. Somehow, he had known all along that the less contentious path would be the one for him.

Uncle Theophilus and Uncle Nii Odartey stood in preparation. Obi dragged the fat, clean goat by a string around its neck towards the elders, half strangling the resistant creature in the process. The crowd at the back jostled for a good view. Obi held it by its tether in front of the old man, who looked at it approvingly. Then Obi pushed the animal on to the ground and pressed its head down hard with his hands; it was bleating as loudly as it could. Robert lowered his head and tried not to hear the desperate cries. Two other men held the goat's legs firmly, and without delay, Uncle Nii Odartey slit its throat with a sharp knife, causing a wave of red to spread over its fur. The knife was not as sharp as it looked, and the animal was only badly wounded; it moaned and thrashed wildly, spraying blood on to the faces and clothes of Obi and his helpers and on Uncle Nii Odartey's hand. Obi pulled the animal's head back, stretching the skin around its neck, and Uncle Nii Odartey cut again with more vigour, this time interrupting the tremulous cries. It writhed aggressively for a few more moments, then became still. The compound filled with the sounds of a satisfied, impressed audience. Blood gushed on to the ground, and the air was filled with the ripe smell of blood freshly warmed by hot earth. Obi held a calabash to the incision and collected some of the blood, which he handed to Uncle Nii Odartey. Robert looked and saw that his shoes and the bottom of his trousers had specks of blood on them; his stomach heaved, and he swallowed a few times to steady himself, trying not to inhale the sickening smell.

Uncle Nii Odartey took the calabash, looking at its contents approvingly, and resumed his incantations, pouring a few drops of blood on the ground each time.

> May . . . the gods . . . and the spirits . . . of our ancestors . . . pour
>   their blessings . . . upon us.
> For . . . we have spilled blood . . . today . . . as . . . a mark of
>   respect . . . to them.
> We . . . ask for . . . protection and health . . . long life and
>   prosperity . . . and . . . plentiful children.
> May . . . the gods and ancestors . . . see that . . . we . . . have done our
>   duty and . . . answer our prayers. Amen!

'Amen!' responded the group passionately.

Uncle Nii Odartey dipped his forefinger in the remaining blood and made the sign of the cross on Robert's forehead. Then he turned to Matilda and did the same. Only then did he pour the remainder of the blood on the already blood-sodden earth.

Obi and his helpers dragged the animal away unceremoniously. Later, it would be gutted and roasted for hungry and appreciative mouths.

It was time to exchange rings. Saint John handed the gold bands that had been specially made for the couple to Uncle Nii Odartey. Uncle Nii Odartey looked at them approvingly.

'We ask the Almighty God to bless these rings and to bless the wearers of these rings.

May any person who comes between this man and this wife be cursed.

We call upon our ancestors to give wisdom to this man and this wife as they embark on marriage and to reproduce and bring forth many times. Amen!

Again, the gathered responded, 'Amen!'

Saint John gave the rings to Robert, who put one on Matilda's wedding finger and then put one on his own. As if on cue, the crowd cheered and clapped, hooting in praise and support of the newlyweds who were smiling, and if they could, would have been blushing too.

'Uncle Nii Odartey, do you have any advice for our newlyweds?' asked Saint John.

Uncle Nii Odartey, still standing, nodded eagerly. 'Well, the best advice I can give the couple is in the form of a saying that our ancestors have relied upon for many generations, and which they will do well to remember. It says, "An ant hill is constructed from inside the ant hill." This means that you are the only ones who can build this marriage, and you must do so from within. No one else will be able to help you to make a good marriage, although rest assured that there will be many who try to spoil it.' As he spoke, Uncle Nii Odartey wagged his finger at Robert and Matilda as though he was scolding them. He had no doubt given this advice to many, many couples, but he spoke with the same fervour of novelty.

The crowd voiced hearty approval, heads nodded, many smiled.

Not to be outdone, Uncle Theophilus stood up and said loudly, 'I too have some advice for the couple. Firstly, we all here present wish you a satisfactory and long marriage.'

The crowd clapped.

Uncle Theophilus continued, grinning, 'But remember always that if you don't disturb the bamboo tree, it will not make any noise.'

172

The crowd laughed.

'Saint John, a full measure of schnapps for an old man, please.' Uncle Nii Odartey thus gave the order for the merrymaking to commence. And in no time at all palm wine and corn wine were being consumed in vast quantities quite quickly in an attempt to quench thirst and quell heat, and the atmosphere soon became convivial.

The couple sat side by side in stilted silence. Robert, relieved that the worst was over, thought longingly of a sizeable whisky. He wanted to leave his wedding to find out the results of the day's racing. Two of his horses had been scheduled to run today; now it was approaching dusk, and the horses would be on their way home. Soon, the stables would be filled with the warm smells of clammy, exhausted animals and the sounds of excited stable boys and jockeys discussing the day's successes – at least, he hoped they had won. This was only the second time in five years that he was not at the racecourse on a Saturday. He thought it ironic that on both occasions, it had been to attend his wedding. No one could object if he slipped away now with Matilda. Surely they would understand?

He motioned to Saint John, his new uncle-in-law, a title that made Robert want to laugh out loud; he paid the man's wages and, as a result, had funded this entire ceremony almost single-handedly. The man's eagerness to please had obviously not diminished because of their new relationship, and he rushed over to Robert's side. Surreptitiously, Robert told him that he wanted to slip away. Saint John winked as if they were in cahoots and told him that it would be most appropriate for the bride and groom to leave the celebration but most inappropriate for them to 'slip away'.

Before Robert had a chance to digest this, he realised that Saint John was knocking on the table in front of him, trying to get everyone's attention.

'Excuse my interruptions of your merrymaking, but I have a very important announcement to make,' he shouted above the din of the party. The impromptu drumming, singing and dancing that had begun after the alcohol started to take effect ceased reluctantly. 'The bridegroom has asked our permission to remove our daughter, excuse me, his *wife* home to consummate their marriage! It seems he cannot wait for the party to be over.'

173

Robert had never seen Saint John this reckless and cursed that he had not realised the man was drunk.

The crowd applauded and began to sing joyously, clapping rhythmically. One by one, Matilda's mother, Aunty Dede and the other womenfolk started dancing around Matilda and Robert, twirling above their heads pristine white handkerchiefs, which they had pulled out from their bosoms. The merry crowd, some sporadically bellowing good wishes and advice to Matilda, who shyly thanked them, thus escorted the couple out of the Lamptey family house, along the narrow alleyway – where the women lifted their skirts to avoid them trailing in the gutter – and up the steps to the street where the couple climbed into Lawyer's waiting car to travel the short distance to his house.

'Go upstairs and wait for me in my room,' Robert ordered as he stepped out of the car into the peace of his compound, pulling the newly acquired ring off his finger.

The yard was empty but for a couple of stable boys who had returned with the horses from the racecourse, and the house was mostly in darkness; apart from Julie and maybe her maids, everyone from the household was still at the wedding. Even Lawyer's sons would enjoy the party until one of their aunts or a family friend carried or dragged them back home later that night.

Matilda was merry from the cups of corn wine that Uncle Saint John had given her towards the end of the day, which she had drunk too quickly. She giggled as she got out of the car, grandly imagining for a moment that she was the madam of this big house. Then she looked upwards and saw Julie. Instantly, her cheeriness faded away. She smiled at her, but Julie quickly disappeared into the house. They had said she was not here. They had said she had gone home. They had made her feel secure in coming here tonight. Matilda stood staring at the house, wondering from which dark room her husband's wife was watching her. How had her mother and aunts been so badly misinformed, and why had they repeated the untruth with such confidence?

She made her way slowly up the stairs, holding her skirt with her hands so she would not trip, and concentrated on each step. Over the

174

past two weeks, she had walked these stairs many times. She had crept up in the dark to his room, without encountering anyone. She had begun to notice that she no longer felt as terrified of him as she had the first time, although her stomach still fluttered with uncertainty and her palms were always damp. And she always left with a lighter step, thankful to be going home.

She hoped Julie would not appear, but as she reached the top of the stairs, she saw her waiting on the landing outside Lawyer's bedroom with her arms folded across her chest. Her pregnancy was still not evident. Perhaps that too was a further mistake, a further false rumour. She was wearing another pretty dress, this time with yellow roses printed all over it. Yet again, Matilda was amazed that she chose to wear such enchanting clothes at home, and at night when there seemed little point, when it was doubtful that anyone would call unannounced to admire them.

'So, you have married my husband. Congratulations!'

'Please, thank you.' Matilda clasped her hands behind her and looked at the ground respectfully.

'God, what is that smell? Where on earth did you get that scent?' Julie had wrinkled her face in disgust.

Matilda shifted her feet restlessly, wondering what might be the appropriate response to such an enquiry.

'I hope my husband has told you that you cannot live in this house.' When she spoke, she raised her left eyebrow as high as it would go.

'Please, yes.'

A plump little girl came crawling into the corridor. Julie picked her up and sat her on her hip.

'I don't want my children confused as to who you are. I have told the boys that their father's marriage will not alter things. They understand their place in this house. And my children only speak English in my presence, like I did with my parents. They will be going off to school in England when they are older. I don't want to confuse them with Ga. Do you understand? And do try and avoid speaking your broken English to them. Is that clear?' The child was stretching a chubby hand towards Matilda, trying to grab at her headdress, but Julie kept moving her away.

175

'Please, yes. Please, I was trying to learn English before—' She stopped speaking. It did not feel right to reveal her true ambitions. She smiled at the child, who she thought looked just like Lawyer.

'I am listening,' said Julie haughtily.

'Please, I was trying to learn proper English before this. God willing, I want to resume my studies.' Matilda maintained her respectful pose, but she felt trapped. She could not possibly turn round and go home. They would shoo her away back to her husband and tell her not to be silly, that there was nothing to fear. She could not go forward, because this woman stood blocking the way and showed no sign of moving. Was that her new status, she pondered, to be suspended in no-man's land? Wanted neither here nor at home?

'Well, that is your problem. I doubt you will be able to change much about . . .' She paused and waved her hands vaguely in front of Matilda.

Matilda waited for her to continue, but nothing more was said. They stood looking at each other in silence. Julie struggled to keep the child in her arms; she was wriggling hard, stretching her arms out to try and grasp Matilda, who decided it best to resist her instinct to take her, or at least to hold her lovely soft arm. Somehow, she did not think Julie would approve. She smiled, and the child rewarded her with a happy gurgle. Even an arrogant person is blessed with healthy children, she thought. Would this girl also grow up to be like her mother? she wondered. This child, as all others, came into the world not long ago without a thing, without a name even, but by the time she grows up, she will have inherited so much, including perhaps her mother's rudeness and pride. Suddenly, she heard Patience's words of advice and tried to imagine that she had her friend's depthless confidence. She swallowed and said, 'I did not choose this to happen to me any more than you. Can we let bygones be bygones? I don't wish to be your enemy. I am Lawyer's wife too—'

'Don't make me laugh.'

'As you know, before God, you and I are equal—'

'Don't be ludicrous, we are not equal. And never will be,' she said through clenched teeth. 'Get in my way and you will live to regret the day that you crossed paths with my husband.' She squinted as if she was squeezing out hatred and anger from her face, then swivelled and walked off, clicking her heels on the polished concrete.

Matilda took a deep breath and walked slowly to Lawyer's room. She sat on his big, soft bed. For the first time as a fully married woman, she was alone with her thoughts. Why did she feel so unprepared? This was what she had been raised for, what the missionaries had prepared her for. She realised that she was shaking. She had never been bullied other than by her mother, which did not really count. What her mother did, the beating, the shouting, the insults, that was only to ensure that she was well raised, well trained. It was done out of love. 'Spare the rod and spoil the child' was one of her mother's favourite verses, and she believed it wholeheartedly.

She had known it would not be easy to contend with the first wife, who thought she was not good enough for Lawyer. Well, she was not dead, was she? She smiled faintly. She had bravely defended herself in front of the first wife, and she was still alive. Even if it had been hard, even if she had not really said very much, not as much as her friend would have, anyway. If things were to continue like this, she would simply have to learn to speak back more forcefully. Little by little, she would do it. Patience was right, she must not let this woman walk all over her, as she just had outside in the corridor. If she couldn't get rid of the fear, she must simply learn to face her afraid.

But she had to accept that despite her valiant display, in only a few moments, Julie had managed to erase the small self-belief that Patience had fostered. It was plain to see how much her family had underestimated the first wife's resentment of this marriage. All of them had miscalculated the extent to which her European education had expunged their traditions from her life. It was obvious to Matilda that this union was hopeless. Perhaps before long, Lawyer too would recognise the doomed state of affairs and discard her like a used food leaf left to rot by the roadside.

As she sat and thought, her shoulders gradually drooped, and her head hung until in the end she had to raise her hands to support it. She would have cried, but she was too tired; the day had been too long.

Chapter Ten

Matilda woke early on her first day as a completely-married-woman and lay on her mat listening to the sound of a cheeky bird singing close to the window. She wondered what kind of bird it was; she heard it often in the mornings, but had never bothered to ask her father, who she was sure would be able to name it.

She relived the wedding. Had she made her parents proud of her? What about the other relatives? There had been joking and laughing in abundance, especially from Uncle Saint John. She had not been able to speak to Patience at all yesterday, but she wanted to talk to her now and see what she had made of it all. And Lawyer? He had told her to stop calling him Lawyer and to call him Robert, but she still found this difficult. He had been particularly broody in his room afterwards and did not say much. On her way home, depleted and exhausted from the day, she had wept effortlessly, only realising she was crying when she found it difficult to see the pavement.

She would not move to his house. It had been agreed by all, after a certain amount of debate, that it would be best if she continued to live in her uncle's house. That wouldn't be unusual at all, they pointed out. And there was no need for her to go, they said, she was needed here as much as there. 'After all,' Aunty Dede had argued, 'is she not still a child that we need to look after?' How much the first wife influenced this decision was unclear, but lying here contemplating the day ahead, she was certain there could be no woman alive more pleased with this state of housing.

She emerged from her bedroom wondering whether she would have to do anything in particular today now that she was a wife. As she sat on a stool daydreaming and eating a bowl of sweetened corn porridge, Aunty Dede came and sat next to her.

'You must go to the market today and cook something for your husband this afternoon.'

'But his wife . . . Their maid cooks for him every day.'

'So what? You are his wife too. And no wise woman lets another woman cook for her husband. No sensible wife lets another perform her duties.'

Matilda looked unconvinced. 'I don't even know what he likes.'

'You know whatever you cook will be delicious, after all, did I not teach you most of your cooking?' She giggled. 'Anyway, I am sure that the first wife does not know how to cook. Look how thin she is! It is not possible that she is fond of eating. We all know that people who are not fond of food cannot cook. And in her condition, the smell of cooking will be as offensive as a gutter in the sun. This is an opportunity you must seize. The next few months are crucial to cement your marriage and reassure your husband that he has made a good choice. With the first wife out of action, you can proceed to claim your rightful place. Make him something special, maybe some palm-nut soup, and take it there this evening. Don't wait for him to ask, show him that you can cook nicely.'

She watched her aunt speak with her usual passion. It was difficult to listen and not have faith in her, to hear and remain unaffected by her eagerness.

She strolled to the market along the open gutters that lined the roads. They were designed to route unwanted rainwater on the occasions that it rained heavily; however, they usually channelled dirty household water, along with urine, spittle and diverse debris thrown in by pedestrians, hawkers and residents alike. At regular intervals, the rubbish – food wrappers, pieces of fabric, newspaper, leaves and old tins – clogged the flow and caused the gutters to swell and threaten to spill their putrid contents.

At the market, there were several women selling fresh palm nuts; clusters of shiny orange nuts with black edges. Matilda chose a bunch, which she put in a basket on her head. She bought overripe tomatoes, onions, some dried fish and chilli peppers. The palm nuts were heavy, and she walked home slowly in the dusty heat, deciding on her way to go past the school and see Patience.

She arrived just as the lesson was ending and watched pensively the girls who came out happily practising the words that they had learned that day.

She waved at Patience, and her friend came running over. The girls hugged. They had not been alone together since the engagement. 'Will you come and keep a housewife company while she cooks her beloved husband dinner?'

'Will you tell me everything? Why do I ask? I know you won't. It's not fair. If I had been the first of us to marry, you know that I would tell you all the details.'

'Well, unfortunately for me, it was not you who married first.'

'So, Mrs Bannerman, what is he like?'

'Me, Mrs Bannerman? Oh, I need time.'

'Does he talk to you? I can't imagine talking to him. He always looks so serious and fierce. Does he shout at you?'

'He is not my father, you know. He is my husband. Goodness me, it sounds strange to my ears.'

'What about your Number One Rival? Is she behaving herself?'

'I haven't seen her again,' she lied.

'Well, she is lucky that her husband picked such a pleasant second wife. And you are lucky to have married well.'

'Well, *you* should count yourself lucky. So far I cannot see the benefits of being married. All I know for certain is that I have acquired another set of elders who will try and tell me what to do and treat me like a child, not a wife!'

'All right, calm down, then. I am sure that will change when you have a baby of your own,' said Patience.

'I don't want a baby.'

'Oh, don't say that, you will curse yourself!' Patience clutched Matilda's shoulder, looking at her in alarm. 'You must have children, you know you must. If you think your life is bad now, woe betide you if you fail to give birth. They will not forgive you for that. They will pull and push you in every direction until you have a child. And you must have not just one but many.'

'Yes, I know.'

'You don't want to give your Number One Rival any cause to break up your marriage, do you? Well, childlessness is not an option, then.'

Later, Patience sat and watched while Matilda cooked the meal. She removed the palm nuts from their cluster using a cutlass, then she boiled them for an hour on a coal pot before pounding them in a mortar with a pestle as tall as herself to separate the orange fibrous flesh from the hard kernels underneath. Then she poured the pounded nuts back into the pan and fished out the kernels with her hands, enjoying the sensation of the thick, slimy mixture. When she boiled the orange fibres again until deep-red palm oil began to escape and settle on top of the bubbling liquid, the compound filled with a sweet, nutty aroma.

In a separate pan, she fried finely chopped onions, garlic and chillies and chopped tomatoes, which she had skinned after plunging into boiling water, until she had a thick red sauce. She poured in the sieved palm-nut extract, gave the pot a vigorous stir, seasoned it with lots of salt and left the soup to simmer for a long while. She was pouring with sweat from all this effort but did not seem to notice, nor did she notice that she had been cooking for over three hours. Just before she thought her soup was ready, she flaked smoked grouper into the soup, savouring the woody smell and allowing herself a little piece of the salty fish as a reward for her hard work.

'Can I taste it?' asked Patience, who had been asleep. 'I have had to sit here inhaling the scent of this delicious food all afternoon. Please let me at least taste it, then I can say that I have shared food with the big Lawyer.' She laughed.

Matilda was too tired to laugh. She ladled a small amount of soup into a bowl, looking with pride at the thick orange-brown liquid, which separated perfectly from the bright-red oil.

'Beautiful,' said Patience after a mouthful. 'I don't think that the Number One Rival can compete with this. I am sure she did not learn how to make this in her British school.'

It had been easy when she was cooking to avoid thinking about anything in particular. Now that her soup was prepared, she had to think about how she would transport it to Lawyer's house, and what she would do when she got there. And what would she say if Julie was in?

Trying to think of only one thing at a time, she put several portions of soup into one of the new enamel cooking pots that her mother used only to serve food. She put the pot into a woven basket, covered it with a new dishcloth and walked with Patience to Lawyer's house. At the gate, they said goodbye, and Matilda entered the compound hesitantly and walked towards the kitchen. She knocked tentatively, peering through the open door. There was no one in the room, so she went in. Her heart was pounding to think that at any moment that woman might appear and find her gawping at her things. But her curiosity had to be satisfied, and she looked around. It was an enormous room, bigger even than Uncle Saint John's bedroom, and it had cream-coloured cupboards and open shelves on almost all the walls. Matilda ran her hand along the shiny green Formica surface of the cupboards, amazed at how clean it was, and admired the stainless-steel sink with its gleaming taps. How blessed Julie was to have water delivered right into her kitchen like this, Matilda thought, as she switched on the tap and watched in awe as an unceasing stream of water gushed out. She opened one of the cupboards quickly and saw that it was full of plates and bowls, all piled neatly, many more than they had at home. There was a large wooden table in the middle of the room, which was marked and scraped with age, and she considered whether she could put her pot of soup on it.

She wondered where Julie did her cooking, sure that the floor, covered in brown linoleum and still wet in patches where it had just been mopped, would not remain this pristine if she used a coal pot on it. She was about to venture further into the house when the maid walked in.

'Good afternoon, Sister Matilda,' she said.

'Hello, Esi,' replied Matilda, suddenly feeling very awkward.

'Did you bring food?' she asked, peering into the basket. 'Madam says we must put hot pans on this table,' she said, pointing at the old table. 'Eh! I say, you have saved me work. Madam asked me to make

182

rice and stew for Lawyer, but as you have brought his food, I don't have to bother. I don't like cooking on that,' she said, gesturing at a massive white lump of metal sitting proudly against one wall, 'but Madam says cooking outside with the coal pot is dirty.'

Matilda walked up to the cooker, which she had thought was another special cupboard. She stood and admired the rings. She touched one of the knobs, which turned easily. There was a faint sound like wind whistling through leaves, and Esi came rushing over, pushed Matilda's hand away from the dial and turned it off.

'The gas will kill us if we breathe it!' she shouted.

Matilda looked confused and stared at the apparatus with increased respect.

'Look,' said the maid. She took a match, struck it, then turned the knob and held the flame close to the nearest ring with her hand stretched as far from her torso as she could manage and her face half-turned away. As the ring exploded into life and was engulfed in blue fire, she jumped back and said, 'Do you see?' She switched off the cooker and continued gesturing with her hands as though she was talking to the cooker. 'And in no time at all, it burns the food. If I turn my back to clean the floor or sweep the living room, then when I return, the food is burned, spoiled, and I have to start again. It is supposed to save time, but you have to stand and guard whatever you are cooking like a watchman as if you have nothing else better to do. What kind of cooker is that?' She made a disgusted sound as she resumed her duties with Matilda watching silently.

The maid put a plate, a bowl, cutlery and a glass on a tray. Just before she walked out of the kitchen, she said, 'Madam has gone shopping. Do you want to see the living room?' Matilda followed her and stood at the doorway of a room across the hallway, which was even bigger than the kitchen and smelled of mansion polish. She looked around curiously. There were two windows behind drawn net curtains, which overlooked the yard. The shutters of the windows were almost closed, keeping out nearly all of the little daylight that was left outside, but the maid did not switch on the electric light.

There were two bulky burgundy velvet sofas and two matching armchairs, all facing a long, low table. The table was covered with a rectangular lace doily and had a floral pink ceramic vase in the centre.

The arms and the backs of the sofas were covered with pieces of matching crocheted white lace. Matilda held her breath as she stepped on to the polished wooden floor delicately, taking care not to slip on the glossy surface, and walked up to one of the armchairs. She rubbed her hand over the velvet cover, fingering the lace, while she continued to look around the splendid room in absolute awe. There was a table by the wall with another gramophone player on it and photographs of Lawyer's children displayed in frames. High on the wall above the gramophone, positioned so that he could smile down on anyone seated in the chairs, was a copy of one of the large studio photographs of Lawyer that she had seen in his office. The picture was browning with age, and although the frame had lost some of its lustre, it was magnificent.

The maid was laying a place at a huge table with several chairs, which stood behind one of the sofas; she placed the bowl upturned on top of the flat plate, then placed a glass, also upturned, next to the plate, and a spoon and fork on either side of the plate.

'Does Lawyer not eat with his hands?' Matilda asked, surprised.

'No!' she said, with her eyes growing in her head. 'I have never seen him eating with his hands. Madam says that is a sign of backwardness. They are all forbidden from using fingers.'

'What a shame. Our food tastes so nice with our fingers.'

She was staring at an odd-looking table with a stool in front of it. It had a sleek veneer and a small pile of books on top of it.

The maid said, 'Piano,' nodding sagely.

They returned to the kitchen, and Matilda noticed that the sun was setting rapidly, turning the sky dark grey momentarily before it plunged into full night.

As she walked home, she remembered that Uncle Saint John had a small set of cutlery, which no one ever used; she wondered how hard it would be to learn to eat with a knife and fork.

That night, Lawyer sent for her. Whenever he wanted her in the evening, he sent someone from his house to call her, sometimes, as on this occasion, late into the night. Her father knocked gently on the window of the girls' bedroom to wake her from her deep sleep, waking most of the household at the same time. She quickly and quietly prepared herself to go and see her husband, but by the time she walked into the yard, she was relieved to see that the only person there was the messenger, one of Lawyer's stable boys; she would have hated to see the look in her father's eyes as she went off to her husband's bed. She walked sleepily, longing for her mat and the warm old cloth in which she slept; hopefully, the visit would be short tonight.

When she walked into his room, Lawyer was standing by the gramophone. He smiled at her.

'I am listening to my new record fresh from London. Billie Holiday; here, listen to her voice,' he said, pointing at the machine. 'Almost drinkable. What do you think?'

She looked at him, bemused, as she listened to the wavy sounds from which a woman's voice, clear and confident, came with the sound of music that she had never heard before.

'Thank you for that food today. I enjoyed it immensely, but what I want to know is how you knew that palm-nut soup is my absolute favourite dish?' he said, as he walked towards her. 'But I do prefer it with rice balls; can you make that for me some time?'

She felt the tension in her shoulders ease slightly, and she smiled to herself. Aunty Dede was always right.

A few days passed, and Matilda went to Lawyer's house again to deliver some more food. When she got there, she was dismayed to see Julie sitting on the veranda outside the kitchen with her twin daughters.

She continued walking as assertively as she could. She smiled and said, 'Good afternoon, Sister Julie.'

'What do you want?'

'Pl— I am bringing some food for Lawyer.'

'And why exactly do you think that you need to do that? I am sure that you have better things to do with your time. Do you think that we cannot cook in this house?' Julie was glaring at her. 'And if you would be so kind, in future do not interfere with my maid. How dare you swan in here as if you are suddenly the madam of this house and tell her what to serve my husband for his dinner, contradicting my strict instructions?'

Matilda was frowning. 'I never told—'

'So now she is a liar? And no doubt I am a liar too. Esi—! Esi, come here now,' she shrieked.

'I never called you a liar.'

'Bernadette, come back here!' Her daughter had toddled up to Matilda to try and get her attention. 'Sylvia, you too, come and sit here.' Julie sounded irritated with her children, who appeared eager to play with Matilda. 'Esi.' Julie turned to speak to the maid who had appeared without the self-assured expression Matilda had seen her wearing previously. Esi stood with her hands behind her back, chewing the inside of her mouth and rubbing the sole of one bare foot on top of the other. 'Esi, she tells me that she did not ask you to serve her palm-nut soup to Lawyer the other day. I want to know who is lying to me.' She was forcibly restraining her daughters, who were beginning to whine loudly.

'Please, madam, Sister Matilda brought the palm-nut soup, and I thought that Lawyer had sent for it, so when I said did I not need to cook and she agreed with me, I did not want to waste the meat,' Esi said without taking a single breath between her words.

'You are my maid. Since when do you take instructions from anyone other than me? Let this be a lesson to you if don't want me to send you back to your village in disgrace. Do you understand me? Now get out of my sight.'

The maid scurried off without looking up. Matilda, realising that her mouth had been wide open for a while, shut it and gulped.

'Your food will not be needed here today. You can take it back to where it came from. If he wants food from you, he will let you know.' Julie waved her hand grandly and turned her back.

Matilda stood rooted and chewed her mouth especially loudly, but not loudly enough to get Julie's attention, and then she left. She kicked at stones when she could, feeling a little cheated. Well, if everyone at home ate at full capacity tonight, then this bean stew would not be wasted. Food was rarely superfluous in Saint John's house. They would be grateful – her uncle and father, her mother and aunts, her cousins – in particular with the amount of fish she had put in it.

And she had kept her fear quite well hidden, she thought. She had been a little insolent, ignoring the instinct to say 'please' when she spoke to the first wife, and she had kept her hands firmly by her sides, not behind her back as would have been more appropriate given their respective situations. This was progress indeed, she thought. People she passed on the road may well have thought she was mad, smiling like this to no one at all, but she did not care.

It was late one evening towards the end of the rainy season, which, although it did not bring a promise of regular rain, just an increased possibility, did occasionally bring some respite from the unremitting heat. But there had been few rains this year, and all around, the dry earth sprouted dehydrated brown growth, and the ground was dusty and crumbling. The sky was black, barely illuminated by the distant moon and feeble stars, and the warm air was still and filled with the noise of crickets and other night insects.

Robert and Matilda had been married for three months, and tonight he was entertaining a group of friends for dinner. The men, Silas Sackey (BA, Oxford) and Kofi Biney (LLB, Kings College, London) were, like Robert, the cream of the elite; highly educated barristers with many degrees between them, stars in their legal world, with status that they took for granted. And there was also Alan Turton, the one real Englishman, currently ADC to Sir Colin, the governor.

Mosquito coils burned silently under the men's seats on the veranda in an attempt to repel the dreaded pests, but every now and then, one of the men slapped some part of his body, killing a mosquito that was too blood-drunk to avoid sudden death, smearing insect and blood on himself in the process. They were eating a sumptuous meal, all of them perspiring copiously as their bodies attempted to cope with the onslaught of hot chilli food on a stifling night.

Robert had sent for Matilda the day before and told her what he wanted her to cook. This was nothing unusual, as he had begun to ask her for food regularly. Married life seemed to mean trips to the market and cooking meals for her husband, which she quickly began to find tedious. It was time-consuming; the coals took an age to reach the right temperature, and the stews he liked had to be simmered for

187

hours. But he praised her food and asked for more. And now, when they were alone, she could feel that he had gained a little weight, which made her proud. She began to tend his food even more diligently, never wandering off in case it burned. In the early evening, just when the sun was setting, before he was back from court, she would take the meal over to his house and leave it in the kitchen.

The first time she tentatively entered Julie's kitchen after she had been sent home with her bean stew, she found the maid alone. Esi looked sheepishly at her and then resumed her work without saying a word. Matilda placed the food on the table. 'Lawyer sent for this,' she said.

Esi was washing dishes in the sink with her back to Matilda. She began to speak quietly, as if to no one in particular: 'Madam is having a bath. This is the time of day she normally has her bath. So, in fact, this is the best time to bring Lawyer's food, because if the truth be known, he has been asking for your food in the evenings.'

But this time, Robert told her he was expecting guests and that he wanted her to serve the dinner. 'By the way,' he said, when she was about to leave his office, 'Julie has gone to her mother's house. I doubt she will return before she has had the baby.' He smiled and winked at her. She grinned back and left feeling quite joyous. She strode home, humming and singing her favourite song, 'Onward, Christian soldiers, marching as to war, with the cross of Jesus going on before . . .' All those apprehensions about serving food to his friends, those big, clever men, what she would wear, how she would comport herself, whether she would be a success, fears which she knew would no doubt impede her sleep, could be dealt with later. At that moment, there was a victory to be savoured, and a magnificent warm satisfaction to relish.

Matilda carried the food to the table on the veranda when she was ready. Spinach cooked in palm-oil with smoked fish, fried tilapia with homemade black pepper sauce, boiled rice and mashed yams. She did not want to interrupt their heated discussions and hoped that they would take no notice of her, that she could be as invisible as a maid, but each time she emerged from the kitchen, they stopped speaking and turned to look at her and the steaming platters she was carrying. She kept her eyes down to avoid all eye contact with them, but she could feel them staring at her. She tried to ignore their admiring looks, but it was impossible not to see how they watched her. She served them quietly, moving as unobtrusively as she could to place the dishes of rich food in front of them. Each time she retreated, they laughed and talked all at the same time, just like schoolboys.

Robert was enjoying the attention his young wife was receiving from his friends. He could only imagine their thoughts as they watched her move elegantly around. He was surprised how proud it made him to see how impressed they were.

'I must say that Matilda is a beauty, Robert. I can see why you picked her. But she must be young, a child still,' said Kofi, when Matilda had retreated to the kitchen once more.

'Young is good, well done,' said Silas.

'Thank you,' said Robert, laughing.

'I must say I do find all this rather perplexing,' said Alan.

'What?' asked Robert.

'That men like you believe in . . . well, in marrying more than one woman.'

'It is not just us men polygamy suits,' said Silas. 'I have three wives, and they'd like to keep it that way.'

'How can you think like that? You cannot seriously believe that women are happy to share their husbands? No woman *I* know would agree with you,' said Alan.

'That's because you only really *know* English women,' retorted Silas, thumping Alan on the back. The men laughed.

'The African family structure has always been non-nuclear,' said Robert.

'And we are not breaking any laws,' added Silas.

'Not yet . . .' said Alan.

'Why do you British want to legislate against our customs?' said Silas.

'For the same reason we got involved here in the first place. To enlighten the people, help them advance and that kind of thing, to share our civilisation.'

189

'Alan, your Victorian-style family life has no place here in Africa,' said Silas.

'Perhaps, but you imitate the Victorian lifestyle, and when the state takes a crack at reinforcing those same values, you balk. I am afraid it just doesn't add up.'

'Alan, Alan! You sound just like those female columnists in the *Gold Coast Times*; they think polygamy is a barrier to female progress. Take Matilda here, don't you think her prospects have been tremendously increased now she is Robert's wife?'

'Well, I can see why Alan is confused,' said Kofi, who had been watching his friends in silence. 'It is men like you who perpetuate the idea that a Christian marriage is the ultimate sign of refinement and elitism. You both had grand church weddings with your first wives, marking yourselves out as progressive Africans, whatever that might mean, then some years down the line, you decide to take subsequent wives in traditional marriages. No wonder Alan is confused. Why do you need to pretend to be an English gentleman when in reality you live like an African chief? I don't believe in mixing cultures; pick out enough threads from the fabric of our tradition and the whole thing will fall apart.'

'Well, the best of both worlds . . . isn't that what everyone is striving for these days?' asked Silas.

'And therewith you illustrate the grave danger this country is in,' said Kofi. 'Yes, our age-old tradition of having several wives at the same time serves to curb fornication and all its ills. Yes, our society is most unkind to women who produce bastards. Yes, we take a pragmatic view about the role of a wife, but you are not living up to these traditions. People like you are diluting our culture by adopting extreme Britishness. Why are we allowing them to persuade us to abandon our religion for theirs? Why allow the Church to interfere in our traditional affairs? Do you remember the trouble in the villages a few years ago when some churches required their members to divorce all their wives but one? Their narrow-minded stupidity left hundreds of women alone and unable to fend for themselves and their children. Who knows how many turned to prostitution and other vices to support themselves? Is that what you call civilisation? I call it denationalisation . . .'

'Well, there is no need for you chaps to have more than one wife, and yet you have three, Silas; Robert has two now. And on that note, I must say I am deeply offended that you did not think to invite me to your wedding, Robert,' said Alan. 'I might have missed my only chance to attend a polygamous marriage!'

'Ah well, you see, those events are saved for family. Robert wouldn't have wanted to inflict the boredom of the ceremony on you,' said Silas.

'Undoubtedly, she is very attractive, and a very good cook,' said Alan.

'You impress me with the way you eat our food,' said Kofi. 'Most of your compatriots never bother to dip into our world.'

'It took a while, but I'm now rather keen . . . It's a pity that I only get it when Robert is kind enough to think of me.'

'Maybe what we need to do is find Alan a local girl. What do you think Audrey would say? A second wife would do you the world of good. Wouldn't you agree, Robert?'

'Heavens, no,' said Alan. 'She hates it here enough already. I'm probably going to have to get on my knees to stop her from getting on the boat home.'

'Another mistake you English make,' said Silas, leaning forward to place his glass on the table so vigorously that he spilled his drink, although he did not seem to notice. 'Obedience! You do not require obedience from your women. You over-educate them and allow them to have opinions, and then you complain when they interfere in your affairs and neglect their domestic duties. God made women to have children, to raise them to be good citizens, and not to go about thinking.'

'True. Julie wants to be involved in every aspect of my life and thinks I need her point of view on every subject. Talk, talk, talk, that's all she wants. Matilda, on the other hand, is nice and compliant.'

'Do they get on?' asked Alan.

'No,' said Robert. 'I keep out of it.'

'Will you go back home if war breaks out as the papers are predicting?' asked Kofi, changing the subject.

'I hope not. Of course, I'll fight if I have to, but they're going to need to man the posts here. The colonies will continue to need governing.'

'Not necessarily by you,' said Kofi softly.

'Kofi, not that old self-government chestnut, it's far too late . . . Robert, we need another bottle,' said Silas.

Robert called Matilda, and she scurried out to the men, flustered.

'Oh, there you are. I thought you had fallen asleep,' Robert said, smiling. 'Bring us another. Look in the cupboard in the dining room.'

When she returned, she placed the unopened bottle in Robert's hand.

'Why don't you join us?' said Alan. He was looking at her with an intrigued expression.

The other men chuckled. 'Matilda doesn't speak English,' said Robert.

She smiled self-consciously and hurried back to the kitchen.

Robert handed the bottle to Silas. 'You are the oldest man here; you'd better do it.'

Silas walked to the edge of the veranda and poured the first few drops on to the dry ground. He mumbled words of honour before returning to his friends, who had remained in their seats, waiting to have their glasses refilled.

Their silence was punctuated by the odd sentence, and gentle laughs. The hum of the crickets seemed to become louder, and there was an occasional snort from one of the horses, who were also feeling the heat. As was typical in the evenings, the breeze had dropped, and the mosquito coils seemed to consume the little air that there was.

'So why won't your governor listen to our demands to reform the system of native administration?' asked Kofi.

'Well . . .' said Alan.

'Traditional rule is regressive,' said Kofi.

'I agree. We, the educated classes, are the natural successors to the British, not the chiefs,' said Robert.

'What makes you think that you represent the views of the uneducated masses?' asked Alan.

'Don't be daft, Alan. Of course we know what's best for this country,' said Silas.

'Well, I would hate to see things go wrong if independence comes too fast. And when we leave, as we inevitably have to one day, we want to leave friends behind.'

'We wouldn't even be in a position to fill the government secretarial posts with women who can speak English acceptably enough to answer the telephone, let alone send a telegram,' said Robert. 'What is the point in rushing to independence so that we can float aimlessly like a life raft that has been set loose from the mother ship without any passengers? I think more harm than good will come to this country if we forget that we have heaps to thank the British for: our concepts of justice, education, individual freedom, quite frankly, civilisation.'

'Civilisation?' exclaimed Kofi. 'You believe that we sat here waiting for them to teach us the meaning of civilisation? Maybe, if civilisation means eating with knives and forks, being able to speak English, wearing pith helmets in the sun and playing polo. But what about the ancient civilisations that existed in Africa long before the Europeans had emerged from their darkened caves? Your government needs to recognise that the sooner we start working together, the more chance we have of containing the extremists.'

'We mustn't allow the radical approach that demands immediate independence to intimidate us. I would not say the British way is better, but—'

'That is exactly what you are saying, Robert. It is their superiority, the loyalty that they expect from us, which you are happy to grant unquestioningly, that is holding us back.'

'Hang on a minute,' said Alan. 'You are being unfair. We have never sought to impose any sense of superiority over you . . .'

'No? Even though the white man has spent centuries teaching us skills he thinks we need, when in order to advance in our own country we have had to learn to read and write his language, and when gradually as a people we have come to believe that he knows better and therefore we have learned to accept instructions from him and we have lost our initiative and self-respect? Tell me, what other possible outcome is there than for the African, slowly but surely, to come to believe that the white man is superior to him? Yes, maybe those skills have helped us, and I concede, maybe they have even improved our lot, but now we actually believe that English is superior to our vernacular; we look to the whites for answers to all our problems. That cannot be right. It can't bode well for when they leave, as they no doubt will.' Kofi sounded breathless.

Robert spoke again, this time more softly: 'They have a lot to offer us. They have our interests at heart. I don't see that it would harm us to adopt some of their more civilised ways of thinking. You can't tell me that you don't see how ancestor worship is holding Africans back. No one will do anything before consulting the dead, the spirits, the fetish priest, you name it; it is really rather uncivilised . . .'

'And pouring libation like you always do? Isn't that to appease your spirits and ancestors?' said Alan.

'That is something entirely different. I am talking about the way we are caught up in the past and bound by a climate of fear and reprisals about what might happen to us if we don't oblige our dead ancestors. Our customs have made us far too fatalistic and reactionary to move forward.'

'Absolute rubbish! Just because you have chosen to abandon your traditions, your religion, even your way of dress, in favour of what you have been led to believe is a superior system, don't expect the entire nation or continent to follow suit.'

'Calm down, Kofi,' said Silas. 'Gosh, I had not realised how anti-white you became in London. Did you join the Communist party as well?' Silas laughed alone at his joke.

'I am not anti-white. I am simply not as wedded to them as you are. No offence intended, Alan. I just want to reclaim my country for my people.'

'And you are a revolutionary, too,' said Robert. The men laughed. '*I* like the British, and not because somewhere way back I have British ancestors – after all, many old Accra families can trace similar heritage. I admire their values, their sense of fair play, their sophistication, and as far as I can see, they are working towards self-government at a leisurely pace, which is fine with me. Cheers,' he said, lifting his glass. 'And God save the King.' They laughed and drained their glasses noisily.

*

In the kitchen, Matilda was struggling to concentrate on her chores. She was amazed at the fire in the men's voices, the passion in their hearts that was spilling out in this uncontrolled manner, in a style, quite frankly, more akin to an argument on the beach between an aggressive market woman and a fisherman determined to get a price for his catch that would justify his weary, aching limbs and would reward him for returning safely to land once more. She was impressed that men who disagreed so fundamentally could be friends like this.

That man Kofi seemed agitated. Before Alan arrived, she had heard him speaking in Ga in derisory terms about the English masters, their language, their culture and how the country would be so much better off once they had left. Perhaps it was only because he could speak the English language that he took it for granted in this careless way. Whenever she heard the crackling voices of the BBC broadcasters carried on waves from London, a faraway place that even her imagination could not conjure up, she would stop and listen to their incomprehensible but wonderful delivery, which to her sounded like soft rain, smooth and eloquent, a language that on its own seemed to make the speaker elegant, and which she knew paved the way to knowledge and understanding. How could this man not see that for now, at least, English held the key to learning, and without it, people like her were shut in the dark? Or did he think people like her deserved to stay where they were, unlearned, ignorant?

And why did he say he wanted the British to leave? They seemed to be the bringers of so many wonderful things; just look around this marvellous kitchen, all these contraptions that made Julie's life so much more straightforward, although, she had to admit, she had never ever spent this long cleaning up after cooking; at home, it took a few minutes to sweep up any coal that had spilled from the coal pot, and the kitchen, with its untreated cement floor, certainly never needed to be mopped.

Even though the British presence was so remote from her life, she was beginning to learn some of their wonderful ways from Robert, like their delectable habit of drinking tea; now whenever she was here and Julie was safely out of the way, she made herself a cup of milky, sweet tea, which she relished, feeling for a few moments what it would be like to be in charge of this house.

Eventually, she was confident that the kitchen sparkled as much as it had when she found it. She went to bid the men good night, anticipating sleep with delight, but Robert asked her to wait a while. His friends were leaving, he said, and he wanted to see her after they had gone.

Chapter Eleven

The summer months dragged Audrey towards winter. Though she could identify little distinction here between hot and cold, rain and dry, she still thought about time in terms of the seasons back in England. Like the climatic changes at home, things that she had taken for granted growing up had gradually gathered disproportionate relevance – the rain, the greenness, the long summer evenings and short winter days, the cool, the cold, the wet, crumpets and tea, the smells of England – her heart ached with longing for the sheer familiarity of it all.

Alan was settled at Government House. Leave was a distant, seemingly fading potential. Just behind her was another Christmas in the colony. Another hot festive season. A pantomime to support. Another series of drunken parties with the same old crowd, this year more withered, more browned, more wrinkled. Ahead, this afternoon in fact, a New Year's Day party at Frances and Brian's house. They were bent on making this event an annual affair. Audrey couldn't understand what Frances got out of endless entertaining. She was forever hosting some function or other. Sometimes, they were impromptu, but at other times, she had everything planned like a military operation, right down to matching food, flowers and napkins. She had been known to make a new set of napkins the night before to achieve that ideal look. And she never appeared flustered or bothered; she never moaned or grumbled. The praise for her perfect home and garden, fabulous food, her imagination and energy was only ever received with a demure smile and an 'Oh, it's nothing much, really' when everyone could see it must have taken her hours of planning and doing to achieve, when everyone could see her ill-disguised delight at having her handiwork applauded. Audrey couldn't bear her falseness and didn't understand why she was this way, even with her friends. It was what continued to keep her apart from them, this need to be something that from within she wasn't.

Audrey was not looking forward to the party. Her head hurt. She could not seem to wake up in any other state these days. Although she periodically resolved not to drink too much, somehow she rarely succeeded; she needed help to get past the memories that otherwise taunted her as she tried to fall asleep, the odours of that afternoon bottled in her mind and released periodically to sicken her.

And ever since Alan postponed her leave indefinitely, at some point in any social gathering, she was overwhelmed by a desire to drown the voices, blur the faces and to transport herself elsewhere. Increasingly, and she felt less guilty revealing this to herself, she hated seeing how happy Alan was at these events. She hated that he didn't know her well enough to see that something awful had happened to her and that his cheeriness was in direct conflict with her own misery. He was able to turn on the charm and joy whenever he was in public, whether or not his private sentiments were rather less jovial. At least he was enjoying his stint as ADC. Whatever it was, the next event in H.E.'s calendar dominated his world and therefore hers. He thought sharing morsels of his day was kind, but the details didn't enthuse Audrey, they only grated. And she begrudged having to experience life through his narratives over dinner, while their servants hovered and insects buzzed.

As they walked up the drive in the blazing sun, they were engulfed by a heady mix of perfectly blended sweet and exotic spices: cumin, coriander, ginger, fennel, nutmeg, ingredients that Audrey would not have recognised if they lay before her. Ahead, glasses chinked and guests chattered through hangovers. Today, Audrey craved buttery mashed potatoes and cold leftover turkey or goose, not curry. Not in this heat. Her arms were folded over her chest. She walked with her eyes on the ground to protect them from the piercing glare overhead but had to squint each time the sun caught the buckle on her sandals.

Beside her, Alan strode with his head up, his hair flopping engagingly over his crown. 'Feeling any better?'

'Yes,' she said, smiling weakly.

This morning over breakfast, he had suggested that she had had a little too much to drink, 'slightly more than usual,' he had added wryly. 'Perhaps you might stick to water or tonic today?' Audrey had tried to appear cheerful, she would receive no sympathy for her self-inflicted illness, but in her head, she screamed. She wanted to shake him and make him see what this place had done to her, was doing to her. How she felt out of control and angry all the time. And not only with the place, the servants, her life, but with him. For not being there when she needed him, for not seeing her sorrow, for postponing their leave. Can't you see? she screamed silently. Don't you care? Why don't you care? Occasionally, she wished she had ignored Polly's advice and told him what had happened when he first got back. Now, months on, the idea of deliberately recounting that event had become abhorrent. She had enough trouble banishing involuntary reminiscences of their whisky breath and raspy laughter from her thoughts.

Alan was whistling. 'Should be a great crowd today.'

'Yes, I'm sure.'

They entered the house, and she picked up a cocktail from the steward who stood rigid at the door. She tasted the blue drink, screwed up her face in disgust and disposed of her glass. Why wouldn't Frances stop all this experimenting? She stopped a passing steward and asked for a large gin. 'No tonic, just ice,' she said twice, quite slowly the second time. Better to be on the safe side, one never knew with these natives whether they simply misunderstood instructions or whether they were plain stubborn. She had formed definite ideas regarding her own crew, but Frances did seem to have the most superbly trained, well-groomed bunch in the entire place.

She turned round and saw that Alan was already engrossed in a conversation with someone whose name she could not remember.

Blood thumped behind her eyes; her head felt fuzzy. She was grateful for her drink and sipped it slowly. Make it last, she thought, I might as well try.

'Yoo-hoo, Audrey.'

Polly and Alice and other women from the club were waving her over. In the background, two maids in ill-fitting outfits carried chubby children on their hips; other small children played in the garden under the watchful eyes of their nannies.

Audrey finished her drink in one fortifying gulp and went to join them. Polly had remained an odd but essential friend. A few weeks after the incident, she had turned up one morning and insisted that Audrey come for lunch at the club, and over the din of the gathered ladies, Polly had encouraged her silently, while the lingering sensations and scents of that fateful afternoon plagued Audrey.

Alice had been a little surprised about this new friendship and hoped it wouldn't affect her close relationship with Audrey. Nevertheless, she was delighted that Audrey had finally come round to seeing things her way. She told Malcolm that her wonderful turnaround, her new calmness, had made all the months of effort worthwhile. 'And isn't it just marvellous for darling Alan that she has finally settled down?' she said, adding, 'I always said she simply needed time, I always knew she was a good egg really.'

Audrey stared at Frances's outfit, yet another creation probably put together last night amidst all the other preparations. It was a halter-neck dress with a deep cleavage, patterned with large blue roses, one neatly positioned over each breast.

'A new dress?' asked Audrey.

On anyone else its main features, that it was actually a little short and too big under the arms, would have detracted from its charm, but Frances could make anything look chic.

'I thought I ought to make some effort as Sir Colin and Lady S. are coming.'

'Oh,' said Audrey, suddenly flustered. She had miraculously managed to avoid seeing Lady Smythe after their chat, then after that horrible day, she had avoided all parties and gatherings, feigning illness so Alan had to go alone. Damn him! She had tried to get out of coming to the party, but he wouldn't hear of it. He said it would be rude to cry off because of a little hangover and told her everyone would be feeling the same way. She stood glumly on the fringe of the ladies' conversation, hearing disjointed sentences here and there.

'Is everything all right?' asked Alice.

'You haven't even got a drink,' said Frances, snapping her fingers at one of the stewards.

Audrey sighed. 'I don't want one.' She could feel tears fill her eyes.

'That's not like you. Are you sure you're all right?' asked Frances.

'Perhaps she simply doesn't fancy a drink, no need to make a song and dance about it,' said Polly forcefully.

When they were alone a few moments later, Polly gripped Audrey's elbow. 'You are probably tired of hearing this question, but *are* you all right?' She worried about her. She was clearly defeated by what those men had done; she had become thinner and faded. She was withdrawn and barely involved with what was happening around her.

'Yes,' said Audrey, her smile tired. 'Just not looking forward to seeing Lady Smythe.'

'Yes, best foot forward and all that,' said Polly, smiling. 'You probably only need more time,' she added gently. Audrey was staring ahead with her face improbably expressionless. Once again, Polly hoped she had done the right thing by convincing her to keep the incident from Alan and anyone else who might have helped her.

Just then, Frances clapped her hands like a schoolteacher seeking attention and hollered that lunch was ready. Guests quickly gravitated towards the table where Frances conducted them into two lines beginning at opposite ends of the table. With impressive symmetry, identical vessels of food had been set out on either side of an elaborate flower arrangement. First, mountains of plain white rice, then steaming vats of yellow curry stuffed with pieces of chicken and garden eggs, then the usual condiments: chunks of freshly chopped banana, salted peanuts, moist tomato and onion relish and peeled hard-boiled eggs. The guests piled their plates and ate heartily. The stewards circulated with glasses and bottles of lager, and a contended hush descended on the room while queasy stomachs and aching heads were soothed with the comforting carbohydrates.

Audrey stood alone next to a large potted palm on the edge of the veranda and tried to drown out the sound of excessively loud drunken laughter that only she seemed to notice. She closed her eyes and swallowed. She breathed rapidly through her nose as she had learned to in an attempt to steady herself while her senses were besieged by the nauseating smell of stale sweat, the sensation of salty sand in her hair. Thankfully, these days, the episodes passed quickly and discreetly, though they left her forehead damp and her face a little pale. She forced small amounts of soaked yellow rice into her mouth, wishing it was something else, that she was somewhere else. She had never had a curry in England and initially had been put off by the sickly yellow of the sauce. But she had had to learn to eat this spicy dish. Whenever they were invited out for Sunday lunch, and often after cricket matches or polo, she had to eat curry. Once, she had admitted to Alan that she did not particularly care for it, and he had laughed and said, 'How can you not like curry? It is food fit for gods, that's what it is.' She had tried to enjoy the meal with the same amount of relish that everyone else seemed to, but today she pushed the food around her plate. The sauce had yellowed the white china bowl and stained the boiled egg with a streaky tie-dye saffron pattern. She pulped cold banana between her tongue and the roof her mouth. As she stood there in the midst of her friends, her life in the colony, she grasped how she would never fit in. She did not even like their favourite meal, for goodness' sake. And for something as ridiculously unchangeable as her taste buds, she felt like an outsider. She abandoned her plate and went to find a drink.

Lady Smythe was pleased to hear Audrey was here. It had been months since she had seen her anywhere, and she had begun to worry that something sinister was amiss. Whenever she had enquired about Audrey over the past months, Alan had been keen to stress that she was just tired, a little off colour, simply exhausted, and Edith had imagined, hoped even for the girl's sake, that she was with child, which was how she preferred to refer to that biological state. She hated the word 'pregnant' and tried never to use it. She experienced a modicum of disappointment as she watched her now. If it was possible, Audrey had lost more weight, and her dress hung on her flat and empty, like it would on a hanger.

She walked up to Audrey, who was staring blankly into a glass. 'I am pleased to see you're out and about again, Audrey.'

Audrey returned Lady Smythe's gaze with sunken eyes. A sleep problem, thought Edith. And even that marvellous hair of hers looked rather weak and tired. A depression of sorts perhaps? 'You don't look very well.'

Audrey was caught unawares by this comment. No one else dared to comment on her appearance, even though she had dwindled in size so that fitting into her clothes was impossible, attempting to disguise her hipbones hopeless. Lady Smythe reminded Audrey of her old headmistress, and she found it difficult to think of her as anything other than a bully. She could see that look in her eyes now, the one that said, 'You can't hide anything from me.'

'What do you mean? I'm fine,' said Audrey defiantly.

'You don't look fine. I suppose the dysentery took its toll?'

'Yes,' said Audrey with a convincing sigh.

'And perhaps you are pining for home just a little?'

Despite her best intentions, Audrey's vision clouded slightly. She stared at her drink and willed the tears away. When would she stop feeling the need to blot out her sensations so regularly? She sipped her drink and wondered how to escape from Lady Smythe's penetrating gaze.

'I believe you are due to go on leave soon, are you not?'

'I wouldn't call "one day" soon,' said Audrey with a sharp laugh that startled even her.

Lady Smythe smiled, pleased that the girl's spark had not been entirely obliterated after all. If she can demonstrate such vehement irritation, she can demonstrate all the other necessary emotions, she thought. 'I will suggest to Colin that he allow Alan to take extended leave when you do go, make sure you have a good long rest so you come back fighting fit.'

Audrey nodded. She had given up hoping that she would go home. She thought the more desperate she was to go, the less likely it was to happen and so in her battle with fate had resolved to take the upper hand and try not to think about it at all. Then the outcome would matter less, she thought. Then there will be no one up there who can have the satisfaction of mocking me some more. But thoughts of home saddened her on days like today, when everything around her reminded her that she was not there: sunshine on New Year's Day, foreign food, black servants. She needed to go and have a proper drink by herself in peace and quiet. She excused herself without looking up at Lady Smythe, mumbling that she felt queasy and needed to go home.

She walked over to Alan. She tugged his shirt to get his attention. His eyes were glazing from too much food and too much drink. Hypocrite, she thought. She told him that she had a bad stomach and needed to go home to bed. He shrugged resignedly and turned back to continue his conversation.

As she walked home, she thought, The old Alan would have left the party with me, made sure I was fine. The old Alan. Did I send him away? Where did he go? She started to cry. And does he search for the old Audrey in vain, as I do too?

Chapter Twelve

Matilda noticed that she was increasingly running into Julie now that she had returned from her mother's house, with her baby sturdy enough to hold her head up. Julie, it seemed, had regained her strength, and no matter what time of day Matilda went there, the first wife happened to be lurking near the kitchen or on the veranda.

She tried her best to walk into Downing House with poise – Robert had decided that his house needed a name and that the name of his old college sounded just right. Well, the pastor at church said that if you persist in behaving as if something is true even when it isn't, eventually it becomes so. She hoped in time that this assurance would become her second skin.

It was then that Julie began to condemn her cooking. First, she attacked the amount of oil in it, although Robert had never complained. Matilda thought it wouldn't hurt to reduce the quantity of oil she used, so she did so. She claimed Robert had said the food was inedible one evening because of the amount of salt in it and that she had had to make him corned beef sandwiches for his dinner. Next, she said Robert was becoming bored with the lack of variety. 'Always the same heavy stews. Don't you know how to cook anything else?' she said.

One afternoon, Julie walked into the kitchen and peered into a deep pot of fried pork smothered in tomato gravy, which Matilda had just placed on the table, liberating a delightful aroma in the process. 'Don't you know that he doesn't like onions?' she asked angrily. 'Look at all those onions in the gravy. We cannot possibly serve this to him tonight.' And with that she tipped the food into the dustbin.

The maid, Esi, who had been hovering and pretending not to be there, gasped audibly. Matilda was rendered speechless. Never in her entire life had she seen food thrown away. There was always a grateful mouth somewhere in her house. What wickedness! And all her efforts wasted in vain. Now she would have to go home and prepare another dish. And it was too late for the market. She quickly ran through the remaining vegetables in the house.

'He keeps complaining about your food, and I thought it was time I took matters into my own hands rather than continue to listen to him bleating on,' Julie said matter-of-factly as she walked out of the kitchen.

Matilda felt her eyes sting. She remembered Aunty Dede's advice to her on her wedding day: 'Under no circumstances must you ever cry in front of the first wife; she will never be your friend, and it is fatal to cry in front of your enemies.' She was determined to follow that sound advice. She opened her eyes wide, pursed her lips and flared her nostrils. She would not let these tears continue to well up or fall in this house.

She resolved to cook as she always had; although it had to be said, she took even more care to ensure that Robert's food was always perfect. If Robert did not like her food, he would tell her. She was sure about that; he was not a man who measured his words, certainly not around women.

A few days later, she prepared him groundnut soup with chicken, which she knew he was going to share with some friends. She lingered over the preparation; instead of using pre-prepared groundnut paste, which was now available in the markets, she shelled and roasted whole groundnuts in a pan over the coal pot, gently, slowly, filling the compound with a hunger-inducing smell. Then she pounded the nuts with a pestle and mortar, adding a few drops of oil periodically until she had a smooth paste. She chopped and cooked an onion in a little more oil and then added several ripe tomatoes, which she had gingerly peeled. To this, she added her paste and enough water to make a soup, leaving it to simmer for a while before adding fresh chicken that she had cut into generous pieces. The soup bubbled for hours on the coal fire, releasing a divine fragrance. She was pleased with her efforts when she tasted the soup, and it was with great confidence that she delivered it to her husband's house.

When Robert summoned her late that night, she anticipated an amorous visit, but he was furious. 'What did you do to the food today? Are you angry with me, and this is your way of letting me know? It was inedible. Did you put a bucket of salt in it? I had guests tonight, and we could not eat the food; we had to send for *kenkey* and fish from the street.'

Matilda was aghast. She knew Julie was responsible for this fiasco. So, after all, that woman had succeeded in getting her into perfect trouble. 'The food was fine when I delivered it,' she said.

'Well, it was not fit for consumption. I am disappointed in you . . .'

'I am many things, but I am not forgetful. I swear that when I delivered the food, it was fine; when you ate it, it was not. I know you are busy and you may not wish to become embroiled in a petty problem between your wives, but I am sure even you can see for yourself what is happening.'

'Are you sure? Can it be that she is being childish?'

Matilda shrugged. 'For my part, I will try and make sure it never happens again.'

She walked home grinding her teeth, seething. That woman wanted all-out war, which was disconcerting. Matilda could imagine being disrespectful here and there, being insolent on occasion, being sullen and difficult even, but vengeful, merciless? That she would struggle with. She could not even easily kill an ant, how on earth would she find the necessary cruelty to retaliate, especially when her opposition was such a ruthless woman?

A few days later, the women met again. Matilda's courage sank when she saw the first wife standing on the veranda. The mere sight of this woman caused her spirit to groan. Julie greeted her cheerily, but

Matilda remained wary. Julie was wearing yet another dress that Matilda had never seen, and she wondered at her limitless wardrobe.

'Hello there, Matilda. How are you?' said Julie loudly, like someone projecting their voice from a stage.

'Fine, thank you,' she said quietly. The compound was full of people, and she did not want to be their public entertainment.

'So, have you still not conceived?' Julie asked, tutting sympathetically. Matilda gasped in shock. 'I really hope for your sake that it is not an unfixable problem that you have.' She spoke at the top of her voice still, but with a caring look on her face, and her head cocked slightly to one side.

Matilda took a deep breath and brushed past her into the kitchen, where she placed the hot pot of food next to the cooker. She leaned her hands on the kitchen surface to support her slouching body for a few moments. This time, she did not succeed in holding back her tears, and large drops began to gather in her eyes. But before she could release her emotions further, Albert came bounding into the kitchen chased by Edward, and the two boys collided into her and as usual seemed to knock her strains away.

She sniffed and smiled. She couldn't bring herself to dislike these children, who were, after all, the older siblings of her unborn children. When their mother was nowhere to be seen, she played with them and fed them with sweets she bought or made. Occasionally, she allowed them to help her make their favourite toffee with condensed milk and lots and lots of sugar in Julie's kitchen. They stirred and sang while the sugar mix turned brown, then wet and frothy and gradually hard. They salivated while she rolled the toffee into long strands, which she cut into bite-sized pieces. When it was cool, she wrapped it in brown paper and gave it to them.

'Aunty, Aunty, he has my train and won't give it back,' wailed Edward now.

Matilda quickly wiped her eyes and crouched down on her knees, blinking rapidly. 'Albert, please give the train back to Edward if it is his. Come on, be a good boy for me.'

'Only if you tell me a story first,' said Edward.

'Oh, yes! A story, a story.'

Soon, the boys were chanting in time. Matilda looked out into the yard to see where their mother was and saw her stepping into the car.

'All right, then,' she said, much to the delight of the boys, who were now pulling her hands and leading her into the living room.

'Promise to tell us a long story. Pleeease,' said Albert.

'Long story, long story,' repeated Edward.

She laughed and, shaking off any remaining doubts she had about sitting on Julie's beautiful furniture, sat comfortably on the sofa with one child on each knee, and she told them the story of a swindling spider who persistently tricked everyone whom he came into contact with, narrowly escaping with his life, as he travelled through the countryside from village to village, earning much wealth and several enemies along the way. The boys listened rapt, squealing with delight. She was just coming to the end of the story when they were interrupted by a loud scream coming from the kitchen, where someone had obviously been badly injured. She pushed the boys off and rushed to see what had happened, half expecting to see a pool of blood on the floor or something even worse. Esi was standing near the cooker with both her hands covering her mouth as if she was trying to still her screams.

'What has happened?' she asked, as she approached the maid.

'Yeeeh! I am dead. For sure, Madam will kill me now.'

She looked at what the maid was staring at. Her heart began to pound wildly. She grimaced and bit her lip. Then, unable to resist, she stretched her hand out to stroke the neat ring that her pan had singed into Julie's Formica.

'What is going on here?' Julie's voice bellowed in the stunned silence. She had returned before anyone in the room expected. When no one responded, she walked up to the cooker, pushed Esi aside and saw for herself what had caused the commotion. She screamed before instinctively lunging at her maid, who darted like an evasive firefly behind Matilda and out of her madam's grasp, causing Julie's hand to strike the top of Matilda's bare shoulder instead. The air of dismay that had previously filled the room was replaced by disbelief. Esi sloped out of the kitchen, aware that she would be better off not witnessing whatever happened next.

Matilda slowly lifted her hand to touch her stinging flesh and glared at Julie, who she thought might display some remorse or apology, but

Julie's face revealed only deep abhorrence. Matilda was stunned and angry, and irritated to find that faced with Julie's clear wrongdoing, she was the one who felt tongue-tied. She knew that within minutes of leaving this house she would be able to have the most lucid imaginary conversation that would put this woman firmly in her place. After long moments of reciprocated glaring, Matilda said softly, 'Don't. Ever. Touch. Me. Again.' Then she turned to the excited boys who had witnessed the whole spectacle. 'I promise I will finish the story next time I am here,' she said before striding out of the room.

She marched into Robert's office without knocking. He looked up, frowning, surprised to see her. She steadied herself; this conversation would be best if she could avoid watering it with tears.

'That woman has crossed the line. No one has ever slapped me apart from my mother and my aunty and my uncle and my cousin. She is not entitled to slap me, and I will not accept it. You must do something about it.'

'Slow down. Who hit you and why?'

'How should I know why? She alone knows why she behaves as she does. I would understand it if, God forbid, you as my husband decided you need to beat me for misbehaving, but she is not entitled simply because she is your wife.'

'Julie hit you? Why?'

'Because she is jealous of me. Because she cannot cook and you prefer my food. Because I am younger than her and they say that you prefer me. Because . . . I don't know what her reasons are,' she said. She realised where she was and took a deep breath. She lowered her voice a little and said, 'Please, I wanted to register my dissatisfaction with the situation. Please, you must speak to her, otherwise I will have to stop coming here . . .'

'Don't be ridiculous,' said Robert, walking towards her. 'How will I live without you . . . your delicious food? Ignore her . . .'

'Ignore her? How exactly am I supposed to ignore my husband's wife? You are the one who put us in this position of intimacy, so please, you have to deal with it.'

'My, my, where has this anger come from all of a sudden?'

'It has been building up inside here,' she said, pounding her chest. 'Every insult, every look, every laughter. I have not said anything to you apart from the time she put salt in your food. The other day, she even threw away the food, your pork and—'

'She what? That woman really has taken leave of her senses. I will deal with her. Come back tonight, I want to see you later. I have some work to finish now and you are too distracting. My pork, eh?'

It took her a number of days to calm down from the hitting episode. She told her mother, her aunts, her friend Patience, and all of them agreed that Julie had crossed over the boundary of acceptable behaviour, that it was Robert's duty to remedy the situation.

Patience shouted out loud when Matilda told her what had happened. 'My goodness gracious me! Who does she think she is? A queen?'

'That was my exact thought,' said Matilda.

'Anyway, this might be a blessing in disguise if it allows Lawyer to see her for what she really is, a snake under grass.'

'A poisonous, wicked snake.'

'Tell me again the part about how you walked into his office and told him that if he does not sort out his domestic problems, you will not step foot in his house again.'

'I said, "Mark my words, Robert, if you don't speak to your wife, I will not step foot in your house again under any circumstances."'

'And what did he say?'

'He said, "I cannot live without you. Leave it with me."'

'You see, there is some of your mother in you after all,' said Patience, glowing with pride for her friend.

Matilda did not see Julie for several weeks, which convinced her that Lawyer must have said something, taken the appropriate action. She was pleased, and wondered only why she had not involved him sooner. She began to walk with the self-possession of belonging, her head held higher and her shoulders back. She introduced herself with composure as Mrs Bannerman – yes, the lawyer's wife – and began to refer to him as 'my husband' rather than 'Lawyer'. It was with this newborn confidence that she walked into the compound at Robert's house one morning, and there, sitting on the veranda, in a dazzling dress made with baby pink and black lace, having a cup of tea with one of her friends, was the first Mrs Bannerman.

Matilda felt her heart descend. Instantly, her steps faltered as she moved awkwardly towards the kitchen.

'Oh look,' Julie said to her friend loud enough for Matilda and everyone else in the compound to hear, 'I see the cloth girl has put on a frock today.'

It was as if the entire cast of Robert's compound suddenly became the subject of a slowed-down motion picture. Matilda noticed the stable boys dawdle further over their already leisurely paced activities. The maid stopped playing with the baby and leaned her ear ever so slightly in the direction of Julie and her friend. The old man and woman who were as usual seated under the neem tree little by little turned their heads and fixed their unwavering gaze on Matilda's dress. Even the chickens seemed to stop clucking; in fact, it was only the dogs, ever dozy in the fierce heat, that seemed uninterested in her dress.

It was a dress she had implored Aunty Dede to make with fabric purchased using money Robert had given her for food, a fact that in itself was best kept shrouded. When Matilda had held the material up in front of her aunt, she had said, 'I have never seen a dress made with such material.'

'As soon as I saw it, I knew it would make a beautiful dress,' said Matilda. It had gigantic yellow roses and green foliage printed all over it, and it was soft and gentle, without the scratchiness of woven cloth or the stiffness of wax prints.

'But what do you need a new dress for? Is Lawyer taking you somewhere?'

'Julie wears a different dress every day and—'

'Ah, I see. Take my advice, a woman like Julie is best left in her own league. You will only wear yourself out if you try to match her.'

'I am not trying to compete. But so far my husband has not given me any additional money for my upkeep, yet I know that he expects me to look like his wife. How else am I to do that if I don't start to make new dresses?'

'Yes, but do they have to be European ones?'

Matilda shrugged and wrapped the fabric around her. 'So, are you going to help me or not?'

'I suppose I don't see the harm in it,' said Dede, who then set to work to make a dress. She commented how she had never sewn anything this short, this small, this fitted or this tight, but Matilda was inflexible about the design. It had short sleeves, a round neck, a tight waistband and a gathered skirt. It took two days of cutting and sewing, and when Matilda squeezed into the dress, she beamed. It was a little uncomfortable, but that was how European dresses looked; it must be simply a matter of getting used to it.

So while the compound silently awaited Julie's next words, Matilda pulled in her stomach, forced her chin up slightly and took fast, small steps shortened by the restrictive dress.

'It amazes me that some women don't realise what suits them. Look how ridiculous she looks in that dress, with bulges in all the wrong places. You would think that she would know to stick to her cloth costumes,' Julie continued. 'Once a cloth girl, always a cloth girl, don't you think?'

Matilda held on to her breath. She tried to drown out their laughter with her thoughts and to deflect the many eyes stinging the back of her neck. She breathed in and out rapidly, cursing her weak tear ducts. God forgive me for hating her, she thought to herself, and if this was the kind of behaviour that one learned in a finishing school, then it was indeed a misuse of money. She slid into the kitchen so she could hide her mortification. But she could not ignore the most painful fact, that she had felt the need to be sophisticated – like Julie, in fact. She stood in the kitchen pulling and shoving her dress, which was fitted closely around her ample buttocks and breasts. She heard Julie's voice from outside: 'I don't think she'll ever make a frock girl like us, do you?' and then more laughter.

When she got home, her mother screeched when she saw the dress. 'What sort of attention are you seeking? How could you go out of the house in a dress that looks like curtains? Have you forgotten your station in life?'

That evening, through bleary eyes, she cut the dress into small squares. She refused to think about how she would explain this waste to Aunty Dede and comforted herself with the fact that the household would have nice clean dusters for a long while yet.

Chapter Thirteen

When she had lived a full year in her married state without any sign of impending motherhood, Matilda knew she faced increasing pressure. 'What use are you if you cannot bring forth?' her mother kept asking. Although she had felt unprepared for children when she first married, she was ready now, and she often secretly wondered if Patience was right and she had cursed herself.

Things became critical when Ama found out that Julie was expecting yet another child, her sixth. She had dreaded her mother finding this out and had kept the news to herself for a while, but Julie was not one to suffer in silence, and her terrible morning sickness was quickly the talk of Robert's household. Soon everyone knew that the first wife was expecting again.

'What is wrong with you?' Ama said one morning. She was discussing the problem with Matilda and her aunts.

'Eh! Maybe somebody has cursed you,' Aunty Amele said fearfully.

'You know, it is true. I have been thinking for a while that we need to take matters into our own hands and deal with this problem before it is too late. His family may even decide that they have to replace you if you don't bring forth soon. They know he is not the problem. After all, he has fathered many children. The blame falls squarely on you,' said Ama.

'Number six? Well, I think we have to go and see the priest as soon as possible. We have delayed enough.' Aunty Amele had never hidden the fact that she was a regular visitor to the fetish priest, asking for solutions to every problem, physical or material, that she faced in life.

'Ma, please, I don't want to go to the juju man. The minister has told us that these are pagan rituals and that they are devil worship. Please don't make me go.' She knew the women believed in their right to harness the support of the spirit world to help them in their daily life and to maintain a healthy balance between the two worlds, but she was attempting to be a true convert to Christianity and wanted to leave the traditional practices behind her.

'Devil worship? What nonsense,' said Ama. 'That man has lost his mind. If he has chosen to forsake his tradition, he is doing so at his own peril. We are not going to go down that same road. When his family is suffering untold curses left and right, he will be the first to go and pour libations and ask the gods and ancestors to help him, but by then they too may have forsaken him in return.'

'It is true,' said Aunty Dede, nodding sagely. 'And if you don't have children, some of our ancestors who are waiting to come back to this life will not be able to. This is a serious matter that affects our entire family. It is not your problem alone.'

'As for me, I have never understood why going to the juju man with our problems should concern the Church,' said Aunty Amele. 'We go to church faithfully twice a week to worship the Almighty and pay Him His dues, but we also have to keep the spirits of our ancestors happy.'

'Listen, does the Bible not say, "Honour thy mother and thy father"? You will obey me. We will go and see the priest before dawn tomorrow,' Ama said, getting up to signal the end of the discussion.

Matilda was forlorn. How would she explain to Reverend Dankwa if he found out? He was a particularly fervent convert who some said was trying too hard to indoctrinate the younger members of the congregation to abandon their traditional beliefs. She realised most of the congregation, including every adult in her house apart from her father, regularly went to see the fetish priest for help in matters relating to health and wealth, and sometimes in order to extract a vengeful curse on an enemy, but she wanted to follow Reverend Dankwa's teachings; she believed the Bible and had been praying and fasting diligently for months now in the hope that she would fall pregnant. But month after month, she menstruated on schedule, and she had become increasingly downhearted recently. Her mother was right. It was only a matter of time before Robert's family decided that he had been duped into marrying a barren woman. If he abandoned her now, no one else would have her. Perhaps she owed it to them all to try the priest. She tossed and turned in her bed all night, thinking about the visit she had to make in the morning.

Aunty Dede woke her up before the cocks had crowed by shaking her violently and whispering for her to get dressed quickly. Soon Matilda, her mother and aunt were on their way to the fetish priest who lived in the Korle shrine, which was in a hut between the Korle Lagoon and the beach. It was dark and eerily quiet, the time of day when few living souls roamed about. They walked the fifteen-minute journey in silence.

Matilda was afraid; she had been raised with a healthy respect and a deep fear of the spirit world and as a girl had heard of countless wondrous and fearful things that the fetish priest could do. She could not recollect ever visiting the priest herself before, although her mother said she had been taken as a child when she had a terrible fever that did not abate after weeks of treatment. Her grandmother had feared that an unhappy ancestor wanted to claim her as payment for a debt, and so they had taken her to the priest for protection.

As the women approached the shrine, Matilda could hear the thunderous ocean crashing relentlessly on to the beach. The air was already warm and humid and tasted of salt. It was a Tuesday, the day Mami Wata, the water spirit that the fishermen believed inhabited the sea prohibited fishing, so the beach would be deserted. Those who claimed to have seen Mami Wata described her as a stunning fair-skinned mermaid-like creature with long, dark hair and com-pelling eyes. Matilda had heard that Mami Wata could bestow wealth but never fertility. She could not help wondering whether Mami Wata would interfere with the priest's work.

When the women reached the shrine, Aunty Dede called out,

'Wulomo, please, we have humbly come to ask for your healing and help in an important matter.'

'What do you bring?' The voice that responded from inside the hut was soft and gentle.

'Please, we bring offerings to the Korle fetish.'

'Come in.'

The women stepped inside the small, square hut, strung together with woven palm tree leaves, bits of string and pieces of wood. The floor, which was laid with palm tree leaves, crackled under their weight. A faint flickering flame from a small kerosene lamp hanging on a nail up high cast a hushed glow over the shrine. Matilda stayed behind her mother and aunt, rubbing her fingers hard into her palms. She could feel her knees trembling.

She looked around in wonderment. There were several feathers and other unidentifiable objects stuck or pinned to the woven walls. The juju man sat cross-legged in a shadowy corner of the room next to the shrine, as though he had been expecting them. He was old and skinny with a thick white beard and moustache and short white hair. He was wearing only a white cloth wrapped around his waist, and Matilda stared for a moment at the wiry white hair that grew all over his chest and stomach. He was wearing several talismans – beaded necklaces and bracelets – on his wrists, around his upper arms and his ankles. She looked at his face but could not make out his features in the murkiness. She could not see whether he had his eyes open or not, and if he was looking at them. The hut smelled of a mixture of old food and incense, and Matilda saw a rickety altar, where the remains of an offering still lay.

When the fetish priest acknowledged them with a nod, Aunty Dede moved forward and placed a bowl of food and a bottle of gin on the ground in front of him. Then she stepped back, and the women sat on their haunches facing the priest.

'Take, drink.' The priest pointed to a calabash of water that was on the ground next to him. Aunty Dede reached for it, took a sip, poured a few drops on the ground, then passed the calabash to Matilda, who was next to her. Each of the women did the same, a few drops of sustenance for them, and a few drops for the spirits.

'What do you want from the fetish today?'

217

'Wulomo, please, our daughter has waited for one year and has still not brought forth. We want to know what the problem is. Are the spirits unhappy with her? Has someone cursed her? Please, we beg you to tell us what to do so that she may bring forth many times quickly,' said Aunty Dede hurriedly.

Matilda startled and almost lost her balance when he suddenly looked at her with very wide-open eyes. He lowered his head and remained quiet for a few moments. Matilda peeked at the women on either side of her. They were staring ahead at the man and did not seem to notice her.

The priest raised his head and said quietly, 'Someone has cursed her.'

There was a sharp simultaneous intake of breath from the women. Ama covered her mouth to smother a cry. Matilda's mouth fell wide open. She breathed rapidly, continuous shallow breaths, which dried the cavity of her mouth.

'I see a serpent blocking the entrance to her womb.'

Matilda screamed and gripped her stomach in horror. She had a deep abhorrence of snakes, and even the image of one terrified her. She felt ill, and her eyes were wide like full moons.

The man spoke gently, looking at Matilda. 'My child. If you are determined and you do what I say, we can remove the serpent and you will bring forth soon. Don't worry, the fetish is more powerful than the evil spirit that has put that serpent there.'

'Yeeh! I told you that we should have come a long time ago,' Ama said, trembling.

'Take this and drink it twice a day – in the morning before you eat or drink anything, and at night before you sleep.' He handed a dark-coloured vial to Matilda, who took it with trembling hands and held it with a mixture of dread and concern. Then he handed her a terrifying-looking wooden carving, which was covered in whitish fluff, probably animal hair and feathers. 'Put this above your bed to ward the evil spirits away,' he said. 'And put this under your pillow to encourage the spirits of childbirth to come to you.' He gave her a little fertility doll with beads around its waist and neck.

She already had a fertility doll that had been given to her when she married. She wondered whether he had put a charm in this one.

'Wulomo, thank you, thank you. We are indebted to you,' Aunty Dede said. 'You must return in one week with a sacrifice. Don't bring the girl. She will bring forth within the year.'

The meeting was over. The women nodded respectfully and left the hut.

Outside, the sun was beginning to rise slowly over the grey ocean, tinting the sky orange. The sea looked dark and ominous; a rare storm was brewing, and the waves were monstrous.

'You see now?' Ama was using her hands animatedly. 'I am sure it is that woman. She hates Matilda. I wouldn't be surprised if she has poisoned Lawyer's family against us. Maybe they too think that Matilda is not good enough to be his wife. They pretend that they are so English with their tea and biscuits, yet they are the first to curse their enemies. You have to be very careful what you say and do in her presence. Do you hear?'

'Yes, Ma.' Matilda was reeling from the information about the serpent. Please may the gods let this potion work, she thought. She was sure she could feel a pain in her abdomen that had not been there when she woke up.

'Where is the medicine?' Aunty Dede had been unusually quiet since leaving the hut. 'Take it right now. You have not eaten anything today, and we cannot afford to waste any more time.'

'But I drank water in the shrine.'

'Ah yes, you are right. Well, don't forget to take it tonight. Don't misplace it. Keep it safe. And don't tell anyone about this, do you understand?'

Matilda struggled to keep up with the women, who were striding home purposefully; each with her own troubled thoughts.

For a week, for that is how long it lasted, Matilda diligently drank a little of the potion every morning and every evening. She needn't have worried that it might be repugnant. It was cloudy but tasteless. Following the priest's instructions, she put the amulet above her bed and placed the doll under her pillow. Her initial reservations about going to see the fetish priest had left her. She knew that the comparisons with Julie, soon to be a mother of six, would be relentless if she remained unfruitful. Again, she wondered what it was that one person needs with six children; she would be grateful with just one. She decided she would simply not mention it to any of her friends at church. And if they found out, she was sure they would understand.

At the end of the week, Aunty Dede and Ama returned to the fetish with a generous sacrifice, and the morning after, Matilda woke up before dawn with crippling stomach cramps. Initially, she thought it was her period, though it was not yet due. She wriggled on her mat, lying in different positions to try and ease the pain, but it got worse. Eventually, she was crying out in agony and woke up the other girls in the bedroom. Her mother and aunts came running in to see what was causing the palaver. She was writhing on the floor in pain and frothing at the mouth, and her eyes were disappearing into the back of her head.

'Matilda, Matilda. Wake up,' shouted Ama, who was kneeling beside her trying to wake her up from what must have looked like a trance. Aunty Amele had retreated to the furthest corner of the room along with the younger girls, terror in their eyes.

Several minutes must have passed. Then without warning, Matilda retched and vomited all over the floor, splattering her mother and aunt with a yellow, foul-smelling liquid. The pain receded, and she opened her eyes and started sobbing.

'Ma, I'm scared.' She gripped her mother's arm, still doubled over and holding her stomach with her other hand. 'The pain was terrible; I was sure I was going to die.'

'Come with me,' said Aunty Dede, taking charge and pulling Matilda out of the room by the arm. 'Everything will be fine. Let us go and clean you up and you will feel better. Eunice, start cleaning this mess up straightaway. Don't mention this to anyone. If I hear that any of you has spoken about this, I will beat you well and proper. Do you understand me?'

Matilda was too bewildered to object to being bathed like a child by her mother and aunt, who seemed unfazed by what had just happened; she stood submissively as they sponged and rinsed her quivering body.

'This is what the priest told us would happen,' said Ama calmly as she scrubbed her daughter aggressively, as if there was some layer of

220

uncleanness on her that she could not remove. 'The potion has removed the spirit that was blocking the entrance to your womb and now you can fall pregnant.' Matilda looked at her mother quizzically, but Ama had squeezed her lips and looked stern.

She spent the rest of the morning sitting on a stool in the yard watching the other women cooking. She rejected a bowl of corn porridge, specially sweetened for her, ignoring her aunt's pleas to eat something, and just sat, picking constantly at the skin around her fingernails, trembling every now and then as if she had a chill. She thought fearfully of what had been living in her body and how it had got there. Her tired eyes stung in the sunlight, but she did not want to go into the dark, lonely bedroom to sleep, preferring to stay in the yard with the others but sitting on her own, silent and dazed. And in spite of her thorough wash, she continued all day to smell lingering traces of a rancid aroma around her. She thought about going to put some perfume on to disguise the smell, but she looked at the bedroom, which looked murky from where she sat, and she changed her mind.

The first time she went to church after the fit, she prayed to God for forgiveness and for protection from evil spirits and begged Him once more for a child. Then she tried not to think again about what had happened. Over the following weeks, she succeeded in keeping herself busy during the day with her duties as wife and daughter. However, when evening approached and the sun descended, she became wary and increasingly anxious of the time when the house would become engulfed in dark silence, and once again, she would find herself on her mat, forlorn and troubled, unable to sleep.

But the weeks passed, and she was amazed one day when she realised that she had not had a period for a while. She eagerly looked for and found the signs she had heard about: the sickness, the tender breasts, the fatigue. When she was certain, she told the women. That night, there was much jubilation in the Lamptey household.

As soon as he had been given the good news, Saint John mobilised efforts to clear out a room in the house, which until now had been used as the storeroom. Robert sent his wife a new bed and a chest of drawers made from mahogany. Her relatives stood astonished as the new furniture was carried into the yard and installed in her room. Aunty Amele stood, open-mouthed, rubbing the carved headboard and admiring the sprung mattress, while Matilda's sisters sat on the bed and bounced their bottoms up and down laughing, amazed that their big sister would sleep in something so soft.

'You can come and sleep in it with me sometimes,' she said, patting Celestina on the head, chuckling when the child bounced even harder at the thought.

It seemed to Matilda as if the first months of her pregnancy passed painfully slowly. She filled her time and her head with advice from her mother, aunts and anyone else who would share of their reproductive success, and she followed all the guidance unquestioningly. She forced her stomach out long before it was ready and often rubbed or held her belly protectively, trying to show the outside world that she too was growing a life inside her, that she too would soon be a mother, and she blossomed, gaining a considerable amount of weight, which pleased them all.

She managed to avoid going to see Robert in the early stages of her pregnancy, because she wanted to avoid any unnecessary harm to her baby. So she developed extreme morning sickness at all hours of the day and night, especially when he sent for her, so that by the time he next saw her, her naked belly was proudly bloated with confident new life. He asked gently if she was well, then he was silent. But she could see he was proud of her and their unborn child, and pleased, possibly even grateful, that things had resolved themselves so perfectly, because later when they lay side by side, he placed a hand on her hard stomach and, with his eyes closed, smiled to himself like a person giving thanks.

The women assured her that she would find giving birth easy. 'You have got big hips; the kind that are meant to bring forth,' Ama said. How she enjoyed these months when the women of the house pampered and fed her constantly. Such pleasure she derived from their collective protectiveness. The few errands that she had been sent on from time to time after her marriage ceased altogether, and during the last stretch of her term, they prohibited her from paying amorous visits to Robert. She hardly ever saw him, even when she delivered food he had requested, and realised again what an advantage her rival had over her. 'Spend not all your time in complaining and grumbling' was this month's message at church. She, like everyone on the pews, had nodded vigorously in agreement with the minister, but here, facing her first opportunity to put that message into practice, she failed. Was it actually possible to be good? she wondered.

She had often dreamed of the moment but did not recognise her labour when it started. She awoke early one morning to go to the lavatory, but before she could get there, she felt a warm wetness trickle down her legs. She rushed to the latrine before she could embarrass herself any further. On the way back to her room, she felt the urge to go to the toilet again. Once more, before she could get there, she wet herself. In a panic, she went to find her mother, thinking that something had happened to allow the baby's life to seep out of her like this.

'Ah, Matilda. Your time has come,' replied her mother, smiling.

'But I don't feel any pain,' she said, joyous and fearful in equal measures.

'Don't be impatient. It will come. For sure, it will come,' Ama said, as she started to gather things they would need for the birth.

The pain came. It built up over the course of the morning, slowly at first, until in the early afternoon, each time a contraction began to rise, shrinking her stomach into a tight rock and compressing her baby, Matilda held her breath, closed her eyes and concentrated on it, praying that it would pass quickly. The contractions became fierce; each sharp tightening spreading like a wave from the base of her womb to the top of her distended belly, where what felt like two great hands pressed down as if determined to squeeze her baby out. The baby seemed to respond and started bearing down on her with increased intensity.

It became clear to the women that the time had come. The women, who had been going in and out of the room where Matilda was now writhing on a mat on the floor, settled down to remain by her side. She tried to make sense of the increased activity in the room, aware that Aunty Dede was giving short, sharp orders, but everything seemed hazy, and the voices she heard were muffled and slowed, like people talking underwater.

Her naked body glistened; rivulets of sweat ran down her face, stinging her eyes and salting her tongue. There was no air, no coolness left in the room. Her pupils dilated. She panted like a hunted animal and groaned like one already dying. Yet in between the most intense, and now nearly constant, contractions, she was overwhelmed by the desire to sleep and allowed her eyelids to droop heavily in search of peace from her ceaseless ordeal. Aunty Dede shouted, 'The baby is ready to come out. You must get up and push now.' When she did not respond, Aunty Dede shouted louder and shook her. 'Matilda, you must push this baby out. Right now! Do you hear me? This baby needs to be born.' The others also uttered encouragement, until eventually, pulling and shoving, they managed to persuade her into a squatting position, with Ama gripping one of her arms and Aunty Amele the other.

But Matilda held on to her baby. For as long as she could, she held on, fearing that if she gave in to these urges to push, she would expel her entire insides on to the floor. Eventually, however, she had to obey her body's overriding desires, and after a few strenuous pushes, Aunty Dede held out her skilful hands to catch the slippery baby. Then she announced, 'You have a son. Well done.'

The women helped her to sit on her sore bottom and handed her screaming son to her. She took him uncertainly, looked at him and cried; this was her own baby, and he was a boy. She held his slimy body against hers while she wept and he wailed, flaying his arms in confusion, tensing his whole body and swelling his stomach with each tremulous cry.

'You must hold him properly,' said Aunty Dede, shoving the baby firmly towards Matilda's chest. 'He is bewildered by all this space, hold him tight.' And amazingly, the baby stopped crying soon after his mother held him as securely as he must have felt inside her.

She looked at him again. He was breathtaking. Warm and soft, like freshly baked bread, his skin was velvety, like dark cocoa paste. His head was long and covered with hair, which was stuck to his head like wet cotton wool. He opened his swollen eyelids and blinked at his mother with large black lashless eyes, revealing irises that were marbled with red streaks from straining to be born. She lifted his body up

224

to meet her face and breathed him in. He smelled vibrant, of smells that she had never smelled before.

Reluctantly, she gave him up to be bathed and dressed, feeling distinctly uncomfortable at being separated from him. But Ama had to wake her up when she returned after a while with the baby, who was now clean and hungry.

Ama sat and patiently taught her how to feed him until eventually she said, 'That's it. You are doing it the right way now. Look how hungry he is.'

She looked at her mother and smiled. 'Thank you,' she whispered.

'I am only doing my duty. After all, have you not given me a grandson now? Anyway, well done,' she said quietly, as she walked out of the room, leaving Matilda alone with her son for the first time.

After a short feed, the baby fell asleep, exhausted by his journey. She sat and stared at him. She uncurled his clasped fist and placed one of her fingers in his palm. Spontaneously, he clutched her, glad to have something to hold on to. She was impressed that he had so much hair and looked so much like his father. She kissed his soft, creaseless lips that looked as if they had been drawn by a master artist and marvelled at what she had brought into the world, wondering was it sinful to take some of the credit for this perfect humbling creation?

Her father came and sat with her when the commotion had died down, when there was no one else in her room. He admired his grandchild from a distance for a while. Then he showed her his diary, and there underneath the date, 13 March 1939, was his indecipherable scrawl. He chuckled and then, after taking one more look at the baby, walked back to his favourite spot in the shade.

When Robert's family heard that his second wife had finally had a baby, they hurried to congratulate her and brought lavish presents: clothes for the baby and bottles of rum and gin for the birth attendants. The main gift-bearer was Aunty Baby, who had not been to Saint John's house since the wedding ceremony. She handed a piece of cloth to Matilda and said, 'This is Lawyer's cloth. He said you should use it to make a pillow for the baby.'

Matilda glowed with pride, aware this was the right way, the traditional way, for Robert to publicly acknowledge the child as his.

For the first full seven days of his life, her son remained nameless and hidden from the outside world. It was unthinkable to her that she should expose her unnamed, unprotected child to the world before the right time. Instead, she remained indoors being looked after by the women of the house, who anticipated and provided for her every wish. Her only job was to breastfeed her baby whenever he cried, which she did willingly, installed in her room, often watched over by her sisters and cousins, who were overjoyed at becoming aunties so young. They rehearsed their titles, calling each other Aunty Celestina, Aunty Eunice, Aunty Pearl and so on, savouring this new indication of their progression up the family ladder, while Matilda smiled, never once taking her hawk eyes off the hands that hovered constantly around her precious baby.

On the eighth morning of the baby's life, Matilda's mother woke her from a deep sleep while it was yet dark and the neighbourhood was quiet. Even in her drowsy state, her heart ached with joy and thanksgiving that this day had finally arrived, grateful that her son would not have to leave this world unnamed and relieved that he had proved that he was not merely passing by but was here to stay. Today, he would be presented to the extended family to be named and protected in an out-dooring ceremony.

In hushed tones, the Lampteys dressed themselves in new white outfits. Matilda wore a special dress made for her by Aunty Dede with some of the fabric that had been used for her wedding dress, and the baby was swaddled in cloths and wrapped in a piece of the same white material.

They were gathering like ghosts in the compound when a loud knock reverberated in the dark and a woman's voice called, 'We are here to fetch the baby.'

Uncle Saint John opened the door to Aunty Baby and one of Robert's male cousins, who had come to escort the baby to its father's house. They poured libation at the step of Saint John's house in thanksgiving before they entered, bestowing smiles and hushed congratulations. Then the group walked to Lawyer's house, Matilda treading carefully in the shadows with the baby in her arms.

226

She was grateful that Julie would not be there this morning. A few nights ago, Ama had relayed to her family how she had courageously told Robert that his first wife was not welcome at the ceremony. 'I told him, "Lawyer, no offence intended, but we don't want any unnecessary curses upon our grandchild. I am sure that you understand our predicament, so if you don't mind, please, only blood relations are welcome." And he could not answer me,' she had said, using elaborate gestures, which confirmed to Matilda that her mother had not spoken to Robert in quite this intrepid manner. But she was immeasurably pleased that someone had remembered to exclude the scheming first wife from her baby's special day, that today she could publicly enjoy her place as Robert's wife, and in his house too.

At Downing House, Robert and the Bannerman family elders were also dressed in bright white cotton. Uncle Theophilus took the baby from Matilda and unwrapped him, while the families formed a circle round him. Then he lifted the naked baby towards the black sky, where stars were still flickering strongly, and said, 'This is the precious guest who has come to us; we are showing him to the heavens.' He lowered the crying baby until his back touched the hard ground and said, 'We show this precious guest to the earth; may he stay here for myriad years.' Three times he raised and lowered the baby in this way, each time repeating the same words.

Mr Peace Nii Aryee Ayitey, the new head of the Lamptey family, was standing next to Uncle Theophilus holding two calabashes, one filled with water and the other corn wine. He held them out to Uncle Theophilus, who dipped his index finger in the calabash of water and put a drop in the baby's mouth. Then, as he put a drop of corn wine in the baby's mouth, he said vigorously, 'If it is water, let it be water. If it is schnapps, let it be schnapps. May this child's "yes" be "yes" and his "no" be "no". Amen!'

Peace Nii Aryee turned to the parents and said, 'What name have you decided for this baby? Nii Aryee sounds good to me.' And everyone started laughing.

'In accordance with the naming pattern of our family, his name will be Nii Kwate,' said Uncle Theophilus, 'and his Christian name will be William.'

227

The gathered family murmured approval, and Uncle Theophilus, still holding William, started the traditional prayers.

> We call on the gods and ancestors to pour their blessings upon us!
> We have formed a circle around this new child to keep him here!
> May he be pleased to dwell among us and never look back from where he came!
> Protect him from evil spirits and curses, and let many offspring come and join him!
> May he be obedient, respectful, honest and honourable!
> May his family be in a position to raise him well, and may he be a blessing to us all!

'Amen,' responded the family solemnly.

Then, while Robert looked on with a stony face and clenched jaws, Uncle Theophilus slaughtered a goat expertly in front of the families and ensured that enough fresh blood spilled into the dry earth to keep all the many ancestors of the Bannerman and Lamptey families happy for a long time.

Cocks crowed, and the sun rose in the red sky, warming the air. Many relatives and friends began to arrive and were ushered towards benches that had been laid out in the compound under canopies erected to protect them from the blistering heat that would otherwise pour down on them later in the day.

Uncle Theophilus took the baby from his mother, interrupting his feed, and said to the guests, 'Welcome, welcome, friends and well-wishers. I present Nii Kwate William Bannerman to you. We welcome him into our family.' The guests clapped and cheered, smiling benevolently at Matilda and Robert. Patience waved to her friend from the back of the crowd, and Matilda smiled. 'Please God, give her also a baby,' she prayed. Now she thought nothing worse than a woman having to endure life without the joy of motherhood.

A few calabashes of corn wine were passed among the guests. Each person took a sip and said the baby's name out loud before passing the calabash on to the next person. Then gifts for the baby, mainly money, were presented and announced loudly by Uncle Theophilus to the rapturous applause of the guests. The crowd applauded more enthusiastically when a particularly generous gift was announced, causing the proud giver to smile and nod in acknowledgement with bogus humility. Then the guests sat chatting well into the day; no one seemed to have to rush to anywhere in particular, and they looked comfortable, as if they were prepared to remain indefinitely to take advantage of the generous hospitality of Lawyer Bannerman.

Chapter Fourteen

By the time they received the letter, Audrey had allowed the joyous anticipation of her impending leave to creep into every breath and every thought. Finally, a date had been set, only a few months away, and Alan had promised that it would not be postponed again. Unhappy memories plagued her less now, and she had learned to cope with them when they did so that they lessened their hold on her mind. Instead images of home flooded her waking mind and effervesced into sparkling eyes and a pleasant countenance. The servants noticed it. Alan came home earlier and left for work later. He even brought her flowers once. A bunch of yellow roses, tall-stemmed and tight-budded. She excused herself quickly and went to the bathroom to cry. She emerged with swollen eyes, which she was grateful he ignored. Good old Alan.

At night, long after she should have been asleep, she planned how she would tell him as soon as they were on the boat that she would not be returning. Or should she let him enjoy the trip and then tell him once they landed at Liverpool? But that would make their stay with his mother awkward. Perhaps when they were at her parents' house? She tussled with the options even deep into sleep, and in the morning her plan was no more certain.

In all this, there was one thing to be pleased about. She had managed not to confide in anyone else, so no one had to know about the devastating humiliation she had suffered. She could think of nothing worse than being pitied now by her friends. Their sympathy would have made things much, much worse, life here truly unbearable.

Then the letter arrived. It was late March, and Alan returned from work in an ebullient mood. He ran up the steps with more energy than seemed right at the end of a working day in the Tropics. He ordered two large gins from Awuni. He seemed not to mind Audrey having the odd gin at home since she appeared to be making some effort to comply with his suggestions about her drinking. And in return Audrey was careful not to drink enthusiastically in front of him.

He stood beside her and put his arm round her shoulders. 'You'll never guess what.' He looked pleased with himself, more pleased than she had seen him for a while.

Audrey felt the heat from his body where their skins touched through thin fabric. Her stomach tightened, and joy bubbled up into her throat. Leave. England. ADC back. In random order, the components of her greatest wish flashed behind her eyes.

'It's Mummy.'

'What?' She coughed gin through her nose, and a lump of ice slid painfully down her throat.

He was grinning at her. 'Mummy's coming to visit.'

The incredulity stunned her. She felt blood rush to her head, and she tightened her fingers around her glass. 'What?' It was barely a whisper.

'I know. I was shocked too.' He was smiling.

Why was he smiling, for God's sake? She drained her glass.

'I got a letter in the mailbag today. She says she cannot sustain her curiosity any longer, and since we seem bent on not issuing an invitation, she has invited herself to visit us for a few months.'

'Months?' The word escaped like a near-strangled cry.

'I know. It's amazing, isn't it? That she would want to sail out to Africa on her own at her age. She really *is* tremendous, my mother.' He was clearly amused, delighted even.

'When?' Audrey steeled herself, wondering how much time she had to foil her mother-in-law's visit.

'Now, that is the most incredible thing of all,' he said, chuckling.

She detected a faint quiver in his voice. Nerves? Excitement?

231

'She set sail last week!'

Audrey drew breath sharply. A faint moan escaped her lips, which only she heard.

Alan was still laughing. 'I can't believe it,' he was saying over and over while he swirled his gin, clinking and clanking the fast-melting ice against his glass.

Audrey wanted to shake him out of his trance-like state. Why the devil did he think this crisis was amusing? His mother here? And what the hell did 'a few months' mean exactly? What about their leave? She looked at him standing proudly, legs apart and shoulders back, and in that moment, she was engulfed by intense irritation that he was thriving in this place like a plant in its natural habitat.

'Audrey?' He was looking at her quizzically. The fear on her face reduced his joy. 'Are you all right, darling?'

'Fine. Fine. A little taken aback, that's all.' She thought, You think it is funny that your bloody mother is coming here for 'a few months'. My goodness, how little you know me, and I you.

Audrey knew his mother from one brief visit to her house after their wedding. She had fussed over Alan interminably and quizzed Audrey relentlessly about the most obscure things relating to her family. Where they came from originally, whether there were any doctors in the family and whether her childhood had been happy, to which Audrey had wanted to respond, 'That is absolutely none of your business.' And children. She wanted her darling Audrey, as she referred to her, to go ahead and procreate as soon as possible, for nothing, she repeated the word slowly with passion, 'nothing comes close to the joy of giving birth to new life'. She had had five children, and Alan was her baby, which she emphasised by patting him on his hand. It irritated and embarrassed Audrey that her husband allowed his mother to treat him in this way. Audrey had smiled, relieved that tea and cake with her mother-in-law would be a rare treat.

But his mother's formidable character stretched over the ocean and remained a silent presence in their marriage. She was redoubtable, a woman whose determination and courage after early widowhood had influenced her son, and he adored her. She sounded as energetic as him, if not more, and considered hard work an absolute necessity for each and every one of God's creatures. Alan

232

often recounted how his mother believed that, if remotely possible, whether by reason of position or privilege, one must serve others – and she had been successful in imparting this wisdom to her own children – one son was a vicar, one a doctor – and of course he was doing his bit for the Empire here in a place that no one in his family could possibly have located on a map without some help. Audrey knew his mother lived by this belief, and even now, at her ripe age of fifty-something, she was indispensable in her parish. If her mother-in-law could see how she spent her days, she would most certainly be horrified. Her dread deepened to complete panic. Who would have to entertain her all day long while Alan was at work for those endless, hot hours? Would she cope with the heat? What on earth would she think of how Audrey ran her house, her life? God! There would be nowhere to escape from the woman. She sighed loudly. 'She's on her way, you say?' she said, hoping against hope that she had misheard him.

'Yes, the boat docks in a few days. My, my, I wonder what she'll make of all this.'

'Awuni, Awuni!' Audrey screamed his name with unprecedented violence, startling Alan.

When the man appeared, grinning as usual, Audrey barked at him to bring her a very large gin.

When Alan's mother arrived in the Gold Coast a week later, Audrey feigned illness and sent Alan alone to pick her up. And when Violet Turton alighted from the car on to the front drive, Audrey clasped her hand to her mouth in shock and quickly pretended she was wiping her face. She had only ever seen her mother-in-law dressed in tweed skirts and delicate knitted jumpers, but the woman was dressed in a long khaki skirt that reached her ankles and a long-sleeved white blouse, fastened under her chin and at her wrists. And she wore laced-up walking boots. She emerged brimming and flushed a delicate pink. She clasped Audrey, oblivious to the fact that her blouse was streaked with dirt and clinging to her like a damp rag.

'Oh, this is enchanting, Alan. Audrey, it's wonderful. I thought it would be. I knew you were keeping me from your little paradise. How delightful.'

Audrey had to restrain herself from laughing. What was delightful? It had not rained for months. The temperatures were soaring in the hottest season, and rain was months away. The gardener could not keep up with the water requirements of the plants; the earth was too parched for moisture to permeate, and when he watered the plants, it simply trickled down every slope and incline in the garden. Most of the grass had died, revealing only more red-and-brown dusty soil. Everywhere, green leaves were hidden behind dust and dirt. Audrey had asked the gardener on several occasions to wash the leaves by watering the plants from a height, like rain. She wanted her garden to look clean, and she thought it might sustain their production of chlorophyll, help maintain their lush greenness; she needed her garden to be green. Hassan had grinned at her, bemused, when she demonstrated what she wanted, but whenever she emerged in the mornings and he had finished for the day, she noticed that he had not followed her instructions. Audrey was beginning to wonder what he did with his time. After all, the garden at the club had not deteriorated like this. Now most of her shrubs were withering, and the flowers they produced quickly wilted and drooped. Thankfully, the large trees were fine, tapping into deep underground reserves that had not yet run dry.

'And you, Audrey . . . Look at you, my dear. You look fantastic. A little thin perhaps, but otherwise so healthy, both of you. This place obviously agrees with you.'

Audrey half-smiled and walked up the steps behind her husband and his mother, her heart heavy like a rock. But she had resolved to make a big effort. Not let the side down and all that. She knew that Alan's mother had struck up a rapport of sorts with her parents, and she feared the account Violet would issue when she returned.

Audrey had heard from Alice that there was a Syrian man who was trying to rear dairy cows several miles from Accra who sometimes had fresh cream as well as fresh milk. She thought an excursion to buy cream would be a wonderful way to fill one day with Violet.

They set off with the driver, Samson. Soon, they had left the sprawling settlements that made up the city and were travelling east along a narrow tarmacked road by the sea. Violet marvelled at everything. Looking out of the same window, Audrey tried and failed to see anything lovely. She remembered family picnics with her parents as a teenager, when she had wished she had a sibling to share the heavy tediousness that had become family time. She knew she looked sullen, but behind the shelter of her sunglasses, she didn't care.

As they passed through a small village with thatched mud huts, where naked children frolicked by the roadside while mothers sat on rickety benches and sold produce from their vegetable gardens, Violet made the driver stop. The villagers could not believe their luck as this woman walked among them smiling and chatting in a familiar tongue that they could not comprehend. 'Oh, they are charming, are they not, Audrey?' Violet asked over and over again. Audrey grimaced. It was not an adjective that leaped into her mind when she beheld the scene. She intensified her surly look to ward off the children. She did not want to be prodded and poked in a manner that Violet seemed to enjoy, and she was flabbergasted when Violet picked up a toddler who had been crawling in the mud utterly naked bar a chain of beads around her waist. The child was snotty, and her hands were grubby, but she was a smiley little thing, and she grabbed and pulled at Violet's hat while she cooed at her. 'Enchanting child,' she said to Audrey, who asked herself what diseases this child might impart. In the end, they bought some green oranges and a tuber of yam from the women and left amidst a resonating farewell. 'Oh, how wonderfully happy they all seem,' said Violet, shaking her head as once again the car filled with the pull of draught. 'They really do have so little, but how content they are, how satisfied. It's joyous to see. A real lesson to us all, what, Audrey?'

They reached the farm, but as soon as Audrey saw the cows, a few dejected-looking things with hipbones sticking out painfully and their tails swishing ceaselessly to thrash away flies, she wanted to turn back. Dairy cows were supposed to be fat and healthy. Black and white with large pink udders, chewing on lush green grass. She looked at the barren field and wondered what the cows were fed on. But they had come this far, and Violet thought it a shame to return empty-handed, so they bought some cream and some butter and a large bottle of fresh milk, which was carefully packed in a box with

235

several large icepacks. On the way home, Violet fell asleep. Her head lolled back with her mouth open, and she snored faintly. Audrey saw Samson hide a smirk. One day, she thought. How on earth do I entertain her for several months?

Audrey invited a group of her friends for tea to welcome Alan's mother. A visitor from England was a rare treat, and they all came willingly. At the last minute, she decided she felt bold enough to invite Lady Smythe. She knew Violet would love the chance to meet the Governor's wife. It would give so much more depth to her tales back in England. Yet she was surprised when Lady Smythe accepted and instantly regretted asking her.

That afternoon, Violet sat and basked in the attention. Yes, she loved it here. Yes, it was marvellous. Yes, yes, yes.

'That's because you don't have to stay here. You can go back,' said Audrey, and everyone but Lady Smythe, who looked as though she hadn't really heard, turned to stare in surprise. Audrey blushed and stood up quickly. 'I'll just check on tea,' she said and walked off.

She had asked Cook to make afternoon tea. She had made a great effort, instructing him that it was important everything be beautiful. She returned to the veranda with the small boy, who was carrying a large tray of scones and pots of cream and jam. Audrey poured tea and watched, impressed with her efforts. She saw Alice eagerly take a bite of scone piled with cream, which looked a strange colour, and strawberry jam. Alice winced as soon as she tasted it, but swallowed what was in her mouth. Polly twisted her mouth and spat on to her plate a lump of masticated scone, jam and cream and wiped her mouth in disgust.

'Audrey, darling, I think the cream is off,' said Alice.

'Oh no,' said Audrey. 'We bought it specially.' She called for Cook, who told her that he had done nothing wrong. He had simply set out the tea things in advance this morning so as to save him time later. Audrey surmised that the cream had been standing in the hot kitchen while the scones baked and had curdled. 'Why is everything so complicated in this place? Why is it all so difficult, so testing?' she said, throwing her hands up in desolation.

'The main thing is to try, and if one fails, to try again,' said Violet, smiling. She was fiercely embarrassed that she had been let down in front of the Governor's wife. Actually, Violet didn't mind that much what the Governor thought of her. It was how this reflected on Alan that concerned her. She wished now that she had interfered with the arrangements. Really, Audrey should have known better than to leave the preparation of such a vital tea to her staff, despite their eagerness. She believed in the maxim 'If you want it done right, do it yourself' and made a mental note to educate Audrey on this before she left. She turned to face Lady Smythe with her most charming smile and spent the rest of the afternoon talking about Alan, who, she explained, was like his late father in every respect – dedicated, loyal and hardworking too. The younger women, especially the brash one with her American hairdo and cheap red nails, kept trying to capture Lady Smythe's attention, but with age on her side, Violet was able to hold them off. Lady Smythe was naturally much more interested in the same topics as Violet, and in the process of their conversation, they discovered, much to Violet's delight, that Lady Smythe had been at school with one of Violet's second cousins.

After she had been in Accra for a few days, Violet felt she had seen enough to have a frank chat with her son. She confronted him one evening while Audrey was in the bath and said in her direct style, 'Is everything fine with Audrey?'

'Why, yes. Why do you ask?'

'Because it evidently is not. I don't understand her. Here she is in paradise . . . listen . . .' she said, closing her eyes, '. . . listen to the sounds, the crickets, the birds, the people. What a wonderful way to live. And smell . . .' she said closing her eyes again, '. . . the heavenly jasmine, a coal fire. Really, I do not understand why she is depressed.'

'Oh, Mother, Audrey is not depressed.'

His mother raised her head and looked at him from the corners of her eyes. 'She isn't? Well then, there is really no excuse for her behaviour. She is rude to me—'

'Rude? I do apologise, Mother.'

'That's quite all right, Alan. Not your fault at all. The thing is she thinks I am too stupid to appreciate her bad manners, which not surprisingly, I am not. But I think she oversteps the mark rather with the servants. They do try so hard to please her. She treats them as if they are her slaves. You really must say something to her. Just because they are servants does not mean she can treat them anyhow. That is not how I brought you up. It saddens me to think you might be acquiring a reputation because of her behaviour.'

'I suppose if she is low, I am entirely to blame.'

'How so?'

'I am loath to say it, but she is not suited for life out here. I mis-judged things rather, didn't I? But since I brought her out here, I regard it as my duty to make her life as bearable as I can.'

'Absolute rubbish. She is a grumbler through and through. I've known my fair share of them in my time. Trust me, she'd moan even if she were the Queen of England.'

'Mother, that's a bit harsh.'

'Perhaps I've said enough.' She patted Alan on the arm. 'Just one last thing, you're not responsible for her happiness. You'll only kill yourself trying.'

'Possibly. But I brought her here, and I am her husband. If I don't make her happy, then . . .' His mother waited expectantly. '. . . and I do love her. Sometimes I wonder why, but I do.'

'Love is a rather strong word,' she said. She ignored his quizzical expression and said, 'Come on, let's enjoy the lovely warm air.'

Audrey stared at the cold scrambled eggs. She had spat out the first mouthful because it was too salty, and now she moved the lump of egg around her plate as if she was prodding a sleeping animal for some reaction. She was well aware that Violet was watching her, but she didn't care. Her coffee tasted funny too this morning, and she glowered at the steward for getting everything wrong when he came to clear the table. She had been feeling a little dizzy lately and was finding the hot season particularly wearisome this year. The only respite from the sweltering heat came once the sun had set, when the temperatures dropped back down into the eighties. By nine in the morning, they had soared once more, leaving the skies cloudless and hazy. She had developed prickly red spots on her chest and upper arms, even though she had three baths most days. Surprisingly, Violet seemed unfazed by the temperatures. Each day, she donned another

clean white shirt and another long skirt and looked set to face whatever the colony might throw her way.

Audrey pressed her temples. Perhaps she had heatstroke. Why
else would she feel this giddy and nauseous? Or was it last night's
dinner? Cook had served spinach stewed with onions, tomatoes and
grilled sardines. She winced when she thought about it.

She puffed loudly. 'What shall we do today?'

'Whatever you wish, my dear. I'll enjoy whatever the day brings,'
she said, patting Audrey's hand. 'And you know you mustn't feel
obliged to entertain me.'

Audrey nodded. Yet another day to be conquered with polite talk.

'We could go swimming? I thoroughly enjoyed that. Seawater is
fabulous for the circulation.'

The first time Audrey had taken her mother-in-law to the club,
she had emerged quickly from the changing room wearing nothing
but a baggy black bathing suit and her straw hat. Audrey was stunned
at how comfortable Violet was in her near-naked state, revealing
blue-veined legs, where punctured vessels marbled her skin like old
Stilton. Then the woman had jumped into the pool shrieking and
laughing like a child, much to Audrey's embarrassment. Polly had
leaned across from the next table and said, 'I hope I have as much
gall when *I* am nearly ninety,' which had made Audrey giggle.

'Yes, we could,' said Audrey, thinking that she might be able to
cool her body in the tepid pool.

But her condition got no better. Twice on the way home she had
made the driver stop the car because she thought she might have to
throw up. She did not want to cause unnecessary concern and continued to blame something she had eaten, but she was afraid that
perhaps she had finally contracted some unpronounceable disease.
That night, sleep came in short stretches as she contemplated this
nameless life-threatening condition.

When Alan left for work the next morning, Violet came out on to
the veranda, where Audrey sat concentrating on her nausea. Violet
was beaming. She sat next to Audrey and leaned forward bursting
with excitement.

'Dear Audrey,' she said, 'do we have some good news, then?'

Audrey stared blankly at her.

Slowly, it dawned on Violet. 'You don't know . . . You have no idea, do you?'

Audrey shook her head and raised her coffee cup. Before the cup reached her lips, the fumes made her want to retch. Here goes to another day with you, she thought.

'But you must suspect something? You're pregnant, aren't you?'

Audrey shrieked with laughter, but Violet looked serious, her earlier jovial expression had faded away. Audrey began to feel alarmed. She swallowed, and her mouth scratched with dryness.

'You've no idea, have you?'

'I can't be . . . It can't be . . . You are mistaken.'

Violet frowned. 'What do you mean? Aren't you overjoyed? Pleased? I presumed you were trying for a child?'

'Oh!'

'Audrey, speak to me.'

She sat in a haze as the facts began to settle in her mind. The nausea, the dreams, the dry skin. Her period was later than normal, but she was sure she had been cautious enough, and in any event, her period had been erratic for a while now, thanks to irregular meals and constant drinking. True, her stomach felt swollen, bruised almost, but she had thought that was because her period was due. She remembered she was talking to Alan's mother and forced a smile. 'I'm just taken aback, that's all. Well, stunned, you know? Very . . . I don't know . . .'

'Quite natural, my dear. Now, the thing to do is to refrain from telling Alan until we are sure the pregnancy is viable,' she said, shuffling in her seat. 'Until things are really rolling along splendidly. I would not even bother with the doctor until then.'

'When . . . Why . . . ?'

'Wait at least until the baby begins to protrude, I'd say.'

'The baby?' Audrey felt the nausea she had tried to control all week rise up. She felt as if she was being slowly lowered into a pool of dark water. She sat still, holding her breath, and waited for the sensation to pass. The nausea reached her mouth, her nose, her eyes, and everything went black.

When she came to, she was lying on her bed. Violet was sitting beside her holding something damp on her forehead.

240

'You fainted, my child. Awuni and Cook carried you here.'

She closed her eyes, repulsed at the image. Had someone thought to hold up her dress so that her servants had not looked straight up her skirt? She remembered the conversation she had been having with her mother-in-law. 'I think I'd like to be alone. Maybe have a nap?'

How could this have happened? She did not want a baby. She couldn't have a baby. There must be a mistake. She had a long, hot bath. By the time she emerged, she felt better, convinced that Violet was mistaken.

Violet was pleased to see her looking so much better and launched into a conspiratorial discussion about 'their little secret', but Audrey told her that if they wanted to keep it from Alan, it might be best if they did not indulge themselves by talking about it at all. In her head, a new mantra played unremittingly: I will not have this child; I cannot have this child, with varying emphases and intensity.

Audrey was woken by a dull tug on her lower abdomen. It was lightening outside, and she could hear the servants sweeping the yard. An early morning bird was toot-tooting in a distant tree. She turned over and cradled her stomach. She pressed it. She pressed it often, and sometimes pummelled it when she was alone. Could one press a baby to death? It was either her or it. She knew that all along, from the very first horrific realisation that she was pregnant; she simply did not have the energy to sustain her *and* a baby in this place. She had been drinking large amounts of neat gin after Alan and his mother were asleep in the hope that she might drown it somehow. Then she would lie awake, her senses animated by the alcohol, wondering what kind of punishment she might face if her murderous thoughts were revealed.

The tug increased. There was a sharp pain and she grimaced. She stood up and felt a terrific pull, as if something was being wrenched from her. Something warm and wet was released between her legs. She gasped and pushed her hand over her nightdress between the tops of her thighs, fearful to part her legs. Her hand came away wet and sticky, and looked as if she had dipped it in red paint. The sound she made was desperate, but quiet. Clutching herself, she hobbled to the bathroom, keeping her knees together, and climbed into the bath. Without taking her nightdress off, she put on the shower and stood shivering under the water. Gingerly, she opened her legs and felt the thing slip down one of her thighs. She started to cry at the horror of what was happening. The pain had receded slightly now, but the tug was persistent, expelling the other life down her legs, washing it down the drain.

After a while, she felt that it might be over, that she might be clean. She turned off the shower and opened her eyes. The gentle dawn sun was filtering through the netted window, streaking the walls with sun shadows. She lowered her head and saw a dark-red lump the size of fist lying in the plughole. She screamed and clutched her sopping nightdress about her. Alan came rushing in looking afraid. There was a trail of blood leading from the bed to the bathroom. He had blood on his legs where he had strayed on to her side of the bed. He put his arms round her and helped her out of the bath and back to their bed. She felt muddled. Suddenly, his mother was there, mumbling something. Then Alan forced a tablet into her mouth and made her drink some water. She closed her eyes. What would Alan do with the thing in the bath? She had not been able to look closely at it, yet had had a desperate morbid desire to see, imagining a fully formed child, only minute, lying there waiting to be picked up and discarded.

When she woke up, the bedding had been changed around her sleeping form and the floor cleaned. The sun was streaming in through cracks in the curtains. The house was hushed. She shivered. She looked at the clock. It was hard to focus, but she saw that several hours had passed. She turned her body slowly. She felt bruised. Something was wedged uncomfortably between her legs. She felt a wad of cotton wool. Had Alan done this? His mother? She was dejected. What now? she wondered. What now?

Alan came and sat beside her when he heard her stir. 'Don't worry, Audrey. We can have another one,' he said.

She screwed up her forehead and watched him. She had never seen him look so sad.

'Why did you not tell me you were pregnant?'

She looked away.

'It isn't your fault, you know. Mother says these things are decisively random, quite unpredictable, but the best thing, once you're up on your feet again, is to go right ahead and try again.'

She blinked at him and shook her head imperceptibly. 'I'm tired, Alan. I think I'll try and sleep some more.'

He kissed her crown and left the room.

They tiptoed around her for the next two days. Violet insisted that she stay in bed, and fed her on meat broth and liver to regain her strength. Audrey hated liver but ate a bit of it rather than argue. In the quiet of her room, with the curtains permanently closed, she began to long for her mother. She wanted to sit down and have an honest conversation with her. But would her mother understand that her daughter had lost a child, willingly, in the bathtub? Would she sympathise, be shocked, scold her? She realised how little she knew her mother. But she too must have had low periods in her marriage – her father was not easy to be around for long stretches. She remembered that awkward chat her mother had tried to have with her about marriage. She realised now how she had been trying to prepare her for things. For this? The distance home seemed to expand as she lay helplessly in her bed, seeping blood into a pad made and installed by her blasted mother-in-law, when she had a very capable mother all the way back in Stonebridge. She cried, and the bed trembled under her shuddering flimsy body, and each time her stomach muscles contracted, she felt blood spurt from her freely.

When she emerged from her bedroom the next morning, they remained hushed and talked about the weather. After Alan went off to work, Violet sat with her.

It emerged that it had been she who had scooped the lump of blood out of the bathroom and disposed of it appropriately. She could see the question in Audrey's eyes. Yes, she had most definitely lost the baby, but the pregnancy was too early for the foetus to be identifiable by the naked eye. It struck Violet anew just how naïve her daughter-in-law was, and she tried to put her arms around her protectively, but Audrey pulled away.

Two nights later, it rained. The first rain of the year. Audrey was lying awake with her eyes closed listening to Alan's deep snore when she smelled the cooler air that preceded rain. She held her breath and watched the curtains. They fluttered a little, and she breathed out. She rolled out of the bed and went to the window. She could see nothing, but she listened to the trees swaying in a seductive dance, enticing the clouds, the rain. She was on the veranda to see the first drops fall. The tropical rain drove hard into the ground in vertical lines. Audrey stuck her hand out into the flow of water spilling from the roof gutter. Quickly, half an inch of rain fell on this desiccated land. The smell was intoxicating: wet soil, fresh green. It would be lovely and clean in the morning, she thought as she ventured down the steps of the veranda. The rain landed on her head hard like hailstones. Frogs croaked above the din of the rainfall. She continued walking. The ground was slimy and muddy. She mashed her toes into the wet earth and lifted her chin up. The rain was warm and delightful. She walked towards the largest open space in the garden and sat on the ground with her legs stretched out before her and her face still upturned. She started to sob quietly. 'Thank you, thank you,' she said over and over. She cried because she did not believe she deserved to have her wish granted, for wishing the thing would die. But she was overjoyed, and she felt no guilt whatsoever, only joy and overwhelming relief, which gushed out in her tears.

The rain eased and patches of light poked through the dark sky. She stood and squelched her way back to the house. Her shoulders were loose, her face serene. It felt as if she had taken part in a ritual, not that she believed in such things. Often, she wished she could believe in God in the simplistic way that the natives did, but she was too intelligent to believe in a God who could sort out her problems for her; that seemed too obvious a solution. But that one of her prayers had been heard was heartening.

She walked through the living room depositing puddles of mud and water on the floor. Suddenly, there was a chilling scream and the sound of breaking china. Audrey turned and saw Violet crouching by the fridge. She had dropped a mug on the floor and it had shattered. When she saw that the mad-looking figure was Audrey, she shouted and screamed even more.

Audrey smiled and said calmly, 'Didn't mean to terrify you, Violet; I just fancied a walk in the rain. It doesn't rain here often, you see.'

Violet looked stunned. She tried to take her by the shoulders. 'Are you all right?'

Audrey was suddenly very sleepy. 'Actually, I have not felt better in a long while.'

'Why don't you get back to bed, dear? Make sure you change out of your wet clothes first.' She stared at her daughter-in-law, frowning. Perhaps it had not been such a marvellous idea to keep Audrey from seeing a doctor. She had heard of strange things happening to women after miscarriages, but nothing like this. Thank goodness she was here. Poor, poor Alan.

Later, they confronted Audrey about seeing a doctor. She sat there staring from one face to the other and was reminded of her parents. How her mother would occasionally report some dire behaviour to her father so that he could reprimand Audrey. Then they would sit opposite her at the kitchen table. Her father with hands folded on the table, her mother with hers clasped on her lap. Audrey would fasten a placid expression on her face and stare from one to the other while she set herself thinking about the most distracting things she could in order to get through the ordeal. Self-preservation, she termed it. She looked past Alan and Violet into the garden. One long shower had spruced it up and made it look temporarily glorious. She looked for clouds in the hazy, cloudless sky. They had vanished, traceless. When would it rain again? she asked herself, sighing.

'Audrey, please,' said Alan, exasperated. He leaned across the table to clasp her hand in his. 'Please talk to us. We are trying to help you.'

But what could she say? She knew Violet was suspicious of childlessness, surely she would think it perverse that she was indifferent to her 'loss'? She was aware of the expectant looks and realised that there was a polite smile on her lips, not a sign of pleasure or contentment, merely an expression that she now wore often, involuntarily. Nevertheless, she realised it was an expression that was decidedly unsuitable, when she saw Alan's eyes cloud up. She looked at him quizzically, wondering, What is the right thing to do if your husband starts crying in front of his equally bewildered mother? She softened and grabbed Alan's hand so that he would not embarrass himself.

The next day, she accompanied them to see Dr Stewart. Alan sat in the consulting room with her and held her hand. Violet waited outside. But there was nothing they did not already know. The pregnancy had aborted spontaneously. There were no explanations for these things. Rest a while, try again, was the advice delivered in monotone.

Audrey nodded obediently. On the way home, they chatted optimistically about what the miscarriage meant – that everything was functioning as God intended, said her mother-in-law – and what it did not mean – that there was anything for her to worry about, said Alan. They agreed that the best thing would be try again as soon as she felt well enough; a child would make their family complete in the most wonderful way that they could ever, ever imagine, said Violet.

When they got home Audrey marched to the house. I will not take orders from her. She stamped up the stairs to the veranda. I will not take orders from him. She was not some child to be bossed about. 'Bullies, the bloody lot of them,' she hissed beneath her breath as she undressed and stepped into the bath.

She returned to see Dr Stewart the following week. Alone. He said he had expected her and gave her the advice she needed. He couldn't believe, and frankly neither could she, that she had managed to avoid pregnancy so far simply by chance. When Audrey left his consulting room that day, she was buoyant. Her body was the one thing she had control over, and she was determined to keep it that way.

Chapter Fifteen

When Violet sailed for England in June 1939, there were less than one hundred days before Alan and Audrey were due to finally go home on leave. Audrey had been counting the days, and as soon as the number had dropped to double digits, she began to allow her excitement to show and could talk of little else. She was thrilled that even Alan seemed to be looking forward to a break. He was looking forward to seeing his family and friends. They chatted and made plans. Audrey drew up a detailed itinerary of their visit. They would have four months. What did he think, should they start in London and then her parents for a week . . . two weeks? Then his mother for the same length of time? 'We mustn't allow either family to feel cheated,' she said, and Alan had agreed. Then maybe visit Freddy, who had joined the army and was stationed up in Yorkshire? Eventually, she had it all mapped out. Each family would have two visits, one at the beginning and one at the end of their stay. That would give them time with his friends and hers. And there would be time to shop – they both agreed they would need several days in London to make sure they had all the things they needed. Audrey began a new list: Items to Purchase. She spent hours revising and adding to the itinerary. Whenever an idea popped into her head, she drew a sheet of paper from her bag, a pocket or a book and wrote. Four long, glorious months in England, she could not wait. It would be early autumn when they arrived. She closed her eyes and tried to remember her parents' garden in September, how the apple trees at the bottom of the garden would be laden with reddening sweet apples. Her mother always picked each apple, including those that had fallen and bruised, and spent hours making apple sauce, pickled apple and apple jam, which she carefully sealed and labelled and stored. She would wrap some of the nicest fruit carefully in tissue paper and place them in boxes in the shed so they had fresh apples during the winter months. There, the smell of the fruit would intensify over the months, forming a heavenly blend with the musty, soily damp of the shed. If there was much fruit, she would press some of the apples and bottle the juice, which over time frothed and soured so that the back of Audrey's jaw tingled whenever she drank it. The walnut tree that Audrey had planted as a child would be covered in large, flat, bronzed leaves, which fluttered to the ground in the slightest wind. Despite her father's valiant efforts, they could not keep the squirrels from the nuts and hardly ever managed to gather more than a few handfuls before the pests had scurried and buried them all over the garden.

At the club, and in the newspapers, discussions were less lighthearted. For a while, the decision of His Majesty's Government to ask Parliament to authorise conscription and what that would mean dominated conversations. Some of the men started a sweepstake on whether or not there would be a war. Whether the fact that Hitler had cancelled Germany's non-aggression pact with Poland and its naval agreement with Britain would result in hostilities. Audrey read the editorials for herself in the newspapers that Alan's office received, usually about six weeks after they were published in London. She had always read newspaper articles and editorials with clinical detachment. Although she could not wait to be back home, the black print failed to engage her emotionally on any level; it seemed all so far away, so irrelevant to her life. As a teenager, she had devoured the newspapers for information and knowledge; now, delivering old news, they were a distraction, something to read when she had nothing else to occupy her.

When, days after Hitler had invaded Poland, Alan arrived home late and told his wife that their country had declared war on

Germany, she felt her whole body start to tremble. She asked in a voice that masked her fear, 'We will still be able to sail in two weeks, will we not?'

'Bloody hell, woman, you really are the limit,' shouted Alan. 'Do you ever think about anything that happens beyond the end of your nose? Do you?'

She stared at him silently.

'God knows what this will mean for Britain, for the colony, for us.' He emptied his glass, slammed it on the veranda wall and poured himself another large measure of whisky. 'You have probably lolled about here all day feeling sorry for yourself for . . . for no reason fathomable to man. England is at war! Do you understand what that means? Do you?' He was shrieking the words; spittle flew out of his mouth and sprayed the air in front of him. He had been unable to rid himself of the sick feeling in the pit of his stomach since he heard the news. They had received a telegram confirming H.E. and his wife had arrived safely back in England where they were due to have four months' leave. It was fortunate that they had been able to go when they did; Alan had heard that their son had gone down from Oxford to sign up. At least Sir Colin and Lady Smythe would have the chance to see him off to war in person. A few weeks later and they would have been stranded here like the rest.

Audrey lifted her glass of tonic water to her mouth. Her hands were shaking, and her insides were somersaulting wildly as she watched him in shock. He had never spoken to her like this before. She had thought it strange that he smelled of alcohol when he walked in from work and marched straight to the drinks cabinet.

'My brothers, my friends, may well be drafted in to fight, to die, probably your beloved Freddy too. And all you can think about is your bloody leave? You can forget your leave. Until further notice, no leave for you, no leave for me, probably no leave for anyone. But while that is no doubt heartbreaking for you, it is not life-threatening. Not in the way a war might be anyhow. Damn you, woman!' He stormed off and slammed their bedroom door.

Audrey saw that the servants were hovering at the steps of the veranda watching. 'The entertainment is over now. Off to bed with you,' she said, glaring at them before she walked into the house.

249

As if in a trance, she went to the cupboard and took out a bottle of gin, got some more ice and sat in the largest chair with the bottle at her elbow and her filled glass under her nose. She was too stunned to cry. Too shocked and angry to feel. Too miserable for words or thoughts other than bitter riddles, like why it was that Polly and Lady Smythe, who needed it less than she did, had managed to go on leave just in time. Who knew, if the war lasted for months and months, they would have no excuse to return to this awful place. She was too sad not to have a large drink. Well, it was Wednesday, nearly the weekend, and who could deny that circumstances had been so radically altered, control so decisively and cruelly ripped from her that silly resolutions about alcohol consumption during the week were now positively irrelevant?

Over the next few days, she moved about like a zombie and laughed inappropriately into the silence of the house. Later that week, she closed off the outside and spent daylight hours asleep in her darkened room. One night, Alan woke up to find her side of the bed empty. He heard swishing in the bathroom and hurried to find her lying in the bath with water up to her neck, her nightdress floating about on the surface. 'Anyone would think you'd just seen a corpse,' she said as he stared, speechless. 'I'm hot. I couldn't sleep.'

The filled bath became her favourite place. She would shut the door and lie in it for hours refusing to answer Alan or the servants. At first, he came often and crouched beside her and talked softly to her closed lids while she held her breath for counts of ten – the first night, she reached 253 before he left. After that, he retreated before she reached the first hundred and by the end of the week, she heard his feet pad out of the bathroom and the door shut on her peaceful retreat before she had even counted up to ten. He stopped interrupting her baths.

One Saturday, she exhausted herself trying to stay in a different room from Alan. She never managed to remain alone for more than a few minutes when he sauntered in and started some mindless task, some pointless search for some imaginary thing. Eventually, she screamed at him, 'Stop following me about, will you? I need some space. Can't you see you're suffocating me?'

'But, darling, I . . .'

'Why don't you go out? Go to the club or to your friends. Just leave me in peace!' She went into the bathroom and started to fill the bath.

There was a soft knock on the door, and Alan spoke through the keyhole: 'There's no need to get into the bath. I'll go out. Get out of your way.'

Soon, the days began to blur one into another, and she enjoyed the sensation of losing all sense of time. She spent long periods asleep during the day, and at night, she sat in the living room listening to her breathing until she heard the cocks begin to crow. That was the only time of day she could be sure about, that the first crack of light was about to appear, that life would begin again: servants sweeping, water running, birds whistling.

One morning, she heard someone walking up the gravelled drive and panicked. It would be one of the girls coming to find her. She ran into her bedroom without looking out of the window to see who it was, and locked her door.

Awuni knocked on the door. 'Madam, please, your friend is here.'

A few moments later, she heard Alice's voice, 'Darling, I am not going anywhere until you come out. I mean it.'

She lay on her bed and shut her eyes, but her heart was racing. Knowing that there was someone out there waiting made her feel claustrophobic and ill.

Alice knocked again. 'Do please stop this, Audrey. We are ever so worried about you. Poor Alan is beside himself. Come on, darling, we are here for you. We understand how you feel. We're not cross, please come out.'

Why would they be cross? What right did they have to be cross because her life was slipping away from her? Why wouldn't they just leave her alone? She didn't want to see them. She couldn't see them. She lay still, barely breathing. Wouldn't it be wonderful if you could will yourself to stop breathing? she thought. She waited. Alice knocked some more but eventually gave up when Audrey continued to ignore her.

Later that afternoon, she gathered her hair in her left hand and with a pair of scissors chopped it off as close to her scull as possible.

251

She flung the cut hair about on her bare feet. It was strange how hair swelled when it was released. She was pleased that the resulting jagged mop ruffled even Alan when he returned from work that evening.

When he saw what she had done to her beautiful hair and the Mona Lisa smile on her face, he turned and walked out. He got in the car and drove for a few minutes. He parked on a quiet road, dropped his head on to the steering wheel and wept. His body shuddered as he poured out unmanageable sadness. He was at a loss as to what to do any more. He didn't know how to make her happy, or well. And he was weary from trying, from wishing there was some way he could stop it, this madness. He lifted his head a little. He had never thought of her in those terms, but perhaps this was what it was; maybe she was going mad. There was certainly no explanation for her erratic behaviour, the indefinable moods, the unpredictable temper. There was nothing he hadn't already tried that would have helped a more balanced person.

It had all been far too much for him recently. Work was chaotic, the war was building, and uncertainty rife. How he wished she could be there for him now, at least occasionally. Someone to confide in that he was struggling with the fact that he would avoid conscription by being out here. But she wouldn't know or care that he might need someone to listen, or simply be. Not with herself on her mind all the time.

It preyed on him, on all of the chaps actually, that they had been spared something. An uneasiness hung around the war discussions at work – whose cousin, whose brother had signed up, where they were based and headed. How long the war would last. They agreed, each of them, that it was unlikely to run as long as the Great War. Without exception, with ease, each vowed that he too would have signed up immediately back home. Alan wondered if any of them felt the cowardly relief he did, that someone else had made the decision, that he didn't have to contemplate going off to war. He admired the absolute bravery of those who would fight, voluntarily or otherwise. Like Freddy. And the tens of thousands of natives who had joined the Royal West African Frontier Force to fight for their colonial masters in a war that was thousands of miles away, while he stayed behind to run the colony. Unable to sign up and fight for his country, unable to make his wife happy, he was here to see this war out from Government House, with his guilt intact. A failed man, useless and unwanted. Wasn't that how she saw him? How she had made him feel over the years?

He must have been in the car for over an hour when he began to feel strong enough to return home. She would be in bed; he would be able to creep into the spare room without being seen. He wished he could call on Polly, she who always had a balanced view of things, who helped him see through the mire that his life with Audrey had become. But she was back in England, poor thing. Even in Cambridge, there would be horrors that none of them here could imagine.

Some days later, at Alice's suggestion, Alan arranged for Audrey to be examined at home by a doctor. He prescribed some tranquillisers and described her condition as a 'delayed and sustained response to a traumatic event', as she sat before him, stone-faced, wondering why Alan was so worried about her taking a few baths.

'The servants are threatening to leave,' he said that evening when he was trying to convince Audrey to try and behave normally in front of them and to remember to take her tablets.

She smiled blankly.

'It is serious, Audrey. They think you might be possessed or something. They are afraid of you.'

'About bloody time,' she said and laughed wildly until tears rolled down her cheeks.

The tablets made her feel happy; consequently, she took them most of the time, sometimes with her hidden supply of gin, sometimes with water; it depended very much on her mood. And the gloominess came and went stealthily. There was rarely much warning. She either wanted to go out or she did not. It seemed quite straightforward to her.

She emerged one afternoon to see that Alan had brought home a sun lounger, which he had placed on the veranda for her. She started to spend her days on it, lying still and thinking of nothing. Most evenings, he came home to find her lying there. Mostly, she felt nothing and she heard nothing, as she watched the garden below. Slowly, she began to notice that out there things moved without pause. Lizards, which she had learned to tolerate, sunned themselves for long stretches in the most mesmerising manner, bobbing their heads incessantly and darting their eyes restlessly. From here, she began to hear the birds and see the large yellow butterflies that lived in her garden. And she could feel the breeze, which rustled through the leaves. From up here, she came to love her garden anew. She watched the plants grow. She saw them wither. She could see where birds were building nests and where dragonflies hovered. On a particularly hot day, she wondered where these creatures went for water and decided she had to erect a birdbath. For days, she pondered what she could use and in the end asked the gardener to make a pile of bricks and stones, and she put her largest serving platter filled with water on it. Now she could watch the delighted birds flit in and out of the dish.

And it was from up here that she saw Hassan leaving one afternoon. She called him up to the veranda to remind him to get some more manure. As usual, he was wearing his woven shoulder bag. As he turned to leave, she noticed that the bag was moving.

'What's in your bag?' she asked.

'No,' he said.

'No what? Show me what you have there,' she said, sitting up.

'Rat.'

She started screaming. She hated rats, and this must be a rather big one, she thought.

Hassan looked perplexed, wondering what he had to do to stop the screaming. They would think he was attacking her. She wouldn't stop, so he moved closer to try and touch her and she screamed louder. He lifted his hands into the air in a sign of despair and took a step backwards, which seemed the right thing to do. She stopped making the dreadful noise.

Breathlessly, she said, 'I hate rats. How dare you bring a rat into my house?' Her hands were shaking with fear.

'Madam, no, not rat, *cat*. Meow, meow.'

She looked puzzled and a little afraid as he reached into his bag and lifted out a teeny kitten.

'Oh, poor kitty. How dare you keep it in your bag? You can't do that to a cat! What is wrong with you?' It was a scraggly tabby, too young to be away from its mother. She held out her hand. 'Give it to me.'

'No, madam.'

'Now.'

'Madam, my food.'

She gasped. There was nothing on the poor animal to make a decent meal. 'Wait here,' she said. She went into the house and returned with a few coins. 'Here. Now give it to me.'

He handed the kitten to her. It felt like a vibrating ball of fluff. 'You poor, poor dear,' she said, sitting down to stroke him. Then she saw that it was covered in fleas. She held it away from her as she ran to the bathroom in disgust. She ran a bath, added some disinfectant and put the kitten in to soak off the fleas. His meows were no louder than a squeaky door, but he was shaking. When the water filled with floating black specks, Audrey lifted him into the sink and brushed his fur with Alan's toothbrush to make sure that there were no fleas left. He was trembling, and his eyes were shut; she was sure he would die. She wrapped him in a towel and fed him warm milk from a teaspoon on the veranda. He revived enough for her to take the towel off and have a look at him. She lifted him to her face and examined his underside. 'You're a girl,' she said happily, kissing the kitten's nose. She laughed and something fluttered to life within her, like delicate wings in a breeze.

When Alan came home from work, they were curled up on the sofa. He sat beside her and stroked the cat that she had named Sheba. Her eyes were alight as she recounted their meeting. He saw how she handled the kitten with tenderness that he had no idea she still possessed. Could he dare to hope?

Over the next few days, she nursed Sheba back to full strength. She fed her biscuits soaked in brandy milk and mashed sardines. She would not go anywhere in case Sheba came to harm. She told Alan that she would want his dogs shot if they harmed her. He smiled. The next time Alice came over, Audrey ignored her bewildered expression and asked her to teach her how to macramé so she could make a little orange collar for Sheba.

When she was sure Sheba was strong enough, she went to the club for the first time in weeks one evening with Alan. She felt shaky as she walked through the entrance, and Alan reached to steady her. She noticed how the doorman stared at the space above her eyes as she walked past him, performing his bow in military fashion.

Alice and Malcolm stood up to greet them. There was an awkward silence, then in a teasing voice Audrey said, 'Weren't you ever told it's rude to stare?'

'I do like your hair. It's very emancipated,' said Malcolm, flustered.

'Actually, you can stare all you like, Malcolm; it's what everyone is saying behind my back that intrigues me.'

'No one is saying anything,' said Alice, hugging her friend. 'We've all missed you so. We are so pleased you are well again. You were a little under the weather, we understand. The most important thing is you're back and raring to go.'

'I shan't be raring anywhere fast for a while.'

'Oh, let's be positive, Audrey. And there's always the pantomime to look forward to in a couple of weeks, we are going to need you to help with the costumes.'

Audrey groaned inwardly. Lord give me strength, she prayed.

'And we thought maybe you could have your debut on stage this time? Nothing tasking, of course. We thought you could muster up the energy to play a tree perhaps, or a cloud?' said Alice with a grin.

Audrey laughed.

Alan reached to touch her. 'It's good to see you happy.'

She smiled. And from here, she realised just how deep was the dark hole she had fallen into.

Chapter Sixteen

Her first months with William – Robert preferred him to be called by his Christian name – passed in a blur of happiness for Matilda. She thought only of her child and his needs, and he responded by being a peaceful baby who never seemed to cry for long. The days passed one like the other, with little change, but she found the monotony comforting and revelled in her role, convinced that only she could provide the care her baby needed. If William was not being fed or cradled in her arms, he was asleep on her back, and at night, he slept with his mother in her new bed. If anyone picked him up, barely would a few minutes pass before she asked to have her baby back.

The women taught her how to bathe him, holding him carefully on her lap while she sat on a stool, massaging his little body with a warm flannel before putting powder into every crease of his body and Vaseline in his hair to make it shine.

And her special treatment as a new mother continued; she did not have to do any cooking or cleaning, no chores whatsoever. 'You have worked hard to bring this child into the world, and now you must work hard to keep him here. Your job is to feed him and regain your strength,' her mother told her whenever she tried to help.

William's cheeks filled out, and his arms and legs grew strong. When he smiled at his mother for the first time, she cried, wondering why she had ever felt hesitant about becoming a mother, why she had ever thought that there was something more worthwhile, how she would ever manage to tear herself away from him, and where exactly she would find space in her heart to love another child so completely.

She dreaded Robert resuming his night summons, anticipating her anxiety at having to leave William. When the first summons came, she feigned illness and refused to go to him. This happened a few times until one day Aunty Dede said, 'Matilda, this is the most important time for you to go to your husband. You must resume your status. You can rest assured that the first wife has done all she can to erase memories of you from his mind.'

'But . . .'

'I know, I know,' continued Aunty Dede. 'But you must go. Go tonight. Make yourself pretty, put on a nice dress, do whatever you need to do, but go. This is not something you can delay unnecessarily. Remind him what he has missed.' She giggled.

'But who will look after my baby while I am gone?' Matilda wailed.

'Shame on you, Matilda! Am I not here? Is Aunty Amele not here? What about your mother? Look at her now, look,' she said, looking at Ama, who was sitting in the shade cradling the baby. 'Have we not all already given birth and raised children? What kind of question is that?'

Matilda scrunched her mouth in resignation. She could not deny that her mother seemed to adore her grandson, always asking to hold him, bathe him, dress him, forever showing him off when they had visitors and talking to him when she thought no one was listening, telling him in a stern voice, 'Don't forget when you grow up you will be a lawyer like your father. The first lawyer from the Lamptey family. Do you understand me?' Then she would pick up the bewildered-looking child and rock him in her arms, singing, '*Atoo*, my lawyer grandson, *atoo*!'

Watching her mother, Matilda wondered where these maternal instincts had been buried all these years, and why they were resurfacing now when it was too late for Matilda and her sisters to benefit from them.

*

258

She was sitting one day, gazing at her perfect child, watching him purse his lips and stretch his little fingers occasionally before settling back into a comfortable sleep position, when Esi came from Downing House asking her to come and see Lawyer urgently.

'I hear that they are having a party for the twins and . . . Anyway, I should not gossip, but I think that they need you to do the cooking.'

Matilda stood up, bound her son to her back with calico and then wrapped a nice piece of going-out cloth under her arm. This would be interesting, she thought, as she sauntered over to the house.

In his office, she sat cradling her baby like an offering to Robert. He glanced at the wrapped baby briefly but did not come and touch him. 'Is he fine? Growing well, etc.?'

She nodded.

'Listen, the reason I asked you to come here is that we are having a birthday party for the twins. It's their mother's idea, but I think it is a fine one. Twins are special, and it's a chance to get everyone together. I am inviting some friends and colleagues too. You know, before I came back to Accra, I planned that I would throw parties regularly, but the years have fled by, and I have only managed dinners here and there.'

'With all the children?'

'Yes, yes. We will make it a lunch party, which is why I wanted to speak to you. Can you do the cooking?'

Matilda stared for a moment, a thousand thoughts flying around her head. 'Yes. You simply tell me what I should cook. Will your English friends be coming?'

'Yes, why?'

'Then I will not put as many chillies in the food . . .'

'Ah, yes. Well,' his face lit up, 'I thought jollof rice, that's a favourite, some fish, some chicken, some goat, you know the sort of thing. I might roast an animal. And one or two stews, spinach, beans and maybe groundnut soup.'

'How many people will there be?'

'I don't know, maybe thirty or forty. Let's say fifty.'

'And . . . what about Julie? I will need to use your kitchen. If Julie—'

'I'll speak to her.'

259

'It would be nice if she could help too,' she muttered to herself.

'Esi can help you. And your sisters are still at home, no? They can help you too.'

On the day of the party, Patience, who when she had been asked for help had responded, 'You're asking whether *I* want to come *into* Lawyer's kitchen? Would I miss an opportunity like that? Surely not! You can count on me,' went up to Downing House with Matilda early in the morning, followed by a collection of relations carrying pots of food in varying stages along the cooking process.

They had begun to spread out their things in the kitchen, and Matilda had set her sisters Eunice and Celestina and her cousins Gifty and Pearl to work in the kitchen when Julie came in to see what all the commotion was about. She was in her dressing gown, her hair, although tucked in a hairnet, looked messy. 'What on earth is going on here?' she asked.

'We are here to cook,' said Patience before Matilda could say anything.

'And who are you?'

'And who are *you*? Are you the new maid?'

Matilda was able to stifle her giggles, but her sisters and cousins were not.

Julie spluttered and shouted, 'Can you kindly tell me what is going on here and what these strange people are doing in my kitchen?'

'Robert asked me to prepare the food for the party today.'

'I could kill that man,' she said and walked out.

'Aiee, she wants to kill your husband!' said Patience.

Then they heard Julie's shrill voice echoing from deep in the house. 'This is a party for *my* children; it has nothing to do with her. Why on earth does she have to be here?' They did not hear what Robert said, but Julie's voice carried out to them again, 'Why did you not at least have the decency to tell me?'

Patience made a loud chewing noise. 'What kind of person is not afraid of displaying her sinfulness for all to see? Not afraid to discuss the killing of peoples so openly? You were wise to be afraid of her. You know, if I were you, I would not trust her around my child,' she

260

said, pinching the baby, who was bound to his mother's back. 'A woman like that was not made to be trusted.'

Matilda continued to chop, stir and pound.

'This baby is your most precious possession. The thing that makes you most weak.'

'If you don't mind, my baby is not a thing . . .'

'Get away,' said Patience jokingly. 'I am serious, take my word for it, she will try and harm you through him. After all, Lawyer must have said something to make her stop interfering with your food. I am sure she will be looking for another angle to attack you. She is a snake under grass; you never know where she is hiding to strike next.'

Matilda was frying, boiling and stewing.

'You are your own person, but if this were my precious child, my flesh and blood, I would take him for protection, to be covered by blood.'

Robert had purchased a pig, which had been roasting for a while outside on a spit that Tetteh had erected, and the smell of crisping pork fat soon filled the air. Tables and chairs were scattered in the yard. There were barrels of cool corn wine in the kitchen and boxes of bottled beer. Everywhere, towering piles of glasses and dishes stood in gleaming readiness.

Matilda stopped what she was doing and turned to her friend. 'My son has been out-doored in accordance with tradition, but I will not take him to a fetish priest for more sacrifices. He goes to church with me. I am choosing to trust the Almighty to look after him.'

'There is no harm in taking avail of all the different kinds of protections available to us. Church is good, but our native priests are also here for a reason. Don't misunderstand me, if you did not have to contend with such an evil woman, then I would not advise this, but—'

'We have food to cook. We have to get dressed. We have a party to attend. I don't have time to discuss such things.'

'You cannot expect God to deal with every little concern that we have, only one person, how can He—'

'God is not a person. He is God. And He can hear every prayer. He is able to answer each one.'

261

'It's up to you, Miss Madam. If it were me that had such a beautiful son . . . All right, don't worry, I am going. I am going to change, and I promise to return looking spectacular. There cannot be many better places to find a suitable husband. I will be eighteen soon, so I have decided that I must take every opportunity there is.'

'Good luck to you,' said Matilda. She wiped sweat from her brow and continued arranging pieces of crisp fried chicken on a platter.

When she returned a while later, Matilda laughed in amazement. 'You look spectacular indeed.'

'The guests are here, you know. You should be there with your husband, not in the kitchen.' Patience held a handful of roasted peanuts and salty *achomo*, which she threw one by one into her mouth. 'All the chairs are nearly full. I think you should go and get ready now. You cannot let them see you in your dirty house dress.'

Matilda looked out of the window. She could see that her friend was right. 'I brought my clothes with me. I will go and change now.'

Patience spoke through a mouth full of nuts: 'I think that woman is taking advantage of the situation, leaving you to do all this, not even with a maid.'

There was a knock on the door, and Alan walked in. Matilda gasped, embarrassed to be seen in her food-stained house clothes by such a distinguished guest.

'Please, no,' she said, waving frantically.

Patience emptied the nuts into her mouth, put her flat palms in front of Alan's face and started to walk towards him so that he had to back out of the kitchen. 'No, no,' she said, shaking her head and looking horrified.

'Do you see what I mean? You are needed by your guests. You are Lawyer's wife, not his maid. You should be ashamed that the *obronie* has come and seen you in this state. Leave it to me,' she said.

Matilda looked up, but her friend had gone. Moments later, she was back with Esi. 'You are very lucky that I have not reported you to Lawyer,' she hissed. 'Your job is here in the kitchen, not joking and laughing with the stable boys.'

Esi scowled. 'Madam told me that I was not needed in the

kitchen. That there were some maids from Sister Matilda's house here today.'

'Do we look like maids to you?' shouted Patience. 'Matilda, let's go. We will be back to check on your work soon. And don't bother muttering about me under your breath. I have powerful ears. Eunice, make sure that she does not misbehave.'

When Matilda emerged from the house, she could tell that many turned to look at her. She wore a dress made from a subtle purple-and-white woven fabric. When her mother saw the dress the first time, she said, 'What is the point of making a simple dress like that with this expensive material?' But Matilda was pleased with it. It fitted in the right places, yet she had enough room to breathe with ease, to eat, to move, and most importantly, it disguised her greater heaviness; she was even sturdier now that she was a mother.

With Patience beside her, she felt able to hold her head high, and together they walked down the stairs into the gathering. She went to stand with her mother and sisters, who were sitting around one of the tables furthest from the house. She looked around and saw Julie talking to the white man. He seemed nice, always much more courteous to her than Robert's other friends and always very happy. He seemed interested in what she might say, though she hardly ever spoke in his presence, and then she didn't believe he understood anything she said. But he sounded, perhaps not surprisingly, like the voices on the radio waves from London, superior and educated. He was the only white man whom she had encountered at close range.

He looked intriguing, with pale skin, which she had been surprised to observe was actually quite pink and covered in a patchwork of brown and white blotches through which she could see his veins when she was close. And he had those odd-coloured, cool-looking eyes that were the colour of the lagoon in the wet season, and thin, wispy hair that could hardly offer much protection from the beating sun, which explained why, as ever, he was carrying a helmet.

Her baby started to cry. She knew his cry when she heard it, although it could have been one of several babies here today. She took him from her cousin Pearl and put him on her back, tying him

263

first with calico, which she covered with a piece of the cloth from which her dress was made. 'There, there,' she said, rocking him, enjoying the warmth and the softness bound to her. When she turned around, she saw that Alan was making his way towards her. She moved to stand closer to Saint John, as if he would be able somehow to protect her from something, though what, she was not sure. Alan reached them, stood before her and smiled. He was clearly impressed by her transformation and examined her closely so that she lowered her eyes and became self-aware.

'You look stunning, Matilda. And, look, there is a happy baby, if I have ever seen one. I should think that's a most comfortable place to sleep.'

'She does not speak English. Yet, might I add. That is the current state of affairs, however, we intend to rectify this, don't we, Matilda?' said Uncle Saint John. He chuckled to himself. 'In our family, there are many beauties, both on the male side and on the female side. Where the beauty comes from has not been determined; however, we are pleased that it is more or less equally shared by all family members. Though it must be said that Matilda received more than her fair share. Anyway, it is my honour to meet you finally, sir, my name is Saint John, and I am trusted clerk to Lawyer.'

'Right. Nice to meet you too, Saint John.' He looked at Matilda again. He had seen her once or twice serving food at Robert's, being treated like a maid, really, and looking like the child she must be. But she was rather breathtakingly beautiful, and he was surprised how startled this made him. 'You are a marvellous cook.'

'Yes, in our family, there are many talents, some hidden, some not. And cooking is something that our females are particularly adept at,' said Saint John, chuckling some more.

'Would you really like to learn English?'

'He said, "Would you like to learn English?" She would like to. You know, my family is very advanced in most matters, including the education of females. We were educating Matilda, as is the right thing to do, when she was requested in marriage by Lawyer. Needless to say, family duties have kept her from her studies, but as soon as the time is right, she will resume them.'

'I am sure I could find someone to teach Matilda English.'

Saint John translated this, and Matilda rewarded Alan with a lovely smile.

Robert joined them, and Saint John took an imperceptible step backwards. 'What is this I hear?' asked Robert.

'Matilda would like to learn how to speak English, and I think I might have just the right teacher for her,' said Alan.

'Oh? Who?'

'Well, Audrey, actually. And by the way, apologies, but she really wasn't up to it today.'

'But she is fine otherwise?'

'Oh yes. She still finds gatherings like this quite gruelling . . . I am trying to find a diversion for her that's not too strenuous. She doesn't like the sorts of things most of the other wives do, you know, tombola nights, quiz nights, music recitals, etc., etc. But I think she might well rise to the challenge of teaching someone like Matilda. And it would be nice for her to meet a nice local woman. Her life is much too confined.'

Matilda stood listening to this talk littered with her name and the word 'English'. She wondered what they were plotting and found it difficult to stand still and smile politely while they discussed her.

'I am not sure how learning English will benefit Matilda,' said Robert. 'But why not? If she wants to, I can't see the harm.'

'That might prove rather a challenge, don't you think?' said Julie, who had walked up to join them in time to hear Robert's question.

Matilda watched how effortlessly Julie took her place next to Robert, how she placed her hand on the small of his back and rubbed it gently, and how Robert's back stiffened ever so slightly, and how within moments, he had seen someone more interesting on the other side of the compound whom he wanted to introduce Alan to.

'You are looking nice, Julie,' Matilda said. She saw from the corner of her eye that Uncle Saint John had retreated further but remained close. She knew her family would be preparing to eavesdrop, and she could sense their bodies shifting into protective postures, their starched cloths rustling, their slippers scraping the ground.

Apart from their encounter this morning in the kitchen, the women had not seen much of each other recently.

'Don't go letting these grand ideas about learning English settle in your small mind. If I don't have the time to sit about reading books, I don't see why you should! You should beware of gallivanting about and reaching above your station, lest you fall and injure yourself and yours!'

Matilda smiled as she had learned to do, even when there was nothing to smile about.

'Well, I think Robert is quite satisfied with the number of children he's got. There's no need to overdo things. And you really shouldn't be carrying your baby on your back like that.'

'Listen here, young lady,' said Aunty Dede, shuffling forward. 'We are all here, many of us,' she said, waving a heavy arm to indicate the formidable presence of Matilda's family. 'If you misbehave today in front of us, you will—'

'Don't you dare threaten me! This is my house. I can do or say what I like here.'

'You see, that is where you are wrong,' said Aunty Dede in a whisper. 'That is how you manifest your lack of wisdom. Respect is required in certain circumstances, yet you choose to flagrantly abuse our traditions. You cannot continue in that vein without tragic consequences. Mark my words, young lady, don't let your tongue be your downfall. Our daughter has done nothing to you, yet you mistreat her at any opportunity you get . . .'

'It's all right, Aunty Dede.'

'No, it is not. And where are you going when I am talking to you?' said Aunty Dede, gripping Julie's arm.

'Aunty Dede, please let her go,' said Matilda, amazed. She was terrified of the scene before her, yet could feel unmistakable mirth bubbling away inside her.

Aunty Dede ignored her and continued to grip Julie. 'Do you want your guests to know the kind of woman you are? Shut up and listen to me, then. Do you know that you are not the first woman to have to share your husband? And you will not be the last. Lawyer has enough for you and Matilda to share. But you don't want to let her live in peace. We have left you alone up until now; however, mark my words, if I hear of any further misbehaving, any further issuing of curses, I will come and find you,' she said, pounding her spare hand against her chest.

'Lawyer's sister is coming,' said someone from behind her.

266

'Mark my words,' said Aunty Dede, releasing Julie. Then she shuffled back to find her seat.

It is true that Matilda's baby's first year was a series of ceaseless miracles that fascinated her and even left her awestruck. She was astounded at the pitch he could reach with his screams, and how real tears spilled from his eyes. She could not have imagined such perfect fingernails could grow so fast. She nibbled them while cradling him, unwilling to use anything sharp near him. She was astonished by how much he fed, proud of how fat he had become. And how she exclaimed when he could hold his head up by himself. She was certain that if she was vigilant, she would see his limbs straighten and stretch, his eyes animate, and his curiosity awaken. But no matter how much she watched over him, she was able only to record his growth after the event, and she never knew for sure when was the moment that he unfolded into a sturdy toddler bent on crawling away from her.

She could not imagine having another, loving another the way she loved this one. Perhaps this was why she allowed the symptoms to go unnoticed for far too long before she accepted that she was expecting another baby.

William was one when she gave birth to a girl. She was overjoyed that she should be so blessed. The girl was named Ruth after a woman Robert had known in England, and she was as perfect as William had been. She was relieved to see how effortlessly her full heart expanded to make room for her daughter.

Ruth had fat cheeks and big eyes and no hair when she was born, but Matilda hoped that she would inherit her father's hair, dreaming already of the different hairstyles she would create on her daughter's head.

When she was nearly two weeks old, Aunty Dede decided that it was time to pierce Ruth's ears. She heated a needle double-threaded with black cotton in an open flame to sterilise it. Then she wiped the baby's right earlobe with boiling water and pushed the needle through the centre of the lobe and into a piece of cork that she held on the other side. Ama tried to steady her granddaughter's thrashing arms, while Aunty Dede looped the cotton and knotted it, biting off the excess thread with her teeth to leave a tiny ring of black thread in the baby's ear. Matilda had retreated to her bedroom from where she still had to tolerate her baby's raw cries. Undeterred, Aunty Dede plunged the needle into the baby's other ear with steady hands before Ama carried her to her mother to be comforted. Matilda grimaced when she saw her daughter's swollen earlobes and tear-stained face but was pleased that it was over.

Every morning and night for the next few days, she cleaned Ruth's ears with cotton wool dipped in boiling water to remove the residue of blood and pus that had gathered, and then gently pulled the thread ring round to make sure that the hole could not grow shut. She was overjoyed when finally she was able to cut the thread away from Ruth's ears and replace it with a pair of tiny gold-coloured earrings. Now no one could mistake her beloved daughter for a boy.

Now she had two children to marvel over. She beheld their every deed with unadulterated delight and wonder. Ruth's first smiles and reluctantly unclenching fists, her floppy head and regurgitated feeds were as enchanting as William's first unsteady steps, his undecipherable babble and contagious laughter. In months to come, she would ask herself if she had gloried excessively in her children, whether she had begun to take her joy for granted, or whether, quite simply, she had been too proud.

When Ruth was three months old, on a night Matilda was with Robert, she became ill with a mysterious fever. Matilda found Aunty Amele pacing the yard with the screaming infant when she returned home. She took her child, additionally distressed that she had not been home when her daughter needed her. She strove unsuccessfully to ease her child's discomfort, sensing that something was terribly wrong. She wished her mother and Aunty Dede had not gone away to visit a relative whose husband had passed away. Aunty Amele thought it might be malaria, but Matilda knew that while she was breastfeeding her, the baby was protected. Aunty Amele spent the next few hours fretting beside Matilda, unable to provide any further helpful suggestions.

She desperately tried to soothe her baby and cool her down, but the baby's cries became more and more shrill and painful, waking up the entire house. She rocked her and paced for hours, crying and begging God to let her child be well.

As soon as the darkness began to fade, she took the baby to the doctor, accompanied by her aunt. 'Go and tell Lawyer that we have taken Ruth to the doctor,' she instructed Eunice between sobs before they left the house. By now, the baby had stopped crying and only whimpered from time to time. Her crying seemed to have exhausted her, and she was dozy and sluggish.

The doctor rushed out to see them when he realised that she was Lawyer Bannerman's wife. Matilda was too distressed to speak, and Aunty Amele explained that the baby had been very hot and had cried a lot. Before she could finish, the doctor called for his driver to take the baby to the hospital. In the car, Matilda began to plead more fervently with God. She implored and bargained for the tiny bundle that seemed oblivious, and which, despite the vigorous rocking, would not open her eyes. Matilda removed all her clothes save for her tiny cloth nappy, but still the child's body was burning. They were almost at the hospital when she realised her baby was not making any sounds at all. She shook her gently first, then harder, shouting her name out loud.

'Driver, faster. Come on!' the doctor shouted. He tried to take the baby from Matilda. 'Don't shake her,' he said.

'God, please help my baby.' She refused to let go of her baby. Her stomach lurched, and she felt a wave of nausea overwhelm her. The baby was cooling down. Matilda screamed, 'Please, no. Please, I beg you, don't take my child. Please!'

The doctor managed to prise one of her arms away so that he could take a proper look at the baby. She was not breathing, and her lips were darkening. Matilda looked at him and saw the look of despondency in his face. She screamed and clutched her baby to her breast. Her lifeless baby. And she cried freely. Tears splashed on to her baby's face, tears her baby could not feel.

Later that morning, it rained for the first time that year. The sky darkened with gathered clouds, and the soil moistened in anticipation, soaking the air with the sweet smell of damp earth. As the trees began to sway vigorously in the strong wind carried over the ocean, the normally sweltering, sedate population closed down their makeshift streetside stores, hurriedly removed washing from lines, carried chairs, food, coal pots and other household objects to shelter, and themselves scuttled indoors to await the rain. Empty vessels were strategically placed to catch rainwater. But for a short while, it would be cooler outside than in, and a few lingered, savouring the unusual coolness and darkness, the reduced heat which made breathing more pleasurable.

The rain came. It fell in thick, fat drops. It bounced off the parched ground and formed fast-flowing rivulets, which poured, along with a layer of the red earth, into fast-filling gutters. Myriad flying insects came too; lured from their nests with newly grown wings only to be pounded back to earth after an abrupt solo flight, where they could abandon their sodden wings and crawl back into their drenched holes. Puddles formed rapidly, and soon a cacophony of toads and frogs was heard through the driving rain. So nature danced in honour of the rainfall, while the empty streets were washed and the ground fed; goats, sheep, dogs, chickens and cats had taken refuge wherever they could and seemed quietened by this unusual sight. When the downpour was reduced to a harmless drizzle, impish children emerged to dance delightedly in the warm shower, which formed droplets on their impenetrable hair and skidded off their shimmering black bodies. Somewhere, distant farmers were probably rejoicing at answered prayers, but in Accra, the rainfall seemed inconsequential to most. To Matilda, it was as if all of heaven too was weeping the tears she could no longer cry.

She felt nothing when her daughter was laid to rest in a tiny white coffin with pink satin lining two weeks later. That is to say, she felt a great deal, too much, and her mind, exhausted and overpowered by the many emotions, in the end simply deadened to the painful sensations.

She was sure she would not survive the slow, unbearable days. She went about in a daze, silent and distraught, unable to do anything useful but sit and stare and weep. She did not feel the heat or the flies on her skin. She did not hear the baffled cries of her son. She did not know when she was thirsty or hungry, and when she was tired, she could not sleep. Often, when she did sleep, she would dream that she was suckling her baby and wake up to the silent reality that her baby was gone, and that her breasts, still producing milk, were heavy and throbbing.

Her body cried out for sleep, her mind for respite from the endlessly circling thoughts and questions. On wakening, her consciousness was immediately hijacked by the sensation of deep loss, of a sharp physical pain where her heart continued to beat in spite of her desire that it would cease. Not a moment passed when she did not think of her child, want to hold her or evoke her smell. Would she be able to do things differently if she could relive Ruth's life?

She was never left alone, possibly because her family feared that she would harm herself, although such a violent thought would not have easily occurred to Matilda. Even when she had to go to the toilet, someone would accompany her and wait outside the latrine. She knew this was only out of concern, and her mother's conviction that a person who has just been bereaved must not be left to grieve alone.

Robert did not ask her to cook for him and thankfully did not request any visits, not that Matilda would have been allowed to attend to him. When he came to see her, he asked her why she had not gone to the doctor earlier, and she was certain that he held her responsible for their baby's death. In any event, she blamed herself, as perhaps any mother would, so she was unsurprised that others too might suspect her of neglect and carelessness. There was no postmortem, because the family did not want the baby's body to be mutilated, so she never found out what had killed her precious child.

The older women wanted to consult the fetish priest immediately to find out who had come to claim the baby and why. They wanted to know what to do to avoid it happening again, whether someone was angry with the family, whether they had been cursed. But Matilda refused to go with them. She was sure that Ruth's death was God's way of punishing her for not trusting in Him and for going to see the fetish in the first place. The minister at church had become even more vehement in his opposition to traditional religion, possibly because after gentle persuasion, the congregation of the Accra Methodist Church gave no indication of heeding his teachings.

He preached of his frustration that although the church was full to the brim every Sunday, that although the congregation sang heartily and donated generously, and although they nodded approvingly and spoke nothing but praise to his face, they had in no way altered their cosmopolitan practice of 'worshipping in two temples' as he put it. He had abandoned all graciousness and now preached fervently about the wrath of God on the 'Sunday-church-Monday-fetish custom', and his sermons had become more and more zealous. Matilda was convinced that she had brought this tragedy on herself. She resolved never again to visit the fetish priest, and never again to allow her mother and aunts to bully her into consulting him.

But the women did not give up.

'What is wrong with you?' her mother asked her after the funeral. 'Don't you want to know who has done this? Don't you want to make sure it does not happen again?'

'Ma, I am a Christian now, and I won't go and see the fetish priest about this or anything else. Reverend Dankwa says fetish priests are demonic.'

'"Reverend Dankwa said this, Reverend Dankwa said that" is all you say these days. Just because he has abandoned our culture to further his career in the Church does not mean that you have to do the same. Where is the problem? I go and see the fetish; I respect my elders and honour the dead. That does not mean that I don't believe in the Almighty. But this is different. The Almighty is not interested in our everyday problems, and anyway, I don't understand why you can't go to church like the rest of us do without abandoning our tradition,' said her mother.

Aunty Dede also seemed genuinely bewildered.

'You are really getting above your station these days. Just because you are Lawyer's wife don't forget where you came from, my girl. Why do you think that you are so special anyway?' Her mother tutted in disgust. 'Let me tell you something. What is good enough for us is good enough for you too. Do you understand me? Or are you trying to tell me and your aunty that we are not correct Christians? You think we are sinners, is that it?' Ama was becoming more and more agitated. 'As your Reverend Dankwa himself would say, "Let he who is free from blemish cast the first stone."'

272

'We have been going to church since before you were born, Matilda. We even baptised you with a Christian name and sent you to a mission school. Why do you think that we would want to compromise your Christianity in any way?' asked Aunty Dede gently.

'You misunderstand me, Aunty. I am not saying that you are sinners; I would never say that. But the time has come for me to make a stand. I don't mean to be disrespectful, but I beg you to respect my wishes in this matter. I can't go and see the fetish priest. I won't go. When have I ever disrespected you or disobeyed you? I have always done my best, but this I cannot do. I won't do.' She was shaking her head, causing sizeable teardrops that had welled up in her eyes to stream down her face. She was quaking inside, but she was determined not to give in. This was the first time she had dared to contradict her mother or any of her elders with conviction. Please let this argument be over now, she thought; she did not know if she had the strength to stand up to them much longer.

'Oh, let the girl go.' Ama waved her away, as though she was an irritating fly. 'She has become so high and mighty these days.'

Matilda was relieved; and she returned to her silent haven – her stool in the shade of the pawpaw tree.

A few weeks later, when she was putting William to bed, she felt something hard in his pillow and pulled out from the pillowcase an amulet similar to the one she had received from the priest. She realised at once that the women had gone behind her back and taken little William to the fetish priest. She was enraged and confronted her mother.

'We had to be sure that he would be protected,' said her mother unrepentantly. 'He is my grandchild, you know? I have duties to my family too.'

'But I told you that I did not want to have anything to do with the fetish any more. How dare you?' she shouted. Her mother was staring at her with a shocked expression. 'I don't care what you need to do for yourself, but don't ever take my child there again. And take this evil thing away from us,' she screamed, flinging the amulet across the room.

Ama gasped and hurried to pick up the amulet. Then she turned and faced her angry daughter. 'Never talk to me like that again,' she said in a whisper, and then she slapped Matilda hard across her face. 'And may the gods pardon you,' she said scornfully and walked out of the room.

Matilda told Robert in between floods of tears about the problems at home. They did not often talk like this; she rarely revealed her true feelings to him since he never seemed interested. But the strain of living in the house with her mother who refused to talk to her, and her lack of sleep, caused in no small measure by her fear that she had indeed offended the gods with her insolent behaviour, was taking its toll. When she explained that she wanted him to intervene and forbid Ama from taking their son to the fetish again, he refused, 'I think this is an internal family problem for you to sort out without my involvement. Anyway, I don't see your concern. This fetish priest nonsense is all mumbo jumbo and quite harmless. If it keeps the old women happy, why don't you just let them get on with it?'

Matilda, who in any event was sure that Robert was not much older than her own mother, was not reassured. But she realised that there was no point discussing this matter further. She did what she thought he wanted. She spoke no more of what was concerning her and, instead, applied herself to his needs.

Time passed. Matilda hoped that another baby would fill the cavernous emptiness caused by Ruth's death. She prayed that once she was pregnant again, the knot of pain in her chest would melt and the desire to hold her daughter once more would recede. But the ache eased only slightly as a new life began to grow in her womb. This time, she did not feel celebratory but weighed down by doubts. She condemned herself for denying her daughter the chance to grow up. If only she had taken her to the doctor earlier, if only she had listened to Reverend Dankwa, if only she had been strong enough – all these and many more ifs plagued her night and day. But the weeks advanced with unremitting relentlessness, and her body blossomed boldly.

PART II

The Gold Coast

August 1946

Chapter Seventeen

It was the middle of a particularly fruitful wet season. The rains had come early, and the earth, which for most of the year looked barren and tired, was less dusty and sprouted life wherever it could; prosperously green tree saplings, weeds and grass emerged from the most sterile-looking cracks in pavements, on roofs and even in gutters, flourishing, until in a burst of productiveness, these random growths were removed by determined house owners with specially sharpened cutlasses. This season, the rains came often, in short bursts mostly in the early mornings, so that dawn was fresher than normal, damp and devoid of the usual morning sounds. But by midday, the air, cleaned by the rain, allowed the sun's rays to penetrate more intensely and shower the land with interminable, tiresome tropical heat.

A sizeable bougainvillea had shot up against one of the walls in Saint John's compound, beautifying the yard with its glowing green leaves and its delicate blooms, which fluttered softly to the ground from time to time in the langorous breeze to form a threadbare purple carpet over the earth. The plant's lean branches had grown unchecked and were twisted and mingled into a bush that ran along the top of the wall.

Matilda was daydreaming on a chair in the dappled shade of the well-positioned shrub, a plant appreciated in a way that might wrongly suggest that its existence was the result of some careful aforethought. She was holding what she knew would be her last baby, suckling him, at an age when her other children had been weaned. She savoured the serenity, the intimacy of the rhythmic tug at her breast as her son sucked greedily; for now, no other responsibility or obligation mattered.

Baby Robert, who the family called Junior Lawyer, was eight months old. He was Matilda's fifth child – 'Four alive, one dead,' she had heard the midwife say at his birth, and the words still echoed from time to time. After Ruth had died six years ago, Matilda had two sons in quick succession – Earnest and then Samuel. Her family had encouraged this, as though somehow the more live children she retained, the less relevant would become the void left by the dead child. At each birth, her heart had ached a little more when she realised that her body had ejected yet another male into the world. The birth had been complicated and arduous, and the doctor explained that her body had been worn out from producing five children in such a short space of time; another baby would be out of the question; 'unwise' was the word he had used. Now she was resigned to the fact that she would not have another child.

'You really need to wean this baby, you know,' said Aunty Dede, waddling slowly towards Matilda, barely concealing the pain that walking now caused her. Years of excess had taken their toll on her body; her stout legs struggled to support her large frame, and she moved gracelessly and in slow motion, placing all of her weight on one flat, wide foot and one side of her body before taking the next step by shifting her weight over to the other side, her feet shuffling along, never quite leaving the ground. Her body thus swayed from side to side, moving like a large ship in rough waters, edging forwards all the time, slowly but undeterred. She sat down heavily in the chair next to Matilda, which creaked under her mass. As usual, she was smiling and did not seem bothered by the fact that she was breathless from the short journey she had just made or that she would need help to get herself out of the chair when she wanted to move on. Aunty Dede was always happy, or so it appeared to Matilda. She had recently returned after a short visit to her husband, a man she hardly ever spoke of, although when she did, it was always in very respectful tones.

'Oh, he is not ready yet, look at how he enjoys it,' said Matilda, hugging her child proprietorially. 'I can wait a few more weeks.' She gazed at him, painfully aware that nothing she could do would stop this baby following in the independent steps of his older brothers that led away from her. And one day, would they lead all the way to England, where their father wanted them to go and study? She shuddered, hoping that when the time came somehow she would have the strength to cope with that kind of immeasurable separation. 'Anyway, Aunty Dede, tell me why are you always so happy? What is the secret in your life that makes you so?' she asked. 'If there is one thing that I could give my children, it would be that they take after you. Nothing seems to bother you. Look at me, I have everything I should wish for: a husband who doesn't beat me, and he is rich and educated, healthy sons, my own health, and yet you are always happier than me.'

'Maybe you take after your mother.' Aunty Dede laughed. She used every part of her bulk to laugh – her shoulders and chest heaved and wobbled, she clapped her fat hands in delight, and her entire face shone with happiness as she produced this deep, happy sound, which engulfed Matilda with warm reassurance. Again, she reminded herself to laugh often with her own children. She rocked her baby gently; he had fallen asleep with her nipple in his mouth. She looked at his peaceful face. Was this not the greatest pleasure in life; feeding a child until, satisfied, he drifts into deep, contented sleep like this?

Her aunt said, 'I have noticed that you seem different. Has something happened? Did you quarrel with him?'

Matilda creased her lips and remained silent.

'I have told you over and over again, the only thing to do is to ignore him when he annoys you. Men are like children, you must take no notice of their bad behaviour.'

'We have not quarrelled . . . but . . .'

'Oh, I see. He is not sending for you often, is that it? You are worried that your days as favoured wife are over, eh? Well, it could not last for ever, and to be honest with you, I am surprised that it has lasted this long. You just have to look on the bright side; you have more freedom and more time to yourself. Don't take it personally, that is how they are,' she said matter-of-factly. 'After all, which man is satisfied with one woman?'

'I know,' said Matilda. Her heart was heavy. 'It is not that I am jealous of her, but things have changed. I think he prefers her company when he is with his colleagues. She converses with them, and I stand there like an idiot. I stupidly allowed myself to become used to his attentions, and without warning it seems I am not needed any more. I have not seen him for weeks now. I don't even know whether I have offended him.'

'Knowing men as I do, if you had offended him, he would have told you. It is only we women who feel sorry for ourselves and conjure up all sorts of plans for revenge in our heads,' said Aunty Dede, laughing again.

Matilda didn't feel like laughing. She looked at her baby with deep furrows on her brow. Sentiments she could not articulate pounded her chest, making it ache. Why, when she had every reason to be contented? And as she did regularly to remind herself of her fortune, she remembered her friend Patience. She had continually failed to secure a marriage, some said due to less than ideal rumours, and then had become pregnant by an unfortunate man who had promised that he would send his family to ask for her hand in marriage, but he disappeared without trace. Patience suspected that he had gone out to Burma to fight with the Royal West African Frontier Force and had perhaps been killed there. When the war ended, she had hoped for some news, but none came. And when Patience's daughter was born, no one had come to declare parentage, leaving Patience bitter in the knowledge that he had gone off without mentioning the pregnancy to his family. She was certain that if the child's family knew about her existence, they would have performed the necessary ceremonies to recognise her. She did not even know who they were or where they lived. She had been completely fooled, left to raise the child as a bastard. Nonetheless, Matilda knew that barrenness would have been a far worse fate for Patience and had stayed close to provide as much moral support as she could. Seeing her friend distressed, appreciating her struggle, and her shame, Matilda had learned to see the good in her situation. Not least of all because eventually Patience could no longer endure Matilda's complaints about what, to her, was a most blessed union. It was only when Patience's daughter died of malaria that they became close again.

'After all, what is it that you want from a marriage?' asked Aunty Dede.

Matilda shook her shoulders and then said, 'Something more . . . I don't know what.'

'You have to distinguish between life and your husband. He is not your life. You have your own life for which you alone are responsible. He is not responsible for your happiness.'

Matilda looked confused. It was true that after several years of marriage, and with her days of nursing children nearly over, she often asked herself whether this was it, whether she had already achieved everything that was required of her. She could not raise her children alone; that was a collective task her children's relations took seriously. There would be no intense motherly relationship that would require exclusive input from her.

'It is common. You are wondering what your role will be if your husband does not need you and your children don't need you.'

'You have read my mind.'

'You are not the first woman to reach this point.'

Was contentment a ridiculous expectation? she mused. And would she know how it felt? Certainly, contentment and happiness were not goals of most people around her. It was destiny that had to be welcomed with open arms, tolerated, if not entertained. She had watched her mother, who refused to live at ease with the yoke of her fate, suffer daily. And because of what? Matilda wondered. Because she could not accept what life had dealt her? Because not a day or an hour seemed to pass when she did not complain about her unfortunate life? After a few short months as a happy, new grandmother, Ama had quickly reverted to her acidic and dissatisfied state, a woman whose insides may well have been eaten up with bitterness and bile, for she did suffer from terrible ulcers. And would she grow in her mother's image and become that way too? Was the inability to be satisfied coursing unfettered in her blood?

'Maybe the time has come for you to do something for yourself,' said Aunty Dede. 'You have done well, bearing your husband children, and in my opinion, you have done your best. You always wanted to go back to school to learn English. Maybe the time is right? Why don't you tell Robert that you want to learn something? I am sure he can pay for you to have lessons, or maybe he even knows someone who can teach you.'

'But . . .'

'You have to do it for yourself. Not because of him. Not because of the first wife. Yes, I concede, maybe for your children, but first and foremost for yourself.'

Matilda had not stopped dreaming of going back to school one day, but for years, it had been impossible to see beyond the needs of her children. In fact, she had expected her elders to be the very ones to tell her to put silly ideas out of her head and concentrate on her obligations. Now here was hope, wedging its way into her mind, energising her in a way that surprised her.

Ama came out of the house and interrupted the women's conversation. 'It is all right for some of you, sitting around doing nothing. I have to go to the market again today to help Celestina. The girl is useless! She cannot cope on her own. I don't understand this generation,' she said, waving her hands aggressively. 'In my day, I just had to manage. Now, when I should be taking things slowly, relaxing a little more, here I am going to sit in the hot sun to sell to people. When my own daughter is married to a rich lawyer. And my husband is still doing nothing to support me. Is that right? Tell me.' She sounded as if she was on the verge of crying. But she was not a woman who cried easily, and without waiting for answers to any of her questions, she walked out of the compound muttering under her breath.

Matilda and Aunty Dede waited until she was out of earshot and then they crumpled with laughter. Junior Lawyer woke with a fright. His startled eyes looked around to see why he had been roused so disrespectfully. His mother, feeling lighter of spirit than she had in a while, rocked him and blew on to his little, hot face and he quickly dozed off again.

Late that afternoon, Matilda walked to Downing House with the baby bound tightly to her back. The sun seemed to have paused in its descent and hung on the horizon like a dim orange lantern, too far for its warmth to feel powerful, but close enough to light the dark-

282

ening sky. Her leisurely pace disguised the drone of awakened dreams that swam around her head. Absentmindedly she smiled and waved at people who greeted her. When had she reached this pinnacle of Jamestown society? Not when she married Robert, so when, at what point during the slow metamorphosis into mature woman had they decided she was worthy of their respect and admiration? And when had she begun to play her role, dressing up just to saunter down the road, watching how she comported herself as everyone else did? When had she grown accustomed to the many unseen eyes that quickly identified her as Lawyer Bannerman's wife and watched her constantly, not always kindly, to the many hidden mouths that reported unacceptable or strange behaviour to her well-known husband or his circle of workers, friends and family? It still amazed her, this transformation.

Two young girls sauntered up and walked beside her for a while. They greeted her shyly then became engrossed in their own private conversation about the baby. They concurred that he was Lawyer's baby but then disputed whether he looked like his mother or his father. 'But you have never seen him properly,' said one vehemently to the other. 'I have seen him closely, and I tell you he looks just like the baby.'

'Foolish girl, you mean the baby looks like him,' said the other. 'How can a father look like his child?' she asked rhetorically, probably pleased to be able to point out her friend's error. Then as easily as they had joined her, the girls walked away and crossed over to the other side of the road.

Matilda kept a serene smile on her face. The kind of expression that came without much effort now, and which allowed her to look pleasant and approachable. She could not have been much older than those girls when Robert first saw her. She looked at them now, their bodies bulging into womanhood, but their faces steadfast to childhood. What did a man see in a child like that? Over and over she had turned in her mind how she could have emitted some imperceptible signal to Robert all those years ago. Her parents could have no inkling that she still questioned why they had let him marry her. Why had it not seemed improper to them? She clasped her hands underneath her baby's bottom. What would she do if Ruth had faced a similar situation? What would Robert have said? What kind of man would Ruth have married? She had to stop. These thoughts went nowhere straight. They led only back to each other. In any event, she knew there was no man on this earth that Robert would allow Julie's daughters to marry so young. He had plans for them, for all his children in fact. He talked at times in a dreamy manner about the degrees they would obtain, the letters that he wanted to see behind their names some day. Wouldn't he have loved Ruth just as much?

No, there was no point revisiting such a distant event, which after all had resulted in all these children. She could not imagine their non-existence. Yet they were the products of Robert's desire for her. Without that they wouldn't be. Those were the facts that made up her life. And was it that bad? As Aunty Dede always said, 'If you look backwards when you are walking forwards, you will fall into a gutter.'

'Good afternoon, Aunty Matilda,' called a woman who was creased with age and black as ink, sitting on a rickety stool waiting patiently for purchasers of her wares. 'How is the baby?' she asked, waving at the sleeping child, smiling to reveal several missing teeth in her receding, blotchy gums.

'Fine, thank you,' said Matilda, not stopping to pursue this conversation. But she smiled at the lady, grateful for bringing her out of her winding thoughts.

'Please, hello, Aunty,' spoke another woman softly, perched in the doorway of her home wearing a piece of old batik wrapped under her arms, her hair covered in a different, equally pattered piece of cloth. Matilda nodded without pausing; she could not favour one stranger over another by stopping to chat to one and not the other. She had even stopped buying anything from the vendors near Robert's house soon after her marriage when she witnessed a fight between the *kenkey* sellers and heard that it had been started by the one she didn't patronise.

Quite close to Downing House, a man stood up from where he was sitting under the shade of one of the old neem trees that lined the road and came bounding up to her with his eyes wide open in surprise. 'Aunty Matilda,' he said loudly, as though he were greeting a long-lost friend. He gripped her hand in both of his and held it tightly. 'Please, how are you, madam? How is the baby? How is Lawyer these days? And the boys, they must have grown by now, how are they? I have not seen them for a while.' He sounded regretful.

She smiled awkwardly. She did not know him; she smiled, told him her family was fine and tried to extricate her hand from his soft, clammy palms.

'Please, greet Lawyer for me,' he said, grinning with sad eyes before he let go of her hand and allowed her on her way.

She had learned not be bemused by this kind of encounter. For all she knew, he was a former employee of Robert's who had been sacked for misbehaving and longed to be forgiven. Early on she had learned not to relay such messages to Robert, who only ever became irate if he was reminded about someone or something that he had decided to forget. She understood that she was the only live connection between those who lived inside the big house and those who lived along its walls. Robert and Julie never walked down these streets. They were never seen by these people except fleetingly as their cars rolled past. But Sister Matilda, although no longer one of them, still talked to them, still walked beside them, and they admired her greatly for it.

Robert's compound had not changed over the years, except that there were numerous children running around all the time. The youngest of Julie's six children, George, was now already seven and only two months older than Matilda's oldest, William. They were great friends and went to the same school. Earnest and Samuel spent more of their time with their mother; however, they too often came to play with their older half-brothers and sisters at Downing House, under, at least so Matilda feared, the malevolent, watchful gaze of their stepmother. Patience often warned her that this was not a good state of affairs. 'To leave your children unguarded in the presence of a witch is not a wise thing,' she said. But Matilda knew it was important for her children to feel as important as Robert's other children: to eat the same food, to be friends with their other brothers and sisters and to spend time around the matriarch Aunty Baby, who was still living in her downstairs room all alone. Aunty Gladys had died after suffering for months with an unnamed illness emphasising to Matilda the need for her children to get to know the living members of

Robert's family. They wouldn't come visiting at Uncle Saint John's house, so she brought them here. And now that they were old enough to go to the same English-speaking mission school as their brothers, William and Earnest dropped by at Downing House most days after school. She wanted them to understand that they belonged to this distinguished family and to know their place amongst them. In any event, she was secure in the knowledge that with so many adult eyes at Downing House all the time it would be hard for even Julie to mistreat her stepchildren.

Several children, hers and Julie's, ran up to her as soon as she entered the compound to give her a joyful welcome, and she stooped to allot indiscriminate hugs and kisses. 'Aunty, Aunty,' 'Ma, Ma,' the younger children cried, tugging at her hands, pulling her dress and her bag, hoping for some treat or some short story, for some of her time, while each of the older children tried to tell her about some important event or achievement from their day.

'Yes, William,' she said, beaming with joy. 'Oooh, it's the beautiful twins, Sylvia and Bernadette,' she said approvingly. 'I love your matching dresses. Come here, Gloria,' she said, giving the child a hug. 'And there is one of my favourite sons. Hello, Earnest,' she said, scooping her son up tightly. And so she stood jiggling Earnest on her hip, while he fondled her face, and listened to each child in turn, smiling, praising, nodding, approving, laughing until, satisfied, they let her disentangle herself and continue.

As she walked towards his office, Julie appeared in the doorway of the kitchen.

'I see you refuse to change your ways, then.'

Matilda was surprised to see her wearing an apron and her hands covered in flour.

'Hello, Julie. I have told you many times, the new ways are not always the best ones.' Her boldness disguised the old, indefinable apprehension that rose up to tighten her belly whenever she saw the first wife. She paused to nudge her baby upwards and tighten the cloth that bound his warm form to hers.

'Ah, why do I bother,' said Julie. 'Only those who know no better carry babies on their backs in public.' She turned to re-enter the kitchen.

'And it is good to see that you are doing something useful for a change,' said Matilda, hoping the words would carry themselves to Julie's ears.

Robert was alone in his office. She knocked and entered. For a minute, he did not notice her and remained engrossed in his book. She watched her husband, ignoring the slight swelling she felt in her throat as she tried to recall when the last amorous visit she had paid him was. She had heard that he had another new woman. He had been seen about town with a glamorous girl; she had been spotted at the races with him, seen in his car, and even in his office. Matilda knew this was different to the other relationships he had had over the years, girls here and there who provided some necessary distraction. This one seemed to be fulfilling the role of wife, her role, Julie's role. Just the other day, his maid tried to give her a pretty, floral ceramic dish thinking it was hers. But when Matilda said she had never seen it before, the maid had mumbled something incoherent and put the dish in one of the cupboards out of sight of everyone who might possibly find it offensive.

Robert's face showed few signs of ageing. There were silver specks in the hair above his ears, and the edges of his face had filled out, rounding it. The extra weight worked well; he looked good. She gazed at his hands. She had always admired them when he was asleep. He had big hands, which were not fleshy, and his fingers, which were strong and lean but not bony, were incredibly long with rounded cuticles and square-cut nails that always looked newly manicured.

He saw her and smiled uncertainly, blinking away the sunlight that filtered in behind her.

'Come in,' he said. 'How are things?' He looked at her briefly and then back at his book.

Instantly, all her intentions to start a light, happy conversation dissolved. 'Oh, I don't really want to bother you. I have something I want to ask you, but I can come at a better time,' she said to the top of his head.

He looked up with a wrinkled brow as though he was surprised she was still standing there. 'Oh, it's fine.' He seemed flustered and looked back at his book, elaborately placing a scrap of paper in the fold to ensure that he did not lose his page.

Matilda considered abandoning her mission, but she clenched her back teeth for courage, and before she could weaken further, said, 'I want to . . . I thought maybe . . . Robert, I would like to learn English, and I wondered whether it would be possible, if it is not too much trouble for you, maybe you know someone you can ask, whether they can teach me English? I will be a good student . . .'

Robert laughed. 'Is that it? All I ever get asked for these days is money. Why?'

'Why not?'

'Why not indeed.'

'I would like to better myself. To help my children with their schoolwork, maybe one day get some work . . .'

'No wife of mine needs to work,' said Robert.

'I am not suggesting that you don't provide adequately for us all.'

'No. But I tell you what, I will ask around, maybe Alan knows someone. Do you remember him? Wasn't it he who suggested something about English lessons years ago?'

'Yes. Yes, I remember Alan. He comes here for dinner.'

'But I think it was Julie who pointed out that you were too busy for anything like that.'

'She is always giving her opinion where it is not needed.'

'Yes. Well, I suppose it is commendable that you want to learn something. I respect that.' He was staring at her. 'I'll have a chat with Alan.'

'Thank you,' she said, wishing she could learn to chat as effortlessly as Julie. She turned to leave.

'How is he?'

She turned to see him looking at the baby on her back. 'He is doing very well. He will walk soon. I think that he is very clever . . . like you.'

'Oh? That's good. See you soon, then,' he said.

'And how are you? I have not seen you for a while now.'

'Ah, yes. I am very busy. Very. The practice is doing well. So many cases.' He beamed. 'I hope you are not complaining that I am working hard to provide for my family?'

'No. But—'

'Anyway, I need to get back to this brief.'

She nodded and walked out. It was sad, she thought, how men were able to spend so little time with their children. Yes, Robert could hear the older ones playing outside and watch them when it took his fancy, but when they were babies, he had nothing to do with them. Take this baby, for instance, she thought, patting his bottom, he had never been held even once by his father. What a tragedy it is to be a father, she thought. How much they miss simply because they are men. Thank you, God, that You made me a woman, that I can carry my baby without anyone thinking that I am strange or weak. At times like this she wondered why it was that she had never had another baby girl. Even Julie had three. If something happened to one of her daughters, God forbid, then she would still have two spare.

Chapter Eighteen

From where Audrey sat on the beach, Alan still looked marvellously youthful; his hair swept over his eyes, his shirt undone to his stomach, his feet bare. Labadi Beach was deserted, and Alan sauntered, kicking sand, splashing seawater, oblivious of her. Closer scrutiny revealed grooves and dents in his skin, greying, thinning hair, tired eyes. Even so, he was not as ravaged as she was. This continent had prematurely aged her. Her eyes had sunk further into her skull, and her mouth had lost its plumpness. She preferred not to look closely these days, and when she did, found it hard to recognise the woman who had embarked on the most amazing journey of her life just . . . God help me . . . more than ten years ago.

In moments of rage, she still cursed them all freely whenever she realised afresh just how long she had lived, existed here, without a break – Hitler and every German, the Jews, Neville Chamberlain, Winston Churchill, the Americans, the bloody Africans for needing to be colonised in the first place. And Alan. She cursed him the most. Blast him. It was entirely his fault. She plucked her leathery brown skin and lifted the tips of her eyebrows so her crow's-feet retreated a little. She should have kept her hat on at all times; now she had indelible squints round her eyes. And her face was one large freckle; over the years, they had spread and joined. She didn't bother with make-up any more; she couldn't see the point. It only made one shimmer and look ridiculous. What she did do, though, was dye her hair with large amounts of henna regularly, so it was bright red.

She stared out on to the horizon wistfully. Even now, there might be ships out there way beyond her natural vision, gliding home to England. A place she now visualised in grainy black and white. She forced her thoughts to change course; she was convinced that it was longing for things that were out of reach that had almost made her mad.

She took deep breaths to fill her lungs with sea-damp air, remembering how for long years she hadn't been able to come to the beach. She had refused to go whenever Alan suggested it without giving him an explanation, and eventually, he had stopped asking her. And when she did go again, she battled quietly with painful and unpleasant recollections of that afternoon. Now, even years after, there remained a dull tension in the pit of her tummy, faint, but present nonetheless.

Alan was beckoning to her, inviting her into the water. He was smiling eagerly, his face radiating. He had never given up on her. He had known something was wrong, and though she was sure he had never quite figured out what had happened, he had remained committed. And she loved him for that, in a respectful, undemonstrative way, with a love that ironically was even less passionate than that she had witnessed between her parents. Funny, she thought, how life can creep over you until you wake up one day and find you've been snared in a net, like a fish.

After the miscarriage, she had a legitimate reason to continue to reject him, and their relationship became sterile. Eventually, Alan did reach for her, but by then it felt as if they had inadvertently crossed a bridge, one that had since been dismantled, obliterating any possibility of return. He moved out of their room, which made sense; after all, she hated being woken up by him, and he hated sleeping with her cats. She had nine now, and they roamed freely in her bedroom, clawing at the eiderdown so that it was ruined, defecating on the bathroom floor and eating out of bowls that she placed in every room in their house.

She walked into the water, which was as warm as a bath. The waves erased her agitation. Each so different from its predecessor, they were mesmerising. Why else did she feel serenity wrapped around her so? Would she remember these wonderful sensations now seeping so freely into her soul when she was back at home? Where she had still not fully mastered the art of doing nothing, where she was at times still uneasy about her idleness? It amused her to remember how she had battled for years with the servants for control of her house, how she had subconsciously tried to live up to the stereotype of wife that her mother embodied, and how when she accepted her redundancy in domestic matters, once she had surmounted her desire to have a relationship with them, they seemed to annoy her less. Just like that, they became less irritating. And they coped well, she might as well admit. They ran things in a rather clockwork manner, actually, and she only seemed to offend everyone when she tried to get involved. She ignored them mostly these days and let them carry on how they wished. There was rarely need for discourse with them. And to be fair to them, especially Awuni, her input was not much missed. They carried on like bees, swarming around her house, doing their work around her, whistling and singing to themselves. Dutifully, they greeted and smiled, but otherwise, she might as well not be there.

It was in the garden she was queen. She tended it daily when she was home. Not all of it, mind, that would be too much, just a nice, manageable portion in front of the veranda, where she had created a rock garden. There were no special plants or anything like that – what would be the point when anything that could thrive in this heat, where rain was an unpredictable necessity, would do just fine? There were the rocks and stones she had gathered over time, arranging and rearranging them until she was pleased with the effect. The servants were used to her arriving home with a stone or two in the boot, which she always insisted had to be positioned straightaway, no matter what time of day or night. Cook once asked her why she didn't simply go to the stone quarry in the hills outside Accra and get a whole load of rocks. 'They can deliver too, madam,' he said, completely uncomprehending that her delight was in the slow unfolding of her garden, the paced creation of a masterpiece.

As they were leaving, Alan bought some small, sweet bananas and groundnuts from a little girl on the beach. She couldn't have been more than twelve or thirteen, yet tightly bound to her back was the sleeping body of a younger sibling. A sweet thing, with pink squished lips and glossy cheeks that he couldn't resist stroking. He paid the girl and watched her saunter off with the chipped enamel tray of fruit carefully balanced on her head.

He still found their childlessness hard. He had always hoped for a family of his own but knew it was unlikely with Audrey so keen to remain childless. Not long ago, he had raised the subject of children one last time, and she had looked right past him, unblinking, while she continued to pick her broken nails. He thought it was what she needed; to have someone else to think about. It would certainly help curb her drinking too, he thought. He knew she drank steadily every day. He had once marked the bottles over a number of weeks, to measure how much gin she was getting through. He had been alarmed when he realised quite how much it was and had raised it with her. In her indomitable style, she had told him he was being a bore. True, she was rarely overtly drunk when he got home from work, but he knew the signs. She would be amenable, laugh easily and smoke non-stop. He had raised his concerns again a few weeks later but had to back down when she started to cry. He could still hear the blame in her voice as she told him she needed a drink now and then to get through her life. He had had to listen to her moan about the endless boredom, the long, dark evenings when he was at work, and the wireless reception was lousy so she could not listen to London, when she had nothing to read because she had devoured every book and magazine she could lay her hands on, and a new shipment had not arrived from home. And when she was with friends, gossiping about old news or at a dinner party with the same lot one had had dinner with the previous week talking about the same things, everyone had a drink. Couldn't he see that she simply needed something to help her through the one long, tedious *déjà vu* that was her life? 'When are you going to realise that it is pointless to compare me to your mother?' she had asked accusatorily.

The next morning, Alan went to the office early to catch up with things, leaving Audrey to dawdle from one room to another, trying in vain to escape the gloominess that pervaded the house. She searched unproductively through piles of papers and letters on the desk in the living room for her mother's last letter so she could reply to it. Her search was fruitless, and she began scribbling a note, more pointless than ever. Ever since she received the letter telling her that her father had had a stroke, brought on by the stress of the air raids, Audrey had found it harder to write home. Her father had recovered most of his speech, but he was clearly a burden on her mother. He needed help with his shoelaces, his belt, his buttons. Audrey felt a little guilty that she wasn't there to help, a little relieved that she didn't need to be. She hadn't cried at all when she received the news. She was sure that was only because she was still coming to terms with the fact that her cousin Freddy was missing in action. His plane had disappeared over France, and he hadn't been heard from. She was sure he was dead and had cried for days for the waste of his young, handsome life. When she heard about her father's descent, well, it seemed trivial compared to the finality of Freddy's death.

Writing letters was hard enough with nothing to tell, and she had learned that written words are terrifyingly able to reveal, to solidify, to immortalise feelings, which otherwise might in time prove transient. From time to time, she would sit and attempt to write a jovial letter, but before she knew it, she had poured out her heart, described her average day and made herself sad. She sat smoking a cigarette and read what she had just written. She was calm about it now, this distance from home, this unending pause on her life. Years back, she would have cried at the encroaching whiff of depression. But she had learned to stop constantly seeking purpose and to embrace what her existence offered: lazy, if predictably boring, days. It was the evenings that were most problematic, especially if she spent them alone or alone with Alan. Then she seemed to need to drink rather more than usual to cope. All in all, it was preferable to pass the hours at the club with others who also had nowhere better to be.

She arrived there after a leisurely bath when the day's heat was beginning to wane. Her body softened, slackening visibly as she walked through the lobby. Her mind cleared a little, and her breathing eased. Before her, gloriously innumerable hours of chat with like-minded souls beckoned; behind her, well, a pointless existence, if one was going to be quite honest about it.

She walked through the hallway still garlanded with dampened photographs of those linked in some way to the club who had been killed in action. Earnest, young faces peered arrogantly through lenses seeing a future far different from the one they had been dealt. Prime position was held by Alexander Smythe, Sir Colin and Lady Smythe's son. He had been twenty-three and killed within weeks of going off to war. Audrey felt for them all, even though she could not claim to imagine what it was like to bury a child. Her dreadful mis-carriage hadn't deprived her of a fully grown person, one with presence and character whom she had loved, but she had known that Sir Colin and Lady Smythe would not return to the Gold Coast, and they hadn't.

Polly and Timo had also not returned from England. In fact, very few who had gone on leave just before war broke out had returned to the colony. The Atlantic was deemed too dangerous for non-essential travel. Audrey hadn't kept in touch with Polly, but she heard of them regularly enough and knew they were doing well back in Cambridge, where Timo was working in his family's business.

'Over here, darling,' called Alice.

'I need a drink,' said Audrey, settling down in a chair next to her friend and looking around for a steward, irritated that one had not materialised next to her already. One came over, nodded in greeting and asked Madam if she wanted her usual. He had barely removed his hand from the tall, icy gin and tonic he placed in front of her, when she reached for it and, closing her eyes, breathed in the com-forting smell. She took a long, satisfying sip. She felt her shoulders loosen further, and she took another sip, then she put her glass back on the table gingerly.

'Margaret is not coming; the baby is sick,' said Alice, taking a sip from her drink carefully so that the large drops of condensation that had formed on her glass did not fall on the tapestry on her lap.

'Nothing serious, I hope.'

'I rather doubt it. You know what Margaret is like.'

Audrey had noticed that in a far corner there was a group of men, commercial types, who were talking and laughing loudly and drinking a lot. They were from one of the mines up country, or perhaps from a timber company or even cocoa buyers. She was always a little nervous when this sort were in the club. She started her deep-breathing exercises, and Alice asked if she was all right. Audrey nodded and continued taking deep breaths. Then two of them started walking towards them. Audrey felt the blood drain from her face, but she plucked up the courage to look at them. She had never again seen Douggie and Derek but harboured a fear of bumping into them. She breathed out loudly as the men approached, relieved that she didn't recognise them. One had long hair and overgrown whiskers, and the other was small, balding, but also very muscular, and both were brown as nuts. For all she knew, they knew of her, thought Audrey, irate.

'Hello there, girls. How are we today?' asked the hairy man in a cheery cockney accent.

Alice looked at them so they would realise that they were as welcome as flies on a hot, sticky beach. 'We are relishing a few quiet moments away from the hustle and bustle of our families. If you don't mind, we would rather be alone.'

'I say, very high and mighty, are we, then?' he said, and he and his friend walked away.

Slowly, Audrey's bad feeling subsided as they discussed problems with their servants, the lack of good teabags and the desire for some proper mustard powder. And so, the afternoon passed. One last drink before tennis, then another. And another cigarette. Eventually, tennis, or anything energetic for that matter, seemed like a silly idea. Better to dip in the pool, stay in the shade, chatter and have one last drink before dinner.

Alan was having coffee on the veranda. All around him, Sheba's descendants were sunning themselves on various pieces of furniture. Sheba herself had disappeared a few years ago without trace. Audrey never found out what happened to her and feared that she had after all been part of a meal. She shuddered when she thought about it. She had quizzed all her staff at the time and warned them that if any more of her cats went missing, she would sack them all.

Cook, who had been affronted, told her that unfortunately her cat had probably been eaten by a snake, run over by a car, killed by a dog or met with any of numerous other possibilities. That one of them might have eaten it was insulting. 'After all, are we bush people? No,' he had said angrily. 'I beg to differ,' she had muttered under her breath.

Alan had had to push one of the cats off a chair before he could sit. When Audrey joined him, he said, 'I hope we aren't about to have any more kittens. I am not sure how much more I could cope with.'

Audrey lifted two large tabbies on to her lap and said, 'Gosh, it's bright this morning,' as she put on her sunglasses.

'There is something that I want to ask you. You know, pick your brain.' He handed her a cup of coffee. 'You remember my friend Robert, don't you?'

'Of course I do.' She poured milk into her saucer and placed it on the table for the cats.

'Do we have to have them up on the table?'

'They like it here. They would only fight if I put it on the floor. What about your friend with the harem?'

'Well, it's not quite a harem, although I must admit, I have seen him lately with a new woman . . . Anyway, do you remember a while ago . . . gosh, a few years now . . . I mentioned that his wife, his second wife, well, that she wanted to learn English, and I had suggested you might, you know, help her a little? She is illiterate, the poor girl, can't string a sentence together in English and . . .'

Audrey stroked her cats and looked at her garden, so marvellously fecund from all the rain. It had started earlier this year, and there seemed more of it than usual. She slept well when it rained, drops thundering down on her little patch, turning it briefly into the paradise she imagined she would be happy in. She watched Alan's moving lips. She had always liked his mouth, plumper and more tender than it looked. She wondered whether he was having an affair like all the other men eventually did. Something was keeping him going and his enthusiasm high. These days, she shivered at the thought of feeling the flesh of another person on hers. That part of her was truly dead, she thought, somewhat wistfully.

'. . . It was a long time ago and all that, you know, but I think it

297

might be something for you to do . . . a challenge, you know, if you taught her a little English? And some etiquette, you know what I mean.'

'Who?'

'You haven't heard a word I said.'

'Sorry, my mind wandered,' she said, looking at him intently.

'Matilda.'

'Matilda who?'

'Robert's wife.'

'I thought she was called Julie?'

'It would be nice if you could give me half the attention you give those bloody cats,' he said. He repeated his suggestion and said, 'It really is up to you. I thought it might amuse you. I sometimes think you are wasting your abilities, Audrey.'

She stirred her coffee. What made him think he could plan her life for her? Beyond what he already had? And what made him think she had so much free time, anyway? Her days were quite full, actually. She was on three committees now and was even the secretary for the steering committee too! All thanks to him. She had only done it to show him that she was capable in the first place, but he had remained totally unimpressed, as if he had expected it of her all along.

She stopped stirring her coffee and stared at him. She lifted her cup and took a few sips, wrinkling her nose when she tasted it. She screamed for Awuni to bring more milk. Yes, yet another of his mother's philosophies by which her own life was to be judged: 'Keep busy, keep happy, you've no reason not to do either.' But she had tried. And failed. At least she no longer castigated herself for it.

'Wasting, yes . . .' It might make some sense to find something useful to do other than organise quiz and bingo nights. But would teaching some wealthy man's concubine classify as useful? And she had never taught before. 'Why does she want to learn English?'

'Ah. Do you know, I have no idea. Didn't occur to me to ask. Perhaps she wants to improve herself, what with Robert's first wife being rather posh and all, for here anyway. I suppose the contrast between them makes her appear all the more primitive. Perhaps you might consider it?' Without looking at his wife, he said, 'Audrey, believe me, I know it is not always easy . . . but don't you think you should lay off the . . . gin a little? You know . . . ?' He looked at Audrey, who was gazing into the garden, carefully stirring her nearly full cup.

'Yes, I know,' she said with her eyes stretched wide in exasperation. 'It might be a challenge, I suppose.' Damn it, she thought, maybe this was what she needed, something to distract her.

'How perfect. She will be thrilled, you know; poor girl can't have much to look forward to. I'll tell Robert,' said Alan. He reached and clasped her hand.

Audrey counted slowly; one, two, three . . . ten, then she pulled free.

'Well, I'd best be off. I might have to work late again tonight . . . rather a lot to catch up with,' he said cheerily. He leaped out of his chair, and for a moment she thought he was going to kiss her on the cheek, but he scampered down the stairs towards his waiting car.

Chapter Nineteen

After Robert told her of the arrangements later that month, Matilda almost danced home, jiggling her baby on her back so that he slept through a rather bumpy ride. He offered to send his driver every morning to take her to Alan's house in the European residential area, where she would have two hours of English lessons with Mrs Turton. After the lessons, Mrs Turton's driver would drop her back at home.

She was most astonished that Robert had remembered. She tried to recall anything he had done for her over the years. But then, she had only ever really asked him for money. Initially, he had sent her money regularly without her having to ask, but in time, she had had to go to him with requests egged on by her mother and aunts, who reminded her regularly that the Bible says, 'Ask and you shall receive.' Unquestionably, it was different for Julie. Just take her many dresses, for instance. Matilda could not even imagine what it cost Robert for his wife to dress so expertly. She sighed. And how much time had passed since she had tried to learn English with Mr Mensah? Her youth, that's how much.

She recalled how bitter she had felt when her mother insisted that she abandon the lessons. But today, none of these thoughts could drown out her delight. After all, Aunty Dede had been right again; it had been worth waiting patiently. She wondered whether such wisdom in all matters, particularly in relation to husbands, came naturally with time or whether Aunty Dede was born with special gifts. And it was not as if she was in a rush; there was plenty of time yet for education. First, she had to learn English, the language she believed would open the door to unknown treasures. She dug out an old English schoolbook when she got home and revised the unfamiliar sounds and words. For the rest of that week, she sang often, smiled frequently and hardly slept.

Mrs Turton commandeered the rest of her waking thoughts. What would she be like? Would they get on? And how difficult would it be to learn the language, which she now heard all the time? She was secretly hopeful that it would not take her long. She had heard so much English over the years that she was sure she would understand much more than anyone envisaged. She assumed that it would be like putting on a new dress that had been made especially for her, at first a little uncomfortable, because the fabric was starchy and inflexible, but one in which she would always be confident because it had been made with her unique measurements to hand.

The day of the first lesson arrived. Matilda was up and ready long before the car was due to pick her up. Travelling in silence in the back, she realised that the last time she had been this exhilarated about anything was when she realised that her first baby was about to be born. That morning, she had felt her waters break and trickle down her legs, signalling the beginning of the most terrifying and rapturous experience of her life. She wondered again what Mrs Turton would be like. Above all things, patient, she hoped.

As the car travelled through the European district, Matilda was impressed with the lushness of the area. There were many more trees growing behind the fences and walls of the houses here, in addition to the large, generous neem trees that lined the streets. Everywhere, black men worked in the gardens digging, weeding, watering. She was bemused that the whites spent so much time beautifying their surroundings. But she had to admit this area did look a lot nicer than where she lived. She thought about the bougainvillea at home and tried to remember who had planted it.

When the car pulled into one of the gravel drives, she craned her neck to look at Alan's wife, who was sitting on the raised veranda that ran along the length of the house, but she could not make out her features through the gauze. The house was typical of the colonial houses. A single-level dwelling erected on pillars to raise it off the ground. She had heard that they built their houses in this manner in the hope of excluding insects and snakes. Well, that was the disadvantage of so much greenery; there were no snakes where Matilda lived.

The building itself was surrounded by a large garden covered mainly with grass. A gardener stooped in the heat tending the flowerbeds and pouring water on shrubs. She remembered her premarriage, most hated daily chore – fetching water. That was before Lawyer had arranged for a tap to be installed in their compound. Here and there, the grass had failed to thrive, either from too much sun or from too much shade provided by one of the many large, flamboyant trees that were dotted around the garden, their majestic flame-coloured petals lying on the lawn like ornaments. Several tall casuarinas lined the plot, their wispy branches swaying with every occasional breeze, causing spiky needles and thorny nuts to drop to the ground.

Matilda was about to get out of the car when two large, fierce-looking dogs appeared and began barking at her door. She jumped into the middle of the seat and screamed. She chanted, 'Jesu, Jesu,' as though the animals might contain some reincarnated evil. For what earthly purpose did they have these unsociable, terrifying animals?

A man came up to the door of the car and told Matilda, first in English, then when he realised that she did not understand, in laboured Ga, that Madam was expecting her and that the dogs were harmless. But she refused to get out of the car while the dogs continued to prowl freely, and in the end, the man gestured to the stairs, which led to the veranda, grabbed the dogs by their collars and pulled them towards the back of the house.

She climbed the stairs trembling. Thoughts of uncertainty filled her mind. Was this perhaps a silly idea after all? But Mrs Turton was waiting for her at the top of the stairs smiling, with one hand under her chin, while she stroked her stomach with her other hand.

'Hello. My name is Audrey. Come in. Sit there. Would you like some tea, some coffee? Or perhaps some water?'

Matilda looked blankly for a few moments, listening to the sounds the woman made and observing in amazement her watery blue eyes, like the colour of the diluted sky on a sunny, cloudless day. Her thin mouth looked hardly more than a slit in her face. And as for her nose, it was tiny and turned upwards so that Matilda could see into her nostrils.

But it was the woman's thinness that shocked her and rendered her awestruck. She was sad to behold bones that protruded from almost transparent skin under the woman's neck. No one became this thin unless they were very poor or very ill. She realised she was gawping and shut her mouth.

She had not expected to understand a word of what the woman said, but because of the names and the exaggerated gestures she had made when she spoke, patting her chest when she said, 'Audrey,' and as for 'tea', 'coffee' and 'water', those nouns had by now made it into the local dialects wherever there were enough English-speakers. 'Hello, Mrs Turton, please, tea,' she said, nodding affirmatively.

'Awuni, some tea please,' Audrey shouted a little too loudly in the direction of the servant who was hovering at the bottom of the stairs. 'You must call me Audrey.'

The women sat in silence for a few moments. Matilda noticed several cats sunning themselves on some of the other chairs.

'It is rather hot today, isn't it?' said Audrey.

Matilda smiled eagerly and wiped her forehead with the back of her hand. It came away wet, and she realised that beads of sweat had gathered all over her face.

'Well, let's start, shall we?' Audrey began looking through the books on the table, which Alice had lent her. She picked one up, the easiest-looking one, and opened it up to the first page. It was a simple storybook normally used to teach very young children how to read. Audrey explained slowly, 'I will read to you slowly, pointing out the words, so you can learn the *correct* pronunciation and intonation, as well as the meaning of simple English words. With a bit of luck, you will also learn to recognise and read them at the same time.' She hadn't really given much thought to how exactly she was going to teach Matilda English. She was counting on the fact that teaching couldn't be that hard.

Matilda was smiling. She was having a lesson. She was learning English. She would never have believed anyone if they had told her how joyful she would be to be sitting here with a pencil and a new notebook listening to an English woman teach her a few words. She was in heaven, truly! How splendid that she had had the courage to ask Robert. You see, it is true, she told herself, if you don't ask, you don't get. Never in his life would he have had the idea to ask her what she wanted, whether there was something that he could give her, something that would not even cost him a penny, and which would make her this exultant.

Awuni interrupted them with a tray of tea and a plate of short-bread biscuits. Matilda watched as Audrey poured tea with her bony hands. She had put on one of her best cloths and was surprised to see that Audrey was wearing what was actually quite a shabby-looking dress, faded and a little too baggy, nothing Julie would let any visitor to Downing House see her in. Audrey offered milk and sugar. Matilda poured almost half the jug of evaporated milk into her cup and then proceeded to help herself to three heaped teaspoons of sugar. When she took a grateful slurp of the delicious drink, Audrey tutted aloud, but Matilda pretended not to notice.

But her enjoyment was short-lived. It took a lot of willpower not to spit out her tea when she saw Audrey allow one of the cats to lick her teacup. Then as if it was the most natural thing to do, the woman put milk in her saucer and put it on the floor for the cats. This was too much for Matilda. She put her cup on the table and looked at it with regret. No, she could not under any circumstances share a plate with an animal.

'Don't you like the tea?' asked Audrey.

She nodded, and her eyes travelled to the drinking cats.

'Ah, yes. Alan doesn't like it either. But they do get washed,' she said, gesturing. 'And I never let them drink from the cups,' she said, shaking her head vigorously while she pointed at her own cup.

Could this be acceptable reassurance? The tea was particularly milky and sugary, so pleasant with such lovely biscuits. She decided that in future she would simply not place her teaspoon on the saucer. She would stir once and then put her spoon on the tray. And the steward looked clean. His uniform was white and starched. His hair was short, and his skin fair. All in all, he looked like someone who valued cleanliness. She glanced at the cats once more and wondered where it was that so many of them went to the toilet. She looked into the dark living room and shuddered.

Audrey began to read and point to the words in the book; 'This', 'is', 'my', 'house' and so on, each time asking Matilda to repeat the words several times until she got the pronunciation right. It did not seem to matter to her whether or not Matilda understood the words.

Matilda found it hard to concentrate; the sounds that came out of the woman's thin mouth were quite delicate. Painstakingly, she copied the words into a notebook in her neat, unsteady handwriting while Audrey watched.

'Excuse me a moment,' said Audrey suddenly. She rose and disappeared into the house.

What on earth had she got herself into? Audrey wondered, once inside the house. This was going to be a tedious and probably impossible task. Yet she had agreed to hours and hours of it! She realised now that she had no idea how she was going to teach this girl, how she would impart knowledge in a way that would make sense or be retained by Matilda. She couldn't remember being taught to read, or how she had learned to. She had always been able to read as far back as her memory allowed her. What *had* she been thinking?

Matilda put her pencil on the table and looked about more freely. She was impressed with the expanse of garden. The area that had been given over to trees and grass, and which had no discernible purpose, was much larger than Robert's compound even. She could hardly see the end of the garden for all the vegetation that grew thickly. She listened to the silence, amazed. In the time they had been sitting on the veranda, she had not heard any cars driving past on the road or indeed any human sounds. There had been the occasional dog bark, but otherwise no noise at all from the neighbouring houses that were tucked somewhere behind the high greenness of Mrs Turton's garden. It must be frightening at night, she thought, and swivelled in her chair to look into the house. It looked bare. Why did they not put more things in all this space, she wondered, looking at the large empty area that was the living room, the uncovered floors and the simple cream-coloured cotton curtains that fluttered in the little wind that made it through. Certainly, they could fit several more chairs and tables in the room, which she estimated was at least double the size of Robert's living room. She was disgusted afresh when she saw another cat eating from a saucer in the living room, crumbs of food scattered on the floor.

Just then, Audrey reappeared. She had put on some pink lipstick, which Matilda thought only drew attention to her lack of lips and the yellowness of her teeth. The lesson continued slowly for about another hour or so, with Audrey sighing periodically. Matilda tried even harder, forcing the unwieldy sounds from her mouth and pressing down hard with her pencil when she wrote. Please, be patient, she willed Audrey.

Soon, Audrey called for fresh tea and some more biscuits. She waved one of the books in her face quite briskly. Matilda could see she was becoming progressively heated and bothered and even sweating a little. Although the humidity was high, the veranda was quite sheltered, and there was more breeze here than at home.

Matilda had no idea how long the lesson had been going on when Audrey abruptly called it to an end and started tidying up the books. She called the driver, and in no time, the women were in the car with Matilda in the front, where Audrey had asked her to sit. Matilda turned around, stunned, when she smelled cigarette smoke and saw Audrey with her eyes closed sucking on a cigarette with a serene expression. She looked sideways at the driver, aware that neither the smoke nor her shock could have gone unnoticed, but he had his eyes fixed on the road so she stared ahead in silent bewilderment.

When the car's wheels crunched up the club's long, palm-flanked driveway, Matilda leaned to look out of the window with unrestrained admiration. The grass was startlingly green and together with the many flowering shrubs and trees – brilliant orange birds of paradise, glossy pink hibiscuses, yellow frangipanis, flame-coloured flamboyants and white jasmines – looked like an exquisite picture. She had never seen anywhere so beautiful, so thriving, or so immaculate, for that matter. There were maybe seven or eight men, all in identical brown clothes, tending this Eden, with large sweat patches

306

on their shirts. Most of them wore straw hats to protect their heads from the midday sun, and those close to the driveway stood up as the car approached and tried in vain to wipe streaming sweat off their faces before taking off their hats in greeting.

The building looked large and full of fun; Matilda had heard that they had a swimming pool inside, and she secretly wished she could go in and have a look at it, imagining for a moment how fearful it must be to be fully immersed in water. When the driver pulled up outside the entrance, and the doorman opened Audrey's door, she jumped out and, after a brief wave, disappeared into the peaceful-looking, dark building. Matilda had been deeply offended by being asked to sit in the front of the car as though she was a servant, and as soon as Audrey was out of sight, she asked the driver to wait a moment while she got out of the car and climbed into the back, which is where she should have sat in the first place. The driver asked, 'Please, where are you going, madam?' in a suitably polite voice that assured Matilda of her rightful stance.

Alone, she relaxed with her thoughts. She wondered what illness Audrey had. Being so bony made her look old. And why did they not have children? But how could a woman so thin bear children, let alone feed them? Perhaps she could cook some food for her as a thank-you. Her food would fatten up even a mosquito, she thought, amused. The poor woman, how empty her life must be without children, how painful to have to wait this long. She hoped they had not given up. In fact, she would encourage Audrey not to give up. Matilda thanked God silently for her boys, and again remembered Ruth. She thought about her every day; after all, a mother cannot forget her child just because she is dead.

She had heard that the Europeans often visited gravesides of loved ones. She never did. No one did. The family had visited Ruth's grave only once, on the anniversary of her burial, to put up the tombstone. They had to wait a year to make sure she was really gone, then they sealed the grave and shut that episode for good. In fact, thinking about it, Matilda was not sure she would remember where the grave was. Cemeteries were frightening places, anyway. Even when she went past one, she would ensure she looked in the opposite direction. No one apart from the gravediggers and thieves who looted fresh graves for body parts required for fetish practices went into cemeteries unnecessarily. And everyone knew that you were bound to meet ghosts and spirits there. She shivered just thinking about it. She could barely think about her daughter lying underneath all that hot earth alone. It was easier to think of her as the six-year-old she should be.

As the car approached her home, she forced herself to think about the excitement in her life and forget her dead child for a while. Maybe in a year or so, she would be able to speak proper English and write some words. How amazing that would be. What infinite possibilities would be open to her! What would she do with it? But she could not let herself think too far ahead. In the meantime, she had to be patient with Audrey. She resolved that she would humour her whenever necessary, treat her like a child, a man actually, she thought confidently. And get as much out of her as you can, she told herself. She is your link to the outside world, the world that Julie and Robert can inhabit whenever they want. Perseverance. And lots of patience, she said to herself, breathing deeply, slowly, as the car pulled to a stop outside her house.

Matilda was keen to share her excitement with someone, but there was no one at home. The house was unusually quiet. Her older boys were at Julie's house, being looked after by one of Julie's maids. Her mother had obviously taken Junior Lawyer and Samuel to the market. She changed into something a little more comfortable and walked to Downing House. For the time it takes to blink an eye, she wondered whether Julie would be interested in hearing about her first English lesson. Why couldn't they have the kind of relationship that other collective wives did? Julie would know she was having lessons; she knew all of Robert's affairs and seemed forever well informed about Matilda's life. This irritating flow of thoughts dried up when the children ran to give her their usual rapturous welcome; eventually, they let her continue on her way.

Julie's two oldest sons were not playing in the yard. Increasingly, they had to have extra English or maths lessons or to practise the piano, which was in itself not a bad thing. As she neared the house, Matilda could hear the faint tinkling of the piano keys. The sound, as pleasant as a flowing tap or falling rain, never ceased to lift her soul, and she smiled. Then she heard a sharp thwack, and the sound of music was replaced by the whimper of a child.

'Not like that, Edward, like this. You must play it like this,' Julie screeched. Then followed the sound of what must have been a perfect rendition of the music that Edward had tried to play.

A snivel, then, 'Yes, Ma . . .'

Matilda had reached the living room and stood in the doorway watching the scene. She wished she could wipe Edward's tears and assure him that she could not tell the difference between his playing and his mother's. She saw Albert sitting at the dining table doing some schoolwork. He looked up and gave her a careful smile.

'We are busy, and we don't want any spectators. What do you want?' asked Julie. Then she turned to Edward and in a more gentle voice, and in English, for she had shouted at him in vernacular, continued the lesson. The boy sat rigidly, his shoulders drooping and his face forlorn. When he peeked at Matilda, she squeezed her eyes hard as though imparting some secret message, and he clenched his jaw and bravely tried once more to get it right.

'That's much better,' said Julie, glaring at Matilda.

She went back into the kitchen where the new maid, Akua, was standing behind the cooker stirring a big pot of stew and speaking to the pot, but in a tone intended for an audience. 'It is not right the way Madam treats her children sometimes. As for me, I find it too difficult to just sit by and watch this maltreatment, but what can I say? If I say something, they will send me back to my village where my father and my brothers are waiting to beat me. Somebody has to talk to her. Someone has to tell her that is not the way to treat children, that if you beat them, you will make their skin hard, their eyes bitter, their heart stony. And when a mother beats her children, they will not remember her when she is weak and old. They will not be at her bedside when she is dying. Then what will be the point of enduring the pain of bringing forth a child?' Matilda ignored the girl and started to make some tea, but Akua continued, 'And it is not just her own children that she beats . . .' She turned and looked at Matilda, fearful that she might have now crossed a line and would be shipped back home having failed as a maid.

Matilda left the kitchen a little disturbed. She walked home in silence with her children, while the boys laughed and skipped lightly.

That night, when she was powdering the older boys after their evening bath, she asked, 'Does Aunty Julie beat you?'

William looked away and said, 'No,' quite firmly.

'He is lying, she does, but she told us if we tell you, she will beat us harder.'

'Earnest! Ma, it does not hurt when she beats us. She beats everybody, not just us. Earnest, now Ma will not let us go and play there. What is the matter with you?' he said, glowering at his younger brother.

Earnest started to cry. 'It's all right,' said Matilda. 'You will not get into trouble. But you tell me if she hits you hard.'

When the boys were out of earshot, Aunty Dede said, 'Earnest by name, honest by nature. That child will only get himself into trouble with his truthfulness. Matilda, don't go running there and stirring up trouble. It is nice and quiet on that front these days, and I would prefer it to stay that way.'

'Yes, but—'

'This is the way things are if you share a husband. She has to treat your children as her own. If she is not sparing the rod with her own children, why should she with yours? After all, they are all brothers and sisters.'

For once, I think you are wrong, thought Matilda, troubled.

Chapter Twenty

Audrey was dripping. Her dress stuck to her back, her hat slipped around on her wet hair and her back was sore from being bent over. The overhead sun was strong, but she was happily tending her patch of paradise. The gardener, on strict instructions, had dumped a pile of horse manure next to her rock garden, and she was mixing it into the soil. She lovingly tilled the earth, distributing the nutrient-rich manure into the soil round her plants. She moved rocks, transplanted plants that had too quickly filled nooks and crannies that she had allocated them. It looked rather dramatically beautiful, she thought, with the almost-white pebbles that she had gathered on the beaches set against the black soil and green plants and the huge black igneous rock that sat towards the back of her arrangement, her last birthday present from Alan. He had enticed her outside early that morning and pointed to the large angular lump on which he had stuck a piece of red ribbon. She had been delighted to finally receive something she wanted.

She stood up and stretched. Her garden looked magnificent at the moment. This project that was born out of despondency gave her so much pleasure now. She walked around stroking glossy green leaves, smelling flowers, checking beds for any moisture at all. The yellow oleander was in full bloom, its funnel-shaped flowers upright like an offering to the sun. She had taken it as a cutting from the

Governor's garden during a party when no one was looking and was proud of how well it was doing. She crouched under her African tulip tree to pick one of the large red-orange blooms it had shed. Dangling from its branches were boat-shaped pods that in a few weeks would burst open to release masses of winged seeds. She admired her deep border of canna lily plants, their glossy leaves almost at right angles to the central fleshy stalk, each standing like a many-armed scarecrow with a fluffy red head. She would tell the gardener to thin the bed a little; it was getting overcrowded. And all around were the delightful croton plants. She loved these, often overlooked because they did not flower. But they were reliably happy in her garden, and each strikingly different. Some with spiky deep-yellow leaves streaked with dark green, others large and oval, glossy green, with red and yellow veins, and yet others thin and delicate, flame-coloured with yellow and green patches. They provided dramatic colour and interest for little effort.

Joy was rubbing her body on Audrey's leg and arching her back for attention. Now that Alan's dogs were old, and lazy, spending most of their life in the shade somewhere, too tired to chase birds, too exhausted to bark, the cats had taken over the garden. They looked alike, each stripy, grey and brown, as they were all Sheba's children, grandchildren and great-grandchildren. But as a mother knows her children, Audrey could identify them, and not simply because they had slightly different patterned collars.

Sheba had had a litter of six, which had astonished and delighted Audrey, and she had begun a quest for suitable names. One morning, she was sitting with the kittens on the veranda, when Cook, on his way to the market, suggested that she name them after the fruits of the spirit.

'What fruit of what spirit?' she asked.

'Madam, the Bible teaches us that there are some fruits of the Holy Spirit. I myself try to have them in my daily life.'

She was amused. 'What are they, then?'

'Please, they are love, joy, peace, patience, kindness, goodness, gentleness, helpfulness and last, but not at all the least, self-control. Nine altogether.'

'And how does one get these fruits?'

'They are a gift from God. If you obey Him.'

'Joy, kindness, what were the others? I think I like that. Wait, I'll get a pencil. Write them down. You could be Joy,' she said to one of the cats.

The others were named Love, Peace, Patience, Kindness and Self-control. As they reproduced and others died, she continued ever after to name them after the fruits of the spirit. What she loved about these names was that, apart from Joy, they suited both boy and girl cats, so there was never any problem. For a while, she had had twelve cats, and she had named some of them after real fruits. There had been a Pineapple, a Mango and a Melon. Today, Joy remained her favourite, and one of only two from that original litter still alive.

As she tilled the earth, she mused how busy she was these days, particularly with those dratted English lessons. She had been surprised when she saw Matilda for the first time. Alan had not said how attractive the girl was, not that he would notice such a thing. But she had smooth, flawless skin, and teeth which glistened when she smiled, which seemed all the time. She was overweight, and Audrey was surprised that that did not detract from her charm. She was what some might call voluptuous, curvy, but to Audrey, there was thin or fat, and this girl was fat. It was a shame, she thought. A little weight loss here and there, especially round her middle, would improve her looks. She could not understand how a girl this young could let herself go like this. But then, she did not wear European clothes, which was just as well, though those traditional outfits, with their quite bizarre patterns and clashing colours, were themselves an eyeful.

Oh, how the first lessons had been painfully slow. She told Alice almost daily that she wanted to give up, that this was a dreadful idea. But her friend had encouraged her to continue, to give the girl time, 'provided she is teachable,' Alice had said. Audrey had no idea what that meant exactly but looked daily thereafter for signs of Matilda's progress. She smiled to herself when she noticed it, and wondered whether the fact that they were making surprising improvements was due to Audrey's innate ability to teach or Matilda's aptitude for learning. Without a doubt, it helped that she sat there each morning in a cloud of calm, happy to be learning English. What else did she have to smile about? A poor girl obviously forced into marriage. How horrific her life must be. And having that dreadful Julie as her co-wife, or whatever the appropriate term was. Matilda had begun to challenge Audrey's outlook emphatically. Was it possible that some people were born without the ability to actually *be* content? Matilda seemed happy all the time. But why? She had nothing in her life that would make Audrey happy, and yet without fail she appeared each morning all shiny and smiley, displaying those magnificent, strong-looking teeth. That too was incomprehensible to Audrey, that they had good teeth when they cleaned them in such a primitive and unhygienic manner. One could see them everywhere with those innocuous-looking chewing sticks. From time to time, they would spit on the ground and then brush their teeth with the tip, which had been chewed into a pulp.

She changed into a clean dress. She didn't bother any longer to have a shower in the mornings. She didn't have time. She would dip in the pool later to wash away the grime and soak the dirt from her nails. She had to attend a meeting of the entertainment committee, which she was chairing, and the agenda was rather lengthy. There was the pantomime next week, and then the Christmas bash. Perish the thought, but maybe Alan's mother was right after all, maybe helping others was a good thing. She did have less time to wallow in her misery. Or maybe it was simply spending so much time in the company of a person who did not appear to need a reason to giggle. Matilda had one of those mobile faces, the kind that used every inch in smiling; the eyes twinkling, the nose wrinkling and twitching, the cheeks lifting and filling out even more, the mouth getting wider and wider; the kind of smile that it was hard to see and not smile with. Really, the smile of a simple person, Audrey thought, smiling herself, her mouth moving only slightly, not in any way that affected the rest of her face, let alone her eyes.

She shuddered again and quickened her steps towards a pleasant afternoon at the club. She walked past the notice board garlanded with decorations that she still thought looked ridiculously out of place in the heat. Why could the other colonisers not accept that Christmas was best left alone? There was nothing at all here that felt Christmassy, no cold weather, no lights, no real Christmas trees, not

314

even any decent presents. She hated using branches of the casuarinas tree; she wanted the real thing, not a poor substitute. Yesterday, like the many years before, she had sat with a festive drink, while Alan and Awuni decorated their Christmas tree, a pathetic cut from one of the trees in the garden. 'How does this look, darling . . . Shall I move it a little more to this side . . . ? What do you think, Audrey . . . ? Audrey? Awuni, what do you think? That side . . . Like this? There, all done. Super, if I say so myself. Now I really am in the mood,' he said, climbing down from the chair while Awuni applauded in delight. The mood for what? Audrey wondered, staring at the limp branches laden with needles that would drop within hours, with thorny nuts that pinched, bare of presents, of lights, of . . . Oh, what the hell! At least there would be lots of parties. And this year, the Acting Governor was throwing a big one.

'Isn't it wonderful how much cooler it is today? Simply wonderful. I was beginning to think that the Harmattan would never come,' said Alice, as Audrey settled down next to her friend.

The dust-laden winds had once again reached the coast, filling the air with the desert sand, which filtered the sun's rays and hid the sky behind a light haze. The dust absorbed humidity, making it the only time of the year when everyone seemed to sweat less. And it covered everything with a layer of delicate dirt. For a few short weeks into the New Year, the weather would be substantially cooler, drier and altogether more bearable before the beginning of the hottest season of the year.

'They make such a fuss about having dry skin for a few weeks. Matilda looked like a greased mannequin again today,' said Audrey, looking around for a waiter. 'Are there no more waiters working around here? Anyway, what about the party? What are you going to wear? I don't have anything decent.'

'Now, that is not the sound of a woman who is looking forward to a party,' said Alice. 'Is something the matter?'

'No,' said Audrey, trying to sound more cheery. 'I was just thinking that I might leave Alan, go home alone, since he doesn't want to go back.'

'How long are you going for?'

'For ever.'

'No! Really . . . ? When?'

'Calm down. It's just a thought,' said Audrey.

'Well, shall we talk about committee business over dinner, then? First on our list, we need a Father Christmas for the children . . .'

'It's too hot for Christmas,' said Audrey. 'It's too hot to think about Christmas. And it's too hot to eat. Look, Alan can be Father Christmas. There, all sorted. Now can we please have a drink?' She had startled herself by voicing her deepest, as yet unspoken desire. Naturally, Alice hadn't been overly perturbed by the idea, probably because she too knew how unlikely it was that Audrey could ever afford to leave Alan. How would she support herself back in England? And the last thing her mother needed was for her grown daughter to return home to be an added burden. Didn't all her letters enumerate the hardship that her life had become? The enduring rationing, the bitter cold, the general gloominess that seemed to have engulfed Middle England?

Christmas morning dawned as every one before it. The sky was clearer than the amount of dust on the furniture indicated it should be. And it was hot.

The night before Alan had stayed up to listen to the Festival of Nine Lessons and Carols broadcast from King's College. Her eyes had filled as the distant, tender voices crackled down the airwaves heralding another English Christmas: 'Once in Royal David's city . . .' Too soon Alan's rough baritone drowned them out, and Audrey sat for as long as she could bear it before she slunk off to bed with a book. He had refused a second drink because he did not want to fall asleep and miss the service, and she could not help but be irritated by his hearty singing. He remained glued to the radio and sang for England, while she listened to him from her bed, unable to block out the grating sound of his voice. The next morning, the King spoke to them crisply from London, so far, so near. He spoke to his people in the British Commonwealth and Empire – as well as from many other countries – and thanked them for advancing civilisation in many parts of the world. And he wished them peace, joy, happiness . . . Audrey stood up, rolled her eyes and went to get ready for the party.

Advancing civilisation? What a ridiculous concept. On the few occasions that she ventured out of the European quarter, it was plain to see how unsuccessful was the Empire's laudable aim of sophisticating the natives. The shacks in which they lived – square cement buildings with very low-pitched corrugated-iron roofs, generally with dirty, blistering paint on which shutters hung open to reveal dank, dark dwellings – were placed haphazardly in clusters separated only by uneven mud paths and open sewers. The sewers, an ingenious theory that had not translated well, were now filled with disease-ridden, putrid filth, beside which the natives slept, shopped, ate, defecated and bathed. And she was always astounded at the number of men and women lounging about peaceably under shady trees, while their laughing children ran around naked or scantily clad on stick-like legs with protruding ribs and bellies swollen with worms and malnutrition, waving ferociously with angular arms and unashamed delight at her white face. At first, she had felt uncomfortable denying them the satisfaction of waving back, but she had been unable to bring herself to; Alan did that. He waved at each person who waved at him or called out in surprise, '*Obronie, obronie,*' never seeming to tire of the predictable reaction his skin colour evoked. Now she either glared at them or ignored them totally depending on her mood, yet still they waved and called out happily, cheerily, clapping and dancing. Hadn't her father often said that stupidity and unjustified happiness were well connected?

Alice had spent a considerable amount of time taking in the Father Christmas costume.

'I hope the children don't recognise me,' Alan said as he rolled up the outfit, some pillows and cotton wool, and stuffed the lot into a duffel bag.

At the club, the mood was festive. This evening, there would be unbridled merrymaking. Children swarmed the place. It seemed an unwritten rule that during the week no one brought young offspring to the club. But it was Christmas, and they had taken over, ridding the place of any tranquillity. How do any of them live to see adulthood? Audrey wondered, watching one child run headlong into a wall so that he had to be soothed for an age by his distressed mother. She observed them in disdain. They were loud and dirty. And demanding. She wouldn't have a decent conversation with anyone today; all these preoccupied mothers, all these unruly children. Why in heaven's name did they allow their maids and nannies to go on leave at the same time?

After a curry supper, Alice nodded to Alan that the time had come. He disappeared to emerge as a fat Father Christmas. The whoops and shrieks were deafening. Alice directed him to his seat. Audrey puffed her cheeks when she looked at him. He was already sweating, and he never sweated. 'I need a helper,' he said to her, blowing the floppy cotton wool that he had attached to his upper lip as he spoke.

'Don't look at me,' she said, walking off to find another cold drink.

Later, she never figured out how, she ended up next to him, helping to place the children on his knee, trying to calm the frightened ones, asking Father Christmas the appropriate questions, giving him small sips from her glass in between children. In fact, it was surprisingly amusing, until one child refused to get off Alan's knee. He wanted a second present. He did not like raisins and wanted something else.

'That is not how it works, Tommy. You go now.' Audrey looked around frantically for his mother or father. They were nowhere to be seen. Wherever it was that they were, they were probably quite merry along with all the other parents who were enjoying Father Christmas's babysitting stint. 'Go on!' Audrey glared at the child. He started to cry. 'Oh, for goodness' sake,' she said, widening her eyes at him, trying to look scary, 'you've had your go.'

'Audrey,' said Alan. 'I think you need to find Susan.'

'Go on, you spoilt little brat.'

The child started to scream. His face got redder and redder. Snot ran on to his top lip. Why, she asked herself, did children manage to produce such copious amounts of snot even in the heat? He was screaming frenziedly, taking large gulps of air in between interminably long shrieks. Alan was bouncing the child up and down on his knee, trying to calm him, higher and higher. Other children started to cry. Audrey grabbed Tommy by his arm to lift him off Alan's lap, and he vomited curry all over her arm.

'Brilliant! Absolutely wonderful!'

'Audrey, he is only a child,' said Alan, standing up and holding his costume so that the vomit did not slide down on to the floor.

318

'Well, where is his bloody mother then?'

'My mother says it's rude to say "bloody",' said a child patiently waiting for his turn.

'Oh, shut up the lot of you,' she said and walked off with tears stinging her eyes. The vomit on her hand made her want to retch. She went into the toilet and scrubbed and scrubbed. Damn Alan! He can sort himself out, she thought, as she walked off to the bar. 'Merry Christmas,' he had said that morning. Well, Merry Christmas to him too, she thought as she lurched in search of adult company. There was no earthly way that she could take much more of this farce that was her life. One more Christmas in this hovel and she might simply have to lie down and die. She had to get out of here. She had to go, and not just on leave. Leave? That was a joke in itself. Leave from what? It would take six years, not six months to rejuvenate her. She would be totally mad to return to this place. Sod the leave. When Alan eventually got round to taking her away from this place, she would not return. She gripped the bar for a moment and took several deep breaths to steady herself from these dizzying thoughts.

Chapter Twenty-one

One balmy night, Matilda was getting ready for bed, when she heard the quiet voice of a messenger. She caught her breath and listened while he asked Uncle Saint John for her. She refused to allow herself to hope. But her pleasure must have shown itself when the boy told her Lawyer wanted her, because he grinned cheekily. Hurriedly, she got ready, taking extra care with her appearance, struggling to decide what to wear, reminding herself that he probably only wanted to ask her to cook something, after all, he had not needed her that way for a while now.

When she arrived at Downing House, Robert was drinking whisky on the veranda with Tetteh, the trainer. Tetteh was a fine-looking man, with reddish hair and skin that was smooth and tight. He had dimples in his cheeks, which were set in a wide, round face. Although he was youthful with a tough body, his hair was receding a little. He had started riding polo ponies for an Englishman as a child, and they became his life. His knowledge of horses and racing was instinctive, and yet he had delivered a modicum of success for Robert right from the start. Now he was responsible for all of Robert's racing staff: the stable boys, who carried out day-to-day chores, and the jockeys, who raced, most of whom shared rooms near the stables, grateful to move away from overcrowded houses and overbearing families.

Although Tetteh lived in a house close by with his wife, her family and several children, he spent most of his time at Downing House.

On Saturday mornings, they discussed the horses' form and strategies in preparation for coming races. Then the stable boys and junior jockeys would walk the horses to the course before it became too hot. Robert always made a grand entrance at the racecourse later in the day, where he was a vivacious and popular horse owner, especially with the punters.

Robert and Tetteh were not friends, but Robert liked his company and sent for him regularly. Tetteh always came. He couldn't decline what in any event was not really a request. Actually, Robert regularly shunned the company of his contemporaries for that of the men he employed, men who had unquestioning respect for him. Many evenings were spent with Tetteh, and sometimes a jockey who had won a race, over a glass of blended whisky. Robert saved his favourite single malt for his friends. What was the point of giving them the good stuff, which they would not appreciate anyhow? After the races, he enjoyed reminiscing with the jockeys who had won or nearly won races. He took pleasure in sharing out some of his winnings with them, convinced that this enhancement of their meagre wages made them want to win even more than he did. They often sat late into the night talking and laughing, until the men were unable to keep their eyes open any longer, when he finally dismissed them. Sunday, the day after the races, was the only day that the Bannerman household remained still until the sun had risen.

Robert was sure the men enjoyed these evenings with him, chatting about the horses and drinking his whisky. He talked, and they listened; he asked the questions, they answered, always politely, sometimes sharing anecdotes or jokes but always choosing their words carefully, saying what they thought he wanted to hear. He knew that it was considered rude to contradict him, so they could not. He knew that it was considered rude to say no to him, so they would not. Somehow, that did not affect their relationship. He could see they were proud to be part of these successful stables, content to have a livelihood and accommodation, pleased to be able to work for Lawyer. But if pressed, it would have become evident that he did not really know much about them: what they liked or disliked, what they thought, anything much about their lives. He saw Tetteh's wife around from time to time, she always nodded respectfully but would never contemplate coming to speak to him, which was the proper way to behave.

Tonight, the men were animated. Robert's eyes danced in the lantern light, and his face was tranquil, revealing his handsome features. She had often seen him like discussing the horses, strategies for coming races, the jockeys and new horses. He now had eight horses and was thinking about acquiring another. And they laughed in a way that Matilda never heard her husband laugh with anyone else, not even his lawyer friends. Their laughter carried far in the dark.

'How is she responding to the extra training?' he asked, just as Matilda reached where they were sitting.

Even she knew that in preparation for the big race they had decided to increase the amount of training for the horse – she could never remember its name – Robert was going to enter for the race. She knew if he won, it would be the first horse from an African stable to win that prestigious race. She stood and listened, grinning at Tetteh who spoke with the animation of a small child. Everyone in Robert's household had begun to feel the tension and excitement of the rapidly approaching Gold Cup race.

'Very well, Lawyer. You should have seen her this morning. I tell you, Lawyer, there is no challenger for her. We are going to do it,' said Tetteh.

Matilda wondered how truthful this man was with Robert, how much he said on this delicate subject because he thought it was what Robert wanted to hear.

Robert looked pleased and chuckled almost self-consciously. He gave her a wide smile. 'So, Matilda,' he said, 'how are you? In the middle of my summing-up in court today I had a sudden urge for some of your delicious palm-nut soup,' he said, winking at her. 'I know it's late now, but maybe you could make some for me tomorrow?'

Matilda forced herself to smile pleasantly and conceal her wounded hopes. 'Yes. Yes, I can.'

'And rice balls,' said Robert happily. 'Oh, and before you go, can you please get us another bottle of whisky? Tetteh, you are drinking slowly tonight.'

As she walked back home, Matilda tried to hold at bay many angry emotions. Look how he had said, 'I know it's late now,' as though she would ever have contemplated cooking for him at this hour! And why did he not consider it appropriate to give her some money to cook these elaborate dishes? And could that other woman, wherever she was, not do the cooking along with everything else? She had imagined that she would not care when this happened. She had never had an undivided relationship with him, but when she had been the favoured one for a long time, she had developed feelings for him. After all, she had never been with another man; this was the man she had been given to, the man to whom in time she had learned to give herself to. Now that he did not need her, it troubled her. And it was not as though it had been discussed; there had been no message to her or her family stating that Lawyer had satisfied his needs and had now found somewhere else, someone else to go to. There had been no warning, there had been no preparation, and now no one could tell her what her role was supposed to be.

Race day came. Robert was taking his entire family with him to the racecourse to witness his triumph. Occasionally on a Saturday, he would take Edward and Albert with him to watch the races. They seemed to enjoy the thrill of the event. He even allowed them to place bets, although strictly speaking they were too young to do so, but they were Lawyer's children.

Matilda had never been to the racecourse before, and she had been looking forward to the day and the prospect of a social outing since Robert had mentioned it. Considering that she was the wife of a prominent lawyer, she too thought it was odd that she had been on very few such outings. She had new clothes made for her sons, including Junior Lawyer, whom Robert had insisted must come along. He said he wanted the whole family in the photograph.

The racecourse was not what she had expected. Actually, she had not known what to expect. As they made their way from the car, several people, mostly men whom she did not recognise, waved and nodded respectfully to Lawyer's wife, some greeting her aloud, others wishing Lawyer good luck today. The driver showed her the way up to the VIP area, carrying Junior Lawyer so Matilda was free to grip hands with Samuel and Earnest, more for her comfort than theirs. They walked through a hallway with betting booths on either side where a mass of people were trying to place last-minute bets, shouting at the officials in order to be heard above the din of the energised crowd, jostling to reach the counter, sweat pouring from their serious faces. The driver explained that the next race was about to start, the race before the big one, and these men were trying to place bets on horses. The atmosphere was electric. She had not realised that horse racing was such a big thing in Accra. She was glad that she had made an effort with her appearance and walked proudly. She wore a new dress today made from a vibrantly coloured cloth; bright cerise silk embroidered on soft, grass-green cotton. The dress was fitted round her curves, which were still bloated from her final pregnancy. Her cleavage was lower cut than she had ever previously dared, and her headdress was particularly fancy; Aunty Dede had starched the material so that it sat at angles, stiff, pointy and hap-hazard. She had left the house with the sounds of exuberant praise and admiration from the women and had swelled with pride and swayed with each step as much as the tight fabric would allow. The driver led Matilda up some stairs to the members' area, where she saw Robert in the bar with a group of his friends engrossed in a heated discussion. He looked up, barely greeting her. Instinctively, she let go of her son and placed her palm on her chest momentarily to still her erratic chest.

The children rushed to join their brothers and sisters, who had secured a spot at the front of the balcony from where to watch the race. Matilda took Junior Lawyer from the driver and held him closely. She followed the others, swaying less. She saw Julie near the front of the balcony chatting with a European lady, both of them dressed up like the women that she had seen in Audrey's maga-zines, with matching hats and gloves. Julie was wearing a fitted hourglass-style dress in banana-yellow chiffon, which had a scooped neckline and a bow that accentuated her small waist. Perched on her head, at an angle, she wore a yellow felt hat with a thin lace veil that stopped in front of the tip of her nose. Even from where she stood, Matilda knew that the dress would rustle when Julie walked, like wind blowing through thick bamboo leaves. Matilda looked around her and realised that all the men were wearing suits, and the women, who were mostly white, to be fair, were in Western clothes. She was the only one in traditional cloth. She walked softly towards the children.

The balcony was large and sheltered, with leather armchairs. It definitely had the best views. She looked at the vast course of hard, dry earth scattered with sprouting grass. It was oval-shaped and enclosed on two sides by a wooden fence painted in blistering white paint, with a barren-looking field in the middle. In front of the balcony, slightly to the left, was an unsteady tower in which she could see some men. To the left and the right of the balcony were stands for the ordinary people. She looked and could not believe her eyes at the numbers of race fans, mostly men, who had flocked here today.

Edward explained to her importantly that they could not move from their spot at the front of the balcony, otherwise they would not be able to guarantee a good view for the short children. 'The start is over there.' He pointed way into the distance at a spot that was not visible from where they were standing.

'And look, Aunty, there is the Gold Cup,' said one of the twins. They had climbed up the first rung of the balcony railings and were dangling their arms over the edge.

'Be careful you don't fall now,' said Matilda. She leaned and saw below, perched in the middle of a table covered with a red velvet cloth, the Gold Cup that Robert had talked about almost incessantly for months now. It was not gold, rather pewter-coloured, like some of the other trophies that he had displayed in his office. But it was much larger. She looked at it and thought it would be big enough to hold a chicken soup to feed her entire household.

Robert had gone back down and was now standing next to a man she did not recognise. She watched him chatting happily, realising that she had few opportunities to observe him clandestinely. She saw how surreptitiously he studied every woman who came into his view, careful not to turn his head from his friend, perhaps not realising that his darting eyes were clear for all to see. Matilda looked around. Everywhere, beautiful people in beautiful dresses. She saw

Alan, and Audrey, as well as some of the other men that Robert often had dinner with. When she saw a tall white man in a starched white uniform with gold and red trimmings and a plumed helmet whom everyone seemed to greet with mighty respect, she thought he must be the Governor here to present the Gold Cup. His stance was regal, and the deference he evoked from the gathering impressive.

A light-skinned black woman in a lime-green dress with matching shoes and a matching handbag approached Robert. Matilda was astounded at the woman's outfit, which was even more amazing than anything she had ever seen Julie in. The dress had a heart-shaped neckline that set off her slim shoulders and was very tight around her waist, but the skirt was heavily pleated and flared dramatically down to her shins and away from her body. When she walked, the plentiful, stiff material swished elegantly. Her hair also moved slightly when she moved, like a white person's hair. It was straightened and flat in the style of some of the women on the covers of Robert's gramophone records, and it reached her shoulders, where it was flicked outwards in a contrived curl. Matilda saw Robert's shoulders stiffen a little, but soon the woman held his gaze while she related some story or other and touched his arm gently. She must have said something amusing, for Robert threw his head back and roared with laughter in a way that Matilda had only heard him laugh when he was dining with his male friends. The woman looked up at the members' balcony directly at Matilda and smiled sweetly. Matilda took a quick step back from the edge of the balcony, ashamed to have been caught intruding.

'I see everyone has made it over in time,' Robert said. He had appeared next to his large family.

Quickly and effortlessly, Julie positioned herself next to Robert and rubbed the small of his back for a moment, gazing up at him. 'You will do it today, I just know you will,' she said sweetly.

Robert fidgeted and moved slightly; Julie took her hand away. The children all started talking at the same time in loud, animated voices, asking various questions about the races, the horses, drinks, treats. Julie conducted a private monologue to Robert, who periodically looked at her with a frown as if he could not hear what she was saying. The twins in particular clambered desperately for some attention from their father, and Robert stooped to give them a quick pinch on the cheek. He was irritable and looked uncomfortable. A white man walked out on to the balcony to talk to Robert. 'Hello there, old boy. All set for the big one today? Brought the family, I see,' he said, shaking Robert's hand and looking at the eager faces of the children. 'Ah, Mrs Bannerman, how lovely you look as usual,' he said, reaching to kiss Julie on the cheek. They spoke in perfect English, the children interrupting politely from time to time to join in.

Matilda stood and watched Robert with all his children and two wives. She chewed the inside of her mouth, wishing she had been learning English for longer, even though Audrey told her she was making progress. Each morning that she was scheduled to have a lesson, she woke with unwavering eagerness. She relished the peaceful, thought-filled drive through the leafy, pretty suburbs to Audrey's house. She anticipated keenly her tea and biscuits on the veranda overlooking the sumptuously verdant garden and the joy of learning new words. And as the weeks passed, her confidence grew along with her vocabulary so that soon she was able to say whole sentences in English, albeit hesitantly, with much pride. Now whenever she heard the BBC on Robert's wireless, she listened carefully, trying to identify words that she too knew, repeating the unwieldy pronunciation in her head over and over again until eventually the word sounded fake, like a word made up for child's play. In fact, Audrey was the only unpredictable factor in the whole matter. Some days, she was as bright as the sun, patient and understanding, even interested in Matilda's life. But often, she looked ill, with dark hollows under her eyes so that Matilda was sure that she had some incurable disease that was eating at the little that was left of her. And on those days, she stank, radiating breath that smelled like rotting flesh. Then she was sullen and less communicative, but Matilda quickly learned that her joyful countenance seemed able to make the lesson go well no matter how irritable Audrey was, and eventually, Audrey would always reward her effort and attention with modest praise on her progress.

But it didn't feel sufficient to introduce herself to this man, or to cope with a gathering like this. Matilda saw that she was not the only one watching Robert and his family. Several eyes beheld the sight, amused or impressed, it was not clear which.

Audrey strolled on to the balcony, and Matilda smiled and waved at her, pleased to see one other familiar face. Audrey looked quizzically at the large, boisterous family first, then their eyes met. She waved vaguely and walked back to the bar.

Robert went off with his friend. He called over his shoulder, 'Watch now, they are lining up, they will start in a few moments. Number eight is my horse.'

And a few moments later, there was a cry in unison from the spectators, signalling the start of the race. Matilda was surprised that she felt some of the excitement that the rest of the crowd obviously did. Most were on their feet, straining towards the right of where they were standing; the direction that Edward had said the horses would come from. She could not see anything. The crowd hushed in anticipation. Then without warning, there were shouts of encouragement and excitement. Hands were waving. And then finally, she saw them, the horses, probably twelve or fifteen. The jockeys, wearing colourful outfits and hats that she sometimes saw hanging out to dry at Downing House, seemed to be standing up, rather than sitting in the saddles. She had never seen horses run so fast, and was rather impressed. They thundered past. The crowd screamed. As suddenly as they had come into view, they were gone, around the far bend of the racecourse. The crowd hushed a little. 'Who won?' she asked the children.

'Aunty, it is not finished yet,' said Albert impatiently. 'They have to go all the way round,' he continued, using his finger to trace the oval shape of the racecourse while he spoke, drawing out his words to last the course. 'The race will finish right here,' he said, punching the air in front of him with his finger.

'There they are,' shouted Edward, shoving his brother roughly. Both boys leaned over the balcony, trying to see if their father's horse was in the lead. The crowd shrieked and screamed. Several flicked their hands in the air to mimic the gestures the jockeys made when they whipped the horses. Others called out the name of their preferred winner.

'What is the name of Daddy's horse?' she asked.

'Moonlight Sonata,' answered Edward, his eyes peeled on the horses, which were now at the opposite end of the course directly in front of the balcony and heading towards yet another bend.

There seemed to be three or four bunched in the front, with no clear leader visible from the stands. The crowd became more frenzied when the horses turned the last bend and raced down the final straight towards the finish. Matilda was caught up with the enthusiasm of the crowd and found herself chanting, 'Moonlight, Moonlight,' along with Robert's children and several others. At one point, she turned to glance at Julie. She and her friend had not moved; they were chatting, coolly oblivious to events around them.

There were two horses neck and neck as they approached the finish. Matilda couldn't see a number eight. The crowd became louder and louder. Everyone seemed to be standing, chanting, screaming. Then the horses thundered past again, one of them the winner by only a short distance. Moonlight Sonata came in third, and Matilda looked to see Robert's reaction. He had watched the race from the lower level, and she noticed that he maintained a very dignified stance throughout the race, showing no excitement at all, and hardly talking. When the race was over, he did not seem sad that his horse had not won. He was beaming from ear to ear and started talking animatedly with the man standing next to him. The man patted Robert on the back, and they seemed to be sharing a joke.

A man Edward and Albert recognised came and said that Lawyer had asked him to get them a drink. What would they like? And would they like some snacks? If so, could they please come with him to the bar? The children ran ahead to the bar eagerly, Matilda followed with Junior Lawyer asleep in her arms. She wished she could put him on her back to sleep.

Several heads turned when Matilda walked into the bar with the children. It was hard enough trying to control excited children and even harder with everyone watching her; she stumbled towards a cushioned bench that lined one wall. The man Robert had sent brought them drinks and some sweets, and for a moment, the children were peaceful.

'Here, I think you need this.'

Matilda turned and saw Audrey proffering a full glass. 'Thank you,' she said. She took a long gulp and grimaced as the bitter drink soured her mouth.

'Gin and tonic. It cures all ills.'

Matilda nodded and finished her drink. She was thirsty. Had she said gin? Was that not what Robert drank when he had no whisky?

Audrey cocked her head and smirked. 'I'll get us another. A few of these, and life becomes rather bearable, even splendid,' she said, wading off through bodies.

Matilda nodded blankly; it was Audrey's style, to expect everyone around her to appreciate if not benefit from her perfect English.

The bar had filled up with people trying to take advantage of this long break before the big race. Stewards served drinks to the other VIPs who loitered on the balcony and the landing between the bar and the balcony. Matilda wished Julie would come and help her look after the children; it would be easier with two adults in this unfamiliar place.

'What is this place coming to when we have to have maids in our club?' said a red-faced, overweight man with unruly whiskers who was standing over Matilda.

She recognised the reddened eyes, which she saw in her father more and more these days. 'I beg your pardon?' she asked in her best English. Audrey had explained to her that the expressions 'What?' or 'Eh?', which were commonly used by Africans and lesser-educated Whites, were most impolite, and she had drilled this question into Matilda. 'Until you speak English well, you will need to ask this question often, so we best get it right,' she had said.

'He asked if we are members,' said Edward quickly in Ga. 'She is my father's wife, and he is a member,' he told the man crossly in English.

'If I had my way, you darkies would not be allowed in here.'

'I beg your pardon?' asked Matilda suspiciously. The man spoke in an accent that made his speech indecipherable. 'Edward, what did he say?'

'Ignore him, Aunty. Leave us alone or I will tell my father,' said Edward.

She felt tension rise to her throat. She was about to tell the man to

330

go away when Alan appeared. 'Shove off, Jackson,' he said angrily and stood between the man and Matilda.

'Darkie lover,' muttered the man before he stumbled away.

Matilda was shocked; this was the first time that she had encountered a bad-mannered white person. True, she did not know many whites, and Audrey sometimes offended her, but really only out of ignorance. She suspected the meaning of the words he had used, but how could she be sure?

'Whatever that drunkard said to you, you'd best just take no notice of him,' said Alan. 'At least he did not wake the baby,' he said, peering into the warm, soft face of the sleeping child in her arms.

She nodded, smiling. 'This is Junior Lawyer.'

'Junior Lawyer,' said Alan, laughing. 'How marvellous. What is his real name?'

Matilda looked surprised. 'Robert, like his father.' Did he not talk about his children to his friends? She looked around to introduce the older children, but they had scampered off.

'Very nice, your . . . erm,' he said, looking at Matilda's head.

She reached up and touched her headdress and laughed.

'And who are you?' Alan stooped to Earnest.

She watched the man tickle Earnest and pretend to take a coin out of his ear. The child thought this was hysterical and wanted him to do it again, again. Matilda watched in awe.

'Ah, Alan, I see you two have met,' said Audrey, handing Matilda a drink. 'Cheers.'

Alan was staring at Matilda again. Audrey opened her mouth to say something but then didn't. Fortunately, Bernadette came running up and grabbed Matilda by the arm and said in the vernacular, 'You have to come now; Albert keeps pushing me.' She tugged Matilda so that her bangles clashed harmoniously.

'Bernadette, say good afternoon to Mrs Turton and Mr Turton.'

'Good afternoon, Mrs Turton and Mr Turton.' Then turned again to Matilda and said, 'Come on.'

'Is this your daughter?' asked Alan.

'She is my husband's daughter, my children's sister, so I have to be her mother.'

'Actually, she is my daughter.' They all turned towards the loud words. Julie was patting her daughter's head.

Matilda saw Audrey and Alan look at each other. She shrugged and had some more of her cool drink. 'You are pathetic,' she said to Julie in Ga.

'Well, I'll leave you to it,' said Alan. 'I'd better go and wish Robert luck.'

'Do you not know that it is rude to speak vernacular in front of a person who does not understand it?' Julie said to Matilda, again in Ga.

Audrey looked at the women bemused.

'I apologise, Audrey. I have just told Matilda that it is rude to talk in our language when you are here.'

'I can't believe Robert brings you both to the same place. It really isn't a secret, is it?'

'What exactly do you mean?' said Julie.

'You know . . . the two of you . . .' She waved her free hand.

'We are not secret,' said Matilda.

'Well, he doesn't usually. You see, she isn't *really* his wife . . .'

'I am a wife, just as you.'

'Just *like* you, Matilda, not just *as* you,' said Audrey.

'You were not married before God, Matilda.'

'In my tradition, I have married.'

'I *am* married, not I *have* . . .'

'I have brought forth just as . . . just like her . . .'

'Do not insult me by comparing yourself to me. You will never be able to match my status, no matter how many times you bring forth,' Julie hissed between clenched teeth.

'Julie, really,' said Audrey. 'You ought to know better. The expression is *to give birth*.'

'Oh, shut up, will you?' Julie turned to spit the words at Audrey. 'What makes you think you have the right to be so supercilious?'

'No need to get all excited, I'm just trying to help you, that's all.' Audrey shrugged and drained her glass.

'Well, I don't need your blasted help.'

'I'd say! Put yourself in poor Matilda's shoes for one moment. It is incontestable that *she* got the raw end of this arrangement. If you must share your husband with someone, I can scarcely think of a better candidate than lovely Matilda here.'

Julie glared at them before walking off dragging her child behind her.

Audrey winked at Matilda. She lifted her empty glass. 'I told you, cures all ills.'

Samuel ran up and announced he needed to go to the toilet. 'Thank you,' she said as she was pulled away.

Audrey wandered off feeling exuberant. She saw Alan talking to a group of black men. Robert towered over the gathering. He really was imposing, she thought, sidling up to them to listen. She sipped her refilled glass slowly as Alan introduced her to the other men. Silas something or other and Kofi. 'We had a boy called Kofi once, didn't we?'

'Audrey!'

'Kofi is a member of a new political party called the United Gold Coast Convention,' said Robert.

Kofi said, 'These are exciting times. We are thinking of appointing a new secretary and have set our sights on a fantastic candidate for the job; he's dynamic, passionate, committed. He is active in London with the African self-government associations . . .'

'Who is he? We must know him. There are so few of us in London,' said Robert.

'Actually, he studied in America . . .'

'Well, not quite to our standard, then. We all know that American education is far inferior to British education. I am afraid I cannot trust a degree from that country unless it is from one of the few top universities there. I presume that he is not a Harvard or a Yale man, otherwise you would have said,' said Silas.

'He went to Lincoln University.'

'Ah, a negro college,' said Robert.

'I like to see you are loyal to your British education,' said Alan.

'I had misgivings initially, but he is proving us wrong. He is a man of vision. We are putting our faith in him. And it is time to put aside our prejudices – introduced to us by the British, I might add.'

'Now, now, Kofi,' said Alan.

'I don't understand why you lot are bent on pushing the British out. It is not what the people want or what this country needs,' said Silas.

'You've been saying that for years, along with the British. Tell me, then, has anyone made any real effort in that regard? Instead of allowing us to progress in the civil service and to learn the skills of democracy, they are strengthening native rule and bolstering the chiefs. How are we ever going to be ready to take over from them when they leave?' said Kofi.

'This is fun,' said Audrey.

'Audrey!' said Alan again.

'Calm down, Kofi, we are being observed,' said Robert. 'By several members of the group you refer to so impolitely as "they".'

But Kofi had not finished. 'Do you think we should wait until the younger factions, the less educated men who served in the forces during the war, who saw that the white man is also weak, decide that they want to seize power? Or do you think we should wait until the British decide they really cannot afford to run their colonies any more? Until Westminster decides it's time to leave us to fend for ourselves? Don't forget that the war cost them a fair amount, and we are beginning to look increasingly like a burden rather than a benefit.' He turned to Alan. 'If self-determination is really your government's aim, then tell me why you don't allow us educated Africans to claim our rightful place.'

'Well . . .'

'Yes, tell them, Alan,' said Audrey.

'Since the war ended, there has been only increased discrimination against us. My brother has been trying for two years now to get into the civil service – don't ask me why – the only positions they offer him are lowly, far beneath his abilities and qualifications. You go and have a look in any of the government departments; white men fill all the senior posts. We are the natural rulers of this country, and we have a duty to claim what is rightfully ours. We must halt this all-pervading obsequiousness that they have come to rely on. We have a duty to fight for freedom.'

'You make it sound as if the people of this country are bound in slavery. You forget that we owe the British rather a lot: our education, our legal system, and I am sure in due course, when the time is right, a well-run democracy. Why boot them out before we are ready to take over?' said Robert.

'Kofi, you really are beginning to sound like a crazed revolutionary, and if I may say so, a xenophobe. It is—' said Silas.

'I'm not prejudiced, and I do not have a chip on my shoulder. There is more to this than that, and anyway, I am neither. Don't forget that I too had landlady after landlady slam her door in my face when I was trying to find digs in London. It was the same story each time. "Sorry, the room has been taken." And yet, the next week, there the advert was again. That is prejudice in its basest form. The kind of behaviour that is easy to ignore when you are educated and have a bright future before you, even when you are standing on the road in the wrong side of London in the pounding rain. When you are young and privileged. When you know that the ignorant, sad land-lady knows no better. But when so-called contemporaries think that they are better placed than us to rule over our own country, just because they are white and we are not, tell me then, why should I accept that like a faithful dog?' Kofi was out of breath.

'Let's not reduce this to prejudice . . .' said Alan.

'Just listening to you makes me thirsty,' said Audrey. 'Over here, boy! Isn't it tiresome how they are never here when you need them?'

'I challenge any of you to find a non-prejudiced human,' said Robert. 'We—'

'We are not xenophobes, are we, Alan?' asked Audrey.

Robert continued, 'We all have prejudices, including you, Kofi. Don't tell me you wouldn't try and stop your daughter from marrying an Ashanti man or, worse still, a Fulani? It's a fact, we Ga people don't like the Ewe tribe because of their juju; we don't like the Fulanis because we are simply more refined and better educated than them, and we don't like the Ashantis because *they* think that they are better than us. And let us not even get started on the Nigerians. It goes on and on. Prejudices in every form are as old and as true as humanity itself, a fact of life. Don't mix it with politics.'

'Listen. I assure you we are working towards self-determination. But we don't want to leave until things are in order.'

'In order?' said Kofi. 'Exactly what do you mean, Alan?'

'Well, the correct systems, you know . . . erm . . .'

'We need to think things through carefully. Don't burn our bridges with the British; that will benefit no one,' said Silas. 'But I admit the ex-servicemen are not helping with their rumours about how they performed better on the battlefield than the British, and about the independence movement they saw in Burma and India.'

'Well, tell me, if the African man is good enough to die fighting for the British, is he not good enough to have a say in his own country's government?' asked Kofi.

'They may have been fighting under our flag, but they were fighting for this country,' said Alan.

'I can see why they might be irritated,' said Audrey. '*I* wouldn't want to fight for this country either.'

'Audrey, why don't you go and chat to some of your friends?'

'Don't tell me what to do, Alan ... I don't understand why we don't give them their bloody country back if they want it so badly, then at least we could all go home.'

'Audrey!'

'It is not even beautiful. It is hot and unhealthy and—'

'Audrey, shut up, will you?'

'—the women dress as if they are stuck in a nightmarish pantomime production with—' Alan gripped her upper arm tightly and marched her out of the bar.

'I rest my case,' said Kofi. 'It is just a matter of time before they are forced out of here.'

Everyone else in the VIP area was headed towards the balcony to watch the big race. Matilda struggled with the two boys in the tiny cubicle, but hard as she tried, she could not make Earnest hurry up. By the time they emerged, she could hear the crowd cheering. She was sure she could hear them chanting, 'Onopod, Onopod,' which she remembered was Robert's horse. She hurried to the balcony but could not squeeze past the crowd that had gathered there to watch the race. Edward had indeed been right about securing their spot. But Matilda was desperate not to miss the highlight of the day. She placed Samuel and Earnest on a table in front of her, then lifted up her long skirt and carefully climbed on to a chair, taking care not to lose her balance with Junior Lawyer in her arms. They could see the horses now. Coming towards the stands. They seemed faster than the other horses in the previous race had been. It was impossible to see which horse was winning, because several were bunched up in the lead. But as they came closer to the finish, it really did look like Onopod – Edward had told her that he was number five in this race – was really in the lead, by a fraction, anyway. Matilda was shouting, her little voice inconsequential in the roar of noise surging around her. She waved her free arm in the air. It looked like Lawyer's horse was going to win. And indeed, Onopod won, and a deafening wall of sound rose up from the excited crowd, which drowned out all else. In the stands, no one was seated. People hugged each other, waved their hands and screamed for joy. Matilda looked around, elated. If she had not been carrying the baby, she might have jumped for joy. Really, she was surprised at her emotions.

'What on earth are you doing?' Julie spewed the words with a look of utter disgust on her face. 'Have you forgotten yourself? Get down from there this instant.'

Sheepishly, Matilda climbed back down carefully, glad that no one else had seen her. After all, she was Lawyer's wife, and he had just won the Gold Cup.

She heard that Onopod was declared the winner. Someone sent by Robert came to gather his family for the presentation and the photographs. No doubt he was busy being congratulated and feted. This after all was historic, so he had told her. No African had ever won the Gold Cup.

Eventually, Robert's excited children and wives were hovering around the cup waiting eagerly for the photographer to arrange them. The Gold Cup would obviously be prominent in the arrangement, as well as Robert of course. The twins were touching it – they loved shiny things – and every now and then, Matilda whispered at them loudly to stop. She could see that they were leaving smudges all over the base of the once-spotless trophy.

Already, several people had surrounded Robert to congratulate him. He beamed happily but in his typical restrained manner. He almost looked shy, even though he must have been euphoric, ecstatic, proud; immensely proud of his achievement today. Now he would go down in the annals of the Accra Turf Club history books, which Matilda knew he wanted dearly. And he was standing there, no doubt contemplating his success with a gentle grin on his happy face with his family gathered around him waiting for the photographs to start, when a group of white men came towards them. They did not look pleased. In fact, the man in front, whom Robert addressed as James and who it later transpired was the president of the club, was frowning deeply.

'So sorry, Robert, but there's been an objection raised that we have to look into before we can confirm the winner. We can't present the cup just yet, old chap.'

There was a gasp from the crowd standing close to Robert. He was aghast and confused. 'Why? Who? What's going on?'

'Listen. It's Jackson. He thinks that you may have cheated by entering Onopod in the race. Says the horse is a thoroughbred. We just have to clear up a few anomalies.'

By now, the news was spreading that something was up, that there would in fact be no imminent presentation of the Gold Cup to Robert Bannerman. The well-wishers started to move away from Robert, back up to their seats in the VIP stands, to get a drink, to wonder and gossip, while they waited for this mess to be sorted out.

'Like what? What anomalies could there be?'

'Listen, this is not the place to discuss it. Why don't you come into the office with us? Hear what Jackson's objections are and then answer them. With luck, we can clear this up and get on with the rest of the day.' James had put his hand on Robert's arm and was firmly encouraging him to walk towards the stairs that led to the committee's office.

Matilda felt ashamed for Robert, who looked like a criminal being marched off, guilty of some awful charge, now under an obligation to prove his innocence before he would be freed again. She was outraged for him and impulsively reached out for her children, scooping up Junior Lawyer, who started crying instantly while he squirmed for freedom. Did they not realise who Robert was? How could they accuse him of cheating? Surely the committee would throw out this objection? They would see the truth. Surely the truth would prevail?

But Robert did not go up the stairs. He stopped and said in a steely voice, 'The committee can go to hell. And Jackson too.' Then he raised his chin slightly and, in a dignified tone, announced that he would save the committee their precious time and disqualify himself from the race. A silent hush descended on the crowd. Robert ordered his wives and disappointed children out of the racecourse to the waiting car. There, simmering, he organised someone to take some of his family home. The children must have realised that it was a time to remain quiet; apart from the twins, who had been so eager to have their photographs taken and were sobbing uncontrollably, oblivious to the glares from their older brothers.

'Never in my entire life have I been so humiliated,' he said softly as he climbed into his car. 'And to think of all that time I wasted preparing my speech.'

Crowds from the stands on either side of the VIP balcony had booed the committee and started to leave the racecourse in protest, even though there were still two more races to be run. As Robert's car left the racecourse, hordes of supporters cheered and chanted, 'Onopod for Gold Cup, Onopod for Gold Cup.' The crowd was so thick that Robert's car could only move slowly, and he was forced to acknowledge the admiration of his supporters.

When Matilda arrived at Downing House later that night, she found it doused in an unfamiliar atmosphere; electrifying yet poignant. Robert was comforting Adotey, the jockey who had ridden Onopod to victory. The man was crying like a baby, snivelling and complaining about the disqualification. It was embarrassing to watch him, so evident was his pain. Horse boys, brushing down the exhausted horses, feeding them treats as rewards for their hard work, were also griping in hushed voices about the injustice of the day. They were hurt and confused, angry actually, that Robert had walked away from what would have been a monumental victory, and without even the slightest fight.

Robert said little, patting the men on the back, nodding his head calmly, offering them each a whisky. Matilda was surprised to see all this activity, albeit calm, for the men were obviously in shock. She had expected Robert to be stomping about, shouting at everyone; she had hoped they would all retire and allow the day to end as peacefully as possible. She went straight into the kitchen, sensing that Robert did not want to talk to her. Julie was in there making some tea with her usually mask-like face distorted in distress. Matilda tried not to look at her streaked cheeks, even though she was surprised that Julie was allowing herself to be seen in this state.

'Julie, the men should have something to eat. I have brought some soup, but I want to make some rice balls to go with it.'

'Yes,' she said softly as she walked out of the kitchen.

Matilda was pleased when she saw Kofi and Silas arrive at the house with a bottle of whisky. While she cooked the rice balls in the kitchen, she heard the men outside talking. She normally loved eavesdropping on their conversations, but tonight they bored her with legal talk, mentioning cases and names that did not interest her and nothing much else. She heard them refilling their glasses frequently. She became distracted with her cooking and tuned into the various indecipherable night sounds – the noise of a wireless carried in the night, a baby crying, two men arguing on the street outside, the horses snorting, the horse boys talking calmly about the events of that afternoon – all punctuated firmly by the men's hearty laughter and the sound of clinking glass.

Robert interrupted her reverie when he shouted for some more ice. Matilda hurried on to the veranda just as Kofi asked Robert, 'Do you still feel the same way about your British friends?'

She stiffened and stared at him. Why was he always so argumentative? Why could he not leave the atmosphere in peace? She returned to the kitchen and stirred the rice furiously with sweat pouring down her face.

'The British introduced us to horse racing. We would not have been able to enjoy the races today without them,' said Silas.

'And you enjoyed it? You enjoyed being humiliated? It is that passive attitude that will be the downfall of Africa. Tell me then, where did your mutual love of racing get you today?' asked Kofi. 'They cannot even bear to have a black man win their blasted prize.'

'Damn Jackson!' said Robert below his breath. 'That bloody miner, a man who in England would never have been allowed into a club like ours. He walks around lauding it over anyone he can. Now the committee will understand why there were so many objections when he applied to join the club. And what was their response?

340

"This is not England." No, it bloody well isn't. If it had been, he would never have been admitted. I can still hear James: "This is not England; we must be more embracing here." So here, they admit any Tom, Dick and Harry miner and lower the tone so categorically.'

'You have every right to be outraged, Robert,' said Silas. 'But I am sure that this mess will be cleared up. The man is nothing but a jealous ruffian; he has no place here. The only reason he is here is because of his mining experience. But this is not Johannesburg, and this is not Obuasi either!'

'You have both always been far more comfortable with everything British: bridge, poker, horse races, to the peril of our own culture. You even share their sense of humour, so tell me then, why don't they allow you into their social clubs?' Kofi was laughing. 'I don't know why their culture is more important to you than yours.'

'I'll tell you, Kofi, why this is important. Horse racing is enjoyed by many Africans, and I have a duty to the punters as a horse owner. It is not just a white man's sport, even if they are the main horse breeders and owners. Winning this race was important to the ordinary men in the stands. I will not lower myself—'

'Hail, an emissary of the King,' said Silas loudly.

Matilda looked out of the window to see Alan bounding up to the veranda. Quickly, she got another glass out of the cupboard and put it on a tray to take outside.

'Hello there,' replied Alan, leaping up the two stairs in one go.

'A man who embodies the reasons I am proud to be a British subject. Whether or not you like it, we owe them,' said Silas.

'Robert, I just wanted to make sure everything is all right. I was appalled earlier today . . . The committee really had no right . . .'

'Alan, that is in the past now. The future beckons brightly. The man does not want to think about it any further,' said Silas.

'Silas is right. I don't really want to talk about what happened today. Here, have a drink instead. Ah, thank you, Matilda,' he said as she placed the glass on the table.

She greeted Alan quietly. He was staring at her again as if she was some sort of apparition, and she became very self-conscious. She hurried back into the kitchen, aware that his eyes were following her. Alan looked at her differently from other men, whose gazes often revealed private, lustful thoughts. He looked in the way she imagined a proud father might look at his daughter, and that made her stir. She put her hand on her chest to steady herself. Her heart was racing in an unfamiliar way.

She continued with her cooking, taking care to eavesdrop some more, but now that they were talking in English, she knew she was missing out on most of what they said.

'What happened today was because of your dark skin,' said Kofi. 'You must accept that.'

'I refuse to stoop that low,' replied Robert tersely.

'We are not all prejudiced,' said Alan.

'Then why do you and your colleagues live away from us, with your separate white-only clubs? And when you have children, why do you ship them off to be schooled like all the other Europeans? What contamination are you trying to avoid?'

'Calm down,' said Robert.

'Well, I'm tired of living under a system in which I have no input,' said Kofi. 'They choose to send any man from anywhere to be our governor and subject us to his whims and his fancies, and when we get used to him, they send him away and send us another one . . .'

'Food at last,' said Robert, as Matilda walked on to the veranda with a tray.

Silas lifted his recently replenished glass unsteadily. 'Well, God save the King, the Governor, the British Empire, and you too, Kofi.' He drained his glass.

Matilda watched, concerned, as the men emptied their glasses at terrifying speed. But she was relieved that they were jolly, laughing, and that the awful events of earlier seemed forgotten.

Back in the kitchen, she pondered what all this would mean. Would her children grow up in a country that had reclaimed its independence from Britain? She could not see anything wrong with the country and was baffled that there were people like this Kofi who were determined to change things. And who knew how the parting with the colonial masters would come about? And how could it bring more hope and prosperity? Would it not rather bring doom and disaster? She only wished for her children that they would know the same peaceful and prosperous world she did. But this talk frightened her. Everywhere, it seemed, people were beginning to talk as if the colonials' departure was inevitable. Why did no one ask her what she thought? And there were many others like her, she was sure.

She put the rest of the food on the table and turned to leave when Robert grabbed her hand. His bulbous eyes were a little droopy tonight, and he said in a gruff voice, 'Wait for me upstairs.'

She sat up in Robert's bed, unsure for a moment where she was. He was standing with his back to her, swaying in time to music. 'Blast the lot of them. How dare they? How dare they?' he muttered over and over again to the wall.

'Robert?' she whispered.

He turned jerkily. 'What are you doing here?' His voice was roughened by whisky.

'You told me to wait.' She got up and started to put her sandals on.

'Where do you think you are going now?'

'But . . .'

'Stay there. I had to stay with Tetteh and the others. Thanks to those bloody men who ruined our day. That idiot James. Damn him!' He started to pull his shirt off, but after struggling for a moment he ripped it open, flinging buttons all over the room.

She was startled. She had never seen his features this contorted in rage, and she was a little afraid. 'It will be all right, Robert.'

'What the hell do you know? I am the one who was educated with them. I am the one who speaks like them. I am supposedly one of them, for God's sake.'

She flinched and whispered a quick prayer that He might forgive her husband for using His name in vain.

'And look how they treat me, like a petty criminal. They can go to hell, the lot of them.'

Matilda gasped. 'Please, Robert, don't say things you will regret.'

'Well, they can. I might as well face it, they . . . they . . . I have been stupid.' He sat on the bed with his back to her and drooped.

'You are not stupid at all.'

'And where was my friend Alan?'

'I don't know.'

'Why did he not speak up for me?'

'But you left, Robert. You walked out. What were they supposed to do? And he came tonight . . .'

'When it was safe.' In a soft and tremulous voice, he continued, 'I expected victory, not disappointment. That venomous Jackson, that spineless James, they have stolen what is rightfully mine. And I have racked my brain all night to find a motive, some explanation I can rationalise. But all I come up with is my colour.'

'No!'

'Why else? What else is it that made it impossible for them to let me win the cup? Have they simply tolerated me all this time? Was I some exotic token? Some trophy for their fancy club, so they could say, "But we have a black man in *our* club, don't you know?" Damn them!'

'Robert.' All this damning made her uncomfortable; it was more or less cursing, and that should never been done lightly, no matter the circumstances, and certainly not under the influence of intoxicating liquors. She wondered exactly how much he had had to drink. 'They are your friends, Robert. I am sure that there is a good explanation.'

'Maybe you are right. I shouldn't really. I can't stoop. I can't let my boys down. They believe . . . We all believe . . . in the system. It is not about colour, it is about racing, isn't it? Everything will be fine. It *has* to be fine. This is my country, after all.' And then he was silent while memories plagued him. He too had suffered petty prejudices. It was foolish to deny it. Take the comment his good friend Charlie Tyson had made in the college bar one night after several drinks. Charlie had said his father was deeply upset that he 'even knew a black man'. Their friendship had fizzled out after that because Robert couldn't understand why his friend had even deigned to repeat such offensive words. 'Maybe Kofi is right. After all, they won't stay for ever. Look what is happening in India of all places. Maybe I should get involved. After all, it won't hurt my career to be an important person in the country's first political party. I should give up the racing. Yes, that's what I'll do . . .'

'You can't, you love the races.'

'Don't tell me what I can and can't do! I will sell the lot of them.'

344

'But they are your life,' said Matilda in disbelief.

He shrugged. 'I have never sought to remain where I am not wanted. Yes, I'll sell each and every one of them. And if I can't sell them, I will give them away.'

'After spending more money on them than your own family, how can you now talk of giving them away for free? And Tetteh, Adotey and the others, what will they do?'

'They are grown men; I am not responsible for them.'

But you are, she wanted to say. And you know it.

He lowered his back on the bed. His eyes were shut. 'Yes. I will.'

Matilda was troubled to see that the hollows at the tops of his cheeks were moist, and in sympathy, her eyes welled. Within minutes, Robert was asleep, snoring sonorously, leaving Matilda awake with her thoughts, apprehensive about the uncertainty that was opening up all around her.

She felt strangely privileged to have shared this time with him, that she had been close in his time of distress. She doubted Julie had ever had a similar honour bestowed on her. After all, how often did a man like Robert shed tears in the absence of death? And this was not something one could talk about. She knew she would never ever tell another soul about her husband's tears, of his humiliation.

Chapter Twenty-two

The English and etiquette lessons had been going on for more than eighteen months. These days, they began by reading old newspapers. This morning, Audrey sat and listened, glowing anew with a fair amount of pride as Matilda read confidently, her soft words undulating in the wrong places. It had taken a while for Matilda to grasp the most basic vocabulary, but then steadily, she had advanced, gathering words and expressions along the way. As she listened to her, Audrey couldn't help but feel immense satisfaction. That she had somehow managed all this with nothing but an instinctive flair for teaching, which she might otherwise have never realised she possessed, made her feel proud and strangely worthy. After a lifetime in this place – she would cry if she brooded over how long it had been, it amounted to a life sentence, for goodness' sake – she had discovered that she was good at something. She could teach, and she had taught one native to speak English. Actually, she reminded herself, as she listened to Matilda's diction, this was no small feat.

Matilda stopped reading when Awuni approached with the tea things. 'This is my favourite thing,' she said, giggling and rubbing her hands together.

'Ah, thank you, Awuni,' said Audrey, sighing. 'Good, he has remembered the extra sugar.'

They sat with their steaming teacups, Matilda stirring her tea delicately in the way that Audrey had taught her, so that her spoon did not keep banging the edges of her cup and the tea did not spill on to the saucer, which Audrey had explained to her was not there just to be spilled on. After seeing how the cats were often fed from the saucers, Matilda tried her best not to use them at all and preferred to place her cup directly on the tray when she had finished with it.

'I have wanted to ask you for a long time now. Is it not yet time for you to have some childrens?'

'Child*ren*. There is no "s" at the end.'

'Isn't it time for you to have some children?' Matilda repeated correctly.

'I can't have any now, but . . .'

'Oh no! How sorrowful for you.'

'Sad. *Sad for me*, not sorrowful, but anyway, I am not sad. I am actually very pleased that I cannot have children. I don't really like children, which is just as well. But make sure you don't mention this to Alan. He too thinks that I am sorrowful about it!'

Matilda had shock written all over her face. 'There are things that can be done; you must not give up. To bring forth is important for a woman. You will regret it. Childrens . . . *children* are the most important thing in this life. What is the reason of life without children? You should just have some before it is too late. Once they are here, you will change your minds, you will be happy. If you don't, you will only regret yourself. As my aunty is always saying, "Had I known never comes at first."'

'She sounds wise, your aunty. I know that you probably think no woman in her right senses would choose not to have children, but that is because of your culture. Where I come from, it is not as important. I am actually extremely thankful to God that I have managed not to have any. Oh, Matilda, the expression on your face is hilarious,' said Audrey, breaking into delighted laughter. 'You should see yourself. Anyone would think that I am suggesting murdering my husband.'

Matilda covered her mouth and drew a sharp breath.

Audrey chuckled. 'Despite what you might think about me, I am not going to murder anyone,' she said, drawing out the words.

Matilda reached for a biscuit and ate it while Audrey poured herself another cup of tea. 'You are the concubine of a married man . . .'

'I am a wife,' said Matilda a little loudly.

'Yes, all right then, a traditional wife . . .'

'Me and Robert's first wife are equal wives.'

Audrey laughed. 'You and Julie? You do not seriously believe that, do you?' she asked, ignoring the look on Matilda's face.

'Yes, I do,' said Matilda with her chin raised. 'In our traditions, there is no difference between one wife and the next wife. Only, she is my senior and I have to respect her for that, but I don't here,' she said, patting her chest.

'Good for you. But what is it like? I'd happily give my husband away, but I can't imagine sharing him with anyone . . .'

'We are not sharing. She has her part, and I have my part. We don't mix our parts,' said Matilda, shrugging her shoulders.

Audrey laughed out loud. 'This is just too preposterous to be true. What about . . . you know . . . behind closed doors and all that?'

It was Matilda's turn to laugh. 'You mean, how do I know when I am on duty? He sends for me and I go. It is very simple, you see?'

'No, not really. And do you honestly see that side of your relationship as no more than a duty?'

'Yes, of course!'

'Gosh! How sad. It should be something special, something fulfilling, something you want, think about . . .' Audrey stared longingly into her garden.

Matilda was shocked. 'In my culture, we do not talk about such things. It is between a man and a wife, for the purposes of the family only.'

'Well, you have been truly deceived. When Alan and I were first . . . Oh, what is the point of reminiscing like this? What about Julie? What did she make of all this . . . Are you all right?'

'I was thinking about what you said before.' She shook her head as though to dispel the thoughts. 'I think Julie . . .'

'She is ever so superior. She must have been angry that Robert married again.'

'Yes. Yes, she was angry, I think. I did not know it, but now I know. But that is how it is. How can I complain about my fortunate life?'

348

'And how old were you when you married? You must have been a mere child. You can't possibly have had much say in the matter? And quite frankly, he should have known better, being educated and all that. Did you . . . Do you love Robert?'

'Love,' said Matilda, 'is . . . What is the word you taught me yesterday . . . ? Splen . . . do . . . rous . . . Love is splen . . . do . . . rous, but not important. Not for children, which is important. And not for marriage, which is also important, but not as important as children. When I was young—'

'How old are you?'

'Now I am twenty-five. When—'

'My goodness,' said Audrey, shaking her head. How many children did she have again? She often talked about them, but it was impossible to keep up with hers and Julie's, as well as the other miscellaneous characters she talked about. Just the other day, she had showed Audrey a new studio photograph of her children, or were they all of Robert's? There had been several smiley black faces in the photograph; she had barely managed to feign interest. 'Well, I can assure you that you are *still* young, my dear.'

'Yes, when I was younger, I wanted love. But now I see that other things are most important. Such as respect, as an example.' She was lying. How could she deny that she wanted a closer relationship with her husband? That she had natural needs that had nothing to do with being 'wayward', as her mother had made her believe when she was younger. They were God-given, these natural needs of a still-young woman. And one of them was companionship, someone to talk to on demand, not only when he wished to, someone she could unburden herself to about her fears regarding their mutual children, his other wife? Look how easy it must be for Audrey, or Julie for that matter, waking up each and every morning within the same four walls as their husbands, not needing good fortune or forward-thinking in order to see him, to talk to him. It had taken her by surprise to realise that it is possible to feel isolated in a busy house, where there is hardly ever peace and quiet. But doesn't loneliness arise because no one really hears you?

'Well, a loveless marriage is tantamount to hell,' said Audrey to herself.

'I beg your pardon?' asked Matilda, startled.

'Oh, nothing. Actually, I have just remembered I have something to give you.' Audrey went into the house and returned after just a few moments with a small book, which she put on the table in front of Matilda.

'*The Great Gate . . . ?*'

'*The Great Gatsby.*'

'Is that really for me?'

'I found it the other day when I was going through some of my things. I thought you might like it. You can now read enough to get through it slowly. You can write down words you don't understand, and we'll go through them when you are here.'

'Thank you. Thank you. Oh, Audrey, you are mar . . . mar . . .'

'Marvellous.'

'I don't receive presents.'

'Neither do I.'

The women were silent for a while. Audrey fumbled for a cigarette and lit up. 'Would you like to try one?'

Matilda opened her eyes in shock, but then took the cigarette and looked at the glowing tip in awe.

'Like this,' said Audrey, pulling on the brown filter.

Matilda filled her mouth and quickly let out the smoke. 'Ah. No.' She coughed and spluttered. 'No, thank you.'

Audrey laughed and took the cigarette.

'It's not nice at all,' Matilda said. It tasted as bad as it looked. Why would anyone fill their mouth with burning smoke? She breathed in enough of that when she was using old paper to set light to the coals. She washed her mouth with a gulp of cold, sweet tea.

'You are priceless, Matilda. Really, you are.'

'I had a price before, you know? Robert paid a lot for me in fact. A lot, but maybe not enough.' She giggled. 'Now, when I open my box of cloths, all I can hear is the scent of dust . . .'

'*Smell* of dust . . . the smell of dust.'

'Yes, the scent of dust, and I don't even have time to sew new dresses. And I have many jewlerries . . .'

'Jew . . . elle . . . ry.'

'Yes, I have plenty of them. But these days I get no gifts. So thank you. I am blessed that I can learn English from such a good teacher. Thanks be to you, my life has opened up before me with several possibilities. I appreciate you.'

Audrey blushed and quickly tried to correct Matilda, who had placed the inflections of the word 'appreciate' in entirely the wrong place, rising with each syllable to a crescendo at the end. Matilda repeated the word several times, and in the end, Audrey said, 'Oh, forget it. So, what will you do with your English?'

'I don't know,' said Matilda, clapping her hands and rubbing them together. 'I have done my duties; now it is my turn. My life is before me. The time has come when I must make my decision. You have given me the means to move forward. My future is brighter.'

In the car, Audrey began to feel unbearably irritated that Matilda was always so full of joyous anticipation. It was baffling that in spite of the fact that her life offered hardly any prospects, she managed to highlight how inadequate Audrey's life was, how stagnant things had become. She looked over at Matilda now. Even if she never achieved anything for the remainder of her life, she would have her children. She would always be able to reflect on them with pride, as she already did. They were her success, her reason for living. It must be rather amazing to have mothered children, Audrey thought wistfully. Was this the beginning of regret? She had often wondered if she would live to see the day she regretted her decision to avoid procreation. She tried to imagine herself the mother of a daughter or a son, the child that had been washed down the drain, and quivered. No, she would never have survived, never have been able to raise a child without causing it irreparable harm, of that she was sure.

Matilda's youth made Audrey realise how old she was. She would be thirty-five next birthday, sliding towards forty. She realised she might have spent her best years here with Alan, unfulfilled and miserable. She remembered her mother's fortieth birthday; she had been sixteen, and rather awed at what seemed a venerable age, and she had vowed then that *her* fortieth would be a glamorous occasion. A big party, the man of her dreams, maybe children, certainly champagne and dancing. Now, it was clear that day would arrive without the key components of those long-forgotten hopes. Instead, she could look forward to looking back on a worthless, unaccomplished life. She fought back tears as she remembered how it had taken all her energy to plod on after what Douggie and his friend did to her all those years ago. The fear of what they might have done had she not crumpled in hysteria, which, it seemed, had brought them to their senses, had haunted her for years. Even though she had tried to believe that she had escaped something even more horrific, the humiliation and helplessness she had felt on the beach that afternoon had reduced her over the following months to an emotional ruin. She could see now that she had allowed them to rob her of much more than her blitheness. They had taken her marriage too, her happiness, really. Damn them and all who love them wherever they are, she thought angrily. A tear escaped beneath her sunglasses and slid down her cheek. Luckily, Matilda was gazing out of the window and didn't notice. Audrey gritted her teeth, determined that she wouldn't break her resolution of old, not to cry over what they had done to her. Now, a new reality confronted her. And it dictated unmistakably that she had to go. She held her breath as she thought about it. Why not? Why not just leave all this behind? Get on a boat and never come back. She could look after herself. Mother had said in a letter how they were crying out for teachers in England. She could get a job and leave home again as soon as she was settled. After all, she didn't *feel* old, her life needn't be over. She was sure that deep down inside she was the same girl who had come out to Africa on an adventure.

That she had ever thought Africa would be an exciting jaunt made her laugh now. She was certain that a few months of the clean cool air of home and she would recover from the exhaustion of languishing out here in the heat. And she needn't leave shamefully. She had after all tried her hardest; no one could take that away from her. And if her mother or Alan's mother, or anyone else, dared to criticise her for leaving, well, let them. Let *them* live here for one year. Only one year with the heat and the grime and the moisture that rotted clothes and wilted hair, that made women perspire like men, and the boredom . . . the interminable, dilapidating boredom. Then, if they too didn't go mad, or try to escape, they could talk and lecture and moan and groan. And she might even listen to what they had to say . . . after she had told them what it was like to live day after day with the knowledge that the men who had harmed her roamed freely, what it was like to be afraid, really afraid, and to keep that deep fear to herself so Alan couldn't understand why she woke screaming in the night drenched in sweat, and why when he offered his arms, she turned him away so often that he stopped trying. No, she sighed. This decision to go was not cowardly in the slightest; she couldn't be accused of running away. To stay here any longer, that would be to abandon who she really was.

Chapter Twenty-three

The invitation to the Governor's party to be held on New Year's Eve 1948 was addressed to 'Mr and Mrs Bannerman', required evening dress and stated that drinks would be served at seven, dinner at eight. But the day before the party, Julie became ill with a high temperature. The doctor diagnosed malaria, and when it was clear that she would not be able to attend the party with Robert, he sent for his second wife. When he told her about the party, she had been excited like a child, but when he handed Matilda the largest sum of money she had ever had in her hands and told her to make sure she wore something decent, she became anxious.

Matilda rushed home to Aunty Dede and her mother, who spent several minutes moaning about how doomed they were until Aunty Dede told her to shut up. 'We need to get the right fabric. We need a pattern. We need a vision, that is all,' and with that, she sent them to the market to begin their search.

Time passed as the two women trawled through numerous stalls looking at the pieces of cloth on display, and then going into the booths where the market women kept additional stock, to look through trunks stuffed with bales of cloth. Matilda did not notice the severe heat, which caused sweat to stream down her face and between her breasts, or the airlessness of the musty stalls, poorly lit with single low-wattage bulbs. She only noticed that she could not find what she wanted.

'We don't have much time, you know. The party is tomorrow night,' said Ama. Periodically, Ama asked, 'What is wrong with this one?' pointing at an expensive batik or other.

Matilda had to admit they were all rather stunning but not quite what she had in mind. She had never before seen anything like she was looking for and could not describe it, but she knew she would know when she saw it.

They found the cloth nearly three hours later. Matilda looked at it, grabbed it and then gasped. Her mother, who was in the other corner of the murky, cramped cubicle, not much bigger than the size of a small bed, turned. Her daughter stood in the doorway, with the light streaming in behind her. Speechless, Ama reached to touch the fabric. It was a deep crimson good-quality cotton, possibly mixed with some silk, with thick, intricate, gold embroidery; fat golden waves ran lengthways down the fabric, between which were elegant swirls of more golden embroidery. It was edged with embroidered half-moons, so there would be no need for hemming. Matilda's heart was pounding, her breathing shallow and fast, she held the material up to her chin and smiled at her mother.

Her mother nodded. 'Thanks be to God that Lawyer gave you so much money.'

Back home, Aunty Dede had installed her Singer machine in the yard and was ready when they returned. Her mouth dropped ungainly when she saw the fabric. She rubbed it between her fingers gingerly and nodded.

Matilda listened while her mother and aunty discussed various styles of dress they could make in the time they had left. After a while, she interrupted them and said, 'I know what I want. I have drawn it.' She spread out a crumpled piece of paper on the table. They were silenced. They looked at each other and then at Matilda. Then back at the drawing. It was a simple floor-length dress, with a wide, round neckline that would reveal no unnecessary cleavage, quite fitted at the waist, and with a slightly flared skirt.

'But what is this?' asked her mother. 'An English dress?'

'Robert would prefer an English style on this occasion . . .'

'He did not marry an English woman,' said Ama. 'He married a Ga—'

355

'He did not say, but I know. Anyway, it is my cloth. My husband. My choice.'

'And I am your mother. Why are you always so headstrong? Why? And so wilful? And disobedient too?'

'Because I am my mother's daughter,' said Matilda. She walked off. 'And this is not disobedience. You will recognise disobedience when you meet it.' She threw the words carelessly over her shoulder.

'And so rude these days. What is wrong with you? Why are you walking away when I am talking to you? Come back here right now! Do you hear me . . . ?'

'Ama, it's enough,' said Dede. 'We have work to do.'

Matilda came back into the yard a while later.

'The youth of today. They are headed for destruction,' said Ama as soon as she saw her.

'Aunty, do you think you can sew the style I want?' Matilda asked with a serene smile. Maybe it was her tone, the assured delivery, maybe it was her body language, the slightly raised chin, the hands on the hips, but neither woman could have been left with any doubt as to what the dress would look like.

'Me?' she laughed. 'You will be the most beautiful woman tomorrow. Your husband will not know what to do with all your beauty.'

Aunty Dede said she had never used such expensive material, and she prevaricated nervously when she had to make the first cut. Then she was off; measuring, cutting, sewing, and, in between, instructing and chatting and laughing. She worked late into the night and eventually shooed Matilda off to bed. 'You need to get your sleep for tomorrow night,' she said.

When she woke in the morning, it took Matilda a few moments to realise why she was excited. Then she rushed out of her bedroom to find her mother and Aunty Dede, who were still sitting at the sewing machine, the yards of fabric seemingly taking shape. They must have been up all night, but there was a look of triumph on their faces. They took Matilda into Ama's room, Aunty Dede asked her to try the dress on for one last fitting before she finalised it. Matilda took a sharp breath; it was more beautiful that she had hoped, but she would not try it on until she had had her bath, which they all agreed was the right thing. Then, refreshed from her night's sleep and holding her stomach in, the women helped her to climb into the dress. Aunty Amele was hovering at the doorway watching. Ama did up the buttons. It seemed to fit perfectly. The sleeves stopped just above her elbows; her toes were poked out from beneath the fabric; the style of the dress made effective use of the embroidered half-moon shapes along the bust-line and the hem, and the swirling patterns seemed to elongate Matilda with magnificent effect. Relieved, and overcome with emotion, she tried to breathe out and realised she couldn't. Aunty Dede had obviously made a mistake with the measurements, and the dress was a little too tight. Not wanting to disappoint them, Matilda did not say anything.

But Aunty Dede noticed and said, 'Don't be stupid, what kind of party would it be if you can't eat because your dress is too tight? Quick, take it off. We have time. Go and do your hair.'

'You can borrow these.' It was Aunty Amele, who had disappeared briefly, but now came towards Matilda holding a black bundle in one of her hands and a bag in the other. She thrust the bundle into Matilda's hand.

Bemused, Matilda held up a pair of soft, silky, long gloves. She looked at her aunt.

'I bought them a long time ago, but I have never had the opportunity to use them. You might as well use them tonight.' Then she added aggressively, 'But I want them back, do you hear? And you could try this too,' she continued, taking a strange item of clothing out of the bag, holding it up for all in the room to see.

'What is that?'

'A corset!' exclaimed Aunty Dede. 'What a good idea.'

'Oh, thank you so much, Aunty,' said Matilda, overjoyed. She would look the perfect lady tonight. Just like in that magazine that she had seen at Audrey's house, the one from which she had copied the style for her dress. The woman in that picture had been wearing long, black gloves, and perhaps even a corset underneath her dress. But how on earth did Aunty Amele come to own a corset and gloves? Matilda was indeed bemused and looked at her aunt hoping to find some clue, but she disappeared into her room or into the kitchen.

'Well, enough time-wasting. Celestina is ready to do your hair,' said Ama, calling out loudly for Matilda's younger sister, who came running.

The rest of the day was spent doing Matilda's hair: several rows of tiny braids, running from the base of her hairline along her skull to converge at the centre of her head, where they were gathered in a bun. The effect was quite stunning, laying bare the loveliness of Matilda's face. And the hairdo showed off her neck. Matilda was quietly confident that Robert would be impressed tonight and found it difficult to resist taking a surreptitious view of her profile in every reflective surface she passed. Then she remembered Aunty Dede's words: 'Pride always comes before a fall,' and reluctantly wiped the confident, steady glow from her face.

That evening, her family accompanied her along the alleyway to the roadside where Robert's car was parked. She walked to suit the dress, with small steps and a straight back, fuelled by the open amazement expressed by everyone who saw her. She felt lofty, as though the air beneath her feet had been pumped up by the unadulterated praise of her clan.

'The dress is first class, if I have to say so myself,' said Aunty Dede.

'Yes,' said Aunty Amele.

'Well suited to a sturdy structure like yours,' said her mother.

'Yes.'

'You have made us all proud, Matilda,' said Uncle Saint John.

'Yes.'

Ama chewed her empty mouth disapprovingly and said, 'Don't you have anything useful to say? What is all this "yes", "yes" for, eh?'

Robert barely greeted her when she got in, and immediately, her spirits began their descent as the car trundled off to Government House. From a distance, they could hear the music from the party floating in the still air. She looked at the approaching floodlit castle, standing tonight like a beacon, fluorescent against the dark vastness beyond that was the ocean. In the black sky, stars flickered faintly, dimmed by the harsh, unnatural light. She had never been to Christiansborg Castle. Unlike Julie. With this thought, she felt a tightening in her chest. She put her hand to her head. Why had her sister stretched the braids so? Perhaps she should have worn a traditional outfit, after all, which would have been more comfortable as well. Well, it was not as though she could expect him to suddenly start admiring her in front of the driver or anything like that, but one word, one look, a proper greeting, certainly even he could manage. Instead, she had to endure his utter silence and his startled expression while they approached a party that she was now dreading.

A lone armed sentry waved the car into the car park. Robert said something about Buckingham Palace, which Matilda did not hear. She was busy gazing at the impressive structure, lit like a Christmas tree. He took the opportunity to admire her surreptitiously some more. He was astounded at her appearance and had been rather taken aback when he saw her, so much so that he didn't know what to say. Without him taking much notice, her youth and innocence had faded. He had certainly never seen her like this, filling a dress like a woman. With a pang, he realised exactly how young she had been when he married her. Not much older than his eldest child. Had he robbed her of her childhood? Seeing her like this certainly made it harder for him to justify himself with the argument that if he hadn't married her, someone else would have. And she was learning English now, at a quite surprising speed, he had heard. He wondered whether spending time with Alan's wife was having this effect on her. What a transformation from the young girl he had married. She must be what, twenty-five or twenty-six now? He could never remember. And he would be forty-five next year. 'My God!' he said out loud as the car pulled to a stop.

'What, Robert?'

'Nothing,' he said gruffly. He was not looking forward to the evening. There would be people here he did not want to meet, including Alan, whom, entirely intentionally, he had not seen for a while. There would be others, like Rose, his current mistress, whose presence could make things awkward for him around Matilda. He didn't usually care about keeping his affairs secret, but he felt strangely parental towards Matilda tonight, more responsible than he ever had. Yet, he thought guiltily, he would have to ignore her for most of the night or else risk a scene from Rose, whose overbearing jealousy was just about beginning to bore him.

Ever since the riots in February, he had become a little uncertain about this part of his life. The disturbances that had taken grip of the country, left more than twenty dead and most, including Robert, bewildered about what was happening in their usually peaceful land. As Kofi had predicted, a group of ex-servicemen went on a protest, probably fired up by *akpeteshi*, a local potent drink, and decided to alter the route that they had previously agreed with the police. Instead, they marched on the Governor's residence with a petition. There their attempts to get past the police guarding the castle had led a white officer to fire into the crowd eventually killing two ex-servicemen and wounding several. The crowd had dispersed but then went on the rampage in the city, rioting and looting, angry that two of their own had been killed in this way. Robert had been agitated by the needless bloodshed. Twenty-nine dead at the final count in various parts of the country. He had had enough by then. He contacted Kofi, who had been jailed following the riots, along with other leaders of his party. Robert told him that he wanted to be involved somehow. He quietly expected that he would be rewarded with a ministerial position in the future independent country, or possibly even with the position of attorney general; he knew he was very able. He was only moderately pleased with the position the party offered him: assistant legal advisor on matters relating to the reclamation of native rule, coastal region. It had taken a while to get used to the 'assistant' element of things, placed there, he was sure, because of his procrastination.

He felt a little like a traitor heading to the castle tonight, not because of his political involvement; no, there would be others like him there. Just because the intelligentsia were fighting for independence didn't mean they had to halt all social discourse with the British. He had an increasing distrust of the British, which he found a little surprising. The incident at the Gold Cup race had done more than upset him. It had begun an adjustment in the way he saw things, which he had previously not imagined possible.

It had taken eleven years of marriage to get an invitation like this, and Matilda knew she might never get another. She stepped out of the car with some difficulty and followed her husband to the entrance of the castle. She lifted her shoulders and pushed them back and pulled her stomach in some more. She raised her nose and placed her usual modest, and less confident, smile on her lips. There was a hot, salty breeze from the sea, and the waves, thundering out of sight, were loud, but not loud enough to drown the sound of the band playing classical music, which kept getting louder.

'Brahms,' said Robert, almost to himself. 'And quite badly, I might add.'

A waiter dressed in a red knee-length jacket with gold tassels and black trousers with white stripes, carrying a silver tray in a white-gloved hand, greeted them. Matilda waited for Robert to help himself to a drink, then she took one too, forgetting to say thank you or to smile at the waiter, thinking only how hot he must be. She took a large sip and wrinkled her nose in a grimace. Robert looked and explained that it was champagne, bubbly alcohol.

They were late, and as they approached the large hall, brightly decorated for the evening and filled with people, Matilda noticed that several guests were already seated at long tables. There must have been more than a hundred people. From behind her serene smile, taut stomach and her well-gripped, well-sipped glass, she hid her true amazement. The floor was covered in lush red carpets, large chandeliers radiated brightly in the ceiling, and mirrors on the walls reflected the glory. Tables were laden with glittering glasses, polished platters and sparkling silver cutlery; so many knives, spoons and forks gleaming next to shiny plates. She panicked; on occasion, she had had to use a spoon but never two implements at the same time. Her heart sank a little and her well-constricted stomach muscles ached.

The band in one corner of the large room stopped for a moment. Matilda looked around, but Robert was no longer standing anywhere near her. And from somewhere in the room, a man with a booming voice said, 'Ladies and gentlemen, dinner is served.' Matilda kept on smiling in between sips of her champagne, wondering where to sit, and decided that the nearest seat would do. As soon as she had lowered herself gently into the velvet, cushioned chair, she noticed a white card in front of the plate, which read, 'John Cummings, Esq.'. She looked to her left and right and noticed that each of the plates had a similar card. She pursed her lips and flared her nostrils in defiance of the tears she could feel pricking her eyes. She wondered how would she find her place in this large room. Looking around desperately she stood up. One of the waiters would know.

'Is that you, Matilda?' said a shrill voice behind her. It was Audrey, who looked exuberant. 'My God, I would never have recognised you. Look at you! Well, well. Look, Alan. Look, it's Matilda. Is Robert here too?' she asked.

'Hello . . . Matilda,' said Alan, staring at her.

'Good evening, Audrey. Good evening, Alan.' Wonderful, someone she knew, she thought, beginning to breathe more easily. Now all they had to do was to stop looking at her as if she was an oddity.

Alan leaned over and kissed her on the cheek gently, which surprised her. She took a small step back. How different they looked all dressed up. She had only ever seen Alan in his khaki shorts and jacket, which seemed to be some sort of uniform, but tonight he was wearing a suit and a bow tie, like Robert, and he seemed taller, more prominent than usual. Audrey was wearing a dress made with a flimsy material the colour of faded green, which clung to her form showing off her lack of curves and excess flesh. But she had pinned her hair up and brushed some of it, although when she looked closely, Matilda could see the tangled mess beneath. At least she had made some effort with her appearance tonight.

'Well, can't stop now. Better dash; H.E. is about to make his formal entrance. Talk later,' said Audrey, grabbing a handful of her evening dress and walking off. She half-turned and winked at Matilda. 'You *do* look spectacular.'

'You do. You look . . .' said Alan. 'You look . . . stunning.'

Matilda looked at the red carpet around his shiny shoes. 'I cannot find Robert.'

'Oh, come with me. You and Robert are on our table. I thought it was time he and I had a chat.'

She walked behind him, keeping her eyes on the small roll of flesh that bulged over the top of his collar at the base of his head. He was nice. She had noticed that before. They had not spoken much ever; they greeted each other in passing on the occasions that he was still at the house when she arrived for her English lesson. And whenever she served Robert, she, unlike Julie, preferred to remain inconspicuous.

At their table, Robert was engrossed in conversation with a glamorous woman seated on his right. She was the mulatto she had seen him with at the racecourse. Tonight, she was polished like a doll with glossy lips and shimmering eyes. She rested her hand on his arm and leaned towards him when she spoke. So was this the woman who had distracted her husband of late? She was impressed with the open tenderness and wondered whether they would have been as comfortable with each other if Julie was here. She felt a twinge of envy. She too had begun to long for something like this, togetherness for the sake of it, affection that was spontaneous. Things she had always been told were not essential for marriage, for a girl like her. But wouldn't it be nice to be thought about kindly, to be touched softly, to be whispered to in the way that Robert was whispering to this woman now, bringing desire to her eyes?

Alan pulled back the chair next to Robert for Matilda, interrupting the intimate scene. She sat and read the name on the card in front of her, 'Mrs Julie Bannerman'. She bit her lip. Next to her, Robert continued to talk to his friend, but she could see that his shoulders were tense. After all, she was his wife, not some momentary girlfriend. She knew her husband well enough to know when he was uncomfortable. The woman next to him, however, seemed totally unmindful of this fact.

Matilda clasped her hands in her lap and wondered how Julie would react if she were here sitting next to her husband – a husband oblivious, it seemed, to all of the effort his wife had made tonight – and staring at a card with another woman's name on it. Anew, she wished Julie a steady albeit unhurried recovery and smiled sincerely at the waiter who placed another drink in front of her.

She looked up at Alan and said, 'Thank you.'

He had been looking at her. He smiled kindly and said, 'My pleasure. It can be a bit daunting at these dos. But you'll be fine. You look . . . stunning,' he said again. His face had lost its usual lightness.

'Thank you,' said Matilda, lowering her eyes. She wondered why he was looking at her so oddly; did she have something on her face, or was her hair out of place? She was pleased when he turned to talk to the woman on his right, Alice or something, whose husband it seemed had kindly swapped places with Alan. She took a long sip and felt the bubbles swim to her head. She breathed out, grateful for Aunty Dede's foresight about loosening the dress. Behind the serene smile, she lectured herself; she deserved to be here as much as anyone else, certainly as much as Julie. Her chin lifted a little. And were the men not looking at her? She lifted her bosom. And the women too? She finished her drink.

'Would you like some more champagne?' asked Alan.

'Oh, thank you.'

'Right, that was the very last thank-you for the evening,' he said, laughing. Their eyes fixed for a moment. She put her hand on her chest. She smiled faintly and blinked in search of relief from his intense gaze. Why did he refuse to look away as she would have considered it polite for him to? It was she who eventually, somewhat reluctantly, which in itself was odd, had to blink and lower her eyes. And he touched her hand often when he was trying to make a point, laying his large, warm hands on top of hers, which did not offend her, because he could not possibly intend anything improper, not with her husband sitting directly under his nose.

When he turned to talk to Alice, Matilda stared at the place card, then at her chatting companions. She reached for it, tore it in two under the tablecloth and let the pieces fall to the floor. She lifted her glass to her smiling lips.

Eventually, when H.E. was installed in his rightful place and grace had been said, several waiters appeared in unison, from some other part of the castle, bearing trays of food. Matilda stared at the plate that had been placed before her, trying to identify the contents, and she wondered which cutlery she should use. She hoped that some-one close to her would start to eat, but they did not seem to have noticed the food. Robert and his woman friend, Audrey and her friends, all chatting and drinking, unaware, it appeared, of their dinner. It seemed to her that she had been sitting there, ravenous, for a while when Alan spoke.

'I always think I must have had too much to drink when I see so many forks and knives, and then I remind myself, start from the outside and work your way in. Works every time.' Then slowly, he picked up a knife and fork and started eating.

Matilda copied him and started to eat a little clumsily. She looked around at her fellow diners; obviously, no one was interested in how she ate. It was a sweet-tasting creamy salad with fish and prawns in it, not like anything she would ever cook, but quite delicious. She said, 'I am pleased to sit next to you.'

'*Owyuradon*,' he said. 'Thank you.'

She snorted with laughter and quickly covered her mouth with her hand. Alan, however, seemed unaware that everyone had turned to look at them.

'Probably the funniest Ga that you have ever heard, am I right? Don't worry, I have no intention of punishing you with it all night.'

The rigidity that seemed to have taken over her entire body earlier loosened as she listened to his non-stop chat. Never had a man spoken to her about such things, and for so long: on and on he went about his family in England, his many sisters and brothers, his heavy sadness that he and Audrey did not have children, and how awful he felt for her, his trips into the bush interior, the first time he ate snake – 'I know H.E. likes it too, so we may be lucky tonight,' he said, then laughed when he saw her face and placed his hand on hers reassuringly – what Robert had been like as a young man, how sad it would be for him to leave this wonderful country, the wonderful people, the wonderful food. As the evening progressed, she found the way he looked into her eyes less disconcerting; he was simply being polite, trying to make her feel comfortable, the only one around her doing so. None of the men she came into contact with had the audacity to stare at her like this. They either considered themselves too inferior, like Tetteh and all Robert's other staff, in which case they looked at their feet or at least away from her face when they spoke to her, or else, like some of his friends, she did not seem to exist. Until she turned her back that is, for then, even she knew that they looked.

'So, how are you, then, Alan?' said Robert, leaning across the table towards Alan, interrupting something Matilda was saying. 'It's beginning to look like independence will be inevitable before long.'

'How are *you*? I've not seen you for a while. I suppose you are a busy politician now?'

'We try. We'd better make the most of this party. Who knows if it will be the last,' said Robert, laughing dryly.

'Oh, I don't think so. I know that you agree with me when I say that this is a country ill-prepared for self-rule. Independence would put Africans with little or no experience of government in authority, and heaven knows where that would lead to,' said Alan, taking a gulp of his champagne. He had watery eyes, which he was blinking rapidly. He lifted his glass again and drained it unhurriedly before he continued, 'If I thought it was the right thing to career towards independence completely unprepared, I would go quietly. Obviously, independence would mean a one-way ticket home for me, and I am not ready to go yet.' Then in a whisper, 'Gosh, I do hope we are here for a little while longer yet. Anyhow, I can't believe the Governor is letting us fraternise with Communist insurgents,' he said laughing.

'Don't believe everything you read. The party had nothing whatsoever to do with the uprisings; the ex-servicemen rioted of their own accord. But you must agree it would have been odd if they had not realised that this was a good opportunity to rally national support for our movement,' replied Robert. 'But I can tell you right now that I have no desire to live in a Marxist state either. Anyway, I think your government—'

'And yours.'

'Yes, well . . . they are the ones acting like Communists. Simply because some disgruntled men go on a march that gets out of hand does not entitle them to curtail our freedoms,' said Robert. 'A few days of riots and we get a curfew and press censorship? Is that what democracy has come to?'

'We do have every right to be suspicious of the Convention. There are rumours they are plotting to overthrow the Government and set up a union of African socialist republics.'

'I can assure you that is completely unfounded. They said that to justify the detention of Nkrumah and the others.'

Matilda was watching them with interest. Alan's face had drooped, and lines that she had not noticed before had appeared around his eyes.

'I didn't think you were that interested in politics, Robert.'

'I had to find something to fill my time. The horses used to keep me busy, you see? I had to find a new hobby to replace racing.'

'You didn't sell them, did you?' asked Alan, aghast.

'I plan to, even though my staff are begging me not to. Kofi approached me after the riots, said the party needed legal advisors.' He leaned in towards Alan and narrowed his eyes. 'I was never an advocate for severing the relationship with the British in this way, I never wanted to make enemies with the people I thought were my friends . . . but things change, don't they, Alan?' He chuckled. 'The idea of defending Communist activists, as you call them, might have put me in a quandary a while back . . .'

'So you joined with them to boot us out?'

Robert was quiet.

'I bumped into James at the club the other day, he was saying what a shame it is that you no longer race your horses,' said Alan.

'Well, what do they expect? Actually, I'd rather not talk about it . . .'

'Robert, it was awkward; they were in a bind about what to do.'

'How about the right thing?' said Robert aggressively. 'They humiliated me,' he whispered. 'I have never in my entire life felt as let down as I did that day.'

'James wants to make amends . . .'

'Does he now?' he said angrily. Robert had dreamed of hearing these words. He missed that part of his life more than he dared show. 'I am sure he knows where I live, where I work; Accra is a small place. If he wants to find me to apologise suitably, I am sure he can.'

'Let's drink to cleared misunderstandings, to old friends.'

Robert lifted his glass but did not drink. He knew it was illogical to allow the despicable behaviour of the committee to taint their friendship, but he had been offended that his friend, although he had expressed disgust that day, had not realised the need to take sides. It had shocked and upset Robert that Alan had continued to fraternise with the very people who had mistreated and humiliated him so badly.

Matilda was unwilling to witness any further this exchange between the men who, as far as she could see, were aching to be friends. She

367

excused herself from the table and went in search of the toilets. The heels of her shoes sank a little with each step into the lush carpet that, to her surprise, went all the way into the toilets. She stood for a moment in front of one of the ornate, brass, oval-shaped mirrors that hung above the sink, too stunned to remember why she was here. There were two sinks and two mirrors, each with lights above them, so that each pore on her face was highlighted. Everything gleamed and reflected in much the same way it did out in the dining room. She could name many people who would be happy to live in a room like this that smelled of soap and shone in spite of the fact that there was no sunlight here.

When she returned, she was surprised to see the guests dancing. She turned in her chair to watch the couples swaying happily, formally, to the music. This type of dancing was so different to what she knew, but it looked elegant, appropriate for the way the guests were dressed tonight, and it would be unlikely to cause everyone to end up dripping with sweat.

'Go on, Alan, dance with Matilda.' Audrey's eyes were wild, and she was holding a cigarette elegantly over her shoulder. She and the woman she had been talking to giggled like schoolgirls.

'Good idea. Robert, hope you don't mind, old chap. But I would like to dance with your wife if she'll have me.'

'Fine with me, but she does not know how to dance. Come on, Rose, let's all dance,' said Robert, pulling his friend up to her feet.

Alan took her hand in his when he saw how her face had dropped. Now this was going too far, Matilda thought, tugging her hand, but he would not let go. 'I should have asked you first. I thought it was a good idea. This is a waltz, nothing complicated. All you have to do is hold on to me, and I will lead you around. I won't embarrass you. Anyway, there are so many people on the dance floor that no one will notice us.'

She wanted to dance. Preferably with her very own husband, which would have been right and proper. They had never danced together in public. A few times, when he had been particularly happy, he had twirled her in his bedroom to one of his favourite pieces. She had enjoyed being held like that by him and loved being pulled around his bedroom while he lost himself in the music for a several minutes.

She watched the dancers swaying elegantly, their feet light on the floor, dresses twirling and sashaying, sequins sparkling. The music seeped into her. Alan stared imploringly. She owed him a reward for his kindness. She allowed him to pull her to her feet. And he kept his word. He held her firmly, guiding her around the floor in step with the music. He held her close; she could feel his stomach on hers, his legs against hers, his breath on her neck.

He whispered in her ear, 'I saw what you did to that card, and I cannot say I blame you.'

She was embarrassed that her crime had been witnessed. Now would he think her childish? She pulled back and said, 'You must talk to him some more, Alan. Tell him to forgive and forget. The horses are his life, and he is suffering. Don't give up.'

Alan nodded and gripped her resolutely; she felt her heart beat a little faster and was relieved when the dance came to an end and she could sit down, because she felt dizzy. When she looked up at him, he looked away. Considering how gently they had danced, she noticed that it took a while for his breathing to ease too. Then he asked her to dance again. It seemed fine to do so, so she did, and in any case, her husband had disappeared. Audrey told them when they sat down for a rest that Lawyer had asked them to give Matilda a lift home.

Alan asked Audrey to dance, but she cried, 'Oh, dance with her, *she* seems not to mind too much. I'm rather comfortable here.' Then she turned to Matilda while Alan was looking the other way, winked and said smiling, 'He must like you.'

Matilda was shocked. This was not the kind of thing one said with a smile. These English people are mad, she thought. They think they have come here to teach us things, many useful things, yes, but really, there is a lot that they don't know. What kind of woman tells her friend that her husband likes her? And we are all married too? She shook her head and told Alan she could not dance with him any more.

A few days after the Governor's party, walking with an extra lilt in her step, she went to Downing House to ask Robert if he wanted to eat anything special for dinner that day; she had taken to calling in on him in his office from time to time, to see if she could tempt him to order some food from her, and generally, this plan had worked. It was as if he simply needed reminding of his other wife and other family.

When she walked round the corner of the office and saw Robert and Julie standing next to his desk with their arms around each other, she froze. She felt like a spy, unexpected and unwanted. How to turn round and leave before they realised that she had observed them with their guard down like this? But her limbs felt distant, not hers really, and in her ears, she could hear the magnified sounds of her body functioning. Her heart palpitated far too loudly, and she tried to compensate by holding her breath as she turned slowly and silently, like a mother creeping away from a sleeping, restless child.

'Matilda?' Robert called.

She turned back and continued up the steps and stood in the doorway of the office. She felt stupid but fixed a nonchalant expression on her face and greeted them cheerily. Julie smiled back a victorious smile, and then glided out of the back door of the office. You witch, thought Matilda, also smiling.

'Do you want something?'

'I just wanted to say hello and to see if I can cook anything for you tonight?' She was wearing what she believed to be her most alluring expression, even though her boldness had begun to evaporate as soon as she heard his question. Why did he always think that she wanted something from him?

'Oh, that is kind, but not tonight. I have other plans . . .' He started to rummage on his desk for something.

He looked a little irritated, and Matilda noted sadly that she rarely saw the composed, happy man she had observed with Julie. It was hard not to take it personally. Oh, but what did it matter? Wasn't she freer these days? Aunty Dede's advice rang in her ears: 'A needy woman is never needed.' She breathed in and started speaking English. 'So, how is work this days?' she said softly.

Robert looked up and smiled. 'I had heard from Alan that you were making a lot of progress. He seemed rather impressed with you . . . well, with how successful Audrey has been, actually. Good.'

'I am trying my best.' Matilda was pleased. 'I want—'

The door banged open, and Julie came in carrying a tray with tea and biscuits. 'Ah, you are still here, then. Have you seen the new tea set that Robert bought me?' she asked with a sweet smile, drawing attention to the fact that there were only two cups and saucers on the tray. 'Did I interrupt something important?' she asked, as she placed the tray lopsided on top of uneven piles of papers and books. 'Was that English I heard you speaking?'

'Yes, she is doing very well. Matilda, is there anything else?' Robert seemed even more uneasy.

As ever, being in a confined space with both his wives made him uncomfortable, and she could see that he wanted her to leave.

'Well, I am going,' said Matilda in English. She was determined not to let that woman get her down. 'All right, I will be sending you some foods tomorrow, then,' she said as she walked out of the office.

She turned the corner and heard Robert and Julie laughing the kind of laughter that should be suppressed but cannot. It was a sound she knew she would never forget till the day she died. Once again, she stopped in her tracks. Evidently, they thought her English was funny. Why should she have been surprised to hear Julie mock her? Wouldn't that be common enough, even with the thin veneer of civility that the years had placed over their relationship? No matter which way she looked at it, they were not friends. But Robert? The father of my own children? Matilda felt her eyes cloud over with tears as she stood there listening to their laughter. Then, suddenly afraid that they might start saying things she did not want or need to hear, she continued on her way, stumbling towards the back gate. Her eyes stung with tears she could not let drop here. How dare they? she asked herself over and over again as she stormed away. When she reached the big gate, she turned and looked at Downing House; her eyes filled with fury and resentment, and she vowed to herself, 'Never again.' Then she turned on her heels and walked home, faster than she had ever walked before, her steps pounding the unpaved pavement to the beat of her sore heart.

She was oblivious to the various greetings and waves. All she could hear were the thoughts that assaulted her mind, the blood that hammered her ears. She would never again place a foot in that house. They may not realise it, but she too had pride. If he wanted to treat her that way in front of that woman, then fine, but there were consequences, and Robert Bannerman, rich, powerful lawyer or not, husband or not, was about to find out that his second wife would not accept humiliation from him; she would not be treated as though she had no status. After all, had she not always been dutiful, obedient to his every command? And compliant? Had she not respected him and asked in return only for respect? Had she not been reasonable in every way as a wife? Having to bear patiently Julie's insulting behaviour. Occasionally, he had become involved to appease the women. More often, however, he had shirked his responsibility, in a cowardly fashion, it had to be said. But until now Matilda believed he had always maintained the only dignified position for a man with multiple wives; he had pretended to treat them as equals, well, more or less, anyway. And just because Matilda had to show deference to Julie because she was the senior wife did not mean she had to allow herself to be humiliated by her husband in front of that woman. She almost spat on the ground in anger each time 'that woman' appeared in her thoughts. Tears were pouring freely down her face. She remained unaware of the stares along her route. Her thoughts expanded as she walked, circling her head, leaving room for little else. After all, had she not been minding her own business, had she not been a schoolgirl with her own hopes too when *he* came to marry her? *She* had not asked him to, yet she had borne him children, many healthy boys. And, let no one forget, a daughter too. Since when does a person's value diminish when she dies? And after all that, was her only reward such utter disrespect? 'Never,' she whispered as she gathered her skirt and climbed over the threshold of Saint John's compound. 'Never, never again.'

Chapter Twenty-four

She continued to cook for her husband dutifully, stirring her anger into the sauces and stews that he liked so much and sent the food to Downing House. She looked after their children devotedly but found reasons to keep them from visiting his house. Her face hardened when his name was mentioned; her heart lamented; her eyes held on to unspilled tears.

Then Robert received her letter. Speaking and reading was one thing, but writing; well, Matilda had a long way to go yet, Robert thought as he read her letter, affronted by the ridiculousness of the missive. At first, he had no idea what she was referring to and thought perhaps one of his maids had been telling tales about Julie. He was somewhat hurt that she should be so insolent, and for no evident reason. And to think that after seeing her the other night, he had resolved that he would pay her a little more attention. Her appearance had been breathtaking, but ever so mature, which had taken him aback, and with Rose there, it had been rather awkward to play a husbandly role. Instead, he had stayed close to Rose, a woman who could be quite unpredictable in those situations, and watched Matilda from afar, noting with a mixture of satisfaction and regret the admiring glances she was receiving from everyone.

Slowly, he began to appreciate his wife's first real show of independence, and it dawned on him that this was not a joke, that perhaps she meant it. Women can be stubborn, he thought. Take Julie for instance, and he had learned that it was better not to get a woman into a position from which she felt she could not back down without loss of face, because, well, then you were done for. But that had never been his experience with Matilda. She had always been compliant, lovely actually. Yet this thoroughly groundless attack, this offensive letter was one step too far. He would not have it. He had never forced his authority on her; he had given her freedom to come and go as she pleased, rescued her from a life of little, elevated her, for goodness' sakes. How dare she? he thought. Who the hell does she think she is?

Later, he would be impressed with himself that he did not simply storm into Saint John's house and demand that she fall into line. He spoke first to Julie, taking care not to reveal the existence of the insolent letter, noting that she was only too keen to identify the offending occasion. Then he realised that there was only one course of action to be taken. He sent for her parents.

Ama and Owusu appeared in Robert's office at the scheduled time in their best clothes and sat on the chairs facing his desk with hands clasped loosely on their laps, his eyes downward, hers wandering curiously, their smiles hesitant.

Robert did not allow his glower to soften. He picked up Matilda's letter and, perching on the edge of his desk, read it out to them: 'Please, I will not be humilliate by you or anyone else for that mater. Should you chose to laugh at me behind my back with your First Wife, then so be it. But I will not partake of such embrasments any longer. I to have pride in myself. I am sombodys daughter, sombodys mother.' He translated the gist of her note into Ga, pausing to look from one parent to the other when he said, 'somebodys daughter'. He noted with satisfaction that Ama's face took on an increasingly distressed expression. Owusu, however, appeared indifferent, even bored, and remained quiet with his unshaven face slumped in his good hand.

'That is why I asked you to come here today. I knew you would want to know what your daughter has done. You must decide what to do about it,' Robert said, as he refolded the letter and placed it on his desk.

In an uncharacteristically quiet voice so that she was almost whispering, Ama said reverentially, 'Oh, my son, we are so ashamed. We are sorry for the disgrace that our daughter has caused us. We did not bring her up to be disrespectful in this manner. And after all the good things that you have done for her, how can she insult your good name like this?' She paused for Robert to say something, but he did not speak so she continued, unwilling to let silence prevail, 'We will talk to her as soon as we get home today. My son, you know her, she can be stubborn. But that is the youth of today,' she said, trying to smile, but when no one in the room smiled with her, she quickly turned her lips downwards and simply appeared more distraught and ashamed.

Robert stared at them and beyond, out into the street.

'My son, we shall not discuss this matter beyond these four walls. We understood that you are humiliated—'

'I am not humiliated. I think that the only person in danger of humiliation is your daughter.'

'Eh! My son, please, I am begging you. Do not divorce our daughter for this. Please, you have the right to, but we beg you, please.' Ama's voice rose and took on a desperately urgent tone. 'I will personally make sure that girl comes to see you this evening. I will not allow her to embarrass our family name in this way. Lawyer, please will you be able to forgive her? Yes, not forget, but please, forgive? We know you as a gentleman. Please.'

Robert had not intended making it so hard for his wife's parents, even though Matilda's letter had annoyed him. He had never liked this woman, and here she was prepared to do anything he bid her in order to seek forgiveness for her daughter. Her ingratiation reminded him of his status. Wasn't he their main source of income? He felt anger rise in him for the lot of them: the insolent man who sat silently throughout looking more forlorn than Robert remembered, and reeking of alcohol even though it was not yet noon, and the annoying woman who caused him to flinch each time she called him 'my son', even though they were probably very close in age. How dare Matilda behave so ungratefully? he thought. Yet her mother realised the gravity of the matter and was here to ensure that sufficient apologies were made. He nodded his head imperially, signalling that he was prepared to be lenient. Then they left, Ama looking visibly relieved.

*

375

Matilda was in her bedroom when she heard her mother screaming in the compound outside, 'Where is that ungrateful girl? Where is she?'

She took a deep breath and steeled herself. She walked out into the glare of the sun. Her mother's face was contorted in fury. The veins in her neck protruded as she shouted at the top of her voice. She lunged at her daughter, but Matilda raised her hand to protect her face and stumbled backwards out of her mother's range.

'How dare you? Are you stupid?' Ama waved her hands around aggressively.

'He sent for you, then?'

'The "he" you are referring to so insolently is your husband,' screamed Ama. 'The man to whom you owe everything. The father of your children. Your husband,' she continued at the top of her voice. 'Have you lost your mind? Do you not realise that he is supporting you? As well as all of us? Have you forgotten your duties? How can you treat him in this way? How dare you write such an insulting letter? What are you trying to do to us? What is the matter with you? What?'

'There is nothing wrong with me.'

'Don't talk to me like that. Owusu, why are you also so useless?'

Owusu shook his shoulders as he made himself comfortable on his stool in a shady part of the yard. Matilda's sisters, cousins, aunts, everyone, had come out of the house and stood around the yard watching silently. Passers-by lingered at the door to the compound and listened openly.

Matilda stood unmoveable, with folded arms. She had written the letter on impulse, the very day that she had heard Robert and Julie laughing at her, and she had sent it before she had the chance to change her mind. But as time passed, she had had ample opportunity to consider her position and was surprised that her resolve only strengthened. For what reason should she allow herself to be humiliated? Because of her duties? No, forget them, she told herself. After all, had she not performed them tirelessly all her life? And forget him too, she thought, a little less boldly. Yes. Forget him. She had not weakened when she had only herself to talk to about this. She had not told a soul about her letter, perhaps out of fear, although she

376

knew now that it could not have been fear, but something else. She would not weaken now.

'Put your hands behind your back when I am talking to you, you insolent girl.'

She placed them on her hips. 'I am not a child any more.'

'Eeeh! God help me. You are a wicked, wicked girl,' Ama said, trying to hit Matilda to the rhythm of her words. Matilda stepped back and blocked the approaching blows.

Ama started to walk up and down the yard, ranting and raving, shrieking at Matilda, her father, her other useless daughters. 'What are you looking at?' she shouted suddenly at the group of staring faces at the compound door and, with unusual energy, forced the gate shut.

'Why are you treating me like this? What have I ever done to deserve such disrespect? And from my own child? What are you being so disobedient for?' Her shrill voice floated in the heavy air.

'Disobedient?' asked Matilda, squinting. 'I have been nothing but obedient to you. And to my husband. And quite frankly obedience is overestimated.'

'Overwhat? Are you mad . . . ?'

'No, I am not mad. He did not tell you why I wrote that letter to him? And you did not bother to ask because no matter what I do, you will always think the worst of me. That is up to you. But I will tell you. All of you,' she said slowly, looking at the family of spectators. 'I . . . you all, have been humiliated by him in front of that woman. And that I will not tolerate. I will not. I know who I am and where I come from. That is what you, all of you, have taught me.' Quietly she added, 'When he is ready to apologise to me, he knows where he can find me.' She had fantasised about how he would rescue her from her pride, how he would come to find her and tell her that he needed her. But wasn't it a silly notion for a fully grown woman and the mother of five to expect the father of her children to come pledging love in that way?

Her mother sat down on a stool and started to cry uncontrollably. Matilda stared at her; she had never seen her cry. Eunice walked over to comfort their mother. Ama's wails became louder; her shoulders heaved with sobs. Matilda tried to touch her.

'Get away from me. You don't see what you are doing to this

family. Have you offended someone that they should curse you like this?'

'What are you talking about? What does cursing have to do with this?'

'You really are a stupid girl! Don't you see how enviable your position is? You are married to a rich, powerful man with healthy children who will also be educated to take prominent positions in society. How many people can boast of such achievements? And you want to throw it all away like a fool.'

'I can take no pride in any achievements that happened to me by coincidence. How can I raise my children to be respectful if I have no respect for myself, because the man that is my so-called husband—'

'"My so-called husband"! God help us. What is wrong with you? It must be that English woman; I knew nothing good would come from you learning English; now look at the airs and graces you have acquired. What they do there,' she said, waving her arm in the air to indicate the faraway place that was England, 'is not what we do here,' she said, pulsing her finger towards the firm ground her feet rested on. 'Now we can all sit back and suffer while you are ungrateful for all your blessings. And because of what? After all, what is it that he did? He laughed at something with his wife, and you have taken that to mean that he does not respect you. So what? What does respect have to do with your duties as a wife, as a mother, as a daughter?'

'Everything. When I was a child, I did what you and my elders required of me. I quietly married a man that I did not know. When I was still a child. Did I complain? No. But I am no longer a child. I need self-respect, just as you need yours and my husband needs his.'

'So, what are you planning to do now without a husband?' asked Ama between her tears. 'What are we going to do? Eeeh! We must send for Saint John straightaway.'

'Send for him, then,' said Matilda, shrugging. She turned to walk back into her room, looking at her father as she passed him. He was looking at her, and in his face she saw something flicker that she had not seen for years. A quivering lip? A sparkle in his eye? She smiled and walked faster so no one would see the tears that had filled her eyes. She was determined to try and shun regret, to avoid having her spirit sapped out of her, leaving in its wake a shrivelled, bitter shell.

She did not want to end up like her mother, or even Audrey. She could not change her mind, no matter what that Uncle Saint John might have to add.

The next day, when Saint John and Aunty Dede were back from a visit they had made to Aunty Dede's now ill husband, the Lamptey household gathered for a family meeting. It was dusk, and stars were beginning to emerge in the distant sky. The Harmattan had passed suddenly, and the dust-laden sky had cleared once more, leaving behind the wet heat of potential rain.

Matilda was surprised that her mother had been able to resist the temptation to blurt out her sins to her elders as soon as they walked in the door, but she had, and later in the evening, when they were gathered around flickering kerosene lamps and mosquito coils, Ama said in a composed voice that belied any internal histrionics, 'Lawyer informed me yesterday that Matilda has written to him to say that she will never again step foot in his house.'

The announcement was greeted with silence.

Slowly, the implications of what his sister had said dawned on Saint John, who felt he had the most to lose if the family angered Lawyer. He looked at Matilda. 'What happened?' he asked her gently.

They all turned to look at her while she recounted the story and described her humiliation.

'But that is not a reason to refuse to do your duties as a wife,' Uncle Saint John replied.

Matilda stared at the insects dancing around the kerosene lamp desperate to reach the elusive flame.

'Maybe a jealous person has cursed you,' said Aunty Amele. 'It could very easily be the first wife. Maybe she does not want you around any longer.'

'That is what I think,' said Ama.

'Or maybe your so-called friend Patience. I personally have never trusted that girl,' said Aunty Amele.

'What are you talking about?' said Matilda.

'In these situations, it does not pay to rule out any suspects until you know for sure. After all, what has she got compared to you? She might be nurturing jealousy in her heart like an open wound, she

379

might be bitter at your success, which *she* may think you do not deserve. *She* may think you do not deserve to have such a nice husband and so many children . . .'

'In which case, Amele, you might also be a chief suspect,' said Aunty Dede. 'Stop talking utter rubbish.'

'Either way, you should go and see the priest urgently,' said Aunty Amele.

'That may well be, but it is up to Matilda whether she wants to go and see the priest or not. That man has broken the one golden rule for a man with more than one wife,' said Aunty Dede emphatically. 'Firstly, he must not favour one wife over the other, and secondly, he must not humiliate one wife in front of the other. He has only himself to blame.' She shrugged.

'Dede, don't encourage the girl,' said Ama angrily. 'She has her duties.'

'Duties, duties. He has duties too, you know? He must apologise to his wife and show her due respect. What does he expect if he cannot do that? I am surprised that you expect your daughter to be humiliated like this. In these circumstances, he should try and understand her side. John, you can go and talk to Lawyer's sisters and ask them to tell him to apologise to our daughter, and this matter will be forgotten. Matilda, am I right?'

Matilda had not considered this as an option, and she panicked a little, but before she could respond, her uncle spoke, in a high-pitched voice, '*Please!* Please, think about what you are saying, Dede. Think, I beg you. Pleeease, think! What you are asking me to do is unthinkable. How can you actually expect a man in Lawyer's position to apologise to his wife? And how can you seriously expect me to be the one to go and tell his sisters that their esteemed brother must come here and grovel to his wife? Would you ask me to pour kerosene on a fire? Would you?' His face was distorted with pain.

'Are you not the head of this house?'

'But how can you send me on such a ridiculous mission? Is this a sign that this family is completely under siege from some evil spirits? *I* should go and ask *Lawyer* to say sorry?' he said, laughing a loud, forced, hysterical laugh. He stopped laughing and started shaking his head and twitching his legs vigorously, like a person with an uncontrollable nervous tic. He played with his moustache, looking at the women, one to the other. In barely a whisper, shaking his head mournfully, he said, 'I will never . . . never . . . never get such a good job again. This is crazy.' He stood up to walk towards the latrine as if maybe some distance from these mad people would make everything fine again.

When he returned, they were still sitting just as he had left them, and it must have been this that made him lose his temper. Shouting and pointing at each of them in turn, he said, 'Look at you, Amele, my own wife, too timid and jealous to be a decent mother or wife, and you, Owusu, a good-for-nothing wastrel, a drunken layabout; and as for you, Dede, you could not maintain your own marriage, you abandoned your husband, and now you are determined to encourage the girl to do the same, to destroy what is left of hers – is this right? Answer me, please. Is this the thanks I deserve? Is this how I am to be rewarded for years of hard work and sacrifice to elevate this family?' He raised open hands to heaven in supplication.

'You better calm down before you drop down dead; I am too tired to organise a funeral, especially of the self-inflicted kind,' said Aunty Dede. She ignored her brother as he visibly convulsed in frustration and anger and said, 'Well, if you are too cowardly to go and face them, I will go.'

'Listen! Stop! This is very serious . . . a very serious matter. You need . . . I mean, we all need to place aside our . . . erm . . . We need . . . Listen, we must just put aside our pride.' He turned to Matilda and pleaded with her, like a man for his life, 'Do you want to destroy me? Do you want me to start looking for another job? If I stop working for Lawyer, then I am as good as unemployable. Is this the way to reward me for all that I have done for you? For all of you? I have worked hard to advance this family. Please think about the consequences of your behaviour on us all.' To any of the people in the compound that night, it must have looked as if the man was about to break down and cry. They all stared at him, some in morbid curiosity, hoping that he would not be able to hold back his tears, but he did.

'What you need to do for yourself is up to you. I know what I need to do for myself,' said Matilda, sighing.

'Do you see what I mean?' said Ama, throwing her hands up in defeat. Saint John's mouth had dropped open. Amele's face showed concern and surprise.

'It is a curse,' said Saint John. 'There is no other way to explain this. I have not done anything to deserve this.'

'In life, we often don't get what we deserve,' said Matilda loudly.

'And since when did you become a woman of such wisdom? You are too known for your own good,' said Ama.

A fearful silence descended, and Matilda sat quietly with her own thoughts. She knew that perhaps as soon as the next morning, they would all be off to make sacrifices to the gods in order to bring their daughter to her senses and perhaps to seek revenge on the person who had cursed her. Although she had kept her old vow not to seek the help of the fetish priest in previous years, it had not concerned her overly to know that incantations might have been said on her behalf. Today, she did not share their opinion that they were on the brink of some disaster. Today, she felt liberated; her spirit strangely freed, in spite of the unyielding knot in her stomach, which she chose to ignore. And for that, only prayers of thanks were necessary.

The cheek of it, Robert thought to himself, when Matilda's aunty waddled into his office uninvited, rested a tiny portion of her large bottom on the very edge of his armchair, because she could not fit between the arms, and told him gently, but in no uncertain terms, that he must apologise to her niece. He was enraged. But the woman was much older than him, and a relative, he could not do what he would have liked most. Instead, he was unfriendly, and his manner verged on rudeness. He would not apologise. He was adamant he had done nothing wrong. Since when was it an offence to share a private joke with one's own wife?

'But the girl is right on this occasion. To be frank, Lawyer, you have wronged her and you have wronged our family, we who have only treated you with the highest esteem that you deserve. If you could just meet her and explain what happened, then I am sure that we can sort this out. Think about her feelings too, how humiliated she must have felt, and after all her efforts to learn English.'

'You are wasting your time. I have received your message loud and clear; your niece means to stand by her letter. So be it. When she is ready, she will come and apologise for her childish behaviour.' He stood up. 'I have to go out.' He watched in disgust as Aunty Dede struggled to get out of the chair, wondering how much a person had to consume to maintain such bulk.

'Lawyer, please, think about it, I beg you. And I will also talk to Matilda again,' she said as she shuffled to the door and out of his office.

Fortunately for Saint John, his greatest fears were allayed when Robert sent for him the next day and, completely ignoring the catastrophe at hand, began to discuss an impending case. He breathed a great sigh of relief and resolved to work extra hard and remind Lawyer how indispensable he was. All day he remained quiet, speaking only when Lawyer spoke to him so that Lawyer may well have thought that he was being particularly respectful. But the truth was that when Aunty Dede had announced that she had been to ask Lawyer to apologise to Matilda, Saint John, who had intended to talk to Lawyer first, but to be honest had not quite found the necessary courage, was apoplectic. So along with his sister Ama, he had been to consult the fetish, only that morning in fact, to find out the reason for the madness that was taking over his family. And he planned to follow the advice given by the fetish, who had confirmed that their household was indeed under a spiritual attack and that he, as head of the household, must do his duty to avert further disaster.

Sitting in Lawyer's car now, on their way to court for the start of a complex trial that was scheduled to last a number of weeks, Saint John, who, to be fair, had assumed Lawyer would no longer require his services, felt treacherous for having sought out the help of the fetish in this way. But it was too late to do anything about it. Prayers had been said, attempts had been made to undo curses, and there was nothing more that he could do. Life was a question of survival of the fittest, and if Lawyer's first wife – after all, who else could it be – had not started this spiritual warfare, he and his sister would not have had to take the steps they had to unleash the spirit world. He sat calmly in the car, but quite frankly, things were now out of his control, he thought, with not a little fear.

383

Chapter Twenty-five

Audrey looked at the tray of breakfast things. Perfectly boiled eggs, fresh toast in a rack, butter on ice, coffee at the right temperature, gleaming cutlery, a bright-red hibiscus flower fresh from the garden. Had Awuni always cared for her this well? She looked around at what had been her home for all these years. Her input had been quite minimal to say the least in the running of this place, apart from the garden, that is. The servants took all their direction from Alan. Wasn't that what these people lacked, direction, a vision? She shook her head. And poor Alan, after all these years, he and his fellow civil servants had failed to instil any of that in them. Well, one couldn't instil vision, could one? It was there or it wasn't. Simple. She smiled to herself. She put her hand over the pocket of her dress and felt the paper rustle. Warmth flooded her. She lifted her face to feel the sun. She thought of rain clouds and gloom, mist and rain and rubbed her pocket again, beaming.

She put her hand into her pocket and held the paper between her forefinger and thumb. She had opened her mother's letter yesterday with trembling hands; it was plumper than usual, and she had been hopeful. She was normally rather half-hearted about her letters, prepared to skim the words, taking in only so much of the information about the apple crop this season, whether the rhododendrons would be as majestic this year as last, how yet again Mrs Bough had managed to avoid whitefly on her roses. She had held her breath and closed her eyes while she split the envelope carefully. Then the money had fallen on to her lap, and Audrey arranged the notes in order and counted. She gulped, held the letter with two quivering hands and read it carefully. 'Dear Audrey, I was thrilled to read your letter. Ever since you left for Africa, I have put aside what I can every month in the eventuality that you should need to come home. I am pleased that I did, and that you were not too proud to ask. I have not told your father, I don't think he would cope well with the disappointment should you change your mind. As soon as you contact me from London, I shall tell him . . .' The words blurred, and she had to wait a while before her eyes had dried enough for her to read the rest of the letter.

She was the first to get to the club that morning, and she lay on a recliner in the sun trying to remember the youthful man who had fallen on his knees and pleaded with her to marry him all those years ago, the man who had promised adventure and excitement. There was no point blaming him now. Joy bubbled in her, bringing the peace that comes from taking a step forward, even if it is in the wrong direction. The burden of lethargy under which she had lived for years had already begun to lift steadily. She remembered the child she had lost. It had taken her a while, but in time, she had learned to think about it, whether it would have provided the needed binding for them, whether her needs would have been changed by the sharp focus of another's needs. She smiled at the waiter when he came to ask if she wanted her usual gin and tonic so that he was rather taken aback. He was even more startled when she asked for a fresh fruit punch. It made her almost giggle to see his bemusement. But she could afford to be gracious and all that now; after all, it wasn't *entirely* their fault, was it?

Alan sat in the wicker chair next to her on the faded cushions that she and Alice had made all those years ago, and together they watched lizards sunning themselves on her rocks. She was listening to the sounds, trying to remember what hot days in England sounded like.

'So, what is it you want to talk about, then?'

'I've decided to go.'

He was pouring coffee into his cup, and she noticed how his hand wavered only slightly, the flow of dark, hot liquid unswerving. When he had finished, he added milk, stirred, sat back in his chair, then looked at her quizzically. 'Where? We sail in two months . . .'

'I'm going without you, Alan. Next month. I'm going home to recuperate, then when I am strong again, I am going to London. To live.' She smiled at him. Strangely, it pleased her that he too had aged. His face had toughened and looked lived in. He too had creases around his eyes, dry lips, thin hair and washed-out eyes.

'Why?'

She laughed. 'Why? That little word sums it all up really, Alan. You have no idea.'

'But we have been getting on fine. What's the point of us parting now? I don't restrict you, you can do whatever it is you want . . .'

'I don't want to stay here any longer. I have decided to take responsibility for myself.'

'Responsibility for what exactly?'

'For my contentment.'

'Ah.'

He was staring at her as if he might cry, and quite frankly, that was the last thing she felt like dealing with today. 'Alan, there is no need for recriminations. I am not right for this place. Never was, never will be . . .'

'Why now? Why not wait till we go off together? It might all be different after a break.'

'I won't fit in here if I stay fifty years. Anyway, it no longer matters. It doesn't matter that I don't like curry or the weather or the people. What matters is that I do something about it. I've tried and failed here. I'm going to try something different.'

'But us, you and me . . .'

'Us, Alan? You would be as miserable back home as I am here. We don't fit any more. Haven't for ages, surely you can see that?'

'I am so sorry if I've let you down that badly.'

Why 'if'? she thought, beginning to get irritated. Take a deep breath, she thought, don't lose your patience with him. 'As I said, there is no point in reproach.'

'But you can't just give up . . .'

'I can do as I wish, Alan! And I am not "giving up", as you put it. I am making a change, seeking some control, some direction.'

In silence they drank their coffee. Audrey ate two eggs. She spread sweating butter on toast and ate fast.

'Where has this come from all of a sudden?'

'It's been brewing for over a decade,' she said, raising her eyes in exasperation. She still thought with pain about the years, time passed, time lost. But what was the point in looking back? What mattered now was that the future looked bright; she must focus on that. 'Even so, you are right in that I decided quite recently that I need to go home. Teaching Matilda has been a huge influence on how I think about things, and do you know, I never imagined saying this, but I believe she has actually taught me something. Perhaps it's simply because I am receptive when I wasn't before. Watching her at the ball and seeing how thrilled she was to be there, how enamoured she was with the attention you lavished on her, made me realise how important it is to live life to the full and to take all one's opportunities.'

'I only danced with her because Robert was beastly to her, and you wouldn't dance with me.'

'But didn't she look splendid?'

'I suppose so.'

'And I can't imagine she has encountered much gentlemanly behaviour with Robert. Anyway, it got me thinking that if *I* was Matilda, I would probably have sulked at home knowing I wasn't Robert's first choice for the party, but instead there she was, grabbing her chance to have fun, and well, that made rather an impression on me, made me want to feel exhilarated again, about *anything*.'

'Right.'

'So, I wrote to mother and, well, asked her to send me the money . . .'

'You what?'

She shrugged. 'If I am going to leave you, I want to do it on my terms.'

'Gosh. And about Matilda, I really didn't mean any offence . . . I was only trying to help the poor girl . . . She is ever so lovely, and, well . . . she was like a fish out of water.'

Audrey laughed. 'Do you know, I thought you were simply being chivalrous, but I think maybe you *do* like her a little. Do you?'

'Audrey, don't be ridiculous!'

'It isn't ridiculous. You would be quite happy if you never went back to England. Actually, I can see you with a native woman. That's what you need . . . an English version of Matilda, or Matilda herself, come to think about it.' She was laughing again.

'Audrey, this is no time for jokes.' He leaned towards her, but she pulled back. 'You're serious, aren't you? There is nothing I can do?'

'I have never been more serious about anything in my life, Alan. I want to be happy again, truly happy, I mean.'

He rubbed his temples and the edges of eyes, as if to massage a pain away. His breathing quickened. 'I never meant this . . .'

'Oh, Alan, I don't blame you.'

'It hasn't been all bad, has it?'

'No. No, I didn't hate it all.' She clenched her teeth. 'Oh, what the hell! Yes, it has been bad. Almost every long, hot and often depressing day, I longed for home in a way that you will never understand. I have given you my best years, Alan.' She spoke with more aggression than she had intended and noticed that the furrow in his brow deepened. 'Well, I have, there is no need to look so perplexed. As long as you were here in your beloved Gold Coast, able to play golf and polo and eat your bloody curry, you didn't care.'

'Audrey, that is unfair!'

'Is it? Look at me, Alan! I have aged here. I am shrivelled and pickled, for goodness' sakes! Look at me properly, if you can bear to! My mother is going to get the shock of her life when I get home. And I am emotionally drained too, exhausted all the time, which for a woman my age isn't normal. I was never a weak child, you know. Even after my breakdown, which you have never had the guts to mention by name, you never wanted to accept how unhappy I was. I did not want to say this, but I *do* blame you, Alan. I blame you for bringing me here to this cesspool, and I blame you for not taking me away. But I have come to realise that I can leave on my own; after all, I came out here on my own. And by God, I'll go with my head held high. I am not the one who is too idiotic to realise that this place is a lost cause. How will you feel after they have successfully booted us out? When you look back in years to come and they are still urinating in their open sewers and still refusing to use toothbrushes? Will you still be *pleased* Alan, *ADC* Alan, *Colonial Administration Officer* Alan, whatever the hell that means? What has been the bloody point of your career? Do you even care?' Out of breath, she stood up and tried to calm her racing heartbeat. She hovered, waiting for him to say something but knew he wouldn't. He was looking at her confused with his mouth agape, blinking slowly, like someone recently awakened from deep sleep. 'I've got to go now, can't keep the girls waiting,' she said, walking to the door. She stopped and turned round. 'We can be friends if you like.' He was staring into space and did not seem to hear her. When she came back out he had gone.

Before they could start their next lesson, Audrey told Matilda that she was leaving sooner than expected, that she would not return, and they would only have a few more lessons.

'Oh? Why?'

'The question on everybody's lips,' she said smiling. It was a much less forced state for her face, effortless even, and she was getting used to this unbiased congeniality. She even found Alan much less grating now that his good nature was being sorely tested and his usually pleasant countenance strained. She had started to write again, to scribble really, about thoughts and hopes for her new life. And she used the word 'new' excessively. It would be rather unlike the life she had left; this would not be a return to anything familiar, this would be a fresh start. She might teach. Maybe. She might just try a course. Hadn't mother mentioned that Jean Hanlon had become a teacher? If Jean could do it, so could she. Not children, mind, she would teach adults. Was there a need for adult educators in England? she wondered.

'Audrey?'

'The reasons are too many to enumerate . . . to list. In the end, it is a question of survival.' Her eyes had moistened a little. 'Alan and I will separate. We don't love each other, and I really don't want to sentence myself any longer to this slow, horrid existence,' she said.

'But you don't need love for marriage. I know you Whites like to be in love, whatever that means. What is important is respect . . .' she shook her head and frowned.

'What is it?'

Matilda shrugged. 'As a matter of fact, I have also decided to abandon some of my duties . . .'

'What duties?'

Matilda recounted her story and said, 'But please don't be sorry for me; it is shameful when a woman has to be pitied.'

'Wise words,' said Audrey. 'And good for you, girl. I think he is frightful.'

'Please don't insult my husband.'

'You are unbelievable!'

'I don't go to him or to his house, but he is still my husband. I still respect him . . .'

'A man who shares his bed legitimately with another woman!'

'It is not possible to understand a culture from the outside. We waste our efforts doing so. For instance, why do you choose not to have children who will look after you when you are older? Why do you choose to leave a man who is kind and who lives in the same house with you? He does not even beat you? So many things he gives you, things a man in my culture cannot give, but it is still not enough for you.' She might have added, why don't you brush your hair? Why do you allow your cats to foul your floor and eat from your plates? And why do you allow yourself to be the object of your servants' ridicule? But that would have been far too rude. 'As you can see, I find you strange. But strange is not bad, or is it? As you said, live and let live.'

'Did I say that?' Audrey laughed. 'So what *are* you going to do?'

'Oh, I will try not to be a woman people feel sorry for,' said Matilda beaming.

They laughed together, and their eyes met. Audrey reached and squeezed Matilda's forearm. Momentarily, their laughter ceased. When it resumed, it sounded clearer and deeper, truer even. And looking at Matilda that morning, there can't have been any doubt that here was a woman who was happy with her life.

'It's funny, I never thought I'd say this, but I think there are things about this place that I might even miss. A few weeks in wet England and heaven forbid, I might yearn for sunshine. I expect the grass is always greener on the other side.'

'The grass is what?'

'Merely an expression, it means things always look better on the other side from where one is standing.'

'What a strange thing to say. You English people love grass too much.'

'Yes. And the neighbour's grass is always greener and healthier-looking than your own. Oh, let's forget these books and have some tea,' said Audrey, sighing as she shoved the books aside. 'Awuni. Awuni, could we have some tea, please?' she yelled loudly so Matilda winced a little.

'And what will you do in England without a husband?'

'Breathe freely for once.'

'I beg your pardon?'

Audrey laughed. 'I might learn to teach. It is deeply satisfying to hear what I have achieved with you.'

'Ah, a teacher. I would also like to be a teacher.'

'Well, actually, I am not sure your English is quite up to scratch yet . . . good enough yet for that.'

'No, small, small children. I can teach in my house.'

Audrey grimaced. 'I could not think of anything worse.'

Matilda was staring dreamily out into the garden. 'And who will tend your garden when you are gone?'

'It will continue much as it did before I came; to be perfectly frank, it looks barely any different from when I got here. Although I might give my rocks away. It's the cats I'm worried about.'

'Who needs rocks?' asked Matilda laughing. 'Books, clothes, shoes, but not rocks.'

'I do believe you've just given me a great idea; I might give everything away, go back with as little as possible. You are wonderful, Matilda! Really, you deserve someone better than Robert. I told Alan that he should be married to someone like you. Someone submissive and maternal,' she said chuckling.

'You think that a second wife is a strange thing, yet you want to give your husband away? You are mysterious,' said Matilda.

'Well, I don't need him any more.'

Matilda looked down at her books. Her face was warm, but not because of the sun.

'You like him, don't you?' said Audrey. 'He is a nice man, and you can have him with my blessing.'

'Audrey! Your husband is a good man and . . .'

'That he is . . . good, whatever that means. But evidently not good enough for me.' Or was it the place? It was impossible for her to distinguish between her dissatisfaction with Alan and their marriage, and her life in Accra; it was all far too blurred. The two were so tangled that she was sure it was best to leave both behind. That was why she was determined to leave without Alan; she did not want distance from this place to affect the decisions she had made.

Just then, his car pulled into the driveway.

'Oh my goodness, talk of the devil,' said Audrey. Since her announcement, it had been difficult to be in the house with him. When he came back from work that first evening, he did not mention their conversation. And he talked about her departure as though he had been the instigator, involved in the concept from germination. Good old Alan, she thought. He must not let anything affect his countenance, even if it is his wife leaving him.

Matilda had not seen Alan since the party and suddenly felt a little self-conscious. And how could this woman call such a nice man, her own husband, a devil? Sometimes she was just too much. She could hear him talking to his driver. He was running up the stairs. She thought how she had never seen Robert run. She kept her eyes on her book, studying it intensely and holding on to it with both hands.

'Hello, Audrey,' said Alan.

'Hello, Alan. What are you doing here?' Audrey asked, barely looking at her husband.

'Hello there, Matilda.'

She looked at him and smiled uncertainly. He was beaming at her. She resumed looking at her book, hoping that he would leave them to continue with their lesson. He sat down at the table and leaned forward. 'Don't mind me,' he said enthusiastically. 'I'm in no rush today, so I'll just listen.'

Matilda was too embarrassed to read in front of Alan and sat dumbly.

'Alan, really, don't be a bore. You must have something better to do,' said Audrey.

'I don't, in actual fact. Great, here comes some well-deserved tea, I am sure.'

'Hello, massah,' said Awuni, placing the tray in front of Audrey.

'Awuni, could you bring me a cup?' said Alan.

Matilda looked up, surprised, and saw that Alan was smiling at her still. She looked back into her book, puzzled.

The three of them sat awkwardly not saying much. That is to say, Alan chattered non-stop about nothing in particular, while Audrey periodically swiped at a fly that was buzzing about and fanned herself, and Matilda drank her tea clumsily until Audrey glared at her reminding her silently of the many how-to-drink-tea-correctly conversations they had had.

Alan helped himself to some tea from the fresh pot Awuni brought, then he settled back in his chair.

Audrey lit up a cigarette and sat staring vacantly at the garden, visibly unaware of the awkward silence. Matilda breathed in the smoke, wishing she too had something to distract her and keep her hands steady.

'Well, I'll go then,' said Alan, draining his cup. 'I can tell when I am not wanted.'

'I've had enough today,' said Audrey, puffing dramatically. 'I think I might just go and take a nap. Would you take Matilda home, Alan?'

'Oh, please, no,' said Matilda, alarmed. Calm down, she thought. 'I'm all right,' she said, smiling unevenly. 'Just let the driver take me alone.' She looked intently at Audrey, hoping that she would understand something, though what, Matilda herself did not know. But Audrey finished her cigarette, stood and, without so much as a glance behind her, walked into the dark cool of the house, calling goodbye cheerily over her shoulder.

In the car, Alan chatted non-stop while Matilda nodded politely. How were the lessons going? Her English was indeed improving all the time. She deserved the prize for Audrey's best student of the year. And he laughed and reached to place his hand over hers.

Matilda held her breath in shock and stared at his hand on hers. She left her hand where it was for a few moments, looking at the many hairs growing profusely out of his fingers and his wrist. She watched blood travel seamlessly along the blue veins that protruded on his hand and noticed to her surprise the contrast of their colour. His whiteness made her hand look a much darker brown, yet in the disparity was a strange lack of disharmony. She removed her hand and wondered whether the driver had seen.

'No doubt Audrey has told you what a monster I am and that she is leaving me. I know that's what they all think at the club.'

'She talks well about you,' said Matilda, nodding to emphasise her words.

'You have no idea how lovely it is to see you again, a friendly face,' he said. 'I feel so all alone these days. Robert is still being awkward, and now Audrey is leaving me, and . . . and my friends . . . My life seems to be falling apart. I wonder where I went wrong . . .'

He was crying. Not like Robert had, with one small tear per eye. Many, many tears were streaming down Alan's cheeks shamelessly. He sniffed and made no attempt to wipe his face. What was it that made all these strong men cry in front of her? Had they not been taught that it was a great sign of weakness? Why all of a sudden did everyone think that hers were the strongest shoulders around? Her shoulders, which also wanted to shudder and shake when she thought of how her husband had betrayed her, when she admitted that she missed her time with him? When she realised afresh how little he must respect her because he had not even bothered to contact her, had no intention of acknowledging his wrongdoing, had not even noticed her absence. His silence was, in fact, the most humiliating thing she had ever experienced. She put her hand on Alan's and said as much to comfort herself, 'It will be all right. Everything will be all right. You wait and see, God always takes care of things.'

When Matilda arrived for a lesson one morning, she was surprised to see a number of ladies on Audrey's veranda. She wondered whether she had got the day wrong and hovered at the bottom of the stairs for a while.

Audrey hollered, 'Come on up. No lesson today.' She was waiting at the top of the stairs with two glasses in her hand.

'Oh?'

'I decided to have a party instead, a going-away-giving-away party. Your idea, really, so I thought it only fair that you should be here.' She handed Matilda a glass of Buck's Fizz and led her into the centre of the veranda. 'Everyone! Ladies! I want to the introduce the lady who inspired me to leave my husband.'

Matilda drew breath sharply and nearly dropped her glass.

'This is Matilda . . . What's your surname again? I don't think I've ever known, actually.'

'Bannerman.'

'Robert's name? I suppose I should have known, silly me.'

What other name would she have as the wife of Robert? Matilda wondered.

'Don't look so affronted,' whispered Audrey. 'I wasn't sure if as his, you know, second wife, you were officially Mrs Bannerman too.'

'You are leaving before you have learned everything we can teach you,' said Matilda.

'Well, ladies, this is Matilda Bannerman, the woman who inspired me to strike out and become more independent. We might think we have a hard time with our husbands, but *she* had to share hers with a ghastly woman.'

Matilda was thoroughly confused to be given the blame for breaking up Audrey's marriage like this.

'She left her husband because he mistreated her.'

Matilda caught her breath and tightened the grip on her glass. She was appalled and uncomfortable. It was clear that Audrey had been drinking, what else would she reveal? But then all the ladies started to clap and cheer, so she nodded a little and forced her dismayed face into a sort of smile.

'Good for you,' said Alice, and there was a chorus of similar acclamation from the others.

'Let's drink to Matilda,' said Audrey, raising her glass. 'To Matilda. I hope things work out as you wish.'

Matilda drained her glass and smiled. These ladies were strange indeed. Applauding a woman who has abandoned her duties? The women at home would faint if they could see her now cavorting with these unrestrained women who were drinking alcohol quite freely in the morning, like drunkards, it had to be said.

'Right, everyone is here now, so I'll make my little speech,' said Audrey, 'Then,' she said widening her eyes naughtily, 'I want you all to go in there and pick and choose whatever you want from my belongings.'

There was a collective gasp.

'You aren't giving *everything* away, are you?' asked Flo.

'I want to feel light and free as a bird,' said Audrey, holding her glass up high to signal to Awuni, who was hovering in the background, that she needed a refill.

'Are you sure this is a good idea?' asked Valerie.

'I have told her I think she is quite mad,' said Alice, shaking her head. 'Polly wrote in her letter how poor everyone seems; how everything is so frightfully expensive. But you know our Audrey, there is no point arguing with her once she has made up her mind.'

Audrey was bristling with ecstasy. 'You have been great friends, wonderful company. I know that I am not always the easiest person to be around, that I have at times needed more than my fair share of jollying along.' Her eyes were welling up. 'But I am overjoyed to be going home, and I want you all to be happy for me.' She took a long sip of her champagne. 'Oh, and look after Alan when I've gone. Make him feel it's quite fine to be happy again. You know what he's like; he might think he has to mourn for a while,' she said, pulling a funny face. 'Come on, Matilda,' she said, linking arms with her and pulling her into the living room where strewn out on the dining table, the sofas, the chairs, every surface possible really, were Audrey's belongings.

Matilda was dazzled by the exclamations of delight from the women, who ran and started picking up things with unabashed covetousness.

'None of my clothes or shoes will fit you, Matilda,' said Audrey. 'But you might like a book or two?'

'Oh, thank you,' said Matilda. She struggled to visualise herself in any of Audrey's loose floral dresses, anyway. She was watching the

396

women exclaim about how they had always liked this or that item on Audrey, and quite frankly, she was surprised. She had never imagined that white women might need second-hand clothes, but looking at them helping themselves to Audrey's things, none of which were especially new, it had to be said, she realised afresh that things are indeed not always as one has been led to believe they are.

She saw a painting propped up against one of the dining chairs and she picked it up. 'I like this.'

'Well, have it,' said Audrey. 'It's a bit tatty now, but I imagine you don't have pictures like that.' She stared at the picture. 'My mother gave me that when I was leaving.' It was a painting of a Victorian parlour scene, which had hung in the bedroom for years. Now it had yellow humid spots on it, and the frame had corroded. Looking at it now, the plump white family with golden hair, the immaculate retriever at their feet, the furious fire, the ornate ornaments on every surface, the gloomy light, a scene that she would have despised before she came here, she ached for home afresh, realising painfully that she might not recognise home when she got there. 'Excuse me,' she said. 'I'll go and make sure lunch is ready.'

Later, Cook, the small boy and Awuni served tiny cucumber sandwiches and fish goujons with tartar sauce and lots of champagne. Someone put on a record, and the ladies were soon swaying around the room in twos and threes, swinging to the scratchy chords. Audrey had a glass in one hand and started to sing along with Ella: 'A tisket a tasket, a red and yellow basket,' while she shook her shoulders and clicked her free fingers. She shimmied her hips suggestively all around the room, radiating. Awuni had never seen his madam dance quite like this, and he looked a little disconcerted, hopping out of her way, which was rather difficult while balancing a tray of glasses in one hand and a platter of food in the other. She reached where Matilda was standing and pulled her arm. 'Come and dance with me.'

Matilda went willingly. Having had had two glasses of champagne, she felt less anxious, and anyway, now Audrey had finished her various speeches, there was little chance of further embarrassment. Her dress did not lend itself to dancing like this, and it was difficult to keep up with the swift, slightly jerky movements that Audrey was making; her own body wanted to move more slowly and much more in time with the music, but she was enjoying the abandonment that came with the absence of men and the bubbles in the champagne. All around, happy, smiling women, here to say goodbye to Audrey, women who were clearly first-class friends, yet another thing that made her decision to go seem a little odd.

Cook appeared carrying a large pink jelly when the dancing was in full flow. Audrey noticed him straightaway and called out, 'Jelly! Girls, it's jelly time. Perfect, Cook. Pop it down on the table.'

Alice looked quizzically at her friend.

'Thought I needed to exorcise the jelly ghost. Made it all by myself, with lots and lots of gin, and it looks divine, if I might say so myself. Cook was under strict instructions not to open the fridge this time.'

'What are you talking about?' asked Flo.

'Long story,' said Audrey. 'Let's just say, this is my signature dish, but it's taken me several years to perfect.'

'Well, it's outstanding,' said Valerie, scooping it into her mouth while she jived around the armchairs nodding her head in time to Glenn Miller's trombone.

Matilda thought it was a little bitter from too much alcohol, but she was beginning to think that was what mattered most to these women.

When the first guest tried to leave, music was still blaring loudly in the background. Audrey went to the veranda and called out for her gardener. He appeared almost immediately from a shady spot under the stairs, wiping his face and blinking rapidly.

'We are ready, madam.'

'Super! Come on then, Alice,' she said, leading her friend down the stairs. 'I have something for you.'

The others followed, curious to see what Audrey was up to now.

'Oh my God!' said Audrey.

In front of what had once been the rock garden was a long row of dug-up plants, soil and roots wrapped coarsely in paper. The gardener had misunderstood her request and dug up the entire rock garden, which was now a mere heap of soil and rocks.

'What on earth is Alan going to make of this?' asked Alice staggered at the mess.

'Ah well. Not quite what I expected, but he'll hardly notice. I thought you could all plant something in memory of me.' She picked up a large bundle of mother-in-law's tongue. 'Here, Val, this was always one of my favourites; it is next to impossible to kill,' she said, stroking the long, leathery leaves, which were marbled light and dark green with yellow edges. She handed out bunches of cat's tails, with their long, red, furry flowers, scarlet-veined, heart-shaped caladium, bright-yellow canna lily, waxy pink torch ginger, and for Alice, a tiny sapling African tulip tree. 'You've always admired mine, so I asked Yusuf to grow this for you when I knew I was leaving. Think of me when it blooms, will you?'

Matilda stood with her bundle of flowering shrub. Audrey had said it was called peacock flower and that it was a small version of the flamboyants growing in the middle of the garden, and she was filled with warm affection for this woman who, in so many ways, reminded her of a lost child, misguided but with her heart in the correct place. She could worry later, when she got home, where she could possibly plant this and what she would say when they asked her why she was suddenly stooping to take upon herself the role of chief gardener. Thankfully, she had had the strength of mind to decline one of the cats. That would have been one step too far.

Cook was the only survivor of the original line-up. Next to him stood Awuni, the second longest-serving member of staff. Then Richard, the latest small boy, and the gardener. Happiness spilled through her, making her stand tall, her chest out, her smile open, her eyes sunny. Alan stood and smiled with her.

'Madam, how my heart is full of aches with pain and grief to say goodbye to you, only God knows the pain that I am suffering right, right now. How wonderful has been my privilege to serve and honour you . . .'

'Oh, Cook, you'll still have Alan for a while yet,' said Audrey giggling.

'Please may God take you safely on each step of your homeward-bound journey,' he said, clasping both her hands in his. Audrey resisted the impulse to pull free. His hands felt smooth and rubber-like, not as soft as she had imagined.

'Awuni, thank you for all your hard work over the years.'

'Madam, madam,' he said and allowed a tear to fall, 'I want to give you a reminder,' he said as he took a crumpled photograph from his pocket. It was a picture of him with one of his wives and three small children in their best clothes.

'Awuni, you did not have to. This must have cost you a lot of money, and how could I possibly forget you? Really, I don't need a photograph to help me.'

'Please take it,' he said, wiping the tears on his face. 'You will do me an honour.'

She held it with both hands so she could not touch him, shake his hand or anything worse.

'Well, then,' said Alan as the car drove off. Audrey turned to look out of the rear window and waved at the smiley faces of the servants' miscellaneous children, wives and girlfriends, who had emerged from the boys' quarters to shout goodbye.

It had been a tiring few days, packing and saying goodbye, and she was relieved to be off. Her case lay lightly in the boot; when Awuni lifted it into the car, she had chuckled and said to Alan, 'Look, my life in a box.'

'Your life is not over, Audrey,' he had said.

'I know. It is about to start.'

She allowed the photograph of Awuni's family to fall to the floor when Alan was looking the other way and clasped her free hands. She breathed deeply, gazing serenely out of the window. Goodbye, she thought at whatever they passed, the heat, the dry ground, the smells; she waved eagerly at a group of children by the roadside. On her face, she felt the pull of warm air rushing through the open windows and breathed in deeply, filling her lungs with these smells, good and bad, one last time.

'I hope you didn't hate it all.'

'No, Alan, not all. In fact, I was thinking last night about what I have achieved out here, what I've learned, and I made a list. And it was rather impressive: I can make jelly, give cocktail parties, chat to boring people as well as interesting people, and to important people. I can swim much better than I could when I came out, and I have learned to garden. Oh, Alan, it has not *all* been dreadful. But a new life is waiting for me, you see. I can't wait for you to make me happy.' She took his arm. 'And it's not as though you haven't tried. You tried frightfully hard, didn't you? But the plain truth is that you are not responsible for my happiness, are you? Each of us is responsible for our own happiness. And I don't hate you at all. I don't want you to think that I do. We're simply one of life's calamities. We made a mistake, that's all. What would be the point of me staying out here when I now know that I can go? Look on the bright side, I won't be able to blame you from now on if I'm miserable! There, that's better. I'd prefer to remember you smiling.'

Chapter Twenty-six

Matilda struggled with mornings that had for so long now been well filled. She had come to rely on the quiet journey to Audrey's house, the chance to float with her thoughts, unaccountable to no one for that short stretch. Then there was the discourse with Audrey, the sense of moving onwards and upwards with her ever-increasing English vocabulary, words used and pronounced in a way that impressed even Uncle Saint John.

She thought often of Audrey. Initially, she wondered how much greener exactly she needed the grass to be. She could not understand what needs Audrey had that her own husband was incapable of tending, a woman who seemed to have lavished more care on her plants, her lawn, her stones than on Alan, a state of affairs that Matilda found greatly disordered. The way she saw it, Audrey was simply being over-demanding. Take her own situation for instance, Robert *had* committed a rectifiable error that he had simply chosen not to rectify. And look how his behaviour confirmed his lack of respect; months had passed without word or sign from him. Just thinking about him still brought heavy pain. The least he could have done was to send his sister Baby to mend some bridges. Indeed, she should have become involved of her own volition, taken steps to save her brother's marriage. Well, it just went to show how dispensable they all thought she was. Now her feet were even more firmly planted in obstinacy, as her mother called it, especially when she considered the possible repercussions of his behaviour. How long before Julie's children also began to deny her the respect she was owed, then her own children, then what? God forbid that she should sit back and just let that happen. When this pain passes, she told herself daily, at least my dignity will still be intact.

Audrey must have arrived safely in England by now. Was it as she had remembered, hoped it would be? Was she missing Alan? And how was he without his wife? Was he not also missing her? She missed the peaceful chats on the quiet veranda, the tea breaks and the biscuits. No one had tea and biscuits at home. And English things were not sold in the markets where she shopped. She decided to go to the Kingsway store, which was opposite the big Methodist cathedral on the way into Accra proper. She had never had reason to go in there, and she imagined it would be expensive compared to the market. But her two sources of tea and biscuits were now unavailable, and the habit was something she did not really want to give up. In addition, it was fair to say that she was curious about what else the Europeans bought. She found it strange that apart from biscuits, Audrey had only fed her once, and then it had been snack food: bread and cucumber, of all strange things. There was simply no way that she would have allowed Audrey to come and go from her house so many times without something more substantial than biscuits.

She asked Patience to come with her to the Kingsway store, and she responded, 'Aha, now your English lady friend has gone, you are looking for your old friends, eh?'

'Don't be like that,' said Matilda.

'What are we going to do there? I don't have any money.'

Matilda shrugged. 'Let's just go and see.'

The shop was small and immaculate. Quiet too, other than the gentle drone of a cooler in the background. The polished linoleum floor gleamed, and there was a smell of disinfectant, which Matilda found rather off-putting around food. The shelves were orderly and filled with rows and rows of tinned foods. They wandered down the aisles nodding politely to two cleaners who were mopping the floors, which most definitely did not look as if they needed cleaning. Matilda

403

peeked into their buckets and was amazed to see that the water was indeed brown.

'How can they do a full day's shopping using only pictures of food and words wrapped around tins and boxes?' asked Patience.

'And with nothing to smell, nothing to feel or taste,' said Matilda. It would quite simply never have occurred to her to buy fresh fish without prodding it, smoked fish without tasting it, tomatoes without pinching them to see if they were firm and fresh, pineapples without sampling the sweet juiciness of the fruit that had been cut to entice customers, or rice without picking up a handful and allowing it to fall through her fingers so she could see whether the proportion of weevils to grain was acceptable. She mouthed the words softly as she walked, aware that her friend was staring at her, impressed with her command of the English language. Together they marvelled at the names, curious as to how things tasted and what they were all for. Some she had seen in Julie's cupboards in the days when she had been nosy enough to look: Bisto gravy powder, Heinz baked beans, potted meat, Hartley's strawberry jam, Bournvita, Gentleman's Relish, Colman's mustard powder, Quaker oats, Camp coffee. She picked a packet of McVities' digestive biscuits and a box of Typhoo tea, which was what Julie used, and clutched them to her chest. She walked round the corner in a trance-like state, reading out aloud, 'Cad berries choco . . .' and walked more or less straight into Julie's arms.

'Watch where you are going . . . Ah, Matilda, what a surprise.'

The women stared at each other in awkward silence. For Matilda, the paramount advantage of her estrangement was that she did not have to interact with Julie, and now here was the annoying first wife to spoil her tea and biscuit shopping!

'Well, well! I have not seen you for a long time, but now I see how you are keeping busy. First, you decide to abandon your domestic duties and your children by studying like a young girl, and now you are shopping like a madam . . .'

Patience chewed her mouth loudly and said, 'Please don't start your insulting nonsense again.' She walked past Julie and beckoned Matilda to follow.

'I don't think I was talking to you. Matilda, I hope you are as well as I am. I never thought I would be able to say this, but thank you –

404

for setting my husband free; I can enjoy my marriage again now there is so much more room . . .'

'I have not set my husband free.'

'That is not what he tells me. He tells me that he has annulled his so-called marriage to you. Anyway,' she said, flicking her hand rudely, 'we are off to England in a few months to take the big boys to boarding school. Well, cheerio.'

'What my husband and I do is none of your business. And you can tell Robert from me that I will not just sit and watch him forgo his duties.'

'Are you threatening us? Don't try and rise above your station, madam!'

Matilda saw Patience readying to strike. She saw each movement slowly enough to intervene, and she watched completely paralysed as her friend shoved Julie with both hands into a shelf, dislodging some tins and boxes of foodstuffs, which tumbled on top of her. Matilda suppressed a giggle as a horrified Julie stood up and tried to pat her hair into shape, pull her dress back down and generally de-tousle herself. Then, with incredible vehemence, she swung at Patience with her handbag, catching her on the arm.

Patience immediately began to scream at the top of her voice for help. Several people came running over and Patience said, 'This mad woman is attacking us for no reason at all. Please help us!'

Julie stood back with her legs apart for balance and her handbag at the ready to strike again. In her best English, she said, 'Take no notice of her. Do I look mad?'

'Come with me, madam,' said the store manager in clipped English, taking Julie by the arm.

'Do you know who I am? Let go of me this very instant! My husband is an important lawyer.'

The man shook his head as if he was used to this kind of behaviour and marched Julie to the door of the shop.

The small crowd of mostly white shoppers that had gathered around them to see the reason for this palaver in their peaceful supermarket started to disperse.

That was when Matilda saw that one of the curious was Alan. He

405

pushed through and stood beside her. 'It is good to see you, but what on earth is going on?' he said, touching her arm.

She moved herself a little to re-establish the gap between them, but he managed to keep his hand on her. Her heart beat loudly. 'Hello, Alan,' she said, swallowing hard. 'How are you? How is Audrey? Have you heard from her?' He was staring at her in that odd way that made her stomach flutter. She grinned briefly when he seemed determined not to answer. 'This is my friend. We are late, we must go.' Matilda tried to get Patience's attention, but she was simply standing there being very unhelpful, grinning at them like an idiot.

'Please don't rush off,' he said, gripping Matilda's arm. 'Was that Julie being marched out like a criminal?'

Matilda laughed. 'Yes. I can never forget the look written on her face.'

'Well, don't rush off. Come, let me buy you ladies a drink.'

'Oh, no, thank you,' said Matilda.

'Yes,' said Patience, nodding vigorously.

'Come on, Matilda, your friend would like a drink,' he said, guiding her out of the shop into the blazing sunshine.

Matilda was flustered and intensely irritated with Patience. She had come to shop, and now, completely empty-handed, they were climbing into Alan's car.

'Take us to the Embassy Hotel,' he said to the driver. He placed his hand on hers again. 'The least you can do is let me buy you something to drink,' he said, looking at her kindly.

She pulled her hand away. It could not be healthy for her heart to beat so fast. She tried to think of something to say but couldn't. She turned to Patience, who was sitting next to her, and said in Ga, 'I want to go home.'

'And miss my opportunity to meet some good men? I have never been to the Embassy Hotel.'

'I will punish you for this.'

'Calm down. I can see that he likes you very, very much.'

'Please watch what you say, I am married and walls have ears!'

'Don't you remember what the first wife said just now? Your husband has forgotten about you.'

'What's all this about?' asked Alan.

406

'Oh, nothing,' said Matilda. 'How is Audrey?'

'Fine, I think. She sent me a telegram to say she had arrived at her parents' house and that she was happy.'

'And you are also going back soon?'

'No. There is no point now.'

She frowned at him. 'But it is your country. How can you leave it for ever?'

'I think there is much more here for me than over there. Don't look so worried. I prefer it when you laugh, you are beautiful when—'

'Please, you must not flatter another person's wife. You know that I am a wife and I am a mother.' She leaned forward to tap the driver on his shoulder. 'Stop the car. I am getting out.'

'Oh, please don't.'

'Matilda, what is wrong with you?' asked Patience in Ga.

When the car stopped, Patience climbed out muttering under her breath. Matilda turned to Alan and said, 'And in our culture, it is rude to stare into another person's eyes the way that you do.' She stepped on to the warm road and started walking briskly, trying desperately to calm her thoughts. How peacefully her day had started, she thought. It goes to show how one moment can change the course of an entire life even. Already, that woman's words were wreaking havoc in her head. Her husband did not want her back? Her stomach somersaulted and knotted painfully with the realisation that she had succeeded in dismantling her entire marriage. Now he was taking Julie's sons to school in England. She gripped her middle and slowed her steps, panting to keep the feeling of sickness at bay. Had she ruined her children's prospects? 'That wicked woman is robbing my children of their rightful place,' she said angrily.

'What else do you expect from a witch?'

'But why is he letting her?'

'Forget him. You have your children. You don't need anything else. Anyway, I am sure she is lying. A man like Robert Bannerman will not leave his children to run around uneducated. I am sure that he has plans for your children too.'

'I never did anything to warrant such treatment. He is not being fair.'

'Matilda, life is not fair. Anyway, William is old enough to be a

407

good spy. Ask him to find out whether it is true that her children are going to England if you are so bothered. Tell him to ask his father when he will go.'

'Yes. That's a good idea. Cunning Patience. What would I do without you?'

'I don't know. The question is what am I doing with a friend who stops me from going to the Embassy Hotel where I might meet a suitable man. A friend who like me is also husbandless but does not want to accept it.'

Two days later, Alan's driver delivered a letter to her. She ignored the curious stares of her family, who were no doubt wondering who was sending letters to her now. She went into her room to read it in peace, fearing that her excitement was already too evident.

> I am sorry if I behaved badly the other day, but I was rather pleased to see you again. Audrey left a pile of books here that she thought you might like; I simply forgot to mention when I saw you the other day. I thought perhaps you could come and get them? I might not be able to buy you a drink, but perhaps I could pour you one? I wonder, would you be able to come on Monday afternoon? A.

She smiled to herself; a joy she had not felt in a long while spread inside her. Robert had never written to her. They had never indulged in the letter writing of young lovers who see each other frequently, notes written lovingly, trustingly. But Patience was right; what did Robert have to do with this now? she asked as she tried to remove his image from her mind. He had made his intentions, his loyalties, rather obvious. She pondered what to do. Her head seemed to be clear as to the right course of action. Her husband might not think that he had a wife called Matilda any longer, but she knew she had a husband called Robert. She couldn't go and visit a man who looked at her the way Alan did. Especially since that look made her heart beat fast and her throat dry out. No, she would not go. She would remember who she was and what was right; she could not go. The fact that she *wanted* to see him was reason enough not to go.

But then other thoughts fluttered up from her heart and wedged themselves in her mind, plaguing her with alternatives. After all, how difficult would such a visit be? Hadn't he said there were books? And to think she had thought Audrey had forgotten her promise to leave them behind for her. She would have to go and get the books. Wouldn't it be rude not to go and pick them up?

Several times a day, she reached alternate decisions. Each time her mind was firm, her decision final, until she changed her mind again. And when she went to bed at night, she fell into a troubled sleep, exhausted by the process; in the end, it seemed easier to just go and get the books. And since she had alerted herself to the possible foolishness of the visit, she was sure she would be able to see danger coming in whatever form it might take and step right out of its way.

Awuni was setting out the tea things when Matilda arrived. She followed Alan up the steps on to the veranda, and there on the table before her lay the books, four of them. She smiled, relieved.

'Thank you, Awuni. Tea, Matilda? Or shall I get us something cooler?'

He was looking at her, but she refused to look at him until he turned away. Then she saw that he was more tranquil than she had seen him before. He had combed his wet hair off his face to reveal the creases on his forehead that matched those around his eyes. Perhaps marks of wisdom learned, of mistakes made. When she didn't respond, he walked into the house and came out with two gin and tonics.

'Thank you. Your wife . . . Audrey gave me this drink.'

'That reminds me, I found her letter yesterday. There was a message for you. Hang on a second, I'll get it,' he said, dashing off.

Matilda took long sips and started to look at the books. She held each, flicking the pages close to her face so her nostrils filled with wordy fumes. Now she could start her own library. After all, most good things start off small, she thought, taking another sip of her drink. It cooled her chest on its way to her stomach, and there, the alcohol smoothed the remaining tension away.

Alan returned with the letter. He was grinning as if it contained news he had anticipated eagerly. 'Listen to this. "You must tell

409

Matilda when you next see her that it is thanks to her show of boldness that I am home and happy, even though it hasn't stopped
raining since I arrived, and the trees are leafless and the ground still
barren from the winter. But the air is remarkably clean and refreshing after the constant muggy heat, and the silence almost deafening.
Oh, Alan, it's wonderful . . ." So, as you can see, she is where she
wants to be.' He chuckled. 'It sounds wet and horrible to me, but
there we go.'

Matilda smiled, not knowing what to say. Why had Audrey
thought she might see Alan again? She would probably be quite
unsurprised to see them sitting here in her house in the middle of the
day when they had no earthly reason to be alone together. That
woman was astounding in too many respects. 'I think of her often,'
she said eventually.

'I know it might seem odd for me to say this, what with Robert
and all that, but I think about *you* a lot,' said Alan.

She was startled and looked away. She was shocked that she
wanted to say, 'Me too.' Was it because she was feeling light-headed?
Was it the drink?

'I heard that Robert and you are no longer together.'

'Who told you such things?' she said, startled.

'Audrey did, before she left.'

She looked at his face. Was it possible to trust someone just
because they looked honest? Seemed kind and true? And interested
in you? Why did she have an attraction to this man, a white man, she
reminded herself, with whom she had nothing in common? Was it not
simply the flattery that he doled out so freely to her only occasionally
unwelcoming ears that had saturated her heart? And her soul? What
else could have given birth to this desire she now had to reach out
and touch his hand, that warm and strong hand that he had offered
already in friendship and more?

'You look so serious; I really am only a harmless Englishman,' he
said, pulling a funny face.

She laughed easily.

He touched her arm and stroked it.

She looked at his hand and placed her free hand on his. It
wouldn't hurt to leave it there for a moment. She pulled away when

410

she heard Awuni running up the stairs. The man must suspect something, she thought, or else he had that sinister sense that some people have that allows them to appear when danger is imminent.

'Thank you, Awuni,' said Alan.

She smiled thinly, relieved that they had not been discovered. Reeling, she gathered the books and stood up. 'I must go, please let your driver take me.' She hurried down the stairs, thankful that he did not try to stop her.

Matilda gasped when she received his next letter, expressing sentiments that he really had no right articulating in this way. 'I can't stop my thoughts from wandering to you frequently.' Had the driver read it? 'You have reawakened feelings that I thought I might never again experience.' Wouldn't her reputation be shredded? 'Can we meet again soon?' The man was mad writing to her like this. 'Perhaps on Thursday afternoon?' She would have to tell him in no uncertain terms that she could not entertain this sort of attention, and with his wife barely gone. 'For a spot of lunch?' What is a 'spot of lunch'? she thought curiously. Anyway, whatever it is, no, I cannot go and have a 'spot of lunch' with him. 'Please.' No. Not on Thursday and not ever. And she could not allow him to write any more letters with similar sentiments flowing freely. She would inform him that this behaviour had to stop. They were not beneficial, these words, which when she was alone at night made her smile, and which conjured up thoughts she imagined she had put to sleep. She couldn't allow him into her heart, into that gap that it was Robert's duty to fill in spite of the illogical yearning to see him again, to meet and talk, and even to touch. But he made her laugh whenever she saw him, and thinking of him brought a warm glow to her heart. How she had tried, unsuccessfully she realised now, to banish the memories of their dance at the Governor's party, the way he had held her and whispered in her ear, and how she had felt frivolous in his arms. What exactly was the point of allowing such dangerous thoughts to sprout and surge through her?

She was perplexed by the feelings, stranger than she had ever experienced. Oh, she had become accustomed to Robert's needs but had never experienced this shivering she felt when Alan touched her.

Her thoughts came to a shuddering stop. My goodness gracious me! What would Robert do if he realised that she had allowed another man to touch her hand? In public too! It had always pleased her that he derived pleasure from her; it had made her feel strangely power- ful. When he abandoned her, as in the beginning she had feared he would, he took with him the self-assurance in her womanliness that she had acquired over the years. And here was Alan, his friend, trying to reinstate that confidence. She was fatigued by her thoughts. No, she would have to go and see him and tell him to his face that they could not be friends. She would go on Thursday.

Her stomach hurt, and her thoughts remained haphazard while she waited for the day to come. It took her a while to choose what to wear. She changed her earrings a few times, put on lipstick, then rubbed it off several times till she finally decided that she would go without any at all. After all, she did not want to give him the wrong idea. Somehow, she already had, she knew, but that would be put right today. She would adjust his thoughts. He could not write such words to her, put his hand on hers; she was not that sort of woman, she thought fiercely.

Alan came running down the stairs grinning boyishly. She felt uneasily excited to see him. She had never noticed before how green his eyes were, how they twinkled. She breathed in deeply and placed on her lips what she thought was a modestly friendly expression. She would not give him any doubts as to the reason for her visit.

He led her up the stairs to the veranda. When they reached the top of the stairs, Matilda saw Awuni getting into Alan's car with the small boy, then the car drove off. She opened her mouth to say some- thing and waved her hand in the direction of the car as if she was trying to stop it.

'I've sent them on some errands,' Alan said, as the car disappeared down the drive. 'I am so glad that you came today. I hoped you would.'

'Alan, I have come only to tell you that we cannot meet like this. If Robert finds out that I am visiting you, I don't know what he will do. Your letter . . . You are mistaken . . . I want to correct your mis- understandings. I am not available to you. I am not that kind of woman.' Matilda swallowed in vain; her mouth hurt with dryness.

'Robert has forsaken you.'

'It seems that way, but until he informs me as such, I am still his wife.' Her stomach churned. It was difficult to maintain faith in her marriage when at every opportunity someone decided to remind her that she was husbandless.

'Yes, but you are entitled to be true to your emotions.' He took hold of her hand.

Tenderly, she tried to retrieve it. 'I am only here to put the record straight.'

'Come inside, I want to show you something,' Alan said, pulling Matilda out of her seat.

She was taken aback. Why would this man not just leave her alone? Was there something in her English that he did not understand? It was disconcerting the way he stared at her, making her self-conscious yet secure at the same time. It was desire in his eyes, and she was fearful of the yearning he had awakened in her. Here was undisguised danger, the kind of temptation warned about from the pulpit, and here was an opportunity to get out of its way, but she stood in the stillness of the living room. Pleased to be alone with him in his house. Enjoying the tranquillity that was overwhelming, wondering whether he could see how her heart was thudding, how her blood had thinned, dizzying her. He pulled her closer and kissed her. She took a sharp breath and opened her eyes wide in alarm. Her lips let out a small moan. Her knees no longer felt strong enough. She had really gone mad now; her mother would be pleased to see that she was right after all. But she did not walk away, even though he was using no force and she had full use of her faculties. Instead, she remained fixed to the floor waiting for this sin to come and seize her, as if paralysed like in those half-asleep half-awake dreams when her legs and arms became heavy and useless in the face of certain danger. And how she wanted him to hold her, to draw her to him and close the circle with his arms.

He gathered her to him, and she closed her eyes to feel the softness of his sweet-smelling skin on hers. She held her erratic breath in an attempt to steady it. And her heart sang. She tightened her hold on him, unsure what had made her this willing.

Throughout, he was tender. She warmed up where he touched her like the earth under the sun's first rays. And in the end, he whispered her name and she held on to him. Then she cried, and though he was distraught, she could not tell him that he had done nothing wrong, that he had only released her from something that had bound her too tight for too long.

Later that afternoon, the sun shone behind the curtains, sneaking through minute cracks on to the bed on which they lay asleep. When she woke, she held her breath, waiting for guilt to crush her. She turned to look at him. She saw he was grinning at her, his sunny complexion unperturbed by this bewildering situation.

Slowly, the horror of what she had done welled up in her. She rolled over and stood up.

'Don't go.'

'I must.' She started to sob. 'This is a mistake. I can't . . .'

'How can you say that?'

She stumbled up, galvanised by his words and gathered her clothes. She rushed into the bathroom to change. She washed her face with cold water, wiped it and smoothed her hair, all of which would have been much simpler with the aid of the mirror. But she did not want to look at herself just yet. You are an adulteress, she said to herself over and over again.

When she was dressed, she entered the bedroom slowly, and without looking at him, said, 'I cannot see you again.' She made her way to the door, but he got there first and put his hand on hers. She looked down at her feet, not wanting to catch sight of his naked body. 'Please, Alan, I have already committed a sin here. I need to go. I don't know why I did this.'

'I thought you wanted . . .'

'No . . . Yes,' she looked at him. 'Yes.'

He exhaled loudly. A moment passed, then he kissed her hand gently. 'Let me take you home.'

It was dusk; the cars they passed had their headlights on. Already, there was little breeze, and Matilda could feel sweat pricking her brow.

They sat in silence. She had managed to compose herself before they left the house. While she had been waiting on the sofa for Alan to get dressed, Cook came in to get something from one of the dining-room cupboards and nodded at her. She had stared at him, unable to say or do anything better. Did he know? Had he been up earlier and seen their discarded glasses? Heard her? There was no point in crying; after all, had she not willingly gone there? Had she not happily embraced this man when she knew it was wrong? Now she was making him feel as if it was his fault alone. Robert had to take some of the blame too. He treated her disgracefully, encouraged no doubt by Julie, who had always had a hand in any discord in their marriage. She glanced at Alan furtively when he stopped at a junction. There was nothing to read in his face; all emotions were now hidden, his face was creaseless and calm. Is it only women who suffer turmoil in this situation? she wondered. Yee! But what *kind* of women have this dilemma to worry about? Not respectable ones, that is for sure.

She asked him to stop the car two streets from her house. She turned to him and said, 'I am sorry.'

He reached over suddenly, pinned her arm down and kissed her hard on the cheek. 'Don't be.'

She pushed him away and staggered out of the car. She stumbled home, sniffing a lot. When she reached Saint John's compound, she heaved open the door with relief, then she feigned a headache and went to bed early, leaving her responsibilities behind. In the peace and dark of her room, she entertained passionate memories of the afternoon, which prevented her from sleep. When she woke with his name on her lips, a tingle on her skin, she was sure he had once more been with her.

Chapter Twenty-seven

It was a hot, humid day. The kind that enters into all conversations and makes people remark about the weather, the closeness that seems to restrict breathing, the absence of any breeze. It was weather that begged for good rain to clear the air.

Matilda was uncomfortable in her church cloth on her church pew. The talcum powder she had doused herself with that morning after her bath had long lost its aridity, and she felt damp all over.

The preacher was pouring with sweat. He paused his sermon regularly to wipe his brow with a wet handkerchief. Matilda shifted in her seat. Her skirt was tight and uncomfortable. She tried to undo the bow to loosen it a little, but it was difficult with Junior Lawyer on her lap. She fanned them both with a piece of folded paper and wished she could persuade him to sit on his own. Today of all days she did not want him on her hot lap.

She had long lost track of what the Reverend was saying, and instead she was concentrating on her breaths. The last time she had panted like this, albeit much more fiercely, had been in labour. It was all she could do, trapped here until the service was over, to cope with the sensation of nausea that was making it impossible for her to concentrate.

Could Alan's latest letter really be the cause of so much discomfort? They hadn't met again after that time weeks back, when . . . She tried not to think about it. She could think about it all the time if she allowed herself. Then the memories alone would weaken her if she let them. He had written to her soon after, telling her that he had been asked to go to Kumasi with some officials to attend a durbar of the Ashanti chiefs and was likely to remain there for a while. She had felt a combination of sad relief that he was going away, and thought about him rather more than she wished. When his letter arrived last week, with an Accra postmark, she had opened it with wobbly hands. He was back. He had not been able to keep her out of his thoughts. Was she well? Would she like to meet him? He had to go home urgently after all; his mother was unwell. But he would like very much to see her before he left. She smiled, excited at the thought of seeing him again and, for a few wishful moments, imagined what might be if she were free.

The service finally ended, and she shuffled outside, grateful for some fresher air. She headed towards a tree trunk where she could lean and watch Junior Lawyer and Samuel play in safety until the older boys finished Sunday school. By the time she saw Julie striding towards her from the car park, dressed in the sky-blue dress made with raw silk with dark-blue piping, Matilda was ready to faint. She stumbled to the tree and panted to steady her spinning head.

'What are you doing here?'

'Matilda, Matilda, Matilda! I should be asking *you* what you are doing here. I was on my way from church when I thought I'd better come and see for myself whether it is true that adulteresses go to church!'

Matilda clutched her heart, turning round to see if anyone else might have heard what she just had.

'Ah, you should see your face. I didn't really think you had it in you, but your face . . . It is a picture of guilt. Apparently, they are right . . .'

'No! What are talking about?' Matilda asked throatily.

'You and Alan Turton . . .'

'Oh, Jesus!'

'Yes, you might well need external forces to help you out of this situation. You see, I will be telling my husband all about your little friendship . . .'

417

'We don't have any friendship! What are you talking about?' Matilda started to cry.

'Crying isn't going to help you. You were seen, you see. You were seen in his car, misbehaving.'

Matilda gasped. 'But . . .'

'You ought to be ashamed! You are a mother, yet you spend your time cavorting with married men as if you have no cares in the world. And then you have the cheek to come to church. For what, forgiveness? I think you are begging at the wrong altar, my dear. Well, your days are numbered,' said Julie, turning. 'I thought it only kind that I should warn you before I tell my husband.'

Matilda stood immobilised and watched as Julie glided back to her waiting driver. Blood screamed through her eardrums; it felt as if something heavy was pushing against her lungs making it impossible to breathe. She took long breaths through her mouth, filling her lungs till they hurt. As she began to breathe more freely, she realised how stupid she had been once again. Could Julie really know anything? If she had seen them, she would not have waited so long to enjoy this moment. Goodness gracious, what is the appropriate behaviour in this kind of situation? she wondered. She could tell Julie that Alan had tried to kiss her against her wishes, and that she had *pushed* him away. Oh, even then, she had been aware that as usual there were those, many, who make it their business to know what other people are up to at all times. Whoever had witnessed them that day would have seen that she had not been willing but had chosen not to relay on that part of the story. Oh, what did it matter now! She wiped her eyes and smoothed her face powder. What could she do? Julie had more than enough fodder to cause the life Matilda knew to come to a dramatic close. She realised with an increasingly sickening heart that she was powerless to prevent her from repeating whatever she wished to Robert, from embellishing the story in any way she chose. As she walked home, she wondered why she cared. It had been a long time since she had seen him. What did it matter what she did with her spare time, if she chose to have male friends as he chose to have female friends? Of what am I so afraid? There is nothing more to lose, she thought, and instinctively reached to clasp a child with each hand. She rubbed her stomach to make it feel better. She needed to have some food; that would make this feeling of sickness abate, it always did.

Later that afternoon, she went to visit Patience with one aim, to share her load, to ease the discomfort, to escape her home so she did not have to look from one face to the other and feel the incalculable doom that was about to be unleashed on the entire household.

They walked in silence towards the sea in search of privacy. 'Whenever you bring me here, I know that you are going to tell me something big,' said Patience grimly. 'Whatever can it be now?'

'Julie saw us.'

'Saw whom?'

'Alan and me.'

'Please, Matilda. I have a headache. I am not in the mood for your bit-by-bit storytelling. Just tell me what happened!'

'All right. Alan Turton . . .'

'Yes, yes, I heard the first time,' said Patience exasperatedly.

'He gave me a lift home one day and kissed me . . .'

'Jesu! Please God, forgive me for calling your name like this on a Sunday too, but I don't think it is vain. Matilda, what is wrong with you?'

'He was nice to me. I was feeling sad. He gave me attention when my husband abandoned me.'

'At least you had a husband to abandon you.'

'Yes, I know. But he was kind, gentle . . .'

'What exactly are you saying? Did you . . . Matilda, look at me! Oh my goodness.'

Matilda was looking out to sea, at the space.

'But Julie doesn't know you . . . you . . . eh! Matilda, I am surprised at you. Well, you must deny it if you are confronted. I am shocked,' said Patience, starting to laugh. 'A white man too.'

'It is not a laughing matter.'

'Well, laughing is better than crying. There is no point crying over something that you cannot change. You know what happens if you play with fire. I wonder what Robert will do. Anyway, it serves him right.'

'He treated me badly,' said Matilda angrily.

419

'Very badly.'

'He abandoned me.'

'In full view of the whole of Accra.'

'Yes. He is to blame too.'

'Well, I wouldn't go that far. So, when will you see him again?'

'I don't know. I don't think it is a good idea.'

'Hmmm. Well, count your blessings; at least you did not get pregnant.'

'Yes,' said Matilda, taking a deep breath of sea air. 'Yes.'

'What will be will be. There is nothing you can do now. But rest assured Julie will get every drop of blood she can out of this situation.'

'What have I done?' whispered Matilda.

The next few days were surprisingly ordinary. Matilda allowed herself to hope that Julie had merely been taunting her, that she had not said anything to Robert after all, and that she did not intend to. She took delight in her daily chores with renewed vigour, as though she was grateful for a reprieve, as though each time it might be the last time that she was able to cook a meal in peace, bathe her children herself, sit around the kerosene lamp, swishing away mosquitoes and enjoying gossip with her aunts.

She was preparing to cook okro stew one morning in the courtyard. She took each hard green vegetable from the heap that lay washed on a newspaper on the floor, cut off the head, then clutching the okro tail down between her fingers, she halved it with her knife, then split it into quarters and eights. She lay it on the flat of her fingers and finely chopped it into the tiniest of pieces, which instantly stuck together when the gluey juice surrounding the seeds was released by her blade so that she had to scrape it off her hand and into the pot. She put onions in a large pan on the coal pot to fry gently while she continued cutting the okro as if in a trance. Her fingers, hardened with years of cooking, hardly felt the blade as it pushed through the vegetable and into her flesh from time to time. There was a strange smell from the onions, which became overpowering. She put aside her knife and peered into the pot, convinced that either the onions were bad or else the oil, which had

420

been previously used to fry fish, had turned. Not wishing to take a chance, she discarded her efforts and started again, cutting up a fresh, hard onion.

Aunty Dede was sitting in the shade of the tree, carrying Junior Lawyer and telling him a story. She looked up at her niece, made a loud disapproving noise and shook her head sadly. 'Matilda. Is there something that you need to tell me?'

'What do you mean, Aunty?' said Matilda, continuing to stare into her pot of onions with a disgusted look on her face.

'I have been watching you for days now, and there is no mistaking the signs, even if you choose not to see them.'

Matilda felt weak. Her legs suddenly did not want to bear the weight of her body any longer. She reached back with her hand to feel for the stool and sat heavily. She looked at her aunt, struggling to conceal the uneasiness in her stomach and the nausea that was increasingly overwhelming.

'And obviously, you have not been seeing Robert so there had better be a good explanation here.' She spoke with a calm voice, but her face quivered in anger.

Her aunt's expression offered no sympathy, and the relief she thought she might feel when her heavy secret became known evaporated before it could materialise. The time had come to confront the disastrous upheaval that would follow the sharing of this news. When they could all face the reality – that inside Matilda was a growing life that in time would show itself before emerging as a person to claim his or her place in this world. Yet, there again was that spark of joy that refused to be doused, even though every part of her rational mind was assured of the madness of her situation.

And over the course of the weeks since she had first suspected this, Matilda had asked herself many more things. She wanted to know whether something happens because it is meant to happen, because there is that thing called fate, which it is of no use to challenge. And does the course of one's life flow like a river meandering determinedly along a set path? But don't even rivers sometimes swell their banks, and at times rebel at the very confinement that has defined their course?

'What have you done? Who is the father? What were you thinking?'

421

Aunty Dede was shaking her head. On her face, Matilda read utter disbelief, confusion and pain.

She was unable to speak and looked at the ground like a child ashamed of something. She shook herself. She would face this head on. Others had played a part in this situation, but as she was carrying the child, the blame would be focused on her. Of all her worries and fears, paramount now was the well-being of her unborn child. Come what may, she told herself, the consequences simply have to be endured; the child's welfare is what matters.

'Are you not going to give me any answers? This thing is not going to go away, you know. How long were you hoping to conceal your condition? Your stomach will show the baby soon; do you think that you can hide this from your mother? I am surprised that she does not know already, the busybody that she is. Now is not the time to bury your head in the sands . . . and don't cry . . . Answer me, who has done this to you?'

'The father is Alan.'

'Alan who?' she spluttered.

'Alan Turton.'

'And how am I supposed to know who that is? God help me! I hoped that there was a simple explanation here, that my eyes and ears were deceiving me. But no, you have to prove me wrong.' Aunty Dede was shrieking and clutching her head. 'Who? Answer me, who?'

'Audrey's former husband.'

'A white man? A friend of Lawyer? Goodness me, what have I done?' She was plainly struggling to keep her voice down; her whole body shuddered, and her voice kept cracking with disbelief. 'When I suggested English lessons, this is not what I had in mind as the outcome. What has he said about this?'

'He does not know, but . . .'

'Oh, help us, God.'

Matilda stared at her aunt. Talking about the situation increased her unrest and further tangled her emotions. Joyous anticipation, fear for her health, her children, their father and Alan jostled for her thoughts.

'How long has it been going on? How did this happen? Why did you allow this? Did he make false promises?' And in a particularly mocking tone she said, 'Is he in love with you?' Her questions hung unanswered in the air; after all, no explanation would change the facts before her: Matilda was pregnant, and her husband, a friend of the father-to-be, who had nothing to do with the life expanding in his wife's womb, was a powerful man who lived just up the road. Aunty Dede's words uttered thoughts Matilda knew she would hear again and again from other members of her family and echoed sentiments that she had lived with subconsciously for the past few days.

'As well you know, evil-doers cannot escape retribution for long,' said Aunty Dede. 'You cannot imagine how disappointed I am in you. I stood by you when you decided that you would rebel against your husband, because I believed that you had been wronged. But now look at how you have chosen to reward me, and your family. I don't know how we are going to explain this, but we need to do it fast. At the end of the day, we have to think about the baby's health; we cannot allow further life to be jeopardised by such a palaver.'

Matilda sat calmly with tight lips. She sat unusually still and felt the sun's increasing intensity on her exposed skin. She looked at her onions, now burned from neglect. It was that time of the morning when people had mostly arrived at their destination for the day; school children were at school, office workers at work, and market traders were in the market. All along the streets, on benches and stools under the shade of trees, people with nowhere in particular to go and nothing in particular to do were lounging in the shade of large trees, lulled to sleep by the dense heat and a heavy breakfast, unbothered by hovering flies. She listened to the usually reassuring sounds of nearby households cooking, sweeping, washing carried through the hot, stagnant air along the alleyways between the tight houses.

'This is new territory for us all,' said Aunty Dede after a long silence. 'I cannot imagine how you can . . . I mean, a man who is not even your husband. That is not to say that I am not a normal woman. In my youth, I too had many offers. But to actually go and do this? Quite frankly, I am shocked.'

Matilda lowered her eyelids. There was a lot she wanted to say, but this woman was her favourite adult; anything she said now would only hurt her more.

'What possessed you to take leave of your senses in this way? Have I been overindulgent with you? I wonder whether my brother and sister were not right after all that you have been cursed. Had I known never comes first, but had I known what I now know, I would have encouraged you to stick to your marital duties.' She puffed forcibly and clutched her head. 'Yeeeh! God, please help us.'

Matilda wondered afresh what Alan would make of all this. She would have to inform him somehow.

'We have to tell them. I will talk to your mother first. Alone. There is no point telling your uncle about this until your mother has had a chance to accept the news. Only when we decide how to cope with this tragedy as a family can we involve your husband.' She squinted at Matilda. 'Don't look at me like that. What else did you expect when you decided to betray him? He will find out about this. It is not as if we can keep a child a secret.'

Matilda knew that her aunty had indeed informed her mother when later that day, Ama stomped out of the house into the courtyard looking for her daughter, her face twisted with rage, her unintelligible voice shrieking of horror and disgust. Matilda, who had been sitting on a stool, stood up to face her mother, but before she could step away, her mother was upon her, slapping her wherever she could, then holding on to her hair and shaking her daughter like a rag doll, all the while screaming rage and loathing. Matilda put one hand protectively over her stomach and the other over her bent head, for her mother had started punching her. Aunty Dede, moving as fast as she possibly could, shuffled out to the women and tried to pull Ama away.

'Stop it. Don't hit her face. She is carrying your grandchild. Don't hurt her.'

'She is a devil, this girl. And this baby is no grandchild of mine. Look over there. Those are my grandchildren,' Ama shrieked, pointing at little Junior Lawyer and Samuel, who were crying hysterically for their mother.

Matilda took advantage of her mother's momentary distraction and quickly pushed her away with great force. Ama stumbled backwards, lost her footing and nearly fell over.

'Now she is trying to kill her own mother! You have brought

nothing but shame to this family. How I regret the day I gave birth to you,' she said quietly.

Matilda was shaking. Tears streamed down her face. She willed herself to forget instantly her mother's words.

'Don't say things you will regret,' said Aunty Dede. 'The girl knows she has been foolish, but she is your daughter, and the child is your flesh and blood. Who knows, one day we will understand why this baby was sent to this family. A baby is always a blessing, no matter the father.'

Matilda had recovered, her hair hurt from being pulled, her arm was sore where her mother had punched her. She spoke with a tremor in her voice, 'I may have disappointed you, but you also let me down. Thanks to you and your greediness, I—'

'How dare you speak to me like that? Are you mad?'

'Not mad, simply foolish. Matilda, think before you speak. You must think about your health, your husband, your responsibilities,' said Aunty Dede.

'Maybe she is planning on moving to England and leaving her children behind. Maybe Lawyer might even pay for their fare himself, eh?' said Ama. 'The child of a white man.' She spat on the ground.

'The child's colour is not relevant,' said Matilda.

'You are even more stupid than I thought. You had the best life of all of us, but you were still not satisfied. You had to go and spoil it all, not just for yourself, but for all of us. You are the most selfish, ungrateful person that I know.' Ama spewed the words like venom. She put her head in her hands and said, 'I know this will kill me, and then you can have blood on your hands too.'

As Matilda listened to the hatred spill out of her mother's mouth, she felt her resolve and anger grow. 'My husband chose to abandon me. Do you know how many months have passed since I saw him? Shall I tell you? Well, it will be eight months next week. What am I supposed to do now that he has no more need for me?'

'Life comes in seasons. He might not need you now, but that does not mean that he never will again,' said Aunty Dede.

'Well, I am young. I don't want to get old and bitter waiting. And I too have desires, which he—'

'Listen to her!' screeched Ama. 'I cannot take this any more.'

'Matilda! We are not here to have desires! My goodness, that English woman has filled your head with strange ideas. We are here to have children and to uphold our family name, which you manifestly want to drown in mud.'

'We must send for my brother. He can come and deal with this. He is the one who organised the marriage in the first place,' said Ama, and with that she dispatched one of her older grandchildren to fetch Uncle Saint John immediately. 'Run and tell him he must come at once. Tell him we have a serious crisis on our hands,' she said. Then she started to wail and cry inconsolably. She put her hands over her ears and said, 'And I don't want to hear any more of your evil noise, as long as I live.'

Saint John must have wondered what disaster his family could possibly be facing now as he rushed home. He shoved the courtyard door roughly and started shouting before he was even inside. 'Sincerely, for your sakes, I hope this is a genuine calamity. I warned you when you sent for me because my son wanted to engage a Fanti girl never to disturb me with matters that I can deal with when I return from work. Today, too, I have left important paperwork behind. So, come on, then, what is it?' But the silence that greeted him must have sounded ominous. Ama had already retired to bed claiming that she was unwell. Matilda was in her bedroom; she had refused outright to join this family meeting. Owusu was sitting quietly in a corner of the courtyard, his face wearing a customary bewildered look. Saint John looked at his wife and sister. 'Well, what is it this time?' he said.

Aunty Dede looked as if someone had died. 'John, sit down,' she commanded.

He obeyed the doom in her voice. 'What has happened?'

'Matilda is expecting,' said Amele. Somehow, her voice sounded victorious, and she would have continued to impart further information, but Aunty Dede looked at her sternly.

'So? This is what you call a crisis? I know the doctor said she should not have more children, but obviously she is able. Is this why you have sent for me? Is this why you have wasted my precious

426

time? You know I have an important job,' he said, preparing to stand up again.

'It is not Lawyer's child,' Aunty Dede said, looking intently at her brother.

Saint John laughed out loud, almost hysterically. 'So what is it then, another immaculate conception?' He laughed some more, looking around at the sullen faces. No one laughed with him. His face transformed slowly, and he leaned forward. 'What are you saying? That the girl has committed adultery? Don't be ridiculous. With whom?' Again, there were no reassuring comments. He rose to his feet and roared for her. His hands and legs trembled visibly, newly formed beads of sweat shimmered on his forehead. Matilda appeared at the doorway of her room, and he thought she stared at him with insufficient humility. Dumbfounded, he pushed himself towards her, his mouth hanging open in complete disbelief. He stood in front of her and bent forwards slightly to study her face. Then he slapped her, in retrospect, probably harder than he had ever slapped anyone, because his hand stung for several minutes, and he noticed that he had left an imprint on her cheek.

'The curse of a beautiful face,' he said. 'Who did you allow to corrupt you, my innocent, obedient niece? Who did this?' he shrieked. When there was no response from his family, he opened his hands as if asking the gods. Then he said, 'Which ancestor is displeased with me? Why is this happening? You see, I can hear the words of my dearly departed mother: "Pride comes before a fall."' Large tears were gathering in his eyes.

For he had indeed been proud of his family's elevated status when Lawyer married Matilda, but not more than anyone else would have been, and he had never intended to boast about it. But she had fallen now, and she would drag the entire family with her. He knew that the neighbours and some relatives who felt that Saint John and his household were overly satisfied with their lofty status would mock him. All of them. And he would not think what Lawyer would do or say, not now, anyway.

That night, Ama, who, as though willing her prophecy to come true, had confined herself to her bed, spoke to her brother. 'We must

427

distance ourselves from her actions if we want to save our family name.'

'But what are we going to do?' asked Saint John.

In a hushed voice, Ama said, 'The only sensible course of action is to ensure that Lawyer does not see her. God help us.'

'Yes, he must see that I, Saint John Nii Quaye Lamptey, do not condone such behaviour.'

'She is only lucky that we are not uncivilised like some of the northern tribes who would stone her for adultery.'

'You are right. She cannot be welcome in my house any longer. In fact, if I were not a gentleman, I would send her away this very night. Lawyer must see that we are taking this matter seriously. He must not think that we Lampteys accept such unspeakable activities.' He sat beside his ill sister in silence for a while. His body was racked with anger, his hands shaking. 'We must go to the priest in the morning; all of us. We must seek further protection for this house. We are under a siege of curses, our situation is worsening by the hour.'

'I am not well, but I too will come,' Ama whispered to her brother, as though she really did not have the strength to live and deal with yet another catastrophe.

'We cannot allow Matilda—'

'Don't mention her name,' said Ama huskily. 'Till the day I die, I don't want to hear her name again.'

Outside, in the compound, where only two lanterns were flickering quietly in the heavy night air, Matilda was sitting alone listening to their murmurs. She felt a shiver start at the top of her head, as if a thousand lice were scampering about on her scalp. It spread over her entire body so that she shook from the cold and had to go to the latrine, where she retched in pain.

In the morning, Saint John asked her to leave his house. He spoke looking at the ground. She stood staring at him unflinchingly with clenched jaws and nodded. Then she packed her bags, careful not to reveal her feelings to the boys.

Aunty Dede agreed that the best thing would be to send Matilda to her house in Tema. 'There is nothing else I can do for now, Matilda. We must avoid the possibility of Lawyer seeing you in this odious condition.'

428

'Let me take Junior Lawyer. He is not four yet, and he belongs with me,' Matilda pleaded, holding the boy tightly.

'You have brought this upon yourself. We have duties to the boys; they are Lawyer's children after all, and they belong here, near his family.'

Matilda began cry. The nausea she had felt last night flooded her senses again. She thought she would pass out and had to hold on to a wall, losing grip of her child in the process so that he slid halfway down her body and started to cry too.

'You go alone until things settle down here,' said Aunty Dede. 'Rest assured I will do what I can so you can return soon. I know, a mother belongs with her children. But can even I convince them?'

Ama remained in bed even after she had been informed that Matilda had gone. She said she was ill and could not get up, and Saint John realised that it was up to him to tell Lawyer about Matilda's situation. He was secretly envious of his sister; he would have preferred at this particular point in his life to be unwell; this burden that the girl had placed on them was too much for even a man like him to bear.

So, later that day, he told Lawyer about the disgraceful behaviour of his niece, in whispers so that no unnecessary ears would hear of their shame, apologising profusely all the while. He was acutely aware that this was one apology that would be futile, and he laid sufficient blame at the door of that Englishman who had forcibly corrupted the girl. Lawyer sat and listened with his arms folded, leaning back in his chair, his face a smooth mask, which concealed any emotion, as though he was listening to the sorry tale of one of his less important clients.

'My sons will come and live here. They will have nothing more to do with their mother,' he said. 'Is there anything else?'

Saint John was speechless. He considered briefly whether now would be a good time to discuss his job prospects, but Lawyer dismissed him, saying he didn't wish to discuss the matter any further, at which point Saint John decided that a written resignation would be the most appropriate action.

Chapter Twenty-eight

Matilda spent every waking moment at Aunty Dede's house hoping for news that she could return home. The days seemed unending, as if the longer they were, the more likely she was to hear something, but she had only the thoughts and memories that taunted her. For long minutes of each long day, her mind was battered with unhelpful reminiscences that made her heart ache intensely so she had to stop whatever it was she was doing and gasp. Her tightly knotted stomach did not seem to want or need food, but she forced herself to eat a little each day for the baby. During the worst nights, she could not help hoping that morning would not come for her, but then spent the first few moments of each new dawn released from the desolation that she knew would drench her later on, and gave thanks for her baby's increasingly steady kicks.

She could not separate her sufferings: being apart from her children, Robert, Alan, her mother's words, which seemed to have etched a permanent place in her mind. As they played and played again, she became progressively enraged at them all, cowards that they were, her mother and her uncle, who could only ever think about themselves. Why would no one see that Lawyer had behaved abominably towards her? That had he not rejected her like this, she could have continued to serve him in peace? And dutifully? Why had they allowed him to take her children away without a fight? They were all part of the same family, after all. And how could he take the last thing that mattered so much to her? After she saw Julie at church that Sunday, she had been surprised that there had been no immediate sign from Robert, but this punishment he had allotted her was greater than she could possibly have imagined and indicated that he had spent his time thinking about the most efficient way to penalise her.

She had been excluded from the only home she had ever known for a few weeks when she received the news that her mother was gravely ill and feared to be dying. She rushed back to Accra, desperate to be with her sons again, fearing what awaited her there.

The silence in the compound alarmed her. There were no children around, and her aunts greeted her with glum, defeated faces. Aunty Dede pointed wordlessly to Ama's room, and Matilda walked the most worrisome steps she had ever taken in her life towards the darkened room. She let out a shrill cry when she saw her mother, skeletal and ashen, with her eyes closed to the apprehension around her. Ama flinched slightly but did not open her eyes.

'Don't talk to her,' said Aunty Dede, who had walked into the room after Matilda. 'She does not want to see you. We did not tell her you were coming.'

Matilda looked at her aunt's sad face and ran out of the room back into the compound, where she shed tears that she had been too upset to cry during her banishment. 'What did the doctor say?' she asked.

'It is a mystery, this illness,' said Aunty Dede, shaking her head. 'She has not been up since the day you left the house.' She ignored Matilda's gasp and continued, 'We begged the doctor to come and see her last week, but he was not sure what the cause was. He gave her numerous medications, which have not helped . . .'

'I have been telling you that these are curses,' said Aunty Amele, looking disdainfully at Matilda's face then her stomach.

'Yes,' said Aunty Dede sighing. 'We called the family head to pour libations yesterday and to say manifold prayers, but she has not improved . . .'

'She is getting worse; we need the fetish,' said Aunty Amele. 'I am not sure why we have delayed like this.'

431

Matilda asked for her children in between gulps of air.

'They are now living at Lawyer's house.'

She gasped. 'All of them? Including my baby? With that witch Julie?'

'Less talk of witches, if you don't mind. He sent for them as soon as you left. They come and go, but they sleep there.'

Matilda bit her lip and tried to imagine what treatment her children might be suffering at the hands of not one but two people who despised her.

Robert knew that Matilda was back. He heard it from Julie, who seemed to know her comings and goings rather well. But he was taken aback when he heard a faint knock one afternoon and looked up to see her form blocking the light streaming in through his doorway.

He stared in stony silence, too shocked to say anything. He could imagine many strange things, but none odder than seeing his pregnant wife here to confront his anger in broad daylight like this. She walked towards him, with the same gait that had caught his eye the first time, that swing, that glide. He looked away. He had often wondered at the extent of the relationship between her and Alan and veered from utter rage at the thought of them together to complete bewilderment about it all. Julie had taken perceptible pleasure in filling him in on the details, the brazen display of affection in Alan's car, and the fact that they had probably been carrying on for a long time under the guise of English lessons.

'Good afternoon.' She paused, perhaps hoping he would say something.

She walked up to the desk, and he tightened his grip on his pencil. He could smell her, a faint whiff of hot oil, lavender, talcum powder. A smell he had liked. She was wearing a smock-like dress, which failed to hide her stomach. He pulsed his clenched teeth.

'I don't know what you have been told, but I can tell you what happened. I made a mistake. Once only . . .'

His pencil broke in two, and he discarded it with disgust. A rage was welling up inside him. He wanted to strike something and clasped his hands instead.

'I will live with my mistake all my life.'

432

He looked up. Her cheeks were wet.

'But my behaviour has nothing to do with my children. They have not done anything to deserve the treatment they are getting. I have seen the welts on their backs, the blisters on their knuckles from her ruler. I have heard the stories. She has even shaved their heads so they look ugly, like criminals, and my children have never had lice. You know what I am saying is true. I cannot sit and watch this, I cannot accept it . . .'

'I don't think what you can or cannot accept is an issue here. You have shown yourself unfit to be their mother.'

'Have you been a good husband? You did not even have the courage to inform me that you did not need me any more. How do you think I felt when I had to hear it from that woman?' Her voice was breaking.

Robert took a deep breath and spoke with a throaty voice. 'You wrote that letter. It seems you have forgotten the opportunities I gave you, the children who will be educated and well provided for.' He glanced at her stomach. 'You had a lot to be grateful for. You had no future when I met you.'

'I was a child!'

Robert bit his lip and looked at her for a moment. She had rubbed away all sign of tears. Her face was stony, but her eyes were pleading.

'I cannot let Julie mistreat my precious children any longer, and neither should you.'

Both of them looked towards the door that led into the house as it creaked open and Julie walked in.

'I thought I heard my name,' she said pleasantly.

Robert shook his head. Her presence would not make this any easier. She had egged him on ever since she broke the news about Alan and Matilda to do something drastic, something violent, he wasn't sure what, but he had remained steadfastly quiet. What more could he do, anyway?

'Is there something you wish to accuse me of directly? I am here now, so you can. Or perhaps you might start with an apology? And then show some gratitude that your children are not homeless, as you are, and for the clothes and food and discipline that I am providing them.'

'That is no more than is their father's duty,' said Matilda harshly.

'What cheek you have to waltz in here with another man's seed growing in your womb! I would have thought you would do anything you could to hide your licentious behaviour from your precious children.'

'This has nothing to do with you,' said Matilda, raising her voice.

'It has everything to do with me. I am the one who has to look after your blasted children. As if I don't have enough to do already.'

'Tell her to leave, Robert,' screamed Matilda. 'Do your duty for once! Please.'

'How dare you come into my office and start to shout at me? Who the hell do you think you are?'

'Your wife,' she screeched. 'I am your wife.'

'You might have been once, in a manner of speaking,' said Julie.

Matilda's face was quivering. She leaned her hands on his desk. 'You have obligations to them. Just because you are a big lawyer does not mean you can pick and choose when to remember your responsibilities.'

'Outrageous,' said Julie, shaking her head in disbelief.

'Shut up for once, you wicked woman,' Matilda screamed. Then she turned to Robert and, pointing a finger in his face, said in a hoarse voice, 'If you could be honest, you would see that you must take your share of blame for these circumstances . . .'

'Get out!' shouted Robert, propelled out of his chair by anger. 'How dare you! Get out.' He strode around the desk, causing Matilda to stumble backwards towards the door. He wanted to strike her beautiful face, marred now with tears and pain, to hurt her for the hurt she had caused him, first with her letter, and then in this irreparable manner with that damned idiot.

Julie stood by with her arms folded across her chest. On her face, her delight was only slightly restrained as she watched Matilda stagger down the stairs and out into the courtyard.

The fetish priest arrived late in the afternoon the next day. The neighbours hushed in awe as he walked down the alleyway to Saint John's house. He was wearing a white cloth around his waist and several amulets around his wrists, ankles and his neck that rattled when he walked. He was a tall, thin man with wrinkled skin, and he looked grave as he asked to be ushered into the room where the sick woman lay. He had not been in there for long when he looked at Uncle Saint John and said in a quiet voice for all to hear, 'There are spirits lurking around the bed waiting.'

Saint John let out a cry that sounded like a forced dry cough, and Matilda reached to grab hold of her father's hand. He did not seem to have registered what the fetish said and stood looking at his wife's body with childish curiosity.

'Please, can't you do anything?' asked Matilda.

'At this stage, it is very expensive, but if you—' said the fetish priest.

'Whatever it costs, we will pay. Our word is our bond. Please, please, perform your rites,' said Saint John in a desperate voice.

They all watched silently as the fetish took out a pot from a pair of large shorts that he was wearing under his cloth and began to smear white paste in broad diagonal lines across his chest and his face. Then he carefully replaced the pot in his pocket and stood for a moment with his arms folded and his eyes closed.

Matilda was trembling and could see that everyone else in the room was equally afraid. After all, had the fetish not said that there were spirits in the room? 'God be with us,' she prayed out loud, and everyone, including the fetish, responded, 'Amen.'

Soon, it was as if the fetish had been submerged in a trance. He began to dance around the bed, stamping his heels hard into the hard floor and making his various charms clatter. Matilda wondered whether he was not hurting himself in the process. When he opened his eyes, it was as if he was seeing past Ama and past all the things that Matilda could see and looking into some distant world. His eyes were glazed and began to roll in his head. His body jerked unevenly, his arms and legs moving like a dancing marionette. Then he began to shout harshly, unintelligibly, in the direction of Ama's head, as if he was having an argument with someone there. No one in the room moved or spoke. Eventually, he became silent, his body looked serene, and his breathing returned to normal.

Matilda realised that she had been holding her breath and gratefully took a few mouthfuls of stale air.

There was a collective gasp in the room when Ama stirred in her

435

bed and opened her eyes a little. The fetish priest, looking very pleased with himself, nodded at Saint John and walked out of the room.

Ama gazed around her bed, blatantly surprised to see all these worried faces staring at her. She smiled. Then, looking at Matilda, said in a rasping voice, 'You evil girl, I hope you are satisfied now. I hope you are proud of what you have done to your own mother.' Then she closed her eyes on the chaos around her, leaving a faint smile on her lips.

Matilda screamed, 'Don't do this to me. Why do you scorn me so? What did I do to deserve your unremitting hatred? Don't die like this. Please God. Forgive me for all my sins. I beg You, don't let her die now. Please . . . I beg of You . . .'

Her mother opened her eyes wide and stared vacantly as she took her last breaths. Matilda started to scream frenziedly, gripped with horror. She shook and pulled at Ama, who just lay, obstinately immobile, with her eyes gazing at nothing and her breath stilled. 'We need to make things right again,' she wailed. 'You need to forgive me before you go. This is your grandchild. *Your* grandchild.' She tugged her mother's lifeless arm while shielding her belly with her hand, as if there was something she did not want her baby to witness. Soon, the entire household was filled with the sounds of tormented women weeping, and the air was imbued with the sense of irreversible loss. The sounds were deeply unsettling and spread an indefinable terror in the house, spilling into the alleyways and adjoining houses. Matilda felt her skin crawl with cold, and she trembled in the heat of the room as the reality of her mother's departure drenched her soul. Her heartbeat seemed to slow in honour of the dead woman, and her spirit sagged until her knees buckled, as if, in response to the sheer awfulness of the situation, life had drained out of her too, and she dropped to the ground heavily, like an overripe fruit falling from a tree. As she fell, she was aware of being immersed in a sea of calm, like a slowly sinking ship, and she succumbed willingly to the dark, unknown nothingness.

The cold numbness that she had felt when her own daughter had died filled every vein in her body, leaving her angry and useless.

Her tears dried over the coming days, and her sorrow was quickly replaced with frustration, and an overwhelming tide of bitterness and resentment, which seemed determined to engulf her, and which she was sure would imprison her unless she resisted.

The preparations for Ama's funeral began on a Friday morning three weeks after she had died. When she heard the wailing that heralded the arrival of the corpse, which the men of the Lamptey family had collected from the morgue, Matilda felt her body chill. She had a tremendous urge to run away, but her feet remained fixed to the ground. Her heart was palpitating, her mouth dry, as she watched the men carry the stiff, shrouded form into the family compound and into the darkness of the biggest room of the house, where Ama would rest in state. Matilda and her sisters and aunts followed the men unwillingly into the room and stood at a safe distance from the bed on which the men placed the body. Uncle Saint John removed the sheet to reveal the corpse, now grey and strangely wax-like, and everyone started to scream and cry out Ama's name. Matilda shuddered, sickened by the poorly disguised smell of dead person that filled the room, but it was the sound of the hysterical wailing that made her swoon, and she fainted again, falling heavily to the ground.

She opened her eyes when she felt a breeze on her face. She was lying on a mat outside in the shade. She hurriedly closed her eyes again. 'Matilda, wake up,' said Aunty Dede, shaking her. She opened her eyes reluctantly. 'You need to pull yourself together, you have duties to attend to. The others will look to you for guidance. No more crying. And no more fainting,' she said firmly.

For the rest of the morning, Matilda, her sisters Celestina and Eunice, her aunts and other miscellaneous female relations who had descended on the house when news of Ama's death had spread spent the next hours bathing and preparing the body, ceasing their crying only periodically. Matilda had hesitated as long as she could before touching her mother's naked body. Eventually, with eyes closed and breath held, she touched the firm, cold, lifeless form, aware now that it no longer housed her mother.

They dressed Ama in her best clothes with all her jewellery and laid her out on her bed with her head resting gently on a pillow, her arms stiff beside her, her eyes closed, so that she looked asleep, and more peaceful than Matilda had ever seen her. Aunty Dede sprayed the body liberally with scent, and the room was filled with the cloying smell of warm, musty perfume.

Matilda kept busy preparing food and drink for the evening and the funeral the next day; there was no way of telling how many people would come, but certainly, there would be hundreds of mourners. The yard had to be tidied and swept, the bedroom in which Ama would receive her last visitors had to be decorated with flowers and lace. A single candle was left to burn on the bedside table so that her face was illuminated with peculiar shadows.

That night, the family dressed in charcoal black and sat with suitably saddened faces in the pristine compound to await those who would come and help them keep watch over Ama for one last night. Matilda sat on a chair next to the bed in which her mother lay quietly. She tried not to look at her, but she saw her from the corner of her eyes the whole time.

The guests began to arrive early in the evening. Some, hoping that no one would notice, avoided going to file past the body, probably hoping instead that the fact that they had come to the house to show their respects would suffice. All night long, mourners wailed and cried intermittently, calling out to Ama, asking why she had gone so early, why she had left them behind and whether she was all right. Matilda shook hands sombrely with the sympathisers, many of whom she did not recognise. She nodded and thanked them for their kind wishes, ignoring their curious stares at her distended belly.

Many settled down to make themselves comfortable in chairs and stools for the night. Some conducted conversations discussing the economy, politics, family, anything really, but in hushed tones so as not to be disrespectful. But there was also merrymaking that night.

Some of the older relatives, who attended funerals every week, sat in groups, unfazed, chatting about the political changes that were afoot, in particular, whether Nkrumah had been right to break away from the United Gold Coast Convention and set up his own party, the Convention People's Party, which called for 'self-determination now'. Out of respect for the dead woman, they restrained their political beliefs somewhat, and only disagreed with each other in loud whispers while they enjoyed the free drink and food.

At dawn, Mr Peace Nii Aryee Ayitey, the family head, came to perform the funeral rites. He oversaw the slaughter of a goat, the pouring of libations, the prayers and incantations to the gods beseeching them to help Ama across, asking for protection for the remaining family and talking to Ama herself, reminding her who they were and not to harm any of them. And everyone, including perhaps some who had despised her when she was alive, understood the need to pay sufficient tribute and honour to the dead woman now that she formed part of the spirit world. She was now an ancestor who could wield power over the living, so the gathering was suitably solemn and repentant. Silently, mourners hoped that she could forgive them for any transgressions that she might harbour against them and begged her not to seek revenge. Again, they filed past Ama, who had now been placed in a coffin lined with red satin. Several tucked money and other gifts into the coffin, taking care not to touch the corpse, telling her as they made their donation for which ancestor on the other side the gifts were intended. Finally, the coffin was closed, and the pallbearers took their positions to carry her to the Methodist church, where mourners sat gravely through the funeral service. When the moment came to close the coffin for Ama's final journey, the congregation erupted in sorrow, lamenting loudly. Matilda sat in the pew, dry-eyed, holding her small children tightly while the coffin closed on her mother's face for the last time. She wondered whether she would ever forget what her mother looked like. And would the painful knot in her heart ever, ever dissolve? What about her mother's last words, would they ever stop their incessant rotation in her head, playing loudly like one of Robert's records? And the words she had not spoken, could her mother now hear them? Where she was, could she see her daughter's anguish?

Then the procession of mourners followed the coffin to the graveside, pausing briefly once more by the doorway of Saint John's house so that Ama would rest in peace and allow them to live without too much fear.

The ceremony at the graveside was a mixture of traditional prayers and the Methodist burial service. The minister wore flowing white robes. He wiped sweat from his brow constantly, and although he delivered his sermon with passion, and although Matilda listened, she did not hear what he said. When the coffin started to disappear into the grave, the mourning became frenzied and hysterical. Matilda thought she would faint again, but she breathed in gulps of fresh air and allowed her tears to fall freely while she said her final goodbye to her mother, unsure what it was exactly that she felt at that moment.

That night, struggling to rid her mind of the images of her mother alone in that box, underneath all that soil, Matilda thought for the hundredth time, For the wages of sin is death. Oh, but can death be as painful as bereavement? Both deaths she had witnessed unfolding, that of her daughter and now her mother, had been prolonged and wrought with suffering, hers and theirs, but then peace seemed to follow for the dead. But she knew that the peaceful, lifeless face of a deceased person masks reality. After all, a dead body no longer houses the person who once lived there. That is plain for all to see. Encountering her first dead person would have convinced her, if indeed she had had any doubt before, that the essence of humanity is in spirit form, and as soon as the body dies, the spirit, whether beloved or loathed, flees elsewhere. Was it somewhere peaceful or not? She couldn't help but remember the descriptions of hell she heard about at church, a place of untold misery, worse even than the worst this world has to offer.

Eventually, she slept. She had gone without much sleep for days now, and even the baby in her womb, who kicked its mother from time to time to remind her of its presence, had been ignored. But Matilda was weary, from her grief and her thoughts, from the silent recriminations of the mourners who had gathered to lament Ama's premature passing. Indeed, enough had been said to place some of the blame for this untimely death squarely on the shoulders of the poor deceased woman's eldest daughter.

Robert was surprised when he saw Aunty Dede standing at the door of his office one morning. Once again, he reflected how unnecessarily accessible his office was. If he closed the door when he was working, the room became too dark and airless, so he had to put up with unsavoury visitors in this way. Thankfully, there were not many who had the courage to brave his door uninvited, like this woman.

A part of him wished he had seen the last of her lot, but these people would always be his relatives now, united by children whom he loved.

She was a sober reflection of her old self; obviously, the family's traumas had reduced her appetite along with her bulk, and he noticed how much more easily she sat in his armchair.

'Lawyer, thank you so much for seeing me. How have you been?'

'Fine.' He glanced at her and muttered, 'My condolences about your sister,' thinking that it was no great loss to humankind.

'Let me get straight to the point and not waste any more of your valuable time, Lawyer. What my family has suffered recently is more than one family should suffer in a lifetime. We have to take responsibility as a family for our mistakes, but we can only assume that the gods are not happy with us. We also know now that we have been cursed, but we are praying. We are praying all the time for victory in this warfare. Matilda . . .' she paused when Robert flinched and then swallowed deliberately, '. . . she has come for her mother's funeral. Lawyer, you should see how she has changed. She is ashamed. Repentant. She knows how stupid she has been, and how she has sacrificed all the blessings she had for a few moments of madness.'

Robert grimaced and looked away. Apparently, they had no idea that she had been here already. Or was it all a ruse? After all, dishonesty seems to run in their family, he thought.

'Lawyer, to be frank, the girl has suffered enough,' she said. She paused a while, undoubtedly hoping that Lawyer would say something. 'Well, I can see that for you she will never suffer sufficiently. That is fair enough. But I have come to beg you for the sake of the children. The children need their mother. I don't wish to offend you or your good name further, but I have heard that your first wife mistreats the boys. And in spite of the unfortunate circumstances, we are your family. I am sure that a good man like you would not expect me to forsake my duties to my sister's grandchildren. So I beg you, Lawyer, please,' she dragged the word out as long as she could before continuing, 'please, reconsider the situation for the sake of the next

441

generation. They have done no wrong. They don't deserve to suffer for her.'

He remained silent, watching her unflinchingly. He turned to look out of the door at the street. On the edge of his vision, he could see that the woman was getting up. He saw her get down on her knees and place one of her hands in the other as though asking for alms, her eyes glistening with tears. 'I am begging you, Lawyer. Please, I beg you,' she said.

'Listen, get up. What are you doing?' he said, jumping to his feet to help her back into the chair. The woman was weeping everywhere and clutching at his arm, still pleading with him. 'It's all right. It's all right,' he said, irritated, as he pulled his arm free and walked back to the door of his office for some fresh air. He had not expected this type of behaviour. How could he allow a woman old enough to be his mother to lower herself in front of him like this? He stood in the doorway of his office listening to the sounds of a neighbourhood preparing for nightfall: the clinking of metal buckets as people carried water home for their evening baths; the smell of freshly steamed maize, frying yam and hot pepper sauce that indicated the street vendors were setting up to sell dinner to those who were hungry; laughing children playing outside in the final moments of daylight before the sun disappeared causing sudden darkness, almost as though God had switched off the light. Robert could not escape the fact that the woman was right. As a child, his contact with his own father had consisted mainly of being summoned for a whipping from time to time because some relative or other had reported some misdemeanour of his. He had vowed that he would never hit his own children, and although he could not say that he never had, seeing Julie beat Matilda's children a little too vigorously on several occasions recently had disturbed him too. 'I'll think about it,' he said gruffly, without turning to look at the woman, who was snivelling rather loudly.

'Oh, Lawyer, thank you! Our family is for ever indebted to you. Thank you. You are a generous man, a good man. I knew that you would understand the situation. It is not for her, it is for the children.'

He shook his head in resignation.

Aunty Dede stood beside him and grabbed his hand in both of

hers. 'Thank you, thank you. What a good man you are. Oh, I will tell them. Thank you! May God bless you for your goodness.' Then she gathered her cloth that had come loose and tightened it under her armpits. 'Lawyer, thank you,' she said smiling, as she danced down the stairs towards the gate.

Typical conniving woman, he thought, as he watched her go. He felt his shoulders stiffen again as he found his thoughts wandering to Matilda, and he recalled the last time he had seen Alan. The wretched man had come to ruin his first day back at the races in two years. Robert had been enjoying the unabashedly welcoming atmosphere, the frisson of excitement in the air, when he saw Alan walking towards him. He felt himself reel anew with the knowledge of his wife's treachery. He was flabbergasted. His veins constricted as vitriol flowed through them freely, and he felt blood rush up to his face. Did the man have no shame whatsoever? He wanted to turn and walk away, anything to avoid confrontation, but there was nowhere he could go. The traitor had trapped him here in this open space in front of all these spectators. And as Alan strode towards him with a thin, unsteady smile on his lips, Robert realised that it was not just the racecourse that wasn't big enough for the two of them.

'Robert, we need to talk,' Alan said hesitantly.

The people who had been standing near Robert moved away slowly, leaving the two men alone.

Robert looked at Alan through narrowing eyelids. He was holding a race programme in his left hand while he clenched and unclenched his other fist, which dangled by his leg.

'Listen, old chap, we need to clear things up. I thought you and Matilda were separated, you know, and the thing is, she won't see me anyway, even though I do care so for her . . .'

Robert, who did not think of himself as a violent man, felt he had been pushed to the limit of his patience and delivered a perfect thudding blow to Alan's jaw, which curtailed his speech. Even he had been surprised at the crack he heard when his punch met Alan's head, and it would be fair to say he hoped he had loosened some of the idiot's teeth. Without waiting to find out whether or not he had wounded his former friend permanently, Robert stepped over him and walked out of the racecourse, leaving behind a crowd that was as stunned as Alan.

Matilda looked up from her cooking when she heard Aunty Dede walking into the compound. She was smiling triumphantly. She told Matilda the good news: 'But make sure that he does not see you. If he sees you like this,' she said, gesturing at Matilda's pregnant body, 'he will remember how angry he is with you and change his mind.'

Chapter Twenty-nine

In the confusion and chaos of the funeral and the joyous relief of being reunited with her children, Matilda thought sparingly of Alan during the day. But at night, he inhabited her dreams clearly so that she woke exhausted with longing. She considered writing to him but deemed it unwise. He would have to know about this child one day, but for now, it seemed easier to wait. For what, she wasn't exactly sure.

A strange, troubled harmony descended on the household. Matilda was uneasy that here and there, shrines to the gods had been erected on which fresh offerings were made daily. It had never been like this before, even Aunty Amele, the most fervent visitor of the fetish priests, had never erected a visible shrine in the house before. She wondered fearfully exactly what it was that her uncle was trying to protect his household from.

It became apparent to her barely a few weeks later, when she had to sit in stunned silence with Uncle Saint John, her father and her aunts, and listen with horror while Tetteh relayed how Lawyer and Sister Julie had been in a car accident on their way back from Takoradi. 'Sister Julie is dead,' he said to the staggered group. 'And Albert and Bernadette too.'

'Oh my God,' screamed Matilda, making a hollow sound that came from near the bottom of her stomach. 'And Lawyer?' she asked from behind her hand.

'Please, Lawyer is severely injured with many broken bones, but he will be all right. It is Gloria who we fear will also go and join her mother.'

'Oh God,' said Matilda, looking around her in total disbelief and horror, while her elders looked at the ground, shifting restlessly and remained ominously quiet. Apart from her father, that is, who did not look as though he had actually understood what Tetteh had said.

Aunty Amele suddenly hugged herself and began shrieking over and over again, 'God help us. God help us.'

Tetteh, who was visibly shaken, continued, 'Sister Matilda, Sylvia is asking for you.'

Saint John looked dumbstruck. 'God save us.'

Matilda turned to glare at him. She opened her mouth to say something, but instead she dismissed Tetteh. When he had gone, she turned to her family and asked, 'What did you do?'

'This was not what we asked for,' said Saint John, shaking his head. 'No one wanted innocent children to be rendered motherless because of their mother's wickedness,' he said with blank eyes, speaking to no one in particular.

'What are you talking about?' Matilda screamed, realising the significance of the shrines. The evidence was all around the house that the family had consulted with the fetish to determine the meaning of the numerous curses they were suffering, why their daughter had acted in such a strange manner, like a crazy person in fact, and why Ama, a woman really too young to die, had died because of all this. Matilda looked from one stunned, speechless face to the other. She witnessed their reaction with a horrendous realisation, and the full implication of what they might have done clutched at her most inner being and spread terror within her.

'But she had been interfering with the marriage, and I was only trying to do my duty,' said Saint John, still talking to himself.

He too must have been filled with the same fear that was engulfing Matilda, making her tremble. It was one thing to believe in unseen spirits and gods and to pray to them, but she knew that no one sitting here still digesting the news had ever had the thing they had indirectly prayed for delivered to their doorstep in such a direct and definite manner.

'Do you see the damage that you have done? She is dead now. And why? What for?' asked Matilda hysterically.

'But it is not as if we asked for her death, we simply wished to undo her curses and allow you and Lawyer to resume your marriage in peace,' Saint John said. His shoulders were drooped, and his voice too seemed to be wilting.

'And why would we ever wish a person dead?' asked Aunty Amele, looking angrily at Matilda. 'Don't you know that to do so would be to court disaster and myriad curses on one's own family for eternity and beyond? Do you think we are that stupid? Do you think that we want Mrs Bannerman's ghost to come and haunt us?'

Matilda looked at Aunty Dede, who had been unusually silent, but her aunt refused to make eye contact with her. She felt her stomach heave again and again and bumps rise up all over her skin. Julie was dead, and who knew, was her spirit now free to roam about unchecked? Was she here? Could she see and hear this unsavoury discussion? Matilda wondered where she would find the strength to keep going. And who or what was it that kept heaping all this misfortune on their household like this? Was it possible to become accustomed to the grief and numbness that absolute loss brings with it? If so, exactly how much suffering did one first have to endure?

Later, she walked to Downing House, oblivious to the stares and the sympathisers who called to her along the road. She was surprised how comfortably her feet found their way there.

She had never stopped seeing Julie's children whenever she could. Just two days ago, in fact, the twins had come to visit her on their way home from school. Thinking about Albert and Bernadette, her chest ached in anguish, and she slowed her steps. Why had she not interfered when she saw that they had been to see the fetish? she asked herself over and over. She should have known that Julie would be the object of their evil wishes, that no matter what was said, her family believed Julie was behind the failure of her marriage. If only she had stood up to them, told Julie, sought the protection of the Methodist church, relented, done anything instead of standing by her pride, then those innocent children would still be alive. And Julie too. Even though she had hated that woman, God, please forgive her for this too, she had never once wished her dead. She could never wish motherless-ness on a child. And the thought of Bernadette, normally inseparable from her twin, an eager-to-please child who was always affectionate to Matilda and her younger siblings, made her weep again. She remembered Ruth and wondered whether she would know her sister when she saw her. It was as if the old wound had been picked open to ooze and now require tending all over again.

Edward, Sylvia and George were sitting hushed in the dark living room. Shadows flitted on the walls, and the velvet chairs absorbed their breaths. Even in the darkness, Matilda could see that Sylvia's eyes were swollen and red. Without a word, she ran to them and put her arms around them. Sylvia started to sob and call out for her mother and sister.

'They are dead and gone,' said Edward.

'It's all right, Sylvia,' said Matilda, clinging to the children. Edward pushed his way out of the embrace and stood up to go and sit behind the piano. But as he sat there tinkling the keys aimlessly and tunelessly, the sound, which everyone in the neighbourhood associated with Julie, caused them to sob.

'I think it would be better if we go to my house, at least for a few days,' said Matilda, who felt a strong urge to get out of Downing House.

'This is my house, and I want to stay here,' said Edward.

Matilda was surprised at his anger but decided to ignore what she would have scolded him for on a different occasion. 'I know, but I thought you might like to be near me for the next few days, at least until Gloria comes out of the hospital, and then I will come and stay here with you until Daddy is home,' she said gently.

That night, when they were safely asleep in her bed, Matilda settled on a mat on the floor beside them. She had promised that she would stay close by them. Even though she was no longer a child, she too could hear the undecipherable night sounds – the squeaks and scrapes of inanimate objects – which on such a sorrowful night had ominous associations. She decided to leave a lantern burning by the door to dissuade any unsettled spirits from flitting through the darkness around them. 'Three or more unnatural deaths in a family, and there is foul play at work,' a minister had boomed from his pulpit once, years ago. These words resounded now in her head. 'Three or more unnatural deaths . . .'

The next day, she was getting ready to go and visit Gloria in hospital when she heard a voice that was instantly recognisable, and totally out of place. She held her breath and listened again, imagining that her dreams were coming to life.

'Excuse me, madam, I am looking for Matilda,' the voice said again, in clear English.

Again, the question was met with deafening silence. She looked out of the window and saw that the women were sitting motionless on their stools gaping at the white man who stood in the doorway of the compound in his khaki suit stroking a hat with his hands. A group of children had followed to see where he, an oddity in these parts, was going, and they stood around him like beaming guardian angels. He grinned at them, and the women before him, and pointed at the house as if he knew she was there. Matilda smiled, delighted. Her hands shook with excitement; inside, everything flickered to life.

It was obvious from where she stood that her aunts were too shocked to understand or respond to Alan, or even to call for her. She quickly put a scarf over her untidy hair and changed out of her drab house clothes into a more presentable dress. She did not dare to put on lipstick or perfume but smudged Vaseline liberally on to her lips before walking out as boldly as she could into the bright sunlight and their astonished, transfixed gazes.

'Hello,' she said. He looked wonderful in real life. Better than in the dreams. She wanted to touch him, to be alone with him.

'Matilda,' he said, taking a few steps towards her and looking with wide, questioning eyes at her stomach. She had forgotten that he had not seen her in this state, and rubbed her belly as if to reinforce what he could see.

'We cannot talk here,' she said, aware of the penetrating looks that her audience was giving her. She tried to steady herself, wiping her clammy hands on her dress surreptitiously.

'Gosh!' he said, still staring.

449

'I hope for your sake, young lady, that you have informed your visitor that he must leave this very instant,' said Aunty Dede too loudly in Ga.

Alan looked at the women, who were glowering at him, and smiled weakly. Without practice, his Ga was now obsolete.

'They want you to leave. You are not welcome here,' said Matilda, shaking her head.

'Gosh! A baby. Why, Matilda, I had no idea. Is this why . . . ?'

'Go,' said Aunty Dede in a booming voice as she stood up and shuffled over towards Alan.

'Alan, you must go.'

'I need to see you. I got back last week from England. Mother is well again. But this,' he said pointing, 'is this why you ignored my letters? You and Robert . . .' He looked pained.

'No. No, Alan.' She wished she could hold him.

'Mine?' He beamed at the people around him.

'I was even sent away without my childrens. They let me come back because my mother died. Now Julie too died.'

'I had no idea. I am so sorry,' he said, reaching out to touch her hand. 'Listen, I have to leave unexpectedly. This time for good. I had to see you once more, to see if you will come with me—'

'Excuse me,' said Aunty Dede, who was standing next to Alan with her hands on her hips looking angry. She pointed at the door. 'Go,' she said, in unfriendly English.

Matilda felt a wave of dizziness. In all the reunions with Alan that she had rehearsed, there was no one else present. Now look at them all, watching, interfering, spoiling things. She sat on a stool and put her head in her hands, hoping the feeling would pass soon.

'This is my baby,' Alan said, smiling at Aunty Dede and pointing to Matilda.

'I said go,' barked Aunty Dede. Amele had come to stand next to her in support. She too had her hands on her hips and glared at Alan.

'Oh, come on,' said Alan, losing his patience, 'I will leave if Matilda asks me to. After all, this is her home too.'

'You will find that you are wrong on that matter,' said Saint John, who had appeared at the doorway of the courtyard. His face was stormy, his body tensed like a boxer about to pounce. 'Her presence is merely being tolerated for the time being. Leave. This. Very. Instant. Do you understand me?' he said, raising the volume of his voice with each syllable.

'This is no way to treat Matilda. She is not a slave, is she? Or a prisoner? Why can't I just talk to her . . . ?'

'Please, which part of my request did you not understand?' said Uncle Saint John, poking Alan sharply in the ribs. Alan was at least a foot taller than anyone there, but surrounded by the two hefty women and a furious Saint John, he felt dwarfed and overwhelmed.

'Matilda, we must meet. Come to the house tonight, tomorrow. Come with me to England. I will look after you there . . .'

'She is not going anywhere,' screamed Saint John into Alan's face vehemently, permitting drops of spittle to fly from his mouth and land on Alan's shirt and chin. Alan wiped his face in disgust. 'She belongs here with her duties, her children. You should be ashamed coming here to cause more trouble. Can you not see what you have done? How you have spoilt things? Now go!' he shouted, shoving Alan hard towards the door.

Alan stumbled and tripped headlong on to the ground. Matilda rushed to help him. 'I'll try and come,' she whispered in his ear.

He stood up and dusted his hands on his clothes. The women were all chattering loudly at him. Aunty Amele started slapping her fat palms together towards his face as if she was trying to shoo him out of the yard like a stray chicken. He looked deflated and distressed as he put his hat back on his head. 'Why on earth is everyone in this blasted colony so aggressive?' he said, before walking out through the door, ducking so that he did not hit his head on the crossbeam.

'You have not finished destroying this family, then?' said Uncle Saint John to Matilda. 'I can assure you that this is your very last final warning. One more digression from you, and you will have to go and find somewhere else to live. Do you want more blood on your hands before you learn your lesson? Your duties? What is the matter with this girl? What?' he screamed at his wife and his sister as if they knew the answer to these questions.

Later that week, Matilda went to see Alan. She could not allow him to leave without the opportunity to say goodbye properly. This was, after all, his baby. But bravery did not come naturally to her. She often wondered when it was that she would stop being so timid and fearful of everything. Hadn't she conquered her husband, his wife and even her mother, the most terrifying of them all? She wished she could be more reckless but trembled whenever she remembered the one occasion she had, and the chaos it had caused. She wanted to break free from the yokes that constrained her like Audrey had but reminded herself that Audrey was not accountable to an extended family all living on top of her in a confined space. Her uncle's threat clanged in her ears. Where would she be without them all? How could she be a homeless mother, a mother with no means of feeding her children? She would rather die than be separated from her children. She would have to put her feelings to death and stay in her uncle's house. And would this deep longing to be with Alan just pass? The illogical and insupportable wish to relive that afternoon? Desires for which there was no room in her life?

As she walked in the blazing heat along the road to his house, marvelling as ever at the peace that prevailed here, she wondered what chaos reigned beneath all this silence. She crept up his drive, hoping to reach the steps to the veranda before his dogs were alerted to her presence, but they came bounding round the side of the house before she had made barely any progress. Matilda froze, too scared even to scream. They reached her and jumped up, pawing her stomach and legs, barking ferociously. She started screaming and waving her arms above her head. Awuni and the gardener came running out to see what had caused this commotion, and finally managed to get the excited dogs under control, all the while trying to convince her that if she stood still, they would leave her alone. But as soon as she was able, she ran towards the veranda to increase the distance between her and the animals. She clambered up the steps and collided with Alan. Still shaking from her close encounter with his dogs, she allowed him to put his arms around her while she broke down and wept.

'Come, come, Matilda. It's all right now, I'm here.'

'I have brought shame to my family.'

'Calm down.'

She told him in a watery voice about the car crash, the motherless children, about Robert in hospital and about her fears for her baby. With all the crying, she was almost incomprehensible.

He put his arms around her, and her stomach kept them apart. She made little effort to push him away.

'But there is some good news in all this,' he said, gently rubbing her stomach. 'This is wonderful. A baby for me?' He pulled her to him once more, and she let him.

She felt her shoulders droop as if letting go of the heavy weight she seemed to carry around with her all the time now. She pulled away and said, 'I must go. We mustn't see each other again.'

Alan didn't let her go. He wiped away her tears, and she clung to him, this man who aroused emotions in her that confounded the pre-conceptions she had been raised with. She filled her lungs with the smell of his body, tried to save the memory of him. His tender hand soothed then awakened her, and later, when it was dark outside and the only light they had was from the weak moon, he made her laugh with his stories.

'There must be another way,' he said, becoming sombre again. 'I have been transferred back, come with me.'

She saw in his eyes that he was serious. What would life be like over there? she wondered. She was curious about England, English people; she admired something about them, something she found hard to pinpoint. But she found it hard to imagine being his wife, living with him as Audrey had. A life with Alan, without her children? That was not a choice she could make. 'No,' she said.

'You know I'd never let you down.'

She nodded. She knew.

Chapter Thirty

Robert Bannerman could not remember being bedridden as an adult, could not remember having so much to contemplate, so much time in which to do it. He kept asking himself where it had all begun to veer out of control, searching for answers that remained exhaustingly elusive.

The one thing he could not recall was the crash itself. One moment, they were driving along the sea road to Takoradi quite fast, the next, apparently three days later, he woke up in a hospital bed to hear that he had killed his wife, one son, one daughter. The front tyre had burst, and he lost command of the car, which eventually flipped over and landed on its side. During the first days after he regained consciousness, he wished greatly that he too could die. He knew this was gutless, but the guilt of curtailing his young children's lives seemed impossible to bear.

Now he had sufficient time to contemplate his imperfectness; he had confronted the fact, albeit unwillingly and painfully, that he had made many mistakes along the way. And it had been hard for him to come to these conclusions when he had been venerated for so long by his colleagues, workers and family members, even if only because they depended on him for their livelihood. He could see that now. None of them could afford to think of him in terms other than greatness and goodness; he was their lifeline, and this was man-

454

ifest in their undying loyalty and passivity. After all, who would bite the hand that feeds him? Over the years, he had naturally come to accept that they were right and perhaps that he did deserve their respect and admiration. Realising that one is not perfect is part of the process of atonement, is it not? he thought to himself. But he knew that he would never pay sufficient penance for causing the death of two of his children and making the others motherless. For the reason that they had been in that car with his family in the first place – the allure of another young woman – was not one that he wished to even think about now. The mere fact that he was analysing the events of the recent past in this manner was in itself surprising to him; he was, after all, not a man prone to self-analysis or guilt. Or even regret. Fundamentally, he did not believe in regret. He had always been quite impulsive and rarely felt much need to explain his behaviour to anyone. But lying in hospital with a broken leg and several fractured ribs, he had had much time to reflect on the misery that had become his. He felt what every driver that survives a crash in which some of his passengers have died must feel. And he faced a painful realisation that morning; his children would have been much better off if their mother had been the one to survive. Doesn't a child belong with its mother? This was the real reason why he had allowed Matilda to continue to raise their children, even though she had behaved abominably and, quite honestly, totally unworthily of motherhood.

Silas came to visit one evening. He told Robert how the government had declared a state of emergency when Nkrumah and his party, the Convention People's Party, had called for positive action in the fight for independence. They had called for a boycott of all British goods, which had been surprisingly effective. 'Thankfully, he has been arrested now, as I believe has Kofi. Why he felt the need to follow Nkrumah with all his pan-African nonsense is beyond me. Nkrumah used the United Gold Coast Convention as a Trojan Horse. While the party leaders were talking to the British and devising a constitution, he was busy galvanising the support of the people for the CPP with his promise of immediate self-government.'

'I am astounded at the support they have,' said Robert.

'That won't last now that the ringleaders are in jail. The British have done the right thing by driving the wolf away.'

'I hear that they are running the campaign from behind bars.'

Silas laughed. 'We'll see about that.'

'The election is going to be some task, what with ninety per cent of the franchise illiterate. It doesn't bode well,' said Robert.

'Historic nevertheless, the first genuinely African election of an African majority assembly. And with Africans, men like you and me, to be appointed to ministerial posts. Something to celebrate, I'd say,' said Silas, pulling out a bottle of whisky that he had hidden in a paper bag. He winked and pulled out two cups. 'I don't go in for law breaking as a rule, as well you know, but there are always exceptions,' he said, pouring them a stiff measure each.

It hurt Robert when he laughed. 'I need that. Anything to numb my mind. I try to sleep, but I can't. I close my eyes and I see her, the children. I—'

'That's why I brought this. Should do the trick.'

'What am I going to do?'

'Try not to think about it; all will become clear in time. Your children need you. And you have your horses, Robert, and an army of staff who depend on you. And we have a country to rescue . . . Well, you know what I mean. We need to make sure that the Convention People's Party support doesn't translate to votes when the election is held.'

'I worry for Julie's children.'

'I hear . . . Matilda is looking after them well.'

Robert waved him quiet. He had heard this too. He had hoped she might, and been quietly confident that she would. For his part, he could not deny his children their wish to have her in the house with them.

'Don't let that scoundrel get the better of your family,' said Silas. 'No doubt he took advantage of her innocence.'

'We were friends,' said Robert huskily. 'I trusted him. What he stood for. I feel so incredibly let down . . .'

'Yes.'

'I can't make sense of things. So much of what I believed in is crumbling out of my reach. I've lost my wife, children. Even my

456

country seems to be slipping away. Nkrumah betrayed us and wants to run away with our future, what is rightfully ours.'

'I know, Robert, times are indeed strange. But the battle isn't lost. He can't win the election from his jail. This country doesn't need a Communist upstart, it needs well-educated, sophisticated and cultured men like you and me.'

'Yes, you're right. I hope you are right.'

Finally, Robert went home. His entire staff and family loitered in the yard, hovering around the car when it came to a standstill. They clapped as he opened the door. Tetteh tried to help him out of the car, but Robert waved him away. Everyone cheered as he struggled on to his feet. He felt rather disingenuous, and their unwavering support made him uncomfortable. Eventually, he stood on his crutches and nodded appreciation, filling his chest with the delightful scent of horses. His eyes immediately found her standing there in the back, defiantly pregnant, his youngest son on her hip. She was looking straight at him as though willing him to read her mind, her sorrow, her frustration. He had let her down, he saw that now, and he knew she blamed him in part for the situation in which they found themselves. He clenched his teeth and swallowed, and then he nodded almost imperceptibly, just for her.

Over the days, he observed the children in a way that he had never before. He saw how naturally Matilda had filled Julie's role. He saw how she loved the other children no differently from her own children. And how they loved her. Sylvia, traumatised at losing her twin, followed Matilda around like a fearful shadow, and for Gloria and George, there could be only one substitute mother. To be fair, he knew that there would never have been any question in her mind that she would raise them. After all, they were the siblings of her own.

Matilda was surprised at how composed she felt when the baby signalled its arrival. Her labour was protracted and intense. Several times during the course of the long, hot day, she tried to close her eyes and allow sleep to take her away. Aunty Dede remained by her hospital bed for the entire time, even though she was too weary herself to help with the birth, encouraging and comforting Matilda until eventually the doctor pulled out a girl with the aid of forceps.

She held her daughter and wept for joy, delighted that the doctor had been wrong all those years ago about her ability to have another child, another daughter. She was amazed how beautiful the baby was, but then which baby is not beautiful to its mother, even when the mother is exhausted or near death, and her baby is wrinkled, with blooded, matted hair and screaming for food? She beheld her child, examining every part of her perfect face and tiny body, her creamy skin, her mouth shaped like a pink, soft heart, her fists clenched in defiance at being born. Tears fell easily as the child screamed loudly, filling her lungs with fresh air, each time pushing out her newly formed bellybutton so that it looked as if it would burst.

Violet. Matilda had decided Violet would be her name. And her second name would be Ama.

Aunty Dede raised her eyebrows in surprise.

'Just because my mother was not able to demonstrate love to me is not the reason to refuse to honour her,' said Matilda. 'After all, the commandment does not say "Honour thy father and thy mother if they are good parents, or if they love you", does it?' she asked through bleary, delirious eyes.

Violet Ama. Her skin was the colour of milky tea, her eyes, when she opened them, were earnest, like her father's, and to the distress of her mother, green like his. Her hair, because her mother lovingly greased it with Vaseline, was a mop of big, soft curls, baby fluff that would soon drop off, making way for new hair, which Matilda would eagerly await. While she sat nursing her hungry baby, she wondered what had she done right for God to send her this perfect creature. She bit her lip and stared at the child whose skin would betray her parentage for all to see. Then she said into her uncomprehending ears, 'I will do everything in my power to give you courage.'

This time, no one would send a cloth to indicate paternity. For all his love of the colony, Alan had actually not learned many of the intricate customs of its people. And anyway, who would bring it across the big sea for him? She remembered their last visit. The pain of reminiscing, the tension, the lack of appetite, the endless, unhelp-ful thoughts, the lack of breath all seemed to be easing, and now she noticed that whole stretches, even hours at a time, passed without unproductive thoughts of him swirling round her head.

She was pleased when eventually Aunty Dede and Uncle Saint John came to see her about the child's out-dooring.

'We cannot fail to observe our traditions just because the child's father is not here. We have obligations. We must perform the ceremony. After all, this child is one of us and must be welcomed as normal. And better late than never,' said Aunty Dede.

'As for me, you know what I think,' said Uncle Saint John. 'Why you have brought untold shame on our family in this manner is beyond me. You, the most obedient of all children, always willing to please your elders, understanding your duties, where did it all go wrong?'

'Please, now is not the time. She knows she did wrong, and as the saying goes, "A resourceful person finds a way out of difficulties without blaming others." We need to out-door the baby as is her due, and move ahead. Matilda does not need us to remind her of her foolishness continuously.'

'Yes. I agree we must perform the ceremony, but she needs to understand what—'

'Enough!' snapped Aunty Dede, and this time, Saint John shut up.

Months after the accident Robert was still in a lot of pain and remained cocooned in his bed for most of the day. The minutiae of his household became his entertainment, and soon he could recognise the squeak of each door, the tread of different feet, the various whisperings. He knew when it was the maid laying the table, hurriedly, normally cursing beneath her breath, and when it was Matilda, gently, silently. He heard the baby cry, feed, burp and then sleep. He heard her mother sing to her and tighten her to her back. And in due course, these comforting sounds carried up to him in the heat of the day, lulled him back to sleep.

Every now and then, he made his way downstairs laboriously to sit in the living room or on the veranda, where he could watch as well as listen. This morning, hearing them discussing in overly hushed tones the out-dooring of the baby that was his children's sister, he realised that he could no longer ignore what he had to do. He called for Saint John.

Saint John, who had once been so gratified that his niece was married to Lawyer Bannerman, who had once dared to think that he and this important man would be friends, able to sit and discuss family matters with pride, but who now had to live with the shameful knowledge that his very niece, his own flesh and blood, had brought humiliation to both the Bannerman and the Lamptey families, was even more subservient and submissive to Lawyer than ever before.

'I understand that you are organising the out-dooring for the baby,' said Robert. 'You have left it rather late, haven't you? Well, it has to be done.'

After his last profuse apology and resignation when Matilda's shame had become known to all, Saint John had studiously avoided discussing any subject that involved his niece, that man Alan or the child. 'Not because we condone her shocking behaviour, you understand, but because of our duties to the child. It is not her fault, after all, that her mother is a harlot, but—'

'Stop.' Robert pointed an irritated finger at him. 'The reason that I called you here is to give you this.' He handed a piece of cloth to Saint John, who took it with a perplexed look on his face.

'Lawyer, please, I don't understand.'

'I have decided to let the child have my name.' Robert said, turning his attention to the newspaper on his lap.

'But, Lawyer, the child . . . the father . . . How can you? I don't understand.'

'There is nothing for you to understand. She is my children's sister. She is growing up in my house. Her mother is my wife. As you yourself just said, because the mother has done an unforgivable thing does not mean that the child should suffer. She will suffer enough because she is white.'

Robert returned to his newspaper in the hope that Saint John would leave. The editorial described the 'landslide' victory for the CPP, marking the 'momentous and historic occasion' of the country's first general election. It stated how Kwame Nkrumah had been released from prison and been invited by the Governor to become leader of government business since his party had won the first general election ever to be held in the colony. The United Gold Coast Convention, Robert's party, had performed quite poorly, actually; the people had after all been captivated by Nkrumah's slogan of 'Self-government NOW!', leaving people like Robert and his party, the party of lawyers and doctors, the 'natural rulers', to ponder how they had allowed their erstwhile party secretary, the man with the degree from the Negro university, to deprive them of their rightful place in history and to thereby sentence them to a stretch in opposition from where they could only wonder why the people of the Gold Coast had not been satisfied with the promise of 'self-government in the shortest possible time'. It cannot possibly last, he thought, infuriated that this same man who had called the United Convention a group of 'imperial lackeys', this ignoramus, hardly qualified for anything, and with no profession, could be given such an important role.

But if he could have seen into the future, he would have seen that this belligerent upstart would indeed lead the country to full independence, the first tropical African country to regain independence, and he would assume with all the confidence of a man born for the role, the office of president of the First Republic of Ghana.

All he could see today was that Saint John was still standing before him flabbergasted. His clouded eyes shining with gratitude, or perhaps adoration, or perhaps simply stupefaction.

461

Chapter Thirty-one

Each morning, as soon as the older children were awake, they came to see Matilda, creeping around her bed in twos and threes to greet her, to hold her, as if to check that she was still there. They rewarded her presence with smiles, with drawings and stories, with wide eyes and laughter. They touched her and fussed over Violet, debating whether today would be the day when she would take her first steps. Sylvia always came last, bringing a cup of sweet tea. She stood at the door and shooed the younger children away in a dramatic fashion that was reminiscent of her mother. 'Let Ma wake up in peace and quiet. Let Ma drink her tea in peace and quiet.'

Matilda smiled gratefully and handed Violet to her big sister. Then Sylvia, puffed up with pride and beaming, would cradle the baby and sing to her, 'My sister, my sister, you are the princess of this house, and we love you, cha cha cha,' as she swayed the child in her arms. Her reward later that morning would be to help Matilda bathe her sister, then smother her in Vaseline and brush her soft brown hair.

When finally washed and dressed, Matilda entered the kitchen to make sure that a good and healthy breakfast was being prepared for the children. Akua, the maid, would greet her correctly and with her hands behind her back, enquire meekly whether Madam had slept well and what she would like to eat for breakfast.

In the beginning, the children were quiet at the table, barely speaking. When Earnest spoke one morning displaying the food in his mouth, Julie's children gaped at Matilda in expectation of an admonition and were surprised to see that none was forthcoming. Today, as it now always was, breakfast was a rowdy gathering. She ate her buttered toast dipped in sweet tea and gazed with appreciation at the many children.

Akua was standing beside her with her hands behind her back discussing the day's meals when Uncle Saint John walked in and handed Matilda an airmail letter.

'For some reason, it was sent to Lawyer's post-office box,' he said. He still found it impossible to look at her without pain searing through him. And now, to top it all, here she was, sitting at Lawyer's table as the madam of the house when Lawyer's sister Baby was still alive and well. That confounded him more than anything else.

She took the letter, trying to disguise her shaking hands. She stuffed it into the pocket of her dress. She could feel it warm her thigh. It rustled when she brushed her hand against it and poked her when she stood up to go to her bedroom.

'My very dearest Matilda,' the letter began. She closed her eyes and lowered the letter to her lap. After a moment, she took a deep breath and continued. The Colonial Office had posted her letter on to him. He had been overjoyed to receive her letter and news of their beautiful daughter, Violet. It was wonderfully thoughtful that she had remembered his mother's name. She had obviously not received his other letters, but he assured her he had written several. He was sorry that they had not been able to meet again before he left. Robert had made things unreasonably difficult. But he thought about her every day. And he was a free man again. The divorce was finalised, and although he had been dismissed from the service, as he had expected, his pension was intact, which was jolly useful. Now she could join him. He wanted them to come to England. She must see that there was no way that he could return there. Robert had made it clear that he would weald all his power. Would they come? The three of them . . . She stopped and reread the sentence. The *three* of them could make a nice life in England. They would be together, which was the most important thing. Enclosed were enough pound notes to cover the cost of the passage and a

463

copy of the Elder–Dempster line timetable. Please could she wire and say yes, and say when they would come? Signed, 'Yours always, Alan.'

Always? That was a long time, she thought. How can one be sure at the beginning what the end will be? And how he had written the word so easily. There was no evidence of struggle, no heavy indentations on the paper. No doubt it had glided off the ink as effortlessly as she knew he would have spoken it. She could almost hear him.

When she had composed herself, she tied the baby to her back and went to lay the table for Robert's breakfast. He had told her a few weeks ago that he preferred her to serve his breakfast, rather than the maid. Matilda smiled, taking the compliment that he intended. Then he had asked her to sit with him while he ate. Initially, they sat in silence, Robert eating and drinking. Slowly, they started to talk about mundane matters, such as the children's needs, their health, their schoolwork. He began to ask her opinion on things. He had already seen that she was making the decisions about clothing, about food, about the house. When a problem arose with the girl hired to help the maid, Robert asked Matilda to discipline her or to sack her if she felt that to be appropriate. 'After all, you are in charge now,' he said without looking at her.

That night, she stared at her sleeping baby for a long while. She had prayed that the colour of her eyes would change over time, but they had not. People must have thought it strange, but few commented on it directly to her. 'The child has strange eyes; have you seen them?' they asked each other. In time, she was sure that everyone would get used to the little half-caste girl with the big green eyes and uncut, curly hair who lived in Lawyer Bannerman's house. Everyone would have a tale about her mother and her father, which in time Matilda was convinced would be so diluted from the truth that people would get bored of telling it.

She sat in the darkness and imagined her trip. What would she take? What would she leave behind? Were her clothes suitable? she wondered. The English preferred such different attire. Would she be cold on the boat? Would her baby? No wonder they learned to knit, these white women. How useful it would be if she could knit some woollen things for them to wear. She listed the many things she must do, the travel documents that she must first acquire, for her, the baby and the boys. It wouldn't be three. He had made a mistake. Theirs would be a family of seven. Then Robert came into her mind with force. She held her breath and closed her eyes tight so her imagination could continue in peace. She tried to imagine how Alan would smile when he saw Violet, as if from deep inside him some joy had burst free through his lips. He would put his arms around them and take them to his house. She tried to imagine what it was like but could not. He had not talked much of his house in England, neither of them had envisaged him leaving. Not when he had considered Africa his home, as he had told her once.

Sometimes, at night, her thoughts ran out of her control. Then she would remember his embrace, his kiss. Agonisingly, she remembered the feel of his skin on hers, and the way he smelled of lemons and Pears soap. In a moment of weakness, she had even bought a bar of Pears soap in the supermarket, but it smelled different on her. When she picked up the translucent bar, it smelled faintly of Alan, but on her skin, it lost all semblance of him. On these occasions, she told herself that in time these thoughts would fade, that she must seek to remember only those things that one day she could share with Violet. One day, she will ask why she looks different from her brothers and sisters, and I must explain.

Around her in the other darkened rooms, the people she loved were sleeping soundly. Could she leave them all behind and go alone with the money he had sent? And then what would become of her? She remembered that Alan had once told her that his mother now lived on her own. She found it impossible to imagine a sadder existence than living in a house all by herself. Such a fate was unheard of for the old people she knew. She opened her eyes to the darkness of her room. She realised that even if she had the money to take them all, perhaps she wouldn't have the courage to go to a place so far away. She started to weep unrestrainedly. It was quite straightforward. It was a case of simple mathematics: there were more people here who loved her than over there. More than ten people who needed her more than they needed anyone else in the world. More than ten people who, for now at least, loved her more than they loved anyone else. And only one person there . . . There was no sense trying, she would never balance the numbers. Maybe one day I will send Violet to go and visit him, she thought. She opened her eyes and said aloud, her voice cracking with pain, 'Don't I have more than I need, than I used to want? Doesn't my cup indeed runneth over?'

One morning, she did what she had put off for long enough. She sat down to write a letter.

> Dear Alan Thankyou for your kind leter. I cannot come to england and leeve behind me all the peepel I love so much. I have choosen to remane hear. One day I will tell Violet about you. God bless you. Matilda.

She put her pen down, folded her letter and put it in an envelope. She struggled to see through her tears to write the address. As she sealed the envelope, which she would post in the morning, her whole body heaved and trembled.

Matilda and her friend Patience were on the veranda drinking cups of sweet, milky tea, which the maid brought to them in Julie's favourite tea set.

'Who told you to use those cups?' Matilda asked.

'Please, that is what Sister Julie always used.'

'You might as well use it rather than let it gather dust for no reason,' said Patience. When the maid had gone, she said, 'Well, the world is indeed round. Who would have thought that your greatest sin would provide your greatest redemption?'

Matilda sighed. 'I don't think about it like that. Too much sadness has been unleashed around here. It would be better if the children still had their mother. For the rest, I am happy with the changes.'

'I am too. All this tea drinking suits us.'

Matilda looked at her friend and laughed.

They were silent for a while, then Patience said, 'Did you write the letter?'

Matilda nodded.

'You made the right choice.'

Matilda bobbed her head, trying not to cry. She knew she had, but feeling she had, that would take some time.